BULL

THE WILL SLATER SERIES BOOK FIVE

MATT ROGERS

Join the Reader's Group and get a free 200-page book by Matt Rogers!

Sign up for a free copy of '**HARD IMPACT**'.
Meet Jason King — another member of Black Force, the shadowy organisation that Slater dedicated his career to.

Experience King's most dangerous mission — action-packed insanity in the heart of the Amazon Rainforest.

No spam guaranteed.

Just click here.

BOOKS BY MATT ROGERS

THE JASON KING SERIES

Isolated (Book 1)

Imprisoned (Book 2)

Reloaded (Book 3)

Betrayed (Book 4)

Corrupted (Book 5)

Hunted (Book 6)

THE JASON KING FILES

Cartel (Book 1)

Warrior (Book 2)

Savages (Book 3)

THE WILL SLATER SERIES

Wolf (Book 1)

Lion (Book 2)

Bear (Book 3)

Lynx (Book 4)

Bull (Book 5)

BLACK FORCE SHORTS

The Victor (Book 1)

The Chimera (Book 2)

1

Zimbabwe

_2005_

The man was six feet tall and a hundred and sixty pounds, none of it fat. His skin, once soft and pale, had long ago turned hard and bronze and calloused. There were deep lines etched into his forehead, caked thick with dirt, and the skin under his eyes had started peeling after a particularly vicious sunburn. He wore cheap denim jeans and a plaid button-up shirt covered in sweat and muck. Nothing but a byproduct of the environment and career choice.

He was thirty-five years old.

He didn't feel it. It was a unique paradox. He somehow simultaneously felt ten years older and ten years younger. Different aspects of his physicality and mindset, blended together into what he was today. Anyone with his past would feel the same. Some of it was believable. Some of it wasn't. All of it had happened.

And all of it had converged to put him here, at this place,

at this time, under these circumstances.

He looked around, and realised it hadn't turned out so bad after all.

He stood at the border of a vast and empty field, on the wooden porch of an old homestead. Everything in sight, as of yesterday, officially belonged to him. There were no crops in the plowed dirt — not yet. That came later. Acquiring the land had been the initial battle. But he'd done it.

Late last night a gang of men had arrived, skinny and slouched and paranoid, and for a moment he'd thought it would all come crashing down around him on the first day. But then he'd spotted the hessian sacks, packed to the brim with maize seeds. A hundred pounds, as agreed. He'd handed over the cash, and they'd left the grain at the foot of his porch and shrunk back into the night.

Now he gripped the balustrade with white knuckles and managed a half-smile. It was the first truly joyous emotion he'd experienced for as long as he could remember. Certainly in the last eight years. Zimbabwe had an alluring culture and an overwhelmingly decent population, but it was the minority that had made his life so uniquely terrible for most of his adult life.

But those were the choices he'd made, and he would make them again if, in the end, they led him here.

A young girl, no older than nine, stepped out through the open front door, and the sun washed over her. She squinted and took her father by the hand. He noted her skin was still soft and pale. He wanted to keep it that way.

She said, 'Daddy, is this our new home?'

He didn't say anything.

His eyes misted over, and he swore not to respond until he had a grip on his emotions. Her life had been wracked with turbulence, and this was the first foundations of something he hoped would become permanent. At least, for her. It was hell outside the boundaries of their farm, and he'd been knee-deep in the conflict for practically a decade. He had no interest in participating any longer. No matter how righteous he believed his cause was. No matter how many injustices he saw with his own eyes. He simply didn't possess the energy to fight any longer.

He stood there, in all respects a battered, beaten, broken man, but he put on a brave front for his daughter.

And for himself.

Finally he said, 'Yes. This is ours.'

'Can I stay here?'

'Of course you can stay. That's what I did this for.'

'For me?'

The man nodded.

'So it won't make money?'

The man shrugged. 'Maybe not, my dear. These are tough times.'

'Why?'

There was so much he could try to explain. He could bring up the past, touching on the crippling guilt that came to him on sleepless nights, reminding him he could have done more to prevent the atrocities he'd seen. He was as far from racist as you could get, but he understood how his prior misgivings could be construed in that light. He could speak of the suffocating new regulations brought about by the Mugabe regime — backwards policies that crippled maize and wheat farmers by fixing the prices at a fraction of market value. He could explain his own desire to persevere in the face of such staggering corruption, maybe to atone for the past, maybe to demonstrate that he'd moved on from a life of conflict. Surely no sane man would try and get a maize farm off the ground in these circumstances.

But he would.

And he couldn't make her understand any of this, no matter how hard he tried. To her, he was a ghost — an absent father who was only just now appearing as a source of stability in her life. She knew nothing of his past. She could only know the future. And he would make it a good one.

A dust plume appeared on the horizon, in front of the purple glow emanating from a distant mountain range. It twirled and spiralled and expanded up the trail, growing closer with each passing second, somehow vague yet ominous at the same time.

The man tightened his grip on the balustrade.

'Go inside, my dear,' he said.

'Why?'

'Just do it. Please.'

She seemed to sense the urgency in his tone. One moment she was clutching his palm between her tiny fingers, and the next she had vanished into the house. He crossed to the door and pushed the rusting mesh screen closed behind her, as if that would deter anyone from entering. But it was better than leaving it open — as far as his conscience was concerned.

The dust plume tightened and swelled as a pick-up truck turned into the endless driveway.

It weaved through the plowed fields, the dust caked so hard onto its exterior that it was impossible to tell which colour it had originally been. The truck was an ancient relic as far as automotives were concerned, but here on the outskirts of the Marange diamond fields it screamed of money. Most people walked around here. Fuel was scarce. And if you somehow managed to afford a vehicle, you'd damn well better know how to defend yourself.

The truck trundled right up to the foot of the porch, and the man made out the logo emblazoned on its side, half-concealed in ochre dust.

The Grain Marketing Board.

He understood why they weren't worried about hijackings.

Out here they were bulletproof.

Out here they were gods.

There was only one reason why they were here. The man risked a glance at the mesh screen behind him, making sure the girl was safely tucked away inside. He turned back to the pick-up truck, unable to make out the details of its occupants behind the chipped windows stained with grime. He reached into the back of his waistband and rested his palm on the hilt of an old-school Smith & Wesson Model 19. Its six round cylinder was loaded.

He cocked the hammer back. He put a finger in the trigger guard. He waited with a pounding heart rate as the doors opened and four men got out, wearing blue overalls, openly wielding firearms.

They looked at him.

He looked at them.

Make an enemy now, and you'll never go back to the way things were.

You'll suffer and rot and die.

Caught between a rock and a hard place, he made the choice.

It was fairly simple.

Both roads led to hell.

But one of them gave him some semblance of independence.

So he took the Smith & Wesson out of his waistband and aimed it at the nearest man's head.

2

Manicaland Province
Zimbabwe
Present day

W ill Slater sprinted flat out for a hundred feet under the relentless sun.

And along the way he whooped and hollered and savoured the relief.

He came to a halt on the wide dirt trail, surrounded by nothing in particular, thinking of nothing in particular — besides basking in bliss. For good measure he stamped his right foot into the earth and skewered it one way, then the other. No jolts. No pangs. No tweaks. No pain whatsoever. He breathed in, then out, then put his hands behind his head and stretched his chest and stared up at the cloudless sky.

All good.

But not for long.

He sat down on the side of the road to catch his breath, resting one elbow on a canvas duffel bag with attached shoulder straps he'd been using to signify a rudimentary finish line. The package consisted of all his earthly possessions, condensed into a tight container for ease of access. He had no pressing need for anything else. Not at this point in his life.

Then a rusting panel van rumbled into view, barely holding itself together as it tackled the uneven trail. Slater turned to it, drinking in the details, surprised to see another sign of life out here. He'd been in Zimbabwe for less than a week, and he'd already grown accustomed to the desolation.

But nothing could affect his mood.

Not after he'd passed his own vigorous testing standards.

So he smiled as the van approached, unable to make out a thing through the windshield. The dust coating the glass seemed an inch thick in places, and he wondered how the driver was able to see where he was headed under such circumstances. He expected the vehicle to bounce and rattle past as fast as it dared, but it slowed.

Something in the back of Slater's brain tingled.

A primal instinct.

You know what this means.

He did, but he pretended he didn't.

He smiled wider.

He spotted the faint remnants of an official-looking symbol on the side of the van. The new owners had sandpapered it off, leaving a murky outline of what must have once been a government vehicle. Now it looked set to fall apart at any moment. It was a miracle the old beast was still running.

The passenger window crawled down, revealing a dim interior, shielded from the sun by the layers of dust on the outside of the vehicle. There was a driver and a passenger, both dark-skinned, both emaciated, both wide-eyed.

They stared at Slater, and he stared back at them, and he imagined what they saw.

They saw a man sitting in the dirt, his back to a barbed wire fence torn to shreds by squatters over the years. Beyond that was an endless field of dead yellow crops from the previous year, a haunting reminder of the toll the old regime inflicted on Zimbabwe. The man himself didn't belong in the surroundings. Sure, he was dark-skinned, possibly a native, but he was built like a professional athlete — his physique was a rippling multi-layered amalgamation of muscle and sinew forged in the fires of religiously consistent daily training. All of this was hidden underneath a thin long-sleeved cotton shirt and a pair of khakis, covering most of his skin despite the heat, mostly as a protection from the sun.

But his face was vibrant and sharp and alive with vigour, including a set of piercing green eyes largely uncommon in the region. They analysed the van with an energy unseen in these parts. The man had vitality, and hope, and he crackled with an aura neither of them could quite put their finger on. But they hadn't seen that sort of energy around Marange in years, if not decades.

There was nothing but misery out here.

So they stayed where they were, loitering, instead of smiling back and moving on.

Slater returned to his own thoughts, and rolled his sleeves up, a perfectly innocuous gesture in an ordinary social setting. Understandable, given the heat. But it gave the two men in the van a good look at his forearms, covered in veins, each muscle exposed, connected to giant hands and thick fingers. There was a noticeable difference between those who had used their fists to get their way in life, and those who hadn't.

Slater hoped these men were alert enough to recognise it.

They were.

But they didn't care.

The passenger barked something in Shona, the language spoken by the majority of Zimbabweans. It was accusatory. Inflammatory. Slater hoped that was the man's ordinary demeanour, instead of a thinly veiled threat.

He shrugged.

The passenger barked something else.

Slater shrugged again.

'You don't speak it?' the passenger said in English.

The man spoke the second language well.

Slater said, 'No.'

The passenger raised his eyebrows when he got a response in English.

The driver craned his neck across the centre, as if reacting to a breaking news bulletin. *Nuclear War Declared.*

The driver said — no, shouted, 'You are American.'

And pointed a finger right between Slater's eyes.

He couldn't hide his sneer.

A ridiculous, over-the-top gesture. But it fit the theme. Slater had only spoken a syllable. These guys were either incredibly perceptive at a whole host of different languages, or despised Americans with venom.

'Yeah,' Slater said.

He wasn't smiling anymore, but he maintained his jovial expression. No hostility. No animosity. Just openness, with his knees up and his forearms resting on them. But he watched them warily, ice-cold under the lukewarm expression. Sociopathic, even. He'd taught himself to mask his true emotions at all costs over a decade in the field, but that didn't mean he didn't have them. Sociopaths lacked empathy, and he had that in spades. Otherwise he wouldn't be celebrating a healed ankle, because without empathy, he never would have destroyed the limb in the first place.

The driver killed the engine and the two men got out of the car in unison.

Slater sighed and stood up.

Still jovial on the surface.

But ready to kill, if that was required.

3

They approached fast, closing the gap in the kind of fashion that, ninety-nine times out of a hundred, led to a fight. Slater had been in enough altercations to recognise it, but he kept his demeanour relaxed all the same.

Men were relatively simple, when it came down to it.

The adrenal gland was the same in all of them.

You either weren't in a confrontation, or you were. When you were, everything about you changed, from the way you carried yourself to the rate your thoughts sped through your mind to the way your fingers twitched in anticipation. These men had all those things in spades, and they came way too close for comfort.

But Slater stayed still, because he either *was* in a confrontation, or he wasn't. There was no middle ground. These men would either never think the same again, or walk away unharmed. When it came to violence, he never half-assed it. And he never started early unless he knew everything about his targets.

So he watched their hands, noting they were unarmed,

and crossed his own hands behind his back. To try and diffuse the tension. It didn't work. They got right up in his face, and one of them stared left and stared right, dramatically, trying to make Slater realise they were alone out here.

'What are you doing out here, American?' the driver said.

No, not said. Spat. Right in Slater's face. Saliva flecks came out of his mouth and peppered Slater's lower lip. The guy's pupils were bloodshot and his collarbones were dotted with sweat and his fingernails were broken. His voice was deep and raspy. He stepped even closer.

The hot wind howled down the trail.

This was the part where anyone else would hold up their hands in a display of innocence, maybe accompanied by nervous laughter, attempting to reason with the madman. It was a consistent universal gesture. It also involved turning your face away, averting your eyes, smiling a scared smile, trying to play the whole thing off like one big joke. It was fairly adept at melting tension away. It was one guy submitting to the other. Letting them know, *Let's not do this, man. Not here. Let's both walk away unscathed. I yield.*

The complete opposite of Will Slater.

He stayed right where he was, and he didn't move his face, and he stared the driver right in the eyes, with a glare that could bore through concrete.

But, at the same time, he didn't activate his adrenal gland.

Not yet.

So his demeanour remained relaxed.

So nothing escalated.

Yet.

Slater said, 'I was running.'

'From us?' the passenger said, and guffawed, and looked

at the driver. Searching for agreement. Trying to diffuse the tension himself. Because he probably wasn't ready for a brawl, not right here and right now.

Because Slater outweighed both of them and looked ready to crush them between his fingers.

But the driver was big-headed. His intimidation shtick probably worked most of the time out here. Slater picked him as a leftover from the Mugabe regime, cast aside as Zimbabwe ushered in a new era of attempted democracy. Trying to atone for the sins of the past. The new guy in charge had just as much blood on his hands, but at least there was some kind of economic competence involved. Concessions were being made. Debates were being opened. Reconciliation was being attempted. Chaos might reign under the surface, but in the public eye everything had taken a somewhat peaceful, reasonable turn.

They'd toned down the public bloodshed, so the old-school no-nonsense intimidators were out. Replaced by people with some level of business acumen. People who had some inclination of how to run a country.

But guys like this couldn't move on easily. It was how they were wired. With Mugabe in power they had their way whenever they wanted, however they wanted. They weren't used to doing things fairly. Which led to frustration, and anger, and resentment. Likely all taken out on the good citizens of the nation, through no fault of their own.

Slater didn't like that.

He said, 'No. Not from you. I was testing my foot.'

The passenger said, 'What's wrong with your foot?'

A normal tone. Or an attempt at it. The passenger even backed off a step. Retreating to an acceptable conversational distance. But the driver stayed right there in Slater's face. Glaring. Slater glared back. Locked in some kind of machismo bullshit. But he didn't care how petty it looked. There was no way in hell he was letting this guy get even the tiniest victory.

Not out here.

Not under these circumstances.

Slater said, 'I broke the ankle a few months ago. And tore two tendons. And tore the tibialis posterior. A very, very nasty injury. Needed stem cells to recover from it. In Tijuana.'

'You got all those injuries at once?' the passenger said.

Slater nodded.

'How'd you do that?'

'Someone got me in a leg lock.'

'What's that?'

'Jiu-jitsu.'

The driver shouted a fake laugh, and said, 'Did you hear that? He's a martial artist. Can you teach me kung fu?'

The passenger took one look at Slater's eyes and said, 'Let's go.'

The driver spun. 'What the fuck are you talking about?'

'Let's go,' the passenger repeated.

'This is an American,' the driver hissed, and he stuck a finger in Slater's face, only an inch from his nose. 'This is not one of us. This is scum in a skin suit. A few years ago we would have dragged him kicking and screaming to the border.'

'This isn't a few years ago,' Slater said. 'It's here, and now. You're an ancient relic. Like your car. You can't call law enforcement to haul me out anymore. Or maybe you were law enforcement. Who knows? Point is, if you want me gone you'll have to do it yourself.'

There was a flicker of hesitation, but only a flicker. Because in that moment the driver had two choices. He could pause for any longer than a second and the confrontation would reach its apex, at which point it would rapidly de-escalate. Just the natural order of things. Slater had graciously offered him an ultimatum, and they both knew it. It was an open invitation to hit him. Because he'd said some inflammatory things. Things that might have gotten him killed a couple of years ago. In the old era.

But now it was just this man, with his fists and no official position in any hierarchy. Bitter and cast out and resentful. Angry at everyone. Especially foreigners. They were the source of all the problems, evidently.

So there was no way in hell he was letting it go.

And Slater knew it.

He knew exactly when the punch was coming, and it was a sight to behold. He'd tapped into the adrenal gland in the midst of his speech. There was no scenario where it wouldn't be necessary, so he'd planned ahead. It meant by the time the driver spasmed like a wild man and threw all his built-up energy into a massive supercharged right hook, searching for a jaw, Slater was more than prepared to deal with it.

He was already on the back step when the driver tapped into his own musculature. Slater noticed the chain activating and darted one stride backward across the dirt. He'd been in so many confrontations — usually an alien concept to the masses — that it had almost become second nature. The fist missed by a couple of inches. Not a whole lot of room. Air washed over Slater, and he noted the power of the swing. If it had connected it might have knocked him clean out. The driver had been in a few fights of his own.

But there were fighters, and then there were technicians.

Slater darted back into range, just as fast, and threw a kick to the leg like his life depended on it. In the movies and the books, leg kicks were pitter-patter strikes, designed to look fancy on the big screen or read good on the page. Slater treated them like the devastating strikes they were. He dug a hardened shin bone into the soft tissue on the outside of the driver's knee, and the whole leg contorted inwards at a grotesque unnatural angle, and the driver panicked and tried to whisk the same leg out of harm's way, but it was far too late. So he planted his foot back and then the extent of the injury kicked in, and he sensed all the destroyed muscle and bone in his joint, and his leg buckled and he went down into an awkward half-squat, eyes almost bugging out of his head as the reality of the situation sunk in.

A single second of actual fighting, and now he wouldn't be able to walk for at least the next several weeks until the swelling went down.

The guy tried to recover from the half-squat, but as soon as he put weight on his bad leg he went down again, nearly tumbling into the dirt on his rear in an ungainly slow-motion fashion. Slater helped him down by slapping him hard in the ear, skirting into range and unloading his open palm into the side of the driver's head. All the man's attention went straight to his head, which took his focus off his legs, which sent a crippling bolt of agony through his knee as he put weight on it in the wrong direction.

He splayed into the dirt, landing hard, thumping down with the sort of finality that signalled the confrontation was over.

Slater turned to the passenger and raised an eyebrow.

The guy shook his head.

Slater nodded. *Good choice.*

'Help your friend up,' he said.

The passenger wrapped both hands around the driver's elbow and heaved him to his feet. The driver's face contorted into a mask of pain, and the bloodshot eyes lost some of their steam. He stared meekly at Slater, then seemed to realise how pathetic that made him look, so he spun it into an aggressive string of insults in Shona. Bringing some of the old fury back. Slater let the words pass him by, smiling at the man instead, which probably made the guy more furious.

He put his hands behind his back again and waited for the passenger to act.

It didn't take long. The passenger hauled the driver back to the car, almost forcibly, looping the guy's arm around the back of his neck for support. He bundled him into the seat, and then the passenger became the new driver, so Slater stopped mentally referring to them as such. The uninjured one clambered behind the wheel and waved a placatory farewell and stared straight ahead through the grimy windshield and put the van into gear and rumbled off back down the trail. The last glimpse Slater caught through the open window was the guy with the bad leg slumped in the passenger seat, his eyes squeezed shut, breathing hard through his nose, both hands on his bad knee.

And then, just like that, it was back to silence.

4

S later paused on the side of the road to survey the landscape.

No-one else was coming.

He was utterly alone out here.

The nearest village was five miles behind him, and he figured he'd walk all day if that was what it took to find shelter for the night. He'd done something similar in Yemen, and he found he savoured the discomfort of the unknown. He'd approached stints in Macau and the Russian Far East through the veil of luxury, and though he could afford it he found it wholly at odds with experiencing life. Because all wealth was the same experience after a while. The five-star hotels across the world were carbon copies of each other, whereas at street level, it was all different. Everywhere he went.

With four hundred million dollars to his name, or thereabouts — it fluctuated each day with the changing markets — he didn't need to skimp and save.

But he did anyway.

Because he got to experience life this way.

So he let the heat wash over him and he slung the duffel over his shoulders, testing the weight on his right leg, and he moved on satisfied with how his body responded. Relief punched him in the chest, even though he'd been on the road to recovery for weeks now. This was the first time he hadn't experienced a hiccup during a test. When he'd touched down in Zimbabwe he'd tried to jog and almost pinched a nerve. His ankle turned sideways in protest and he went down in an awkward heap, panting, experiencing those few seconds of shock and awe as he listened to pain receptors and tried to work out whether he'd re-injured it. Then he picked himself up and dusted himself off and made his tentative way to a bed for the night, lying as still as he could and picturing the limb fully functional in his mind.

Sometimes, the mental battle was harder than the physical on the road to recovery.

But he'd used his bad leg to kick the shit out of the driver's knee, and nothing had tweaked or snapped. He felt whole for the first time since the madness that had unfolded a few months ago. He hadn't received a word of information from either Shien or the Nazarian family, but that was the way it needed to be. He hadn't left any of them his number. He'd vanished into the background and let them start to build the foundations of a normal existence.

Because his life was as far from normal as you could get.

He continued onward, aiming for the mountain range on the horizon, still surrounded by nothing but dead yellow fields. The old regime was out of power, but that didn't mean it was all sunshine and rainbows. As far as he could surmise, taking snippets of gossip from every civilian he encountered across the continent, it would take years to rebuild the vital infrastructure and clamber rung by rung out of famine. He got the sense the country would be feeling the effects of Mugabe for long into the foreseeable future.

But the people he'd met were tough. Strong-willed. Determined. They'd survived the descent, and the trough of the valley. They could handle themselves during the subsequent climb out.

But he wasn't here for politics, so he turned his mind off that particular avenue and concentrated on what he could control. The dirt road ran for as far as the eye could see, and there seemed to be no sign of the terrain changing, aside from the occasional small dwelling slapped into the middle of a dead field, likely by squatters. They were cement structures, thrown together haphazardly, but serving the purpose they were designed for. They provided shelter, and that was enough.

The GPS on his smartphone told him he was approaching what constituted the outskirts of the Marange diamond fields, and he gave thanks for the simple fact that he knew his location this far off the grid.

He relished the progress of technology, and he wondered how useful state-of-the-art advancements were proving to the covert world of government black operations. He was over a year separated from that life, but he couldn't fathom the kind of aid a rapidly changing technological landscape could offer to elite operatives in foreign territory. He knew the stereotype of the old-school warrior detached from the times, but he had to stay up to date with all of it. It used to be a job requirement. An absolute necessity.

If he didn't ensure his every move was anonymous — in terms of leaving a digital trail — then they would find him without much effort.

He was wanted by the entire U.S. covert world, after all.

He shrugged that train of thought off, too.

No use dwelling in the past.

Concentrate on the future.

He strode between dead fields and empty land, the entire area coated in the feeling of desolation. Aside from the encounter with the two men earlier, his time in Zimbabwe had been largely isolating. His own fault. His own doing. He was avoiding people like the plague, even if they seemed friendly. He figured he was trundling through a particularly sensitive portion of his own life, and he deemed it best to lay low until the government put what happened in Maine on the shelf and swept the remnants of the Lynx program under the rug, where they belonged.

Until then, he had to stay quiet. If he found trouble — which he knew he undoubtedly would — it had to be somewhere so detached it all but guaranteed he wouldn't be pursued. He figured Zimbabwe fit the bill. If he got in deep with the wrong crowd out here, the government wouldn't jump at the opportunity to follow him into the diamond fields. Too politically sensitive. Too reminiscent of sticking their nose where it didn't belong.

He figured he could stay out here for as long as he pleased, like a wandering nomad.

The lifestyle suited him fine.

So, in the preceding months, he'd recovered in private with his head down and his veins flowing with someone else's stem cells, and then he'd arranged off-the-record transportation from Tijuana to Zimbabwe. It was hard to do in principle. Not much of a bother in reality. Slater had enough experience with the world that existed under the surface of society's fabric. Most didn't dare venture into it, due to the inherent dangers. But Slater could smash a guy's nose into the back of his skull with an elbow, so he figured he was suitably equipped to take the risk.

There was always ample unused space on cargo planes.

If Black Force had taught him anything, it was the gargantuan size of the international transport industry.

There were all kinds of deals that could be worked out under the table.

So now he was here, unofficial in every sense of the word, a ghost as far as any kind of trail was concerned.

He walked for what had to be hours into the diamond fields, sweating in the heat but barely noticing. He'd become particularly intimate with silence and calm over the last few months, as always seemed to be the case in the aftermath of violent conflict. And that was the summary of his existence — an explosion of turbulence, followed by a solitary period of recuperation.

Repeat ad infinitum.

It was almost becoming routine, and there'd been many times when he'd wondered whether he had been bewitched in a past life to attract chaos like a magnet. But then he broke it down practically, and realised it was very much his own doing. He wandered into places like this, where he most certainly wasn't welcome, and he didn't back down from confrontation. In fact, he witnessed an injustice and then pursued it ruthlessly. Anyone would run into the same amount of trouble in his shoes — just most wouldn't survive it for any longer than a couple of days at most.

So he was unique in that regard.

Then the terrain changed. His phone told him he was approaching the eastern edge of the fields. The dead crops faded away, replaced by endless swathes of dirt to the west, and lush green plantations to the east. A dichotomy if Slater had ever seen one. He reached a fork in the trail and headed east, figuring with his current wealth he had no pressing urge to set up an illegitimate diamond mining operation.

Only a mile into the new trek, he came across a setting straight out of a storybook. A wide, carefully cultivated path with smooth dirt packed hard into the earth. Green fields on either side, spiralling up to a gorgeous homestead with an ornate, carefully curated exterior, three storeys tall and large enough to fit a small army within its walls.

Slater automatically assumed it was government-owned property, and figured he wasn't quite ready to storm into places he wasn't welcome.

Then he spotted the sign.

Ron and Judy's Bar & Backpackers'.

All Welcome.

So he shrugged and shifted the duffel on his back and started up the trail.

He could use a drink.

5

H e made it to the front lot in less than a minute, striding hard, breathing fast, tantalised at the prospect of shade and a cold drink.

There were six vehicles parked in front of the homestead, all pick-up trucks, all coated in enough dust and muck to paint them a uniform orange. It seemed to be the only method of transportation out here. The panel van had been an anomaly, and Slater hadn't realised until the sample size had increased. He sauntered past the trucks, flashing an inquisitive glance through a few of the windows on the way to the front porch. A couple of the drivers' windows rested down at sill height. One of them had the keys in the ignition. If Slater wanted, he could be a mile away in less than a minute.

The brand new owner of a reliable automotive vehicle.

But he didn't, because he had morals, and because the entire homestead lay shrouded in an atmosphere he couldn't quite put his finger on, but it felt homely and warm and inviting all at once. So he stepped away from the door, but it seemed someone caught him in the act.

A voice said, 'The hell do you think you're doing?'

Slater looked up. An old white guy stood on the porch, with a wiry frame and baggy clothing that looked like it had been sewn hundreds of years ago. He had a strange accent — partly British, partly something else entirely. Maybe a bit of South African in the mix. The giant wooden front doors — a pair of them, set into a dark oak frame — swung on their hinges behind him, like the place was a saloon. Slater had no particular inclination to encourage racists, and he thought he saw some kind of manic glint in the guy's blue eyes, so he took a step toward the porch, away from the car.

'Are we going to have a problem here?' he said.

The old white guy cocked his head. 'I don't know. You tell me.'

'We're fine, as far as I'm concerned.'

'We're very far from fine if you're going to steal my truck.'

'I'm not stealing anything.'

'Where's your ride?'

'I walked.'

'From where?'

'The last village.'

'Five miles?'

'Around about that.'

'How long did that take you?'

'All day.'

The guy took a look at his dirty watch, with a chipped face and a faded leather strap. He said, 'Christ, you must be thirsty.'

'I am.'

'Then head on inside and get a drink.'

'How long has this place been here?'

'It closed down for a few years. They barricaded the

windows during a particularly nasty stretch. But then they started up again, late last year.'

'How's it working out for them?'

'There's still problems. But the way you're talking seems to insinuate this is a white folks' haven.'

'Seems that way. Not that I've got anything against that.'

The old guy smiled. 'Seems we got off on the wrong foot. I thought you were stealing my truck. You need to head inside and have a drink. Make yourself at home. Talk to Ron and Judy. Not often we get an American around here.'

'What are you?'

'I'm a mix of everything.'

'How long have you lived here?'

'Couple of decades.'

'You enjoy it?'

The old guy chuckled. 'Sounds like a loaded question, my friend.'

'I'm not like that.'

'Good, because neither am I. Obviously I enjoy it. Or I'd be somewhere else. That's how life works.'

'Noted.'

'Well, you enjoy yourself in there.'

Slater nodded. 'Appreciated.'

'You're quiet. I hope I didn't offend you.'

'I'm just a quiet guy. Trust me, you didn't offend me.'

'How would I know?'

Slater stared at him. 'You'd know.'

Ordinarily something to scoff at. A private joke between friends, feigning the tough-guy demeanour of Hollywood blockbusters. But Slater meant every word of it and the guy could tell, so there was no misunderstanding between them. Instead of laughing and shaking his head at the intensity he just nodded and smiled and sauntered over to his car. He opened the door and fired the ignition up and backed out of the makeshift parking space and waved a calloused hand through the open window, resting his elbow on the sill.

Slater waved back.

The old guy drove away, kicking up a dust cloud as the back of the pick-up disappeared down the dirt trail. It might have been Slater's imagination, but he thought he saw the hood swinging back and forth across the track. The road wasn't uneven. The old guy probably had a few too many at the bar.

Slater played the conversation back in his head, searching for undercurrents of anything distasteful. He lingered on certain phrases, turning them over and over as he stood in the hot sun and admired the giant homestead. Then he realised that wasn't his style, so he dispensed with the analysis and climbed up onto the porch and threw the double doors open and walked into Ron and Judy's Bar & Backpackers' with an open mind.

6

I t was a bar, and a communal area, and a lounge, all rolled into one.

The entranceway didn't exist. Slater figured the walls had been knocked down years ago to make the ground floor a vast sweeping space, open-plan, with orange-and-brown tiles covering the floor. He could see all the way to the rear of the homestead, where latticework doors stood open across the entire wall. Beyond that he saw more green fields, and a smattering of mopane trees dotting the otherwise flat landscape. A hot breeze filtered through the house, and soft lo-fi ambient music filtered through the air, emanating from speakers tucked somewhere out of sight. The furniture was nothing spectacular, certainly not up to par with some of the designer condominiums Slater had laid eyes on over the past year. Aside from the house itself, none of the decorations stood out as overly lavish.

It was simply a beautifully maintained property with owners that had a great eye for detail.

Slater stood a foot inside the door and surveyed the occupants with a quick glance. He didn't want to linger any

longer than necessary. He saw a curved wooden bar countertop in the back corner, with an old white couple behind
it, and he saw three wizened black men clustered around a
pair of sofas near the front door, deep in hearty conversation, each clutching a chipped mug of beer. There were a
group of square wooden tables in the corner opposite the
bar, and a deeply tanned white man sat alone at one of
them, cradling a glass of what looked like apple cider in
one hand.

And only one hand.

Because his other hand didn't exist.

His right arm ended at the shoulder joint, nothing but a
stump, with no prosthetic to make up for its absence. He'd
covered the old wound by cutting the sleeve of his button-
up shirt three quarters of the way past the elbow and tying
the remaining fabric into a tight knot. Slater drifted his gaze
away from the missing limb, making sure not to linger on it
in case the man caught him staring, and then he noticed the
guy's right leg ended at the knee. He had a prosthetic to
allow him to walk, but his cream pants hung loosely around
the metal pole. He wasn't trying very hard to mask the
extent of his disabilities.

Slater respected that.

He looked away and noticed the old couple at the bar
staring at him expectantly. Open, warm, welcoming expressions on their face. No tension. No hesitation at the fact
they'd never seen him before. He respected that, too. He
nodded politely to the group of old men on the couches on
the way past, and they nodded back. They resumed their
conversation straight away. Slater realised the ambient
music did wonders for the atmosphere. With nothing in the
background, the house would feel old and silent, making
conversations awkward, making voices echo. Now, everyone

had their own privacy. The music seemed to divide the open-plan area into four separate quadrants.

Slater approached the bar, and dropped his duffel down on one of the stools.

He wiped sweat from his brow.

The old woman said, 'Hello.'

She might have had an accent in the past — possibly British, or Australian, or even American — but now it was gone, lost to the long years spent in Zimbabwe. It came out strange, with a certain inflection that sounded almost like it was her second language. But it wasn't. It had just lost its polish over the years. Maybe she conversed mainly in Shona these days.

Slater said, 'Hello.'

The man chuckled. 'Is that an American accent I hear?'

'It sure is.'

The woman said, 'Whereabouts are you from, dear? My brother lives in California.'

Slater dropped onto one of the stools and rolled his shirt sleeves up and rested his forearms on the countertop. He raised his eyebrows and nodded in the direction of the bar shelves behind the couple and flashed his trademark smile and said, 'How about a drink before we get into specifics?'

The woman smiled back. 'Well, aren't you a charmer?'

'I try my best.'

'Watch it,' the man said, but jokingly. 'Beer?'

'Please.'

They had a couple of brands on tap, but Slater barely looked at them. The mileage he'd covered and the short detour to throw a single strike at one hundred percent capacity had taken the energy right out of him. He figured he'd lost conditioning, but not to that extent. He chalked the fatigue up to the heat and the marathon of a trek, and graciously accepted a tall mug of the homestead's finest brew.

He drank greedily through the foam and wiped his lip.

Just as refreshing as he thought it would be.

He said, 'Are you Ron and Judy?'

The man said, 'That would be us.'

Judy said, 'And who might you be?'

'Will.'

'Pleasure to meet you, Will. May I ask you something?'

'Sure.'

'You said that reluctantly. It's my job to be around people. So I pick up on those things. Do people call you that? Or are you trying to be polite by offering your first name?'

'People don't call me anything, really.'

'You're not a people person?'

'Not particularly.' He didn't want to seem standoffish, so he added, 'But you two seem lovely.'

Ron scoffed and said, 'You can be honest.'

'I'm always honest,' Slater said.

Judy said, 'So what should we call you?'

'Slater's my last name. People usually call me Slater.'

7

'So you do interact with people,' Judy said, shaking a finger at him. Then she winked. 'Even if only occasionally.'

'Occasionally I have to,' he said with a smirk.

'So what brings you all the way out here, Slater?'

Slater paused. He thought long and hard about it. Then he said, 'I was going to make something up, but you two seem genuine enough. So I won't pretend I'm something I'm not. But at the same time I won't spare you the trouble of knowing, so I'll just clarify that I'm a nice guy and not looking to harm anyone. Just looking for a drink and maybe a bed. And then I'll be on my way. Sound good enough?'

He expected a certain trepidation to follow. He assumed Ron and Judy had adequate imaginations. Maybe they were picturing a serial killer on the run, or an escaped prisoner, or any number of other unfortunate souls.

Instead, Judy smiled and said, 'Trust me, I don't think anything would surprise us.'

'I beg to differ,' Slater said.

'You sure about that?'

'Fairly certain.'

'I think I could surprise you, if we all sat down for an evening.'

'We would love that. Are you hanging around?'

'I've got nowhere to be.'

'Stay a few days.'

'I might.'

'How much can you tell us?'

'I'll figure that out as I go along.'

Ron said, 'You seem like the mysterious type. This isn't the kind of situation where we get killed if we know certain details, is it?'

Slater smirked. 'Not out here. Not this far from civilisation.'

Judy said, 'How can you be sure?'

They both had a twinkle in their eye. Enraptured by the conversation. Delighted by the mystery. Slater imagined after years of the same certain handful of "another one of those" scenarios, they were tantalised by the prospect of a fresh story. Maybe they'd hear things they'd never heard before. He figured that was a novel experience in its own right.

He weighed up the risks. But there weren't many. He could be vague. He could generalise. And most of his life story was so fantastical they probably wouldn't believe him in retrospect. They'd stay at the bar, talking all night with him, and then they'd head upstairs to bed and scoff and shake their heads at each other and muse about the wanderers who drifted into their homestead who had long ago lost their marbles.

So Slater said, 'I'm ex-military.'

'Here?' Ron said, with a dark look in his eyes.

Slater shook his head. 'U.S. government.'

'And the nature of your career means you have to make up a fake story every time someone like us asks you about it?'

'Something like that.'

'Isn't that hard on you?' Judy said.

Slater paused. 'No-one's ever asked me that.'

'If I did important things, I'd want people to know. Maybe I'm selfish.'

Slater shrugged. 'It's not that important to me.'

'Then why did you do it?'

'Because I was good at it. And it paid well. And then it became habit, and then it never left me.'

Ron said, 'Have you killed people?'

Judy hit him lightly in the shoulder.

He looked over. 'What?'

She said, 'Ever think he might not want to talk about that?'

'I'm okay with talking about it,' Slater said. 'I lived it.'

Ron said, 'So you have?'

'It was rare, but it happened.'

'How rare?' Ron said with a raised eyebrow, seeing right through the guise.

Slater shrugged. 'Every now and then.'

'You don't want to talk about it, do you?' Judy said.

He shrugged again. 'I don't mind. I just don't know if...'

'We're ready for specifics?'

A third shrug.

Judy laid her palms flat on the countertop and gave Slater a grandmotherly smile. She said, 'There's no rush. We're always here. Don't worry — I get it. We're a stereotype. We're the lovely old couple full of innocence. We couldn't handle it.'

'It's not that. You live out here. You could probably handle it.'

'But...?'

'I don't know if—'

Ron said, 'We can relate?'

Slater nodded.

Judy smiled again and said, 'Then how about you go and talk to Rand?'

Slater said, 'Who's Rand?'

And some invisible switch in the back of his head flipped from off to on.

As if to say, *Here we go.*

8

Thanks to the ambient music, the ground floor had enough background noise to mask each isolated conversation from the rest of the room. The three gentlemen near the front door kept chatting away, but Slater couldn't make out a word they were saying. Equidistant to them was the disabled man by the array of tables behind Slater's back, so by general principle the man wouldn't be able to hear their conversation either.

So Slater leant forward and said, 'The guy behind me?'

Judy nodded. 'He's a regular.'

'Who is he?'

'I think you should go find out for yourself, dear. I've been in this business long enough. I know people. You're a lone wolf, aren't you?'

'Generally.'

'Which means you're sitting on a mountain of stuff you want to get off your chest.'

'I wouldn't put it that way.'

Judy said, 'I've been in Zimbabwe for long enough. I know there's two worlds. There's this world — which is quite fake, I admit — where people greet each other politely, and talk amicably, and throw up a bunch of smoke-screens and generally hide how they really feel for the sake of seeming nice. And then there's the other world, where all that falls away and laws disappear and men and women fight and kill each other and display all their emotions on their chest. There's something primal about it, but that's what makes it real. It's your survival instincts coming to the surface, and nothing else matters except staying on top, because if you don't stay on top you die and you lose power and you and your loved ones are in danger every single day you don't have control. So you need to be ... like animals. That's how I'd describe it. I haven't been a part of that world, but I've seen it, and I've seen the consequences of it. It used to be a daily occurrence around here. And from what I can deduce, it seems like you used to live in that world. Which is a strange thing to figure out. It makes me think — how do you feel in times like these? When there's nothing going on, and you're just sitting here talking to the pair of us. Are you wishing you were playing the game of life or death? Does all this feel like some kind of carnival game to you? It fascinates me.'

Slater said nothing for a long twenty seconds, digesting. Then he said, 'You're very perceptive, Judy.'

'I try to be,' she said with a smile.

'You practically hit the nail on the head.'

'So what do you think of this world?'

'I think it's great. I wish we could live in it forever.'

'But we can't.'

'Most can. But then there's people like me who have a particular talent that only has any use in the other world.'

'That's why I suggested you talk to Rand.'

'Why?'

'He used to live in that world.'

'He doesn't anymore?'

She lowered her voice and said, 'You didn't see him on the way in, did you?'

'I saw him.'

'I'm surprised you're not already over there.'

Slater raised an eyebrow. 'You think because I'm from a certain line of work I have an obsession with war wounds?'

'They weren't war wounds,' Judy said.

Ron held his palms up. 'Well…'

Judy shrugged. 'A different kind of war.'

'Would he want to talk to me?' Slater said.

'I think so. I'm sure he gets lonely. A new face would be refreshing.'

'You sure?'

'You seem unconvinced.'

'Sometimes people want to be alone for a reason.'

'Like you?'

Slater nodded. 'I like the solitude. I like the road. I can't stay in one place, because that means there's something going on in another place that I'm not addressing.'

Judy frowned, puzzled. 'Are you a vigilante?'

'I guess you could call me that. I don't describe myself as anything, though. I just interfere when I see bad shit happening.'

Ron smiled a sad smile. 'You're about ten years too late, I'm afraid.'

'Something happened to you two?'

'Not us. Rand.'

'Will he want to talk about it?'

'Does it matter?' Judy said.

'I'm rather enjoying my conversation with you and your husband, ma'am. I don't see an urgent need to hustle over to this new guy unless there's something he needs urgent help with.'

Judy shook her head. 'The past is the past. You can't help him.'

'So then...'

She reached across the table and put a hand on his wrist. It was warm, and caring. Grandmotherly.

She said, 'Go talk to Rand.'

Slater got the cue. There was something she couldn't put into words, and she could spend hours scratching at its surface but never quite articulate exactly what she was trying to say. But she understood people, and she had a grasp on the world of violent lawlessness despite never actively participating in it. So Slater trusted her intuition. He drained the rest of his beer and asked for a refill. Ron happily obliged.

The first mugful settled in his stomach and set to work cooling his body temperature.

Taking the edge off.

The only way Slater knew how.

Ron passed the next round across and Slater gulped half of it down.

'Careful,' Judy warned. 'It's a strong brew.'

'That's a good thing,' Slater said.

'Just make sure not to go overboard. You've got all night, my dear.'

'I don't do things slowly,' Slater said.

Then he swung off the stool and headed across the tiled floor to talk to Rand.

T he man watched him approach.

Slater eyed him with as much subtlety as he could on the way over.

He put Rand at roughly six foot — they were the same height, give or take. He had a rough weather-beaten face, sunburned over and over again in the past. Now it seemed perpetually damaged — under the eyes his skin was the colour of wine, and around that it was pale red. He had broken capillaries on his nose, and cracked lips, and deep freckles on his cheeks. But under the worn surface he was a handsome man. A strong jawline, full colourful eyes, and peculiarly long lashes.

Ten years ago, the ladies might have swooned.

There was something cold and calculated in his eyes — unrestrained judgment — but Slater didn't blame him. He'd read between the lines of what Judy had said.

A different kind of war.

He tried not to speculate. It led nowhere. Instead he quickened his pace for the last few strides, bridging the awkward no-man's-land, and pulled to a halt beside the chair opposite.

'Mind if I sit down?' he said.

Rand regarded him warily. Then he gave a single nod. 'Be my guest.'

Slater sat. He put the beer down on the table and wrapped his fingers around the glass.

Rand said, 'Looking for company?'

'I was curious about your wound.'

'That's forward of you.'

'Judy says we might share a similar background. I figured I'd get straight to the point.'

Rand smirked. 'Oh, I doubt that.'

'Try me.'

'Why don't we have a polite man-to-man conversation first?'

'About what?'

'You know — the weather, sport, politics. Whatever.'

'Not my style.'

'Mine either.'

'But you still go through with it.'

'It's tradition. I don't want to seem antisocial.'

'I wouldn't take it personally if we moved right along.'

'And yet,' Rand said, sipping his cider, 'we should still do it. Because pleasantries are pleasantries. And I don't know a thing about you. So why should I talk to you in the first place?'

'I'm the only new guy here.'

'I'm perfectly comfortable on my own.'

'As am I,' Slater said. 'I told you — we're not too different.'

'You can't have had a similar life story to me,' Rand said. 'Or you wouldn't be sitting here.'

'And I could say the same for my own story.'

'Then it's a stalemate.'

'Let's agree that we're very similar, and very different.'

'Let's agree on nothing. I don't know you, and you don't know me.'

'So who starts talking first?'

'You do. You sat down here. By all intents and purposes this is my table.'

'It's Ron and Judy's table.'

'You're buddies with them, are you?'

'Nowhere close. I just met them.'

'The three of you seemed real cosy over there.'

'You insinuating something?'

'You're a charmer. That's what it is, isn't it? You wànt to be friends with everyone. It must be something of a game to you. Be as amicable as you can to everyone in this place. I'm not the type to play buddy-buddy with you. You can go back to the bar if that's what you're looking for.'

'You couldn't be further off the mark.'

'Is that an insult?'

Slater paused, then he said, 'Are you usually this angry?'

'Alright — you can leave.'

'I haven't done anything to warrant a reaction like that.'

'Why'd you come over here?'

'Judy said we should talk.'

'Well, I don't want to talk to you.'

'Why not?'

'Don't you understand conversational cues?'

'Oh, I understand them just fine. Doesn't mean I have to respond to them.'

'I'd like you to leave.'

'And I'd like to stay.'

'Why?'

'Because I've lost count of the amount of people I've killed over my career, and it seems like you might be uniquely predisposed to understand that concept. Just a rumour, though.'

'I understand, alright. Doesn't mean I want to chat about it.'

'How often do you talk about it?'

'Never.'

'And I never talk about my life, either. Not outside very, very narrow windows of time. Like blips on the radar. Other than that it's all silence and overthinking. I get bogged down in my own mind, and sometimes I want to let it out in a setting where my life isn't at risk. I only ever spill my guts when I'm in a life-or-death situation. And I think it's about time I broke that trend. I don't know if you feel the same, but if you don't, then I'll get up right now and go back to the bar and pretend we never had this conversation.'

Rand paused, and looked Slater up and down, and gulped down half his cider, and said, 'Okay, let's talk.'

10

'How far back do you want me to go?' Rand said.

'I don't want you to do anything you don't want to do.'

'That's awfully sweet of you.'

Rand smiled, and sipped again at the cider. He rested his palm flat on the table. The skin was tanned, and the knuckles were calloused, and the fingers were wound tight with sinew. A big powerful appendage. Making up for the absence of its twin.

His entire body seemed a testament to a life of hardship.

The missing arm and leg included.

Slater said, 'How'd you get your wounds?'

'That was a relatively recent development.'

'How recent?'

'Eight years ago.'

Slater paused. 'How far back does your career go?'

'I'm forty-six now. How old are you?'

'Early thirties.'

'You're a pup.'

'I sure don't feel like it.'

'Trust me, you are.'

'Trust me, I'm not.'

Rand regarded him with the judgment of a man whose total sum life experiences trumped anyone he usually came across.

Silently, Slater found himself confident he could give the guy a run for his money.

Slater said, 'Try me.'

Rand said, 'Okay.'

'This shouldn't be a competition.'

'It's not a competition. You're sitting there in peak physical condition without a shred of body fat on you, with all your arms and legs, and a look in your eyes like you're just getting started experiencing the life you want to live.'

'I got out of my particular game before it all went to hell,' Slater said.

'See? You call it a game.'

'Only way I can stay sane.'

'But you're out now,' Rand said.

'Doesn't feel like it.'

'Why not?'

'Do you watch the news?'

'When I can. Used to be hard to find anything unbiased out here. Now it's getting better.'

'You keep up with major international incidents?'

'I try to.'

'Remember all those bodies they found at Mountain Lion Casino & Resorts in Macau? They shut the whole place down after that. What with its owner dead, and most of the security.'

'I remember.'

'That was me.'

'So you're a psychopath.'

'There's a story behind everything.'

'I'm sure there is.'

'Remember the botched peace demonstration in the Bering Straight half a year ago? Between the U.S. and Russia?'

'The icebreaker they found drifting? The one where they figured the whole crew decided to massacre itself?'

'That's the one.'

'You're going to try and convince me that was you too?'

'I don't need to convince you of anything. And I'm not going to explain the motive behind any of it. You can dream that up in your own time. I'm here to tell you there's people who share a similar level of consistent madness in their lives.'

Rand dragged the mug of cider across the table in a hypnotic rhythm. He stared at the condensation on the glass. 'I haven't experienced anything like that in a long time.'

'But you did.'

'And you're way too interested in it.'

Slater cocked his head. Noted the shift in tone. He sensed … something. Guilt?

'What'd you do?' Slater said.

'Nothing I want to talk to you about.'

'Because I'm black?'

A touchy subject, but Slater was starting to piece it together. The hesitation, the wishy-washy stance, the inability to give a shred of detail.

Rand lifted his gaze to meet Slater's and said, 'I'm not a racist.'

'I didn't say you were.'

'If I tell you the truth — which I have every intention of

doing — you could misconstrue what happened. It sounds bad.'

'How bad?'

'Nothing awful. I mean, I killed people. But never because of their skin colour.'

'You don't need to justify it to me. I didn't ask for that. I just want to know what happened.'

'You left bodies in Macau?'

'I did.'

'You left bodies in Russia?'

'I did.'

'I think I'm worried you might leave a body here.'

'I'll hear you out.'

'I think it's a good idea if we never have the conversation in the first place.'

Slater smiled. 'You're overcompensating, Rand.'

'You know my name?'

'Judy told me.'

'What's yours?'

'Will Slater.'

'Pleased to meet you.'

'Likewise. And I mean it. You're not a racist. A racist wouldn't spend this long stressing over how his story sounded. He'd just come right out and say it, because he'd believe it was the right thing to do all along.'

'Maybe I'm a reformed racist.'

'I don't think you are. A reformed racist wouldn't mention it at all. They just wouldn't talk about it, period. I think you killed a lot of people because it was in the job description, and because it's Zimbabwe they happened to be predominantly black. And because you're white, you think I'll think that makes you racist.'

'Pretty much.'

'Give it to me straight.'

'I was a Selous Scout.'

'A what?'

'Back when this place was called Rhodesia.'

'I see.'

'Before I proceed — how much do you know about Zimbabwe's history?'

'Enough.'

'Is that bullshit?'

'I'm familiar with it. I've got a close personal connection with the land.'

'And what might that be?'

'My father is Zimbabwean.'

11

R and mulled over that for a beat, and then he said, 'Yeah, I really don't think we should be having this conversation.'

Slater smirked. 'That shows how little you know about me.'

A pause.

Rand said, 'You two had a tough relationship?'

'To put it lightly.'

'Is he still around?'

'No.'

'What happened, if you don't mind me asking?'

'My mother was taken by human traffickers when I was a teenager, and he couldn't handle the fact that he sat around and did nothing about it. He was wracked with guilt. So he wallowed around in depression for a couple of years and then put a gun under his chin and pulled the trigger.'

Rand froze. The mug of cider halfway to his lips. His only hand froze there, the fingers trembling ever so slightly. He said, 'I'm so sorry.'

'I got over it.'

'That's not something to get over.'

'Isn't it?' Slater said, then raised his eyebrows. Almost mockingly. 'I thought you said I was fine. Because I had all my arms and legs. And an energetic spark in my eye.'

'I shouldn't be so quick to judge.'

'There we go,' Slater said, and drained half his beer. 'Now we're on the same page.'

'How long did your father live here?'

'He grew up here. Back when it was called Rhodesia. Led by a white minority government. The black majority didn't like that. Hence the war. Hence the Selous Scouts. I know all about them, Rand. They were Special Forces for the Rhodesian Army.'

'I told you it was a bad idea to have this talk.'

'Why would it be?'

'Your father...'

'He wasn't your enemy. He wasn't part of the black majority. He wasn't part of any majority, or minority. He didn't have a dog in the fight. He understood the situation as the complicated beast it was. He didn't throw himself at any cause. He sat back and observed what happened with a keen eye, and when the blacks overthrew the whites he paid keen attention to the way they ran the country instead of the colour of their skin. In fact, he didn't celebrate when it happened. He fled to America only a couple of years after the civil war in 1980. Because he saw the trajectory the country was headed. He didn't see skin colour. He saw competency. So he sensed what was coming and he got out before it all went to absolute hell.'

'Smart man.'

'Or lucky. He told me he could sense competency, but that was a load of shit. He couldn't do a single competent thing in his life. I doubt he was the political fortune teller he claimed to be.'

'Did you mean for me to open this can of worms?'

'There's no can. That's all I have to say about the man. I raised myself and I'm better off for it.'

'I can see how you turned out the way you are.'

'I don't know whether to take that as a compliment or an insult.'

'A compliment,' Rand said.

Almost too fast.

Slater smirked, and said, 'What did you do in the Selous Scouts?'

'Plenty.'

'For the right reasons?'

'I was like your father. I wasn't looking at colour. I was looking at doing what I thought was best for Rhodesia. And that meant fighting ZANLA.'

'There were extremists on both sides,' Slater said. 'I'm familiar with the history.'

'We had unorthodox methods. We would take the guerrillas behind the buildings, one by one, and tie them up, and shoot the dirt near their heads. It didn't take long for the last ones standing to cave in and tell us everything they knew.'

'That's better than the alternative.'

'There was plenty of the alternative. We didn't kill unarmed hostages. But there was fighting. Against armed guerillas. There was killing. Lots of it. It probably seemed like a race war. But it wasn't that to me...'

'But it looked like it. From the outside.'

Rand nodded. 'And then they won. And I accepted it. I moved on and put my past behind me and had a lot of time to myself. So I stewed over what I did. And day by day I started to convince myself that I'd been racist. The new government didn't help, of course. I got some spoils of war in the Scouts, and when I parted ways with them I bought a swathe of land right near here. It was fertile and irrigated and ready for crops. I bought a load of maize seeds, and got to work. By then I had a daughter. A little girl. She'd been born when I was in the Scouts. She was nine when I finally settled down.'

'Who was the mother?'

'A fling. Neither of us intended for a pregnancy. But it turned out to be the best thing that happened to me.'

Slater sensed foreboding, and he tried to hide a grimace. 'Where's the girl now?'

Rand looked down at his mug. He blinked hard, over and over and over again. It didn't help. Tears welled in his eyes. Fast. Far faster than Slater anticipated. A couple of drops fell into his lap. He scoffed, embarrassed, and wiped his eyes with a dirty sleeve.

He said, 'She's not around.'

'As in — you two don't talk anymore?'

'As in — I lost her when I lost my arm and my leg.'

12

'**D**o you want to talk about it?' Slater said.

'You asked.'

'I can leave.'

'No, stay.'

'You sure?'

'Positive.'

'Why?'

'You hit the nail on the head the first time.'

'You don't have anyone to talk about this with?'

'You're goddamn right I don't. Just make sure we don't get interrupted.'

Slater glanced at the bar. Ron had a wet glass covered in soap suds in his left hand, and an old tea towel in his right. Judy was nowhere to be seen. Perhaps she'd headed upstairs for some housekeeping work. Perhaps she'd sensed the aura of the conversation emanating from their corner, even if she couldn't hear it. The three men by the front entrance were still a few dozen feet away, nowhere close to earshot. All of them were firmly involved in their own chat. They weren't even glancing in Slater's direction.

He said, 'We're fine.'

Rand said, 'I think I became a maize farmer out of guilt.'

'I'm sure it was profitable enough, if you did it right.'

'It wasn't.'

'Then why did you do it?'

'I just told you.'

'Atoning for your past sins?'

'Something like that.'

'You sound like a man who feels horrendous about what he did. Just how bad was the civil war?'

'Didn't your dad tell you?'

'He told me of it. But he wasn't in it. He was on the sidelines. He didn't experience it up close, in the flesh.'

'You been at war before?'

'For most of my adult life.'

Rand paused, estimating age, running through timelines. He said, 'That doesn't make any sense.'

'I wasn't in Iraq, or Afghanistan, or anything you could classify as an official conflict. But you can read between the lines. You can imagine what I did for my country. You can work it out yourself.'

'How many people have you killed?'

'I lost count in my first year.'

'When was that?'

'I was twenty-two.'

'Shit.'

'Exactly.'

'You ever feel guilty?'

'I don't feel anything I could put into words. It's complicated, isn't it? You wonder if you killed people who were too brainwashed to know any better. You wonder if they really deserved it. You wonder a lot of things.'

Rand drained the rest of his cider, and said, 'That sums

it up. Most of it. It was a war. To me, it had nothing to do with race. To some, it did. And I couldn't murder my own brothers-in-arms because of their opinions. So I stewed silently and did my job and got out when the war ended.'

'Why maize farming?'

'Because it was the most heavily regulated industry, and also the most corrupt, and therefore the most likely to keep me barely above the poverty line.'

'You did that to yourself?'

'The mind is a tricky thing to decipher.'

'I understand.'

'I figured it was karmic punishment.'

'Self-inflicted karmic punishment.'

'I thought maybe if there was anyone upstairs, they'd see what I was doing to myself and forgive me for it.'

'I think if there's anyone upstairs, they'd know your motivations behind all of it anyway. If you're telling the truth about them.'

'I am. From the bottom of my heart.'

'Then why worry?'

'Quite a simple question for something as complicated as a human being.'

'True,' Slater said.

He finished his second beer in one gulp, and pressed the empty glass down on the table. He wiped his lip and assessed his inebriation.

All good, he thought.

A slight buzz, but nothing spectacular.

Ron and Judy had clearly underestimated his past penchant for substances. He figured he'd built a tolerance for the ages.

'Another round?' he said.

Rand nodded. 'We'll need it.'

'Is this conversation about to get heavy?'

'You could put it that way.'

Slater fetched Rand's empty mug and carried it with his own glass back to the bar. He put his elbows on the countertop and leant toward Ron and said, 'How much do you know about Rand?'

Ron eyed the man warily over Slater's shoulder and said, 'Enough.'

'Should I be digging deep?'

'I'm trying not to pay too much attention, but he seems okay. He's been through hell. If he wants to talk about it, let him talk.'

'I think I was too forward at the start.'

'Maybe he needed that.'

'Maybe.'

'If he's sharing, then don't cut him off. Judy knows people a hell of a lot better than I do. She read between the lines. She saw you were similar, under the surface. She seems to always know what people need. I think that's half the reason this place has been so successful.'

'The sign says it's a backpackers'.'

Ron smiled, almost sadly. 'You see any backpackers on the way here?'

'Just me.'

'Sign of the times. It's getting better, though. This place serves as a drinking hole for neighbours who have some coin. It keeps us afloat. But tourism is increasing. Step by step. The country's trying to dig itself out of where it used to be. It's working. Slowly.'

'Too slow for Rand.'

Ron nodded as he finished refilling both glasses. 'You might not want to know the story.'

'Why not?'

'It doesn't have a happy ending.'

'Most stories I hear don't.'

'Is that a character trait?'

'I don't know what it is. I think I keep putting myself in positions to hear those kinds of tales.'

'So you can do something about it?'

'Occasionally.'

'That's not an option here. It's ancient history.'

'You know that for sure?'

Ron stared at him. The man slid the beer and cider across the countertop, and Slater accepted them graciously.

Ron said, 'No, not for sure.'

'Some of the characters might still be hanging around these parts?'

'Those aren't people you want to interfere with.'

'There's nothing I'd want more.'

Ron looked at Slater the way a sheltered family look at a caged lion in a zoo. Then he scoffed, and shook his head, as if in disbelief.

He said, 'Tread carefully, my friend. I'd prefer you stayed above ground while you're here.'

13

S later carried the drinks back to the table, and eyed Rand as he sat down, judging the man's expression. The guy seemed complacent enough. Certainly not angry, certainly not flared up by a righteous cause. He seemed reserved and muted and accepting of what had happened to him.

Slater imagined losing two limbs would take the fight right out of you.

He slid the cider across, and Rand reached into his pocket for cash.

Slater waved it off.

'Don't worry about it,' he said.

'I'm a man of principle,' Rand said. 'How much do I owe you?'

'You owe me a story.'

Silence.

Then a shrug.

Then a nod.

Rand said, 'It started on the first day I officially acquired the property. Paige was just settling in. My little girl. I wanted the first few weeks to go smoothly. She'd had a turbulent life. To put it mildly. I didn't want her traumatised right from the get-go. And then a truck from the Grain Marketing Board decided to show up.'

'And they were...?'

'Mugabe's outfit. Run by the state. They were deemed the only entity that could buy and sell maize in all of Zimbabwe. Farmers had to go directly to them, and no-one else, or they risked their freedom and their lives. I'm not exaggerating that.'

'I can't imagine you would.'

'But they didn't know what the hell they were doing. They fixed prices all wrong. Way, way wrong. I would lose money hand over fist if I tried to work with them, but I had to, so I did.'

'To atone for the past?'

'In some twisted way, yes.'

'So you agreed with yourself that you'd play by the rules. But you didn't want them disrupting everything in the first few days, for the sake of your daughter. You'd cop a beating, if it was required, but not so soon.'

'Right.'

'So what did you do?'

'I pointed a gun in their faces. An old-school revolver. I told them to come back later. I told them I'd have no trouble doing anything they wanted for me, and I was about to explain why, but then I figured it was better for them not to know about my daughter at all.'

'So it got real awkward, real fast?'

'They did what I said. Mostly because of the gun in my hand. They hadn't expected such brazen resistance so quickly. I'd beaten them to the draw. So they turned around, and they left. And then it all went to hell.'

'How quickly?'

'It went on for years. They made my life miserable. The regime was a propaganda machine, and they used it to its full extent. I apologised as many times as I could for the first incident, but they never forgot it. The whole thing was built on whites being the epitome of evil. And I was willing to deal with that. So I worked seven days a week, twelve hours a day, just to give all my profits to the Grain Marketing Board, and I'd hope that at the end of the day there'd be some food left over to feed Paige.'

'You managed?'

'Barely.'

'And then?'

'And then Rangano showed up.'

Slater said nothing — he just sipped his beer. He waited for Rand to compose himself. The man bowed his head, cleared his throat, took a drink, and massaged his temples with his only hand.

Rand said, 'Rangano was a Political Commissar. He showed up out of nowhere. He worked directly for Mugabe. He said the region was now his, and I was to pay him an additional toll or to get off his land. He was a big, powerful man. Far bigger than me. I put him at roughly six-six. And he had muscle, too. He wasn't built like most of us are out here. He was built like a truck. So he showed up, and told me there was a new fee, almost the same amount I brought in with pure revenue. There wasn't a chance I could find the money. And then it really started.'

'I assume he could twist those words easily.'

'Far, far too easily. He went with the popular line of

thought Mugabe was spewing everywhere. I was a rich white farmer, taking land from poor black settlers, hoarding wealth for myself and pretending I didn't have any.'

'But the government was bleeding you dry in the first place.'

'No-one cared about that. They were angry. Angry at everyone. And everything around me was going to hell at the same time. Armed gangs of settlers were invading farmers' land. A couple of my close friends were slaughtered. A few others were beat half to death. And most of them were black, too. The gangs didn't care about that. They care about oppression. In their eyes, those who had land were evil. Rangano made a point of stressing that as much as he could.'

'Did you fight it?'

'I couldn't. I didn't have time. I was working every waking moment to scrape together enough money to pay the government. Just to stay on my land. Which everyone was claiming didn't belong to me in the first place. I didn't have the time or energy to defend myself from the accusations.'

'Any sane person would have left.'

'I'm nothing if not stubborn.'

'You should have done what my father did. You should have got out when you realised where things were heading.'

'I want to say something, but I fear it might offend you.'

Slater said, 'Go for your life.'

Rand said, 'You said your father didn't do a single competent thing in his life.'

'More or less.'

'That's not who I wanted to be. I believed in what I was doing, and I didn't want Paige to think I was a coward.'

'Did she know what was going on?'

'I kept most of it from her. But she knew enough. She would put it together, eventually. She would remember life on the farm, and start to realise why her father took her away from that place in her early teens. It was because he got scared.'

'I don't think so.'

'I told you. I'm stubborn.'

'So Rangano makes your life hell.'

'For a long time. He was expecting me to snap, I guess. So he had an excuse to cut me down where I stood. He didn't need much, but I never bit at his feints. And I tried my hardest to make the payments he was asking for. So there was money coming in. Which meant he was in no hurry to throw me off the land.'

'But surely you had to know it was going to happen, sooner or later?'

'I was blind to it. Blissfully oblivious. It worked to an extent. And then Simba showed up.'

Slater said, 'What? Like the Lion King?'

'The very same name. He was a ZANU-PF official.'

'And they are?'

'The Zimbabwe African National Union — Patriotic Front.'

'Mugabe's goons?'

'More or less. Soldiers, trained to carry out anything their guy wanted. More ruthless than the Political Commissar. Rangano was a terrifying man, but he never did the dirty work himself. He was a politician through and through. He got others to do it for him. So he brought in Simba — a psychopath, all the way down to the core — and he let him have his way with me.'

'What happened?'

Rand lifted the cider glass to his lips and drank greedily. He sighed. The exhale started in the pit of his stomach and shook as it came up his throat and out through his mouth. Slater could tell the man was still rattled by what had happened.

Rand said, 'The worst thing you could possibly imagine.'

14

'When?' Slater said.

'Eight years ago.'

Slater said, 'Your arm...'

'And my leg.'

Silence.

Rand said, 'And my daughter.'

'Is she still alive?'

'No way to know for sure. But I figure it's about the same probability as my arm growing back.'

'Was it Simba?'

'The one and only.'

'How'd he do it?'

'He wasn't so unlike Rangano. He didn't want to bear the whole burden himself. But they seemed to come to a mutual understanding that the game had been played for long enough, and now it was time for it to come to an end. They'd squeezed me dry of all my money. They knew I probably wouldn't put up with it for much longer. So they went to their next phase. Simba rounded up a gang of settlers. Maybe twenty or thirty of them. They stormed onto my property, they trashed the irrigation pipes, they built themselves thatch huts in the middle of my crops, and they destroyed all my produce.'

'But they didn't come after you?'

'Not yet. They thought I'd get the message. It was staring me right in the face. You can't grow crops anymore, and we're still going to be asking for our fees, so you should pack up and get out before we make you. But ... well, I told you before...'

'You're stubborn.'

'To the bone. So I barricaded myself into the house, with Paige. It was too late to send her away without putting her in harm's way. And there was no-one I could turn to anyway. I'd been ostracised by everyone in the community. In their hate-fuelled eyes I was an evil white farmer, just like the rest of them. Rangano came to the door late one night, alone. I opened it. He told me to make my next choice very wisely. He was giving me the opportunity to walk away. Right then and there. But he wouldn't give it again. I looked over his shoulder, and I saw settlers crouching in the ditches with metal pangas. They're knives. Machetes. I saw the moonlight glinting off them. And that was when I knew I was done for. Even if I accepted his offer, they'd take me on the trail out of the property. Which would add to the humiliation. So I slammed the door in his face.'

'And?'

'He disappeared. And then Simba came back. With all his muscle and all his settlers. Like a cult. They smashed the windows and kicked the door in, and I put Paige in the basement and told her no matter what, she wasn't to come out for any reason whatsoever. And I locked the door to the basement and sealed it. Then I went to confront them. They took me, and I'll never forget the look in their eyes. It was like I was the devil incarnate. I don't know what Simba had told them. Or Rangano. They were both extraordinarily adept at churning the wheels of the propaganda machine. But they shoved me down on my stomach on the front porch, and one of the settlers took his panga and sawed my leg off at the knee. They used a cloth as a tourniquet to try and stop the bleeding. To keep me alive. Then one of them wanted to know if he could be more efficient with the motion. He didn't want to waste time and energy sawing. He said he had the sharpest panga in the group. So they held my arm out, and the guy swung down with the panga like he was using an axe to chop wood, and he took my arm off at the shoulder in one blow.'

Slater paused with the beer halfway to his lips. He gulped back apprehension.

He said, 'How are you still here?'

'They managed to stop the worst of the bleeding by stuffing rags over my wounds and using a couple of makeshift tourniquets. And I was holding on with every shred of energy I had in my body. Because my fate was sealed, but Paige's wasn't. Do you have kids?'

'No,' Slater said, but he thought of Shien.

'Then you wouldn't understand. People are capable of unbelievable things to protect their kids.'

'Trust me, I understand.'

Rand looked at him. 'Something happened to you recently, didn't it? Something to do with being a father. I can see it in your eyes.'

'We could get into that,' Slater said, 'but we'd be here another few hours.'

'I've got time.'

'I need to know how your story ends.'

'Not well.'

'I didn't imagine it would.'

'There isn't much more to it.'

Slater sipped his beer and gestured for Rand to continue.

The man said, 'I almost bled out. I lost so much blood. It was all over the porch. The settlers started celebrating over me. They swung my arm around in the air. I was barely staying conscious, but I needed to somehow get them away from the house. Because sooner or later Paige had to come out. There wasn't any food or water down there. If they took up residence in the house, it was over.'

'So what did you do?'

Rand looked at him, and shrugged. As best he could. He said, 'This isn't a fairytale.'

'I never said it was.'

'There's no happy ending.'

'I never expected there to be.'

15

Rand said, 'I lost consciousness. I woke up hours later, and realised they hadn't killed me. They'd driven me miles away from my property, and dumped me on the side of the road. There was dirt in my open wounds. I was covered in muck and blood. I couldn't keep my eyes open for more than a few seconds at a time. I looked around and saw nothing except crops, and no sign of passersby, so I gave up. I closed my eyes and gave myself permission to fade away.'

'And yet, here you are.'

'A family picked me up. All native Zimbabweans. The black majority. I tried as best I could to plead with them. To tell them, *No, just leave me here.* I thought they would take me back to the farm. I didn't want to know what they'd done to my daughter. But they spoke Shona, and nothing else. I couldn't communicate with them. There was a husband, and a wife, and a little girl, and a little boy. I'm ashamed to say I judged them prematurely. Because the only people I'd seen for the last couple of years — when I wasn't working, that is — had been looking to exploit me, and lord over me.

I wasn't expecting anything other than more torture. But the guy was a rural doctor. They took me back to their house and stopped the bleeding, and the guy made a trip to the local clinic, and stole almost half the inventory, and set to work patching me up as best he could.'

'Your daughter...?'

'I couldn't check on her. I was too weak to move. I'd lost enough blood to reach the limit of what the human body can endure. I couldn't get out of bed. No matter how motivated I was to protect her. My body simply didn't respond to my mind.'

'I've been there,' Slater mumbled.

Rand shot him daggers. 'Not there. You have your arms and legs.'

'You ever had a brain injury?'

'No.'

'It's your own personal little version of hell. Like being on the worst psychedelics of all time. You try and command yourself to do something, but important connections have been shattered. So you're left flailing like a dying fish. That's what it feels like.'

'Where did you get a brain injury?'

'Russia.'

'How?'

'Someone stomped on my head.'

Rand paused, then nodded, as if accepting the comparison. 'Well, that's what this was like.'

'How long did it take you to get out of bed?'

'A few days. It should have been weeks, or months. But, like I said, the love a man has for his child...'

'What'd you find?'

'I tried to get the family that saved me to go back there. They had some broken English after all — the wife was learning it. I imagine she's practically fluent by now. She was a fast learner. But they didn't dare involve themselves. Their eyes went wide when I suggested it. They said Simba had set off on his own personal crusade through the region, and he was slaughtering any farmer he could get his hands on. Black or white, it didn't matter. It doesn't usually matter to someone like that.'

'I see,' Slater said.

'So after three days I took the family's car and drove back to the farm, and it was like I was in a fever dream. I was delirious. My temperature was through the roof. I was pale and sweating and almost passed out a couple of times on the drive. But I made it. And the farm was abandoned. They hadn't seized it for their personal use. They'd seized it for the thrill. They had no intention of actually using the land. They were just angry. Angry at everyone, especially what they thought constituted the "upper class." No thanks to Simba, and Rangano. I never saw either of them again. Or any of the settlers that ransacked my place.'

'And Paige?'

'They burned the house to the ground. Just to spite me. There was nothing left. They wouldn't have known she was downstairs. The basement was sealed tight from the outside. They just lit it all aflame, until it collapsed in a pile of embers. I sat there and looked at the wreckage and figured it would have been better off if they'd just killed me. So that I didn't have to ever think about her final moments.'

16

S later noted the pain still seared deep across Rand's face, and then he said, 'Did they find remains?'

'Who?' Rand said, and he managed a cruel bitter laugh. 'Oh — do you mean the investigators? The police? Is that who you might be referring to?'

'Anyone,' Slater said.

Rand shook his head. 'No investigation. It was probably off-duty cops that hacked my arm and leg off in the first place. I didn't have access to any of that. And I was still public enemy number one. The only thing that stopped me eating the nearest gun was the thought of Paige looking down on me.'

Slater opened his mouth to speak, and then hesitated.

Rand said, 'You ever thought of doing something like that?'

Slater said, 'Never.'

'Then you might be uniquely suited to your lifestyle.'

'I think so.'

'Honestly — you've never failed?'

'I've failed plenty.'

'Were the stakes high enough?'

'Always.'

'But maybe not personal to you.'

'I try to keep everything impersonal.'

'Sounds like you've recently been through something that changed that, though.'

Slater said, 'I don't want to talk about that.'

'I think I deserve an explanation.'

'I helped a kid. I left her with someone I trusted. He did the wrong thing. So I made an enemy of anyone and everyone to make sure she got the help I wanted in the first place.'

'Why'd you help the kid?'

'That's what I do.'

'Like what you're building up to here?'

'I'm not building up to anything.'

'You have to be — otherwise you wouldn't have come over here.'

'I just want to know the rest of the story.'

'There's nothing else. That's it.'

'There's always more.'

Rand clenched his teeth together, and cocked his head, and visibly shivered despite the heat. A cold chill was working its way down his spine.

'There's nothing more,' he said. 'No-one cared about what happened. Where you're from, maybe it would have been different. There might have been outrage in the media, and a thorough investigation, and the correct people brought to justice. Out here, there's none of that. They were the media. They were the police. They were the judge, and the jury. So I spent a few days in a rage, driving around the country with no particular aim, trying to find anyone responsible, and then infection set in and I couldn't do very much of anything for a few months. I came out the other side alive, but stripped of any motivation to do anything. I made a deliberate effort to find out as little as possible about where Rangano or Simba are now. I know they're thriving, somewhere. Other than that, all I hear is the odd rumour. I keep the same routine and try not to think about what happened. And that's it.'

'There's got to be someone you could approach now.'

Rand shook his head. 'No.'

'Why not?'

'Just no.'

'Where's the farm now?'

'Gone. Or rebuilt for the new wave of farmers. How should I know? I've never been back.'

'You don't care?'

'Not anymore. I used to care.'

'You just can't do it anymore?'

Rand shook his head. 'I can't do any of it. It's all too much. Besides, what could I do? Look at me.'

Slater looked at him.

He saw a man defeated by Father Time, wallowing in some kind of purgatory state where he felt nothing and said nothing. Slater understood. Sooner or later, the oppressive weight of corruption bore down on you. Sooner or later, you broke.

'Did it happen to other farmers?' Slater said.

'Probably. I stopped wondering a long time ago.'

'It must have.'

'Because of what happened afterward?'

Slater nodded.

Rand shrugged and said, 'Zimbabwe went to hell for a lot of reasons. So that's my story. Make of it what you will. But there's nothing you or me or anyone can do to bring back my daughter, or my arm, or my leg. So I'd advise you to get up and leave, because otherwise you'll get wrapped up in something you have no business being involved in. And it won't change the past anyway. So go.'

Slater stayed where he was.

17

He gave the information time to sink in.

It was a lot to take on board — a fairly simplistic narrative, sporting a surprising lack of twists and turns considering the dark subject matter, but it hit like a gut punch all the same. He made sure not to take the story lightly. He ruminated on what Rand had described, stewing over it image by image. Pictured the man arriving back at the farm he'd poured his heart and soul into, finding it burnt to the ground — but on top of that, finding it abandoned.

Slater didn't underestimate how deep that would have cut.

It had been Rand's life's work, a muddied attempt to atone for a stint in the Selous Scouts. And the settlers hadn't even ransacked it for supposed economical reasons. They hadn't done it for the good of the country. They'd done it because they'd been taught to resent those who had something. Slater had spent half his career in the depths of the Third World, surrounded by poverty and oppression, alone in a hostile environment, with nothing to rely on but his own thoughts. He'd taught himself to look at every situation objectively — he had to, for his own sanity. It had taught him everything about the nature of the world. About how people worked. About how resentment stewed. About how dictators stayed in power. Because they fed off weakness. And they latched onto doubt. And they stoked the fire, and fed it, and encouraged anything that kept them worshipped.

Slater said, 'I assume the farm attacks led to the famine.'

Rand nodded. 'You can imagine by that point I was disillusioned. I didn't care about anything. Or at least I thought I didn't. But even in my darkest days I could feel the anger building. I don't know why. I don't know why I cared at that point.'

'Because it didn't just affect the bad eggs. It affected everyone.'

'They drove away every competent farmer. Or, at least, the overwhelming majority of them. They said they did it to reclaim the land for those who were abused and taken advantage of in colonial times. Which sounds like a noble cause, on the surface. But they had no intention of trying to pick up the pieces. So the country starved, because there were no decent farmers left.'

'I'm familiar with recent history.'

'It's getting better. Slowly.'

'So what do you do now?'

'I do contract work for the resurfacing maize farming industry. The new regime's trying to bring it back from what it was. The new gig pays fairly well. I know how to leverage my expertise. But I only do the bare minimum. I just don't care about making a living. Otherwise, I come here, and I drink. And that's about it.'

'Do Ron and Judy know the full extent of your story?'

'Not all of it. Even you don't know all of it. I'd have to talk to you for a week straight. I've glossed over a lot of it.'

'A lot of the good, or a lot of the bad?'

Rand said, 'Look into my eyes and tell me what you think.'

Slater obliged. They were bloodshot and detached and wracked with a myriad of emotions he couldn't begin to decipher. There was nothing hopeful in there.

Slater said, 'I'm sorry.'

'For what?'

'Wanting to know. It was selfish of me.'

'No, it wasn't. Because all I've done for years is sit around and watch people. People who come through this place with that inspired look in their eyes. They're wanderers. The crazy kind, too, otherwise they wouldn't be out here. Most are spoiled rich kids looking to branch away from what's considered the social norm. Their friends go to Europe, and they come to Africa. But they don't stop there — they seek out the ends of the earth. So you can imagine the relief when they find a place like this. Because sooner or later they all realise there's a reason no-one comes out here. And then when they stumble across a safe haven like this — relatively safe from random acts of violence — they head straight to the bar and book a room. Most end up staying weeks. That's how Ron and Judy get by.'

'I don't see what that has to do with me.'

'These kids don't want to talk to the guy in the corner who's missing an arm and a leg. Neither does anyone else, as a matter of fact. They pretend not to notice me. Even though I'm right here. Social conventions brings in all kinds of excuses. They look around, they admire the view. Looking anywhere but me. They pretend they've seen something fascinating on the other side of the room. They go over there, and they stay there. Because no-one wants that burden. No-one wants to hear the story. They can probably see the look on my face when they glance at me. They know it's not going to be a nice story. I haven't told it to anyone in years.'

'Because everyone knows they're helpless to change it?'

'Something like that.'

'They wouldn't know what to say?'

'Exactly.'

'You think I might be different?'

Rand shrugged. 'That's not my position to judge.'

'You think I'm going to ask you if Rangano and Simba are still around?'

'I don't expect you to ask me anything. And if you did ask me that, I'd consider you a fool.'

'But would you give me a truthful answer?'

'I told you — it's a stupid question to ask.'

'It was a stupid idea to come over here in the first place. If we're looking at it from a social convention standpoint. My day would go a lot better — from a normal perspective — if I did the same as everyone else who steps foot in here. I had the option to. But I didn't.'

'Because of your past.'

'Because of a lot of things.'

'Is this all hypothetical?'

'If you want it to be.'

'I don't know what I want.'

'Consider it an eternal "what-if." I'm not the type to stay in one place for long, so I'm not going to hang around this place for more than a night. I'll be on my way, and it doesn't make a difference one way or the other what information I have. You'll never know what happened.'

'You sound awfully confident for someone who's adamant they're not going to go out and seek revenge.'

'Trouble has a way of finding me.'

'That's a line straight out of a B-movie. That shit doesn't happen out here.'

'It might.'

'I don't want to cause any more problems than I already have.'

'Is that why you haven't tried anything yourself?'

Rand stared at him. He left his glass on the table. He didn't touch it. He drummed his fingers against the wood. He took a deep breath. He said, 'Things change.'

'You were a Selous Scout.'

'With two arms and two legs.'

'I assume, from the way our conversation is heading, that Rangano and Simba are still around. Or one of them. Because you're explaining why you haven't gone after them. Which means they exist. They're within reach.'

'Not within my reach.'

'Why not?'

'You've never lost a limb.'

'I'll concede that point.'

'It changes you.'

'I can imagine.'

'And other people's circumstances change too. Ever since that day on the farm, I went down. They went up.'

'Both of them?'

A nod.

Slater said, 'They're still in Zimbabwe?'

'They're not far from here at all.'

'You must have been tempted. Over the years.'

'You don't know the half of it.'

'Tell me about it.'

Rand smashed an open palm into the table, hard enough to almost break his own fingers. The wood rattled, and the sound punched through the ambience of the background music. At the bar, Ron's eyes darted to their table, flashing with a menace Slater hadn't anticipated. He realised in an instant the demeanour of a caring host was just one side of the man. Judy too, probably. They had to be ready for anything out here. Life would be civilised the majority of the time, but Ron had to be prepared for a standoff at the drop of a hat. Maybe he had a gun under the bar.

Rand shook his head, a subtle *stand down* gesture.

Ron nodded, and went back to washing dishes like nothing had happened at all.

Rand clenched his teeth and said, 'Sorry.'

'No,' Slater said. 'That's my bad.'

'I don't like talking about this stuff.'

'I understand.'

Then he closed his eyes, and muttered, 'But I need to.'

When he opened them again, he sported a steely resolve Slater hadn't seen before.

Slater figured he might get enough information in the coming moments to put himself in a precarious position. Either he would act, or he wouldn't.

He leant forward to hear what Rand had to say.

18

R and said, 'You have to understand I've been deliberately distancing myself from this kind of thing for the last few years.'

Slater said, 'I understand.'

'I don't know enough to help you.'

'But you know something.'

'I hear rumours. Whether I want to or not. Sometimes talk gets through.'

'What talk?'

'I hear Simba, or Rangano, or both, are trying to transition into legitimate business. They've got the kind of money from the old system to keep them afloat, but I imagine they both have enormous expenses. They'd need private security, and housing for all that security, and food and clothing and everything else that comes with the territory. They're powerful, well-established figures in a country that no longer recognises their positions. They're basically outcasts, but they struck the region with so much terror that no-one would dare retaliate. And there'd be no shortage of men from the old regime lining up to protect them, now fresh out of work, but they won't work for free. So that money's going to run dry within a few short years, and these are smart guys who can reasonably foresee the future. They'll be planning ahead.'

'What are the rumours?'

'There's talk they're spending a lot of time at the bull auctions.'

Slater paused. He sipped his beer. 'Bull auctions?'

'The beef industry is going through a resurgence too. Well, I guess every industry is going through a resurgence. But the auctions are always popular. The genetically pure bulls go for a pretty penny. Types like Rangano and Simba are probably the only people in the region who can afford them at this point. So there's talk they're getting in early. Snatching up all the premium pickings. I imagine they're trying to be big players in the beef industry within a few years.'

'What else can you tell me?'

'That's about it. Like I said — I've avoided specifics like the plague. Because if I know where, and when, I won't be able to stop myself confronting them. And that wouldn't go well for me.'

'You have combat experience.'

'Combat experience in a functioning body. Now I'm a wreck.'

'You can still hold a gun.'

'And they can pay fifty men to hold guns. I can't touch them, and if we're being honest, neither can you. I don't have a location, or good intel, or anything I can feed you that would help. If you really want to do this — which I think you do, considering the glint in your eye — then you'd be walking in blind against an entire army of dispossessed psychos from the old regime under the control of a couple of men with enough money to buy up half the country in its current state.'

'How did they get so much money?' Slater said. 'If all they were doing was ransacking farms and driving out farmers?'

Rand smiled. One of the saddest smiles Slater had seen. 'Because that's not all they were doing.'

'I'm sorry if this is hard on you.'

'It'd be harder not to talk. But I'm not the man to tell you about what else they were doing.'

'Why not?'

'I know what they did. But it's all unsubstantiated in the court of public opinion. And I'm only comfortable with commenting on what I've experienced first-hand. Otherwise I might say something untrue. I aim to be very careful with my speech.'

'Could you point me in the direction of someone who'd be willing to talk about it?'

'Walk outside and ask the first person you come across.'

'In detail.'

Rand paused, mulling over it. He said, 'I don't usually think about this.'

'I couldn't imagine you would.'

'I need you to promise me you won't do anything stupid.'

'My life has been one consecutive string of stupid acts. I'm not about to change that.'

'Don't be reckless.'

'That's all I know how to do.'

'Then we should bid each other farewell and go our separate ways.'

'I just want to talk to someone else. I need a better sense of who I'm dealing with.'

'Why are you doing this?'

'I told you.'

'No, you didn't. Not really. Is this for me, or is it for you?'

Slater didn't respond.

He just sat there, cradling his beer, draped in the fog of alcohol.

Then he said, 'It's both.'

'Is that the truth?'

'Yes.'

'I'm glad you're man enough to admit you're not entirely selfless.'

'No-one is.'

'Why is this your problem?'

'I have a habit of making everything my problem. For better or worse.'

'If you fuck it up, and it comes back to haunt me, I'll never forgive you.'

'That's the last thing I want to happen.'

'So how can you assure me it won't?'

'Because no-one will know why I'm involving myself. I won't mention your name. It's my burden, and mine alone.'

'Why?'

'Because I don't like people like Rangano, and Simba.'

'That's it?'

'I'm a simple man.'

'I can see that.'

'Are you going to help me?'

'I thought you were the one helping me.'

'Not anymore.'

'Is this what you do? Find someone who's been wronged, and try to get yourself killed setting it right?'

'That's the general gist of it.'

'You won't set this right.'

'You'd be surprised.'

'I won't be surprised. I won't be anything. Because as soon as you walk out of here I don't want to hear from you again. Ignorance is bliss. I hope you succeed with whatever the hell it is you want to do exactly, but I won't be around to cheer you on.'

'What are you going to do?'

'Same thing I've done for years. Drink and eat and sleep, and lend my knowledge out to farmers who need it so I can fund my simple existence.'

Slater let the silence drag out, and then he said, 'I hope you don't take this lightly — that sounds like a decent life. Considering the circumstances.'

'You should try it.'

'I never could.'

'You could force yourself to. Same way you forced yourself into your career. I assume nearly getting yourself killed over and over again didn't come naturally to you.'

'That's where you'd be wrong.'

Rand shrugged. 'Not my business anymore. Nothing is.'

'You want it to be that way?'

'More than anything.'

Slater nodded. 'Then tell me where I can find out more.'

'You probably won't get there unharmed. Most of Zimbabwe is great these days. The country's recovering. But the parts I'm talking about shouldn't be approached lightly. They're still stewing with resentment over the way things are changing. And that makes for a select few dangerous individuals. That's why I do the same thing every day. That's why I don't venture outside my bubble. There's nothing good out there.'

'I think I'm allergic to living in a bubble.'

Rand said, 'Then I want you to meet the family that saved my life.'

19

S later said, 'Are you sure that's a good idea?'

'If you want answers, that's where to go.'

'Why would they talk to me?'

'They felt sorry for me. They helped me. That means they're reasonable people.'

'I thought you said you couldn't communicate with them.'

'I told you — the wife had broken English. We managed our way past a few barriers. And then I found my home burnt to the ground, and it was like I had nothing to live for anymore. So I gave them their car back, and then I never went back.'

'What did you talk about while you were there?'

'They told me their story, as I lay in bed trying to come to terms with the fact that two of my limbs no longer existed.'

'And?'

'It involves Simba. Which I imagine will lead to Rangano. They're inseparable, only in the way a Political Commissar and a ZANU-PF official could be.'

'Why are you sending me in that direction?'

'Because if the family is even slightly involved in what's going on around them, then they'll have a wealth of knowledge I don't possess.'

'You're not sending me on a wild goose chase, are you?'

'No. If I didn't want to give you anything, I simply wouldn't give you anything. I'm way past caring about being polite.'

'Okay.'

'Their names are Akash and Danai. Their kids are Rudo and Zendaya.'

'You still remember?'

'Always.'

'Have you made sure to remember?'

'Those days were the last unique memories I have. Everything since then has been resignation and acceptance and misery and wallowing in self-pity. That's the best way I can describe it.'

'You ever told anyone that?'

'No. I keep that to myself.'

'Where can I find the family?'

'You got a phone?'

Slater passed his smartphone over. For someone detached from society, Rand proved extraordinarily adept at navigating through its menus. He found a map application in seconds and zoomed in on Slater's current location, a pale blue dot hovering over an empty patch of land deep in the heart of rural Zimbabwe. From there he estimated a route with long sweeping tracks on the touch screen, dragging his finger one way, then the other. After a few moments of pensive rumination he came down on a winding trail further east of the Marange fields, but close enough to walk.

Slater kept a watchful eye the whole time, and figured

he could cover the distance on foot in a single day if he loaded up with supplies here at the homestead.

For tonight, he needed a room.

Rand's finger came to rest on a single point on the map, and he made sure Slater saw before passing the phone back.

'There,' Rand said.

Slater dropped a virtual pin on the map and came away with an exact set of co-ordinates. He showed the screen, with the bright red dot included, to Rand. He looked a question at the man.

Rand nodded. 'Spot on.'

'You don't have their address?'

'Never asked.'

'But you remember the way.'

'I told you before…'

'You remember all of it.'

Rand nodded again. 'Those memories will never go away.'

'Unless you make new ones.'

'Not interested.'

'To each their own.'

'Have you ever lost someone you cared about?' Rand said.

Slater thought of Shien.

He chose his next words carefully.

He said, 'More or less.'

'What does that mean?'

'That's a conversation for another time.'

'But there won't be another time.'

'Exactly.'

Rand stared at Slater, and Slater stared back. They both seemed to recognise the reality of the situation. Rand could give nothing more than a hint as to the current state of affairs, and he'd summed up the most traumatising aspects of his past with a certain succinctness that Slater expected hadn't come easy.

There was no need for anything else.

Slater got to his feet as the sky darkened outside, draping most of the homestead in shadows. He'd barely noticed the sun setting as they talked. Too consumed by the detail. His mind populated by imagined flashes of the past.

He took a deep breath, and then he offered Rand his hand.

A farewell gesture.

20

S later said, 'I hope you're incorrect. I hope I meet you after all this is over.'

'After what's over?' Rand said.

'What was it you said before?'

Rand managed a half-smile. 'Ignorance is bliss?'

'Maybe that's best here.'

'You sure?'

'It's your call.'

Rand waved a hand in Slater's direction. Dismissively. 'You're right. Better I don't know. Better I keep doing what I'm doing, or I'll go insane.'

'What if I bring old secrets to the surface?' Slater said. 'Would you want to know?'

'The past is the past. Nothing you tell me will change that. So keep me in the dark. Do what you need to do for your own twisted sense of self-satisfaction, and then move on with your life. Forget I existed. That's best for both of us.'

'What would you want me to do?'

'Nothing.'

'Hypothetically.'

Rand looked at him. 'After this I'm going to pretend you were a figment of my imagination, but right now I'm going to tell you to make both of them hurt. If you can find them, and get past their security, and avoid making enemies of half the country.'

'Rangano, and Simba?'

Rand nodded. 'You won't be able to touch them. All of this is wishful thinking on my part. I'm choosing to engage with someone with delusions. There's something wrong with me. But I can fully accept that. Given the way my life has gone. So therefore, I don't really care if there's something wrong with you either.'

'What do you think's going to happen?'

'You'll think you can treat this situation like you've treated all the others, and you'll get in too deep, and you'll more than likely die a slow painful death. And no-one will ever know about it, because they'll sweep it under the rug so effectively that it'll seem like you never existed in the first place.'

'That wouldn't be ideal for me.'

'Not at all. But it's the way things go. The old regime still exists. They didn't magically change their opinions when the new government came in. They're still all over the place — they just can't talk about it in public anymore. Some of them still do. Most don't. They're adapting with the times.'

'Can this family point me in the right direction?'

'They'll know more about Simba's current whereabouts than I do. They'll know details. They'll be more actively involved.'

'Not Rangano?'

'Their story concerns Simba.'

'Do I want to hear it?'

'Did you want to hear mine?'

'It was necessary.'

Rand nodded. 'There you go.'

'Is it as brutal as yours?'

'I'll let you find out for yourself.'

Slater shook his hand, and left him there cradling his cider. He went back over to the bar and didn't look back. Small talk wouldn't have sufficed. He and Rand had pierced through that right off the bat. Neither of them were in a talking mood. They could discuss pleasantries, but they'd both see straight through the veneer, and each seemed to mutually understand their introversion without having to make it explicitly clear. Alone time was crucial after such a heavy conversation. So Slater went to the bar and slotted himself back onto the same stool and ordered a fourth beer from Ron, and returned right back to mutual pleasantries with the same mask he'd put on when he stepped into the homestead.

Then dinner was served.

He ate corn paste sadza and fried mopane worms served in heaping quantities as soon as Judy returned from the kitchen out the back. They tasted good, despite the ingredients, and he wolfed them down with reckless abandon, replenishing his system after the staggering trek earlier that day. Ron and Judy watched him in pensive silence, seeming to understand how deep he was in his own mind. He could have put on a pleasant demeanour if he wanted, but he knew Judy would see right through it, and neither of them seemed to take it personally.

At one point Judy said, 'Are you glad you spoke to him?'

Slater nodded through a mouthful of food.

'Are you hanging around?' she said.

He read between the lines.

He said, 'I'll be out of here in the morning.'

'Chasing old rumours?'

'I've got nothing else to do.'

'I could think of a thousand better ideas.'

'You're the one that sent me over there.'

'I thought you could vent to each other. Therapy, of sorts. I don't think I expected this.'

'Deep down, I think you did.'

'You're that kind of guy, aren't you?'

'What you see is what you get.'

'We'll set you up with a room for the night. And we'll leave you with one piece of advice.'

'What's that?' Slater said.

Ron put down a clean glass covered in soap suds and said, 'Don't do anything you might regret.'

21

S later slept straight through the night, blacking out from the moment his head touched the pillow to the pale glow of dawn stirring him from slumber the following morning. He sat up and wiped his eyes with calloused fingers, swivelling his frame onto the edge of the thin mattress. The room was sparsely furnished, but it had everything he needed.

He took a moment to clear the grogginess, breathing fast and sharp in the isolation of the one-person bedroom, then he stood up and tugged on a fresh set of thin clothing from the bottom of his duffel bag. The gear was crinkled, but it was clean, and it smelled satisfactory. It consisted of a plain white tee and khakis that hugged his thighs. He rarely strayed from the same fashion choices. He was a man of routine, instilled through years of repetition. Nothing fancy. He'd tried it all, and came away dissatisfied. Life was not material possessions.

He'd discovered that truth only in the way a man with four hundred million dollars could.

He scrolled through a series of smartphone applications

with a pace forged from a habit of doing the same thing every morning. He checked the local weather, he checked his investments, he swiped briefly through a couple of websites to assess if there was any news he deemed important enough to take notice of. Then he tucked the phone away and nodded to himself.

The world wasn't ending, and he hadn't gone broke overnight.

He swung the duffel over one shoulder, moved past the small bathroom he'd used to shower the night before, and went downstairs to the ground floor of the homestead. Ron and Judy were already up, re-positioning some of the furniture, preparing the bar area for the day's visitors. There was no sign of Rand.

Slater approached the bar and said, 'How much do I owe you?'

Ron eyed him warily. 'Have some breakfast first.'

Slater shook his head. 'I don't eat in the mornings.'

They both looked at him as if were insane.

Judy said, 'Why not?'

Slater said, 'Intermittent fasting. Keeps the fat off. Works for me, at least.'

Judy looked him up and down, and said, 'Well, keep doing whatever it is you're doing. It seems to be working.'

Ron seemed a tad disgruntled by the remark.

Slater smiled and peeled a pair of fresh hundred dollar bills out of his pocket. He placed them on the countertop, and touched a finger to the U.S. currency to skewer it in place. He said, 'I figure this goes further out here?'

Ron nodded. 'Exchange rates are all over the place, so we take what we can in USD. We always wait for the right time to cash it in. It's been working out well for us.'

Slater nodded.

Ron said, 'But we don't have change.'

'I didn't ask for change.'

Judy stared down at the bills. 'You owe us a fifth of that.'

'I'm a generous tipper. And I'd like you to answer a few questions for me.'

Ron slipped the money into his pocket and said, 'Anything.'

'Is Rand in here often?'

'Almost every day.'

'Is he always as glum as he was yesterday?'

Judy nodded. 'That man never changes.'

'Do you know the extent of his story?'

'Most of it,' Ron said. 'Nothing specific, though. He left out any details that could be chased up by a noble benefactor. He didn't want interference.'

'Do you know a man named Rangano?'

Judy shook her head.

'Do you know a man named Simba?'

Ron shook his head.

Slater said, 'Has Rand ever mentioned either of those names to you? Try your best to remember.'

They both shook their head in unison, and then Judy's eyes widened, and she gripped the countertop with white knuckles, and she said, 'Did he tell you?'

Slater nodded. 'But I got the sense he didn't name-drop often. He seemed sickened by speaking the names into reality. Like he'd tried to forget about them for years, but was finally deciding to bring them to the surface.'

'Why?' Ron said. 'Did you ask him for them?'

'Yes, but it's easy to lie.'

'Maybe he did.'

Slater shook his head. 'I don't think so. I think, deep down, he wants to see what I'll do.'

'What will you do?' Judy said.

'Try to find them.'

'Who are they?'

'Civilians, now. But they used to be a Political Commissar and a ZANU-PF official.'

Judy went pale, and Ron got a dark look in his eyes, and they both shook their heads at the same time.

Ron said, 'You should walk away.'

Slater glanced at the double doors in the distance. 'I am.'

'Not away from here. Away from this whole situation.'

'Too late.'

'I'm serious,' Ron said.

'So am I.'

Judy said, 'Please don't get yourself killed, Slater.'

Slater shrugged. 'I thought those days were over around here.'

'The days of those types having official power are over. But there's many more forms power can take.'

'I'll take my chances.'

'Where are you headed now?' Judy said.

Slater took out his phone — its battery replenished overnight — and opened the maps application, still displaying the same checkpoint Rand had dropped the night before. He held it under their noses. Judy took the phone in a tight grip, stared down at it through the glasses resting on the bridge of her nose, and zoomed out with two fingers acting as pincers.

She sucked in air through her lips.

Ron shook his head again. 'Not that way.'

'Why not?'

'That entire region is as backwards as it comes. There's ex-Green Bombers hanging around everywhere. They're like a plague. They just won't disappear. Some of them even wear the old uniform.'

'I take it the Green Bombers were some kind of militia for the old regime?'

Judy nodded. 'Exactly right. The old hatemongers went away, but that didn't mean an entire government militia changed its ideals. They're still around. And they're not even trying to hide it. We don't stray out that way. It's a cesspool of dispossessed folk living in the past. And this country hasn't recovered yet. ZANU—PF are still in power. They just changed leaders. So the hatemongers can still get away with a whole lot.'

Slater said, 'Would folk like that be in need of jobs?'

Judy nodded.

'Would certain wealthy parties like the two individuals I mentioned before feel the need to employ a private army for … unsavoury behaviour?'

Judy shrugged.

Ron shrugged.

They both started to speak, then Ron clammed up and passed the metaphorical microphone to his wife. She said, 'We hear all kinds of rumours from people out that way. They come here to escape the tension. But we run a haven, so we don't involve ourselves with it. We make a firm point of that. With no exceptions. So we're the last people to share details with you, because we don't know them ourselves.'

Slater nodded and said, 'That's what I'm hoping to find out today.'

'Who are you visiting?'

'Some of Rand's old friends.'

'From the Selous Scouts?'

Slater said, 'No.'

Ron nodded, as if relieved.

Slater said, 'You don't like those types?'

'There's a lot of controversy around that time.'

'I know,' Slater said. 'It's been eating Rand up inside for decades.'

Judy paused, frowning, puzzled, and said, 'Rand never mentioned that to us.'

'Then you were right,' Slater said. 'He overshared with me. You called it when I first spoke to you. I was the type to bring the truth out of him. Did he ever tell you why he became a maize farmer during a time when literally anything else would have proved more profitable?'

Judy froze, and Ron said, 'He never put it like that.'

'The past can be ugly,' Slater said. 'Some people want to try and make up for it. You can figure out the rest for yourselves.'

They nodded, suddenly quiet, picturing the solitary disabled man in the corner in a different light.

'Any other words of wisdom?' Slater said.

'The Green Bombers are easy to make out,' Ron said. 'The ones holding onto the past wear olive uniforms, and berets. Usually red and green. They had an ideology, and you don't lose your ideology in a heartbeat. For some of them, it's all they know. Stay away from the fanatical ones. Try your best to stay away from all of them unless it's absolutely necessary. And good luck. I hope you find what you're looking for.'

'Thanks for the room,' Slater said.

He shook their hands, one after the other, first Judy's quaint delicate grip, and then a sturdy interaction with Ron. He nodded to both of them, and smiled, and they smiled back. But it wasn't as warm as when he'd arrived. He sensed something in the air, and he felt he could pinpoint it without much effort.

It was disbelief, and trepidation, and puzzlement, and confusion.

It was both of them wondering if, by letting him leave, they were participating in sending a lunatic to his inevitable death.

He should have been more vague about what he planned to do.

Ignorance is bliss.

He picked up his duffel, turned on his heel, and left the homestead.

22

Call it intuition, but Slater knew he wouldn't make it to the family home without running into an altercation first.

As soon as he stepped off Ron and Judy's porch and set off in the direction of the Marange diamond fields, the balmy early morning weather receded from his perception. Instead he could only see cold ahead, an observation that came to him when he knew conflict was all but guaranteed.

It was the nature of what he did.

He wasn't welcome around these parts. On the off chance travellers or wanderers found themselves in rural Zimbabwe or a similarly deserted location, they would keep their head bowed and their eyes turned to the ground and their guard raised and their manners in tip-top shape. Because offending anyone out here was a recipe for disaster. And Slater had never shied away from that in his life. Which was probably most of the reason he found so much trouble in the first place. The quiet confidence that came with his life experiences put him on steady footing to stare an aggravated local right in the eyes, and ask them what they wanted, and be fully prepared to back up his confidence as soon as the situation demanded it.

So when a faded, gunmetal grey pick-up truck rumbled and jolted past him a couple of hours into the hike, he tensed up in anticipation. The dust cloud washed over him, and he watched the vehicle closely. There were two men in the rear tray, and a man in the driver's seat, and another in the passenger's seat.

They wore olive uniforms.

They had berets on their heads.

Red and green.

Slater stood deathly still, and shoved his hands in his pockets, and watched them like a hawk. If pressed for details, he would likely have to admit that he was encouraging confrontation. On a subliminal level. He wasn't doing anything except sticking his chin in the air and sending a withering gaze in the direction of the truck. An oblivious bystander might chalk it up to simple curiosity.

But the men in the truck didn't.

The pick-up got a few dozen feet past Slater, barreling toward Marange, before one of the guys in the rear tray noticed him staring. The man on the right had his gaze averted, whether deliberately or coincidentally, staring out at the sweeping fields of maize and wheat on either side of the trail. The other man gave the semi-circle behind the truck the once-over, probably not expecting anything other than a quick view of a solo traveller staring at the ground, not looking for trouble, ignoring the alpha males of the region.

But he noticed Slater's accusatory glare, and he paused a beat, unblinking, and then he lurched his upper half over the lip of the rear tray and manoeuvred himself round to the driver's window and screamed a command inside the cabin, drowning out the noise of the loose earth rumbling under the pick-up's tyres.

The truck slammed on the brakes.

Slater stood still.

There was an awkward distance between the two parties. Enough to warrant the driver backing up, nosing up to the twisted and rusting barbed wire fence on the left, backing up again, turning another small arc, finally passing parallel, now nosing toward Slater's solitary form, then hitting the accelerator and bouncing back toward him.

Slater stood even stiller.

He drew an imaginary line in the dirt trail. If the pick-up truck crossed it without slowing, he would lunge for the fence to his left, and hurl himself over the barbed wire despite the consequences. The fencing methods farmers had employed years ago were failing anyway — patches of the barbed wire were missing, either stolen by settlers or dislodged over time. He figured he could make it to the other side without serious injury, and that would lower his chances of getting crushed by the oncoming truck.

But the pick-up — an ancient Ford Bronco that must have been imported a couple of decades ago, at least — hit the brakes again, and Slater stood where he was.

All four men got out at once.

Olive uniforms creased and wrinkled.

Berets perched at random angles atop their heads.

Kalashnikov assault rifles on leather straps over their shoulders.

Slater had four guns aimed at him before he could move.

23

One of them yelled at him in Shona, a long venomous string, and a wave of déjà vu hit Slater in the chest.

He decided to rattle off the same conversational transcript he'd used for the last two men.

He just shrugged.

The same man yelled another string of indecipherable insults. His eyes were wide, his gaze piercing.

Slater shrugged again.

Action for action, gesture for gesture.

The same.

Then it all changed.

One of the men on the outer perimeter of the four-man line-up stepped forward and cut his colleague off by holding up a flat palm. He said, 'This guy doesn't speak the language. What's the bet he came from Ron and Judy's? What's the bet he's a tourist?'

Slater said, 'How do you know about Ron and Judy?'

The outer man looked at him with a raised eyebrow and said, 'English. Fucking told you.'

Slater repeated the question.

The outer guy said, 'Who doesn't know about Ron and Judy?'

'Are they well-known?'

'They're scum who are ruining the region. They pretend this place is a fairytale. They bring their drinks and their cooking and their old money and act like everything is happy and golden because they're living in a storybook. They're disgusting.'

Slater didn't say anything.

The four men just stood there.

But they lowered their guns.

Slater hadn't moved the whole time. They must have dismissed the threat. Figured he hadn't gone for a weapon yet, so he would continue being meek and timid for the rest of the conversation, even if they provoked him. Which tantalised them far more than a tense shootout. They'd prefer to lord over him until he either submitted to them or scurried away with his tail between his legs. It confirmed he was adequate at holding back emotions. Because right now he had a suppressed rage stewing under the surface.

He said, 'Why haven't you done anything about it?'

Acting like he might agree with them.

If they elaborated.

The outer guy jumped at the suggestion, almost salivating, and Slater figured he was the only one of the four who could speak English.

The guy said, 'Maybe you're not so bad after all.'

Slater gave a wicked smile. 'You think I enjoyed that place? It was a piece of shit.'

'Tell me about it.'

Slater said, 'Why can't you fuck them up? They're both dinosaurs. I didn't see any security.'

'That's their whole motto,' the guy said, his face shrivelled in disgust. 'They have an open door. They welcome anyone. Makes me sick. That's not what we are here. They can go back to Australia or America or England or wherever they're from. No offence to you. Sounds like you're about as American as I am, if we're on the same page.'

'We're on the same page,' Slater said.

The guy grinned devilishly. 'We can't go after them because they made friends with most of the farmers in the region. The new breed. The fucking scum that drove us out in the first place. If we flay them for everyone to see, they'll cut off our food. Some kind of pact.'

'When did all this happen?'

'Over the last few months. We were out of work before then, brother. Where are you from?'

'America,' Slater said, but he let false disgust creep over his face, too. 'But like you said — I'm just as American as you are. That's why I came out here.'

Please bite, he thought.

The man looked at him, and shrugged, and said, 'No work available, I'm afraid.'

'It's okay.'

'Where are you headed now?'

'Just walking.'

But Slater didn't want to drift too far from the original topic, so he said, 'They're a stuck-up bunch, aren't they?'

'Who?'

'The dinosaurs.'

The man gave a cruel laugh, and said, 'You want the truth?'

Slater said, 'Always.'

'Our boss is getting fed up with the dinosaurs, too. He says they've been putting up with our tests for long enough.

We do what we can without getting blamed for it. Destroy their supplies. That's fun. They used to have bucks on their land. Like an animal farm. To show the vermin they give beds to. This is not a place for foreigners, and it's not a zoo. It's not a storybook. So we went in one night with pangas and backed them all up to the fence and hacked their legs off when we cornered them. You've gotta go for the hamstrings. That's always the most effective way. Then we let them bleed out on the lawn. All over the grass. Imagine their old faces the next morning!'

He cackled, almost doubling over with exertion, and the man's three friends joined in with glassy eyes, separated by the language barrier but unwilling to be excluded.

Slater laughed too, but it took every morsel of his acting ability. He found himself seized by a silent admiration for Ron and Judy. They hadn't so much as mentioned the ongoing tension threatening to tear apart their intimate relationship with the land and its people.

As relaxed as he could, he said, 'Who's your boss?'

A silence hung in the air. The dust cloud had settled over the trail, and all the intimate sounds of the gathering came to the forefront. The shifting of dirt underfoot. The laboured breathing under the hot morning sun. The slick sweat under palms clutching automatic weapons. The chugging of the idle motor in the Ford Bronco as it sat in park, abandoned on the trail a few feet behind the four-man line up.

The outer man narrowed his eyes, and paused, and breathed hard, and then he said, 'Why?'

Slater shrugged, hands out. 'Just asking.'

'No,' the man said, his voice cold. 'Why do you want to know?'

Slater shrugged again.

'And you defended them at the start,' the guy said. 'Ron and Judy. You asked what was wrong with them. And then you changed your tone. I didn't notice. I was too caught up in it all.'

Slater didn't say anything. Then he shrugged a third time. And he said, 'Come here.'

Hands flew to weapons out of instinct. But Slater stood completely still, keeping his own hands out, the duffel secured firmly to the middle of his back, its rough canvas running down his spine. They could see clear as day he had no hope of reaching for a weapon, even if he had one concealed in the bag. He barely breathed.

The hands froze on the Kalashnikovs.

Slater looked at the guy who spoke English and said, 'Come here.'

A little more urgently.

With raised eyebrows.

As if he had all the secrets in the world to share.

The man couldn't resist.

He adjusted the beret on his head and stepped forward.

24

S later let him approach. There was nothing he could do anyway. The guy skewered his boots into the hot earth, advancing with a level of interest he couldn't mask.

Slater leant forward imperceptibly and said, 'They sent me here.'

'What?'

The guy kept coming forward.

He raised his Kalashnikov and jabbed it into Slater's chest. Slater glanced down at it, just for a second. It was shorter than an AK-47. He spotted the compact barrel, and recognised it as an AKS-74U. A smaller, more efficient version of the bulkier assault rifle. The safety was off. One pull of the trigger would tear his insides to shreds. He wouldn't even have time to blink. He figured he'd get a couple of seconds of hyper-awareness, feeling each impact as the lead tore its way through his heart and lungs. Then there would be a short, sharp fade to black, and that would be that.

So he proceeded with the utmost caution.

Because, as inexperienced as these four were in regards to visceral, life-or-death combat, an automatic weapon had the same result regardless of who wielded it.

Slater feigned agitation. 'I'm sorry, man. I didn't mean to do this.'

'Do what?'

'Ron and Judy, man. They know what's coming their way. They've been planning a counterattack for a while. I did a couple of years in basic training at West Point, a dozen years ago. They met me a few days ago. I said I'd go and stick my nose around and see what I could find. I thought they were good people, man. I didn't know…'

He allowed the edge of panic to creep into his voice, his pitch wavering and cracking with each sentence. He let the words spill out with no restraint, doing his best impression of a guy treading water in an ocean of fear.

The man sensed weakness.

He smiled his sinister smile again.

He jabbed the barrel tighter, and it came to rest wedged between Slater's massive pectorals.

The man held it there.

He said, 'You've made a big mistake.'

'I know,' Slater said, scrunching up his face in disappointment.

'You're going to come with us.'

Slater slumped his shoulders. He injected as much defeat into his posture as he could.

'Okay,' he said.

The guy said, 'We'll show you a thing or two about how valuable two years of basic training is out here.'

'I'm sorry,' Slater said. 'I should have thought it through.'

'You thought you were a tough guy?'

'I guess.'

'Because you work out?'

'I try to stay in shape.'

'You have no training. A dozen years ago is a long time. You're an old man now. And you must be lost. Or crazy. If you're out here trying to stick up for a couple of old dinosaurs. But you're a good actor. I believed you before. Why would you think you could do this?'

'I've never done anything with my life,' Slater said, almost on the verge of tears. 'I thought I could help someone. I guess I'm weak.'

'Ron and Judy sent you?'

'I offered to have a look around for troublemakers. They told me they would appreciate that. They said they didn't like the lot of you.'

The man's eyes lit up, almost manic in his fervour. He said, 'I'm going to enjoy this.'

Slater lowered his voice, and lowered his eyes to the ground, and mumbled, 'What are you going to do to them?'

'Teach them a lesson for what they did. Who do they think they are — sending someone pathetic like you to irritate us? They are scum. They will always be scum.'

'I'm sorry,' Slater said again.

'Want to know exactly what we're going to do to them?'

Slater shook his head, and put on his best performance, and forced a couple of crocodile tears from his eyes.

'No,' he said, choking up.

The three men milling around in the background started to laugh. It echoed down the trail, and they cackled to each other in Shona, no doubt insulting Slater's masculinity.

The fourth man turned around, craning his neck to face his cronies. He laughed and spat something to them in Shona, and they laughed harder. It was now an uproar.

Slater's eyes darted like a hawk to the man's finger on the trigger of the AKS-74U.

Not yet.

He relaxed, and regained his previous demeanour. Slumping down. Doing his best to appear meek. Forcing tears again.

But one of the men noticed.

The guy on the far left of the trio. His beady eyes locked onto Slater, and he cocked his head, and his hand tightened on the stock of his Kalashnikov. He'd seen the brief flicker in Slater's face. He might have noticed it was all an act. But as quickly as it happened, it was gone, and after another few beats of Slater crying silently on the side of the trail, he slackened his grip once more.

Slater nearly breathed a sigh of relief.

The man who spoke English said, 'You're in good shape.'

Slater said, 'Yeah.'

'That sure helped you here, didn't it?'

'I'm sorry,' Slater said again.

'There's a difference between you and us.'

Yes, that's it. Keep going.

Grateful for the line of conversation, Slater said, 'I thought I had enough skills.'

'Not compared to us. Do you know who we are?'

Slater shook his head.

The man said, 'You're in way over your head.'

'I know. Can I turn around and go back to the homestead?'

'No. I told you. You're going to come with us.'

'Okay.'

'And then we're going to pay Ron and Judy a visit.'

'No, please...'

'Our boss doesn't care about them anymore. He's in the

process of finalising new deals with surrounding farmers. We don't need these ones anymore. They can all die, as far as we're concerned. You know what that means?'

'No.'

'It means Ron and Judy's safety net is gone.'

The man jabbed the Kalashnikov harder into Slater's chest.

No, Slater thought. *Not that.*

Then the guy's confidence spilled over. The knowledge that he had more combat training than Slater, the general difference in their demeanours, the reassurance of his three comrades behind him offering protection, the overall safety in numbers, the fact that Slater had seemingly dipped into the throes of a nervous breakdown.

It all bundled together, and the Kalashnikov's aim drifted to the left.

The barrel passed over Slater's right nipple, and then the edge of his chest, and then it drifted into empty air.

The guy took a hand off the gun, milliseconds from reaching for Slater's shirt.

He planned to snatch a bundle of the material and drag him toward the pick-up truck.

But overconfidence was the death of many men.

The guy should have kept a loaded weapon trained on Slater at all times.

He shouldn't have taken his words at face value.

Slater cocked his right forearm horizontally across his stomach, like a crowbar rippling with corded muscle, and he jerked at the waist, transferring kinetic energy up his frame, and he threw from the shoulder, bringing his forearm up like a club, still horizontal, and he lined up an imaginary set of crosshairs at a tiny target on the very precipice of the guy's nose, and he punched his forearm right *through* the target with all the fast-twitch muscle fibres he had available.

He didn't just break the guy's nose.

He shattered it completely.

Crushed it.

Punched half of it inside his skull, and mangled the other half beyond all recognition.

There's no coming back from an injury like that.

25

The guy forgot all about his weapon. He forgot all about everything. He simply dropped the rifle and both hands flew to his face, every aspect of his consciousness concentrated on protecting the wound from a follow-up shot.

His legs gave out at the same time, and he hunched over at the waist, minimising his target area. He squeezed his eyes shut, and his mouth sealed in a hard line. Going through his own personal version of hell. Probably in more pain than he'd ever been in his life. A level of agony he hadn't considered feasible.

Slater caught the AKS-74U in mid-air and went through a series of moves he'd planned in advance, deep in the back of his brain.

He lined up with the guy on the left of the distant trio. The one who'd seen him drop his guard for a brief instant. Slater shot him in the face with a quick tap of the trigger, savouring the efficiency of movement that the compact frame provided. Then he twisted to the second guy and dotted his chest with three rounds, and then he kept the same sweeping movement running for a single second longer and emptied the rest of the clip into the final man standing.

The Kalashnikov clicked in his hand and he threw the useless gun aside, hurling it over the barbed wire fence. It disappeared into the wheat, vanishing from sight.

He straightened up and let an intense calm settle over him.

Ridding himself of the terrified, submissive demeanour he'd used to coax the men into dropping their guards. He stepped over the only man left alive. The guy who spoke English. His hands were over his face, and his eyes were still shut tight. Slater thought he heard a moan, some sort of mixture between anguish and pain and defeat, but he couldn't be sure. He couldn't hear properly. The AKS-74U's barrel offered a moderate level of suppression, but the sharp *thwack* of the rounds had still given him an invisible punch to the eardrums all the same.

Temporarily deafened, he left the guy to squirm and moved to the three bullet-ridden bodies.

He snatched the first man by his olive uniform, now coated in blood, and hauled the deadweight across the trail to the fence. The corpse dragged through the dust, which coagulated with the blood. Slater adjusted his grip when he reached the waist-high wire perimeter, and heaved the body over into the field. It thumped down into a shallow ditch, burying itself under grass and stray crops and weeds, and lay still.

Slater repeated the process with the other two bodies.

By the time he made it back to the original guy, he had a thin sheen of sweat on his forehead. Other than that, he was no worse for wear. Veins pumping in his arms from the exertion, he squatted down by the man with the shattered nose.

The guy was lying on his back, staring up at the clear sky, eyes now open. The whites of his eyes were bloodshot and wracked with horrific discomfort.

Slater said, 'That didn't go the way you thought it was going to go.'

The guy didn't even have the energy to shake his head.

Slater said, 'Do you work for Simba?'

The guy said nothing. But there was something in his eyes. Some glimmer of recognition.

Slater knew he was headed in the right direction.

He reached out and pressed a finger gently into the tip of his mangled nose.

The guy screamed.

Slater said, 'Next time I'll punch it.'

'Yes. I work for Simba.'

'I'm going to let you run back to him. You tell him there's a guy in the region who would very much desire to speak with him.'

'He won't speak with you. Not after this.'

'That's his choice. I'll give it to him. I think he might want to talk if he sees your nose.'

Unmoving, in shock, the man said, 'How bad is it?'

'Bad,' Slater said, staring at the swollen pumpkin already ballooning between the guy's cheeks.

'You shouldn't let me walk out of here.'

'Why not?'

'Not if you know this country. You should be ruthless out here. You need to be.'

'I think I'll let you crawl back to your boss. That's ruthless enough. Tell me more about him.'

'What do you want to know?'

'Who is he?'

'A private man.'

'Who did he used to be?'

'I'm sure you already know.'

'I want you to confirm it.'

'He used to work for ZANU—PF.'

'And now?'

'He was no longer welcome after the coup d'état last year. He chose the wrong side. Now he's out on his own. Self-employed.'

'Did you used to work for them too?'

'I was a Green Bomber.'

'What did you do?'

'Anything we were told to do.'

'Would I reconsider letting you go if I made you describe some of the worst things you did?'

'Of course.'

'Then let's not go down that path. Because I need you to walk out of here alive. And if you make me angry that might not happen.'

'Seems like you're already angry.'

'This isn't angry. You should see angry.'

'What if I come back with reinforcements?'

'Then I'll get angry.'

'Okay.'

'So how is this going to go?'

'I'll get out of here.'

'Do you think you can manage?' Slater said, grimacing as he noticed the state of the man's nose.

'I can't feel anything right now. I think I'm in shock.'

'It'll kick in later. You'll be okay. You can drive. There's not a lot of traffic out here.'

'What are you going to do?'

'I'll keep walking.'

'Where are you headed?'

Slater gave him a disinterested look. 'Nice try.'

The guy picked himself up, slowly. Halfway onto his knees he blinked hard and gasped in pain and tumbled straight back to earth.

Slater heaved him upright.

The guy stumbled a couple of steps in place, like a bowling pin struck with a glancing blow. Then he righted himself. Then he doubled over and put his hands on his knees and breathed deep rattling breaths.

Slater said, 'Get out of here before I change my mind.'

26

The guy levered upright, and there was a clarity in his eyes. Slater knew what it was. Something about mind-numbing pain stripped you of all defences. In that moment in time you found yourself grateful for everything, open to all interpretations of life, savouring the simple fact you were alive.

The guy said, 'I guess I should care more about the fact you killed my three friends.'

'You four hang out outside of work?'

'Not really.'

'Then you're not friends. I killed your colleagues.'

'I should still care.'

'You're in shock.'

'I want to say I'll be back to hunt you down, but I don't know if I will.'

Slater shoved him toward the truck. 'You're delusional. Go back to your boss before you convince me you're going to go AWOL, because I'll put a bullet in you if I determine you're no use to me.'

The guy shrugged, his face expanding by the second. His lips started to swell. He mumbled, 'I'll go back to my boss.'

'What are you going to tell Simba?'

'That there's a black American running around causing trouble, wanting to speak with him.'

'What will you say happened to your three colleagues?'

'You shot them.'

'How fast?'

'Very fast.'

'What did I use?'

'My own gun.'

'How are you going to explain that?'

'You stripped it off me.'

'That doesn't sound believable. How are you going to convince him?'

The guy pointed to his own face.

Slater said, 'Noted.'

A hot wind howled down the dirt trail. Slater pointed to the pick-up truck. The guy nodded and set off toward it with a leisurely gait, taking his time. He put each foot down carefully, as if terrified to experience the vibrations of moving too fast across the earth. Each step was as delicate as possible. Slater had no idea how the man would handle the potholed, uneven trail for the drive back. The ancient Ford Bronco would provide no relief from the bumps and jolts. The suspension would send mind-numbing pain through his face.

But he was alive.

So he had that to be grateful for.

The man clambered into the cabin. Slater snatched up one of the fully-loaded AKS-74Us discarded across the trail and aimed it square through the rear window. The glass was stained with dirt and grime, but Slater figured he would still be able to make out the outline of the guy pulling out a concealed weapon from the glove box or the centre console.

But nothing happened.

The Bronco rumbled into gear and the tyres spun and the old beast lurched off the mark. It kicked up a fresh dust cloud and its suspension kicked in and it turned around and set off back the way it had come. Slater watched it fade into the distance until the dust blew away in the wind and he was left alone on the trail.

He exhaled and gave himself the once-over. Adrenalin was a powerful, intoxicating tool in the arsenal of the human body, but it had the ability to cover up significant injuries that could prove detrimental in the long-term. Slater didn't want to make it halfway to his next destination before discovering he'd broken his forearm in the scuffle.

But years of putting his body through the ringer had paid off. He wasn't cut, or bruised, or broken. His skin was calloused and tough and drawn tight over the dense muscle underneath. He gathered up the three remaining AKS-74Us, and took one long look at them in his arms, and then tossed them all over the fence.

Strolling into new territory with an automatic weapon would do him no good.

He'd made enemies, no doubt. The guy with the shattered nose would slink back to Simba's hideout and inform his boss about the breaking news. That would spread like wildfire through the ranks of Simba's private mercenary force, but any further than that it would fall on deaf ears. If Slater kept his wits about him, no-one would discover his true identity for the next few hours. If he kept his mouth shut he could make it to the family's home undetected, and then he could properly deduce the circumstances.

Right now, carrying a Kalashnikov through the neighbouring villages would only incite multiple conflicts he had no intention of stimulating.

So he adjusted the duffel on his back and carried on down the dirt trail.

Moving ever onward.

Leaving three dead bodies in his wake.

By now, his life had become such routine madness that the confrontation had passed his mind after a quick mile of striding it out under the hot Zimbabwean sun.

27

The only signs of life this far from civilisation were stray cattle wandering aimlessly through the dirt.

Slater sidestepped them, occasionally making eye contact with the wild creatures. They carried on past, rail-thin, nearly starved to death, with no owners or farmers in sight. Slater figured they had some form of foot-and-mouth disease, and he kept a wary distance from them as they trickled by in intermittent bursts.

Eventually the fields of maize and wheat gave way to long undulating plains of gravel and silt, all grey in colour, all running for miles in every direction. Slater eyed the horizon and paused along the side of the trail, ankle-deep in dead weeds, soaking in the scene. He figured this was what the edge of the world looked like. In the distance he spotted a smoking maw in the earth, spilling natural gases into the sky.

He pressed forward.

His smartphone told him he had to straddle the outskirts of the Marange diamond fields for a couple of miles before branching away to locate a small village further east of the perimeter. Like a subdivision in the shadow of a lord's lands.

But as he sauntered down desolate winding tracks he realised he'd held a very different mental image of the diamond fields. The reality was harsh and unimpressive. He found no bustle of activity. Instead the fields seemed dead, and he figured the same principle that applied to Rand's maize farming endeavours was playing out its consequences here, too. The corruption, the hoarding of wealth, the obscene concessions.

It applied to diamonds just as much as it applied to maize.

Slater checked his phone again under the scorching sun, and noted his proximity to his destination, and paused to ruminate.

Something told him the story he needed to hear would be intimately connected with the diamond fields.

Especially considering the state of his surroundings.

He tracked the GPS checkpoint along the edge of the fields, passing a beehive of activity at the mouth of what appeared to be a construction site. It was fenced off from the rest of its surroundings by a corrugated fence made of sheet metal. Above the top of the fence, the peaks of giant mounds of dirt and gravel speared high into the sky. Battered trucks and rusting sedans raced through the gates in a frenzy of commotion, each of them packed with locals draped in high-visibility vests. It took Slater far longer than it should have to realise *this* was a diamond mine. He wasn't sure what he'd been anticipating, but he didn't class it as a positive sign that the first glimpse of activity came half an hour into his trek along the edge of the fields. The rest of Marange seemed like the opposite of an oasis — instead of a lush haven, it appeared as something eerily similar to a volcanic wasteland, yet still surrounded by roiling bright green hills.

Slater figured he'd missed the times of prosperity by at least a few years.

He drew no odd looks from passers-by — in fact, nobody bothered to give him a second glance. They were too preoccupied with meeting their deadlines, racing back and forth from the lip of the diamond mine's perimeter. Slater continued past, returning to desolation as if he'd never left.

He met another couple of miles of rural trails, surrounded by unchanging scenery, plagued by unchanging thoughts.

Then he reached the family's home.

He moved through a rural village jam-packed with cement huts and larger residential dwellings, then reached a somewhat more luxurious outer perimeter with a series of interconnected streets housing what constituted a small neighbourhood.

He came to rest at the top of a street that sloped gently downward, made of clumps of earth packed hard and flat into a smooth surface. On either side of the road he saw wide lots with grass lawns and simple rundown one-storey dwellings sporting thatched roofs and stone walls.

Slater tried in vain to recall the names Rand had provided him with, but it proved futile. He should have written them down. He paused a beat, wiping sweat from his brow, and fished a water bottle out of the duffel bag. He drank greedily, sucking down the liquid in anticipation of what he figured would be a long and difficult conversation.

That was, if it proved anything like his talk with Rand.

He located a series of three houses that could include, within reasonable estimation, the dwelling he was looking for. He zoomed in as far as he could on his digital map, but

Rand had estimated the checkpoint, and hadn't bothered to point out a particular number.

Not that the houses had numbers in the first place.

He set off down the street, drawing to a halt in front of the three ramshackle buildings. His eyes swept from one to the other, and he froze up. The duffel weighed down heavy on his shoulders. Almost out of guilt, he flashed a glance back up the street he'd just descended.

Perhaps paranoid that the Green Bombers had followed.

Because the last thing he wanted was to bring chaos to more innocent people.

That wasn't what he'd been put on this earth to do.

He was meant to fix situations.

He took a deep breath. He started for the house on the left. Might as well work his way across the row. Process of elimination. He found himself at a loss as to what he might say. Then the front door of the middle house opened. A short, plump woman with dark skin stepped out into the sun. She had her hair tied up in a knot and a tan headband wrapped around her forehead. She wore a simple thin dress that hung loosely and unshapely off her frame. Slater put her in her early sixties, but she could have been twenty years younger. Just the nature of the environment, and the unrelenting weather.

He stared at her.

She smiled and nodded a polite greeting to him.

He said, 'Do you speak English?'

She said, 'Yes.'

'Have you been learning it over the last decade?'

She said, 'How did you know that?'

'Did you help a man named Rand eight years ago?'

She didn't say anything.

Slater said, 'He was missing an arm.'

She looked him up and down, as if noticing his appearance for the first time. She said, 'Are you here to hurt me?'

'Far from it.'

'You look like you're here to hurt me.'

'I'm just a traveller. Looking for an explanation.'

'About what?'

'Something that happened to you a long time ago. Rand said you would know what I was referring to.'

'Many things happened to me a long time ago.'

'He says it might be connected to what happened to him.'

'We never spoke about that. Our family hasn't seen him since.'

'He's never come back here?'

'Maybe he didn't want to.'

'I think he has his own issues to deal with.'

'You met him recently?'

'Just yesterday.'

'Where?'

'About twelve miles south-west of here.'

'What's there?'

'Not much.'

'Has Rand been there this whole time?'

'Yes.'

'Then he's been close to us the whole time. Which means he really doesn't want to talk to us.'

'He's grateful for what you did for him.'

'It caused us a lot of trouble.'

'It saved his life.'

'Tell him it's quite alright. We try to help as many people as we can.'

'Does that lead to problems?'

'Out here — of course.'

'Do you think I might be here to bring you more problems? Is that why you're hesitant?'

'I have to be cautious.'

'I'm just looking for a story.'

'About what?'

'Rand mentioned a name.'

'And what name might that be?'

'Simba.'

The woman said nothing for an impressive length of time. She just let Slater stand there, baking under the hot sun, sweating from the twelve miles he'd spent all morning and most of the early afternoon covering on foot.

Then she said, 'You'd better come inside.'

28

She ushered him into a shadowy hallway with a low ceiling and tight walls, but he savoured the escape from the heat all the same. He smiled as he stepped past her, kicking his shoes off amidst a pile of footwear near the straw rug just inside the door.

'Do you mind if I put my bag down here?' he said.

She shook her head. 'Of course not.'

He propped the duffel bag up against the wall beside the shoes and moved through to a small kitchen and dining room with an island separating the two halves. The floor was cheap linoleum, suited best for wiping down fast. There was a square window with an old wooden sill fixed into the wall at chest height, allowing natural light to spill into the enclosure. It looked out onto a small grass field resting in the lee of a hill coated in lush vegetation. The sloping land-scape served as an impressive backdrop to the village.

Slater sat down at a small rickety table in the corner of the room, and wiped perspiration off his forehead. He sweat non-stop out here. Just a byproduct of the climate.

He said, 'Are you the only one home?'

She froze in the doorway, one hand on the frame, and he spun in his chair to meet her eyes. Guilt stabbed through him as he noticed the raw fear in her eyes.

He said, 'I'm sorry. I didn't mean it like that. I mean you no harm.'

He minimised his muscle mass as best he could, slumping his shoulders and tucking his chin down, trying to subtly convey some sort of submission. The last thing he wanted was to put her on edge.

She nodded, her eyes still wide. 'I'm sorry, too. I'm just ... very cautious about visitors.'

'I understand.'

'It's just me here today. Akash is out working. Visiting his patients.'

'Your children?'

She smiled. 'Not children anymore. They are both eighteen. Rudo works in the mines, and Zendaya helps at the nearest school. She is a teacher's assistant. Such a smart young girl.'

'How close is the school?'

'Five miles on foot.'

'That's a long way to travel for work.'

'It's what we must do.'

Slater nodded. 'I can understand that.'

'And what is your name?' the woman said politely.

'Will.'

'It is lovely to meet you, Will.'

'You too. Rand told me your name, but I'm afraid it's slipped my mind.'

'I am Danai.'

'Pleasure to meet you, Danai.'

'Can I get you anything to eat or drink?'

'Both would be great.'

'Water?' she said. 'And I have some leftover *bota* from this morning. Flavoured with peanut butter. You will enjoy.'

Slater bowed his head in acknowledgement. 'Thank you.'

She brought him a giant bowl of the thin porridge and he wolfed it down, then drained a few glasses of water to satiate his thirst. He sat back, replenished from the hike, then started to rise to take the dishes to the sink. She waved him back down, and snatched the bowl and glass out from underneath him. He thanked her for her hospitality. She sauntered around the kitchen for a few minutes, and he sat in comfortable silence. A lifetime of experience had taught him sometimes the best thing to say was nothing at all.

She returned to the table, and sat down across from him, and said, 'I'm sorry I was so hesitant to let you in.'

'Perfectly understandable.'

'Our life has not been easy for over a decade.'

'I can't imagine it's ever been easy out here.'

She shrugged. 'True enough. But it seemed to get worse and worse for a long time. We thought it would change with the new leadership. But it's still the same party. It's still much of the same.'

'Can I ask where it started?'

She sat back in her chair, nearly tipping the front legs up off the shiny floor, and pondered his question for a moment. Her expression was an open book. She wasn't leaving anything hidden. But Slater sensed the intense curiosity all the same.

Danai said, 'How is it that you came to meet Rand?'

'We were having a drink in the same place.'

'Twelve miles south-west of here?'

'Yes.'

'Ron and Judy's?'

'You know them?'

She smiled in a way Slater found oddly sad, and shook her head. 'Do you think we're the type to sit around and drink all day?'

'That's not what I was implying.'

'I know you weren't. I'm simply stating a fact. We don't have the money. But everyone's heard about Ron and Judy.'

'I got the sense they might be in some danger.'

'What gave you that impression?'

'Just some things I overheard on the road.'

'Who did you overhear?'

'They didn't seem like nice people.'

'Did they wear berets?'

'They did.'

'Did they talk to you?'

'I kept it brief.'

'Then you're a lucky man. You shouldn't associate with those men.'

'I wouldn't dream of it.'

'Did that happen today?'

'Yes.'

She cast a dark look over his shoulder, subconsciously putting her attention on the front hallway.

He said, 'Are you expecting company?'

'Not today.'

'But you know these men in berets.'

'They are the source of most of our problems.'

'Is that part of the story?'

'They feature heavily.'

'Then I might be able to help you.'

She went back to the same near-hypnotic state. A vacant smile on her face. A million questions in her eyes. Her gaze fixed on him.

Then she said, 'No. You should leave. Right now.'

29

He sat still.

She gestured to the front door. The same expression on her face. But a coldness behind her eyes. 'Please.'

He said, 'Why?'

'You will not be able to help me. That is the last thing I want you to try and do.'

'What if I promise just to listen?'

'You don't seem like the type.'

'You're a good judge of character?'

'I like to think so. You are a man of action.'

'You can tell that from a brief introduction?'

'You walked all the way here.'

'That doesn't reveal much.'

'There is raw skin on your forearm. You haven't noticed it or you would have covered it up. And there are almost no people out here. If you were walking on one of the trails, you didn't overhear anything. You talked to these men in berets. There's no other reason for you to have been within earshot of them. Which means you know who they are, because you hit one of them. You don't seem like the clumsy type. I don't think you caught your arm on a fence. I think you hit one of them in the face. I can almost make out an indent on your arm. Did you hit him in the nose?'

Slater cocked his head, surprised, and said, 'I did.'

'Should you be telling me the truth right now?'

'Probably not. You might be more likely to throw me out.'

'I'm already considering that.'

'You shouldn't.'

'Why not?'

'What do you know about the Green Bombers?'

She said, 'Everything.'

'You don't think I can help you, and I'm not going to promise you anything. I just want to hear your story, and how Simba is involved, and then I'll decide how to proceed from there. But it won't have anything to do with you, and I won't drop your name anywhere. It'll be my responsibility and mine alone. I already don't like this Simba character, and I doubt what you know about him will change my opinion in any way. If I'm any judge of character myself, I think you are a kind woman, and I think my opinion of Simba only has room to go downhill. So really, I'm only looking for confirmation. If you throw me out, I'll respect that, but I'll probably still go after this man all the same. For what he did to Rand. So I guess you need to decide whether you think any additional knowledge will aid me or not. I'm looking to confront him regardless. Do you want me to have more motivation, or do you want to just send me on my way? Your call.'

Danai let the silence drag out. Slater respected that about her. She didn't rely on social norms. If she needed to process something, she took her time, and she didn't rush into anything. She sat back in her chair again, and rubbed her cheeks with her plump wizened fingers. Some sort of nervous tic.

Slater let her think.

Then she said, 'This is putting a lot of unnecessary stress on me.'

'I'm sorry.'

'Don't be. If you hit a Green Bomber, and you're sitting here unharmed, then you are more impressive than I thought you were.'

'Thank you.'

'You have a good body.'

'Thank you.'

'I thought it was all for show. I thought you were a hothead looking for a fight.'

'I guess I am, if you break it down. But I have a bit of experience to put behind that hotheadedness. So I usually come out on top.'

'I don't expect you to here.'

'No-one does.'

'Did Rand ask you to do this?'

'No. In fact, he warned me not to.'

'And you didn't listen to him.'

'Not for a moment.'

'So why would you listen to me?'

'Exactly.'

'So if I tell you my story, it really won't affect the outcome either way.'

'Glad to see we're on the same page.'

'Then I will tell you.'

'Your English is fantastic.'

She shrugged. 'I have made it a priority to teach myself.

That's the way Zimbabwe is headed. Everyone uses U.S. Dollars now. Times are changing.'

'Is that a good thing?'

'It's definitely a lot better than the past.'

'The past...'

Danai said, 'Is this the part where I talk about it?'

'Only if you want to. It doesn't affect me either way.'

'Yes it does. You are a troubled soul. You can't sit still. You're looking for any excuse to justify going after this man, no matter what kind of protection he has. You want me to tell you a horror story, so you are full of righteousness, and this will make you motivated to go charge through his defences. Am I on the right track, Will?'

Slater shrugged. 'Partly, yes. Partly, no.'

'Where am I wrong?'

'You're right about my head. It's messed up. I'm wired differently. I can't go long without doing something like this. But I don't need to pump myself full of righteousness. I'm long past that. I don't need motivation anymore. Motivation is fickle. I built habits nearly a decade ago that have locked me on a certain path, and now I walk down that path no matter where it takes me. So, no, it doesn't need to be a horror story. It doesn't need to be any kind of story. But I like to know what I'm walking into. I like to know the kind of man I'll be dealing with.'

Danai nodded. 'You are a reasonable man. I didn't think that at the start.'

'Do you know a man named Rangano?'

She paused. 'The name reminds me of something. A whisper, in the past. But I have never interacted with him. Is he attached to Simba?'

'Yes.'

'Then he's probably involved with my story.'

'You don't need to exaggerate it for my benefit. Just tell me what happened. In your own words. In your own time.'

She smiled the same smile. Sad. Forlorn. Resigned. She said, 'I don't need to exaggerate anything. It's a horror story all the same.'

30

She said, 'Did you see the diamond fields?'

Slater held a hand out, palm facing toward the floor, and tilted it back and forth. 'Some of it. I walked along the perimeter. I only saw one mine, and the rest was empty land.'

She smiled the same smile for what felt like the millionth time. 'That's all of it. You didn't miss anything.'

'What happened to it?'

'There's no concrete answer,' she said. 'But I moved here with Akash in 2007. We came from Gweru. A city west of here. Akash had been practicing medicine for ten years, but we dropped everything for the chance at true prosperity.'

'Why?'

'That's when the diamonds were discovered. It was like nothing the country had ever seen before. There were tens of thousands that came to sift for them. Us included. And we were considered upper class when we left Gweru. We had a luxurious life compared to most of the country. But we couldn't resist. I can't tell you why. It was something unspoken. I don't think either of us ever addressed it properly. But we both knew. We were doing well in Gweru, all things considered. But the country was falling apart around us. The economy was dying, the famine was sweeping across everything, and all because of the actions of the people in power. They were choking the life out of Zimbabwe. So there was this feeling of *hope* when the diamond find was made. The fields could generate billions in revenue every single year. Some government department confirmed that. So I guess we wanted to show solidarity. We wanted to show the rest of the country that it didn't matter whether we had a stable life or not. We were prosperous as it was. But we wanted to show them that anyone could achieve it. We thought it might lead to a brighter future for Zimbabwe as a whole. We packed up everything, and we brought the kids here to Marange, and we started sifting for diamonds along with the other thirty thousand people who'd come.'

'So what went wrong?'

'Those billions of dollars in revenue that I mentioned...'

'Yes?'

'No-one ever saw it.'

'What do you mean?'

'It disappeared. All the money, all the profits. Vanished.'

'Where?'

'There's rumours. But that's all they are. Rumours.'

'How do you know for sure it all vanished?'

'Because we both saw with our own eyes how much death and destruction and famine there was when we were all supposed to be getting ... what is it you Americans say? Filthy rich.'

'Is that what it was about?'

'Does it look like I'm the type of person to care about getting filthy rich, my dear?'

Slater shook his head. 'I understand why you came.'

'Hope.'

Slater nodded. 'Hope.'

'And then we ended up seeing the worst despair you can possibly think of.'

Slater didn't say anything.

Danai said, 'Have you ever seen a famine up close?'

'No.'

'It's worse than the worst thing you can imagine.'

'Where did the money go?'

'The government only gave out five licenses to companies allowed to mine the fields. These companies got filthy rich. They bought armies of security. Private mercenaries. Soldiers for hire. All of it. And they patrolled the fields. And they shut down anyone trying to sift for diamonds on their own. If they wanted work, they had to earn it legally. So those five companies hoarded all the profits. Which was fine. It wasn't our version of hope, but it was good enough. There was enough money in the fields to revitalise the entire economy. Billions of dollars a year. U.S. Dollars, too. Not our useless currency at the time. If all that money flowed from the companies to the economy, the country wouldn't have crumbled.'

'Where did it go?'

'Associates of the president. Politicians who sucked up to the right people. The inner circle at the top. They got rich. All of them. Because they controlled it all.'

'How did they justify it?'

'They pretended it wasn't happening. They simply couldn't explain where all the money was going. But we knew.'

'Did anyone believe you?'

'No. We were the bad guys. We were the dirty thieves

trying to steal the diamonds away from legitimate businesses. Mugabe was good at that. We were the enemy.'

'Rand told me something similar. He was a farmer, and he was the enemy. Because he had something, and the settlers didn't.'

'That's how dictators hold onto power. They convince the population to *hate* a certain group of people, for any reason they can come up with.'

'So what happened?'

'We were outcasts. We were the ... what is the expression? The laughing stock. Is that it?'

Slater nodded. 'That's it.'

'We were the laughing stock of Gweru. We couldn't go back. We shared a house with fifteen other people. We did anything we could to make ends meet. And we ended up supporting the MDC. Which ruined our lives.'

'The MDC?'

'The Movement for Democratic Change.'

'A political party?'

'Yes.'

'They opposed the old regime?'

'Yes. And they were popular. Because the country was dying. Zimbabwe was a disaster zone. People were starving on the streets. So the MDC grew, and grew, and grew. And that's where the Green Bombers came in.'

'The militia?'

'Yes. They were Mugabe's soldiers. They were brainwashed to worship him. They all started as youths, and they were raised in training camps, and now they don't know any better. Which is why they're still around. Just because Mugabe went out, doesn't mean their beliefs will go out with him. They thought the MDC wanted white rule, and nothing else. Really, we just wanted to stop people starving.'

'What happened to you?'

'Akash tried to practice medicine. To scrape out a living. The Green Bombers knew he was a supporter of the opposition. Every time they found him outside his house, they beat him and left him in the street like a dog. If you meet him, you will see the left side of his face doesn't move like the right. They did nerve damage over the years. They beat him so many times.'

'Did they hurt you?'

'They tried to rape me. But I was so scared. I never left the house. I never gave them the opportunity.'

'And your kids?'

'They beat them too.'

'Why didn't they just kill you?'

'They made Akash work as their private doctor. Like contract work. They needed him to patch them up. They were torturing anyone associated with the MDC, making them disappear, killing them or beating them or throwing them out of their homes.'

'Jesus,' Slater muttered.

Danai smiled the same smile, and shook her head. 'That wasn't the worst part.'

'I don't know if I want to ask.'

'It was the famine. You've never seen one. You've never seen people that are practically skeletons, crawling in the street. With distended bellies. With flies all around them. There were fields of dead crops everywhere you looked. Because no-one knew how to grow them properly. Because all the farmers were killed or excommunicated for having too much. But nothing has made me angrier than what happened with the diamonds. I could let it go that the regime was destroying the country. I could say it was due to them being naïve. That would have been understandable.

Stupid, and foolish, and murderous — but at least understandable. Maybe in some sick way they thought they were doing the right thing. *That* was the hope I was holding onto. And then they made the diamond find. And so many of us swelled up with that same hope. Because we all thought, *this* could be the thing that sets it all right. With this they could set up the foundations of an economy. They could start growing crops. They could feed the country. Instead they took it and hoarded it and pretended it never existed. And that way I got to see my closest friends and family starve to death in the street. And while I was watching that happen, the government labelled me the enemy. Can you even imagine how that felt?'

'How did Simba come into this?'

'He was in the inner circle. He knew the right people. He made our lives a living hell, because he knew we supported the MDC. He co-ordinated a year-long tactical assault against us. He would send Green Bombers to our house regularly, to beat us and torture my husband. And at the same time he would buy up most of the land around here with the money he was hoarding from the diamond mining companies. That's why he's so rich now. That's why he's hired an entire army of ex-Green Bombers to do his dirty work. Because he has an endless amount of funds from what he did in the past, and that mentality will never change. They will always smile and laugh and gorge themselves as the rest of the country succumbs to slow deaths by starvation.'

Slater sat in silence, aware of every minuscule sound in the quaint little house.

He closed his eyes, and breathed in, and breathed out, and said, 'Where can I find him?'

31

Danai said, 'I'm not sure I should help you.'

'You told me it didn't make a difference either way.'

'It didn't make a difference if I told you my story or not. I don't know if I should help you find him.'

'Why not?'

'You will almost certainly fail. Who are you?'

'Just a passerby who didn't like what he saw.'

'You will have to give me more than that if you want my assistance.'

'What do you need from me?'

'Reassurances.'

'Such as?'

'If you're telling the truth about what you want, then you seem delusional from my perspective. I do not know anything about you. I've risked everything by telling you this story. You have some kind of spark in your eyes. I cannot work out what it means. I'm still not sure whether you're a contractor from overseas. You might be. It would fit in Simba's budget. He was high up in ZANU—PF for a reason.

Given his position he was not supposed to be on the ground doing the dirty work, but he liked it. Which is why we helped Rand, all those years ago. We stopped by the side of the road out of curiosity, but we saw corpses and those close to death every day. If we wanted to be benevolent, we would have had hundreds of tortured farmers recuperating in our house. But we didn't do that. We only took Rand. Do you know why?'

'I don't think he knew himself,' Slater said.

Danai nodded. 'I heard him mumbling a name over and over again. When we stopped. He was delirious by that point. He probably wasn't aware of what he was saying. He kept saying "Simba" under his breath, like some sort of incantation or spell. And then, when we showed him compassion, the name changed to "Paige."'

'His daughter,' Slater said.

Danai stared at him. 'He left a few days after Akash stabilised him. He took our truck without asking. To go back to the farm. To find her. He wasn't fit to drive. He wasn't fit to get out of bed. It's a miracle he survived the journey, even though it wasn't far. And then he brought the car back the next morning, and he was as pale as I've ever seen a man. He didn't say a word. He just left. We never heard from him again. He didn't leave us a number, or any details whatsoever. We had no way of contacting him. And we were too busy trying to stay afloat for that level of good-will. We didn't have time to track him down. So we left it for a few weeks, and that became a few months, and now it's been years. And we still don't know what he found when he went back.'

'He locked his daughter in the basement when Simba and the settlers came to take his farm. To try and protect her.'

Danai blinked hard and sat still. There was no sign of her trademark sad smile. 'Did they burn the house down?'

'Was that common?'

Danai nodded. 'It sent a message. They did it to many farmers. Especially the successful ones. It was like a beacon. An alarm to all the surrounding farms. They'd reclaimed it back from the white suppressors. But that didn't make any sense, because all the black farmers were assaulted and driven out too. I think they just hated anyone who had something. And that's what kickstarted the famine in the first place.'

'Do you think they were brainwashed? Or truly evil?'

She shrugged. 'You do not share the same experiences I do. You do not know what the Green Bombers have done to our family. I resent them with all my heart. I can't imagine it any other way. If they believed in what they were fighting for, they would stick to that. But they took it further. They were a militia, but they got used to the power. For even daring to oppose them, our lives meant nothing.'

Slater said, 'I hear Simba's still around.'

'He's untouchable.'

'I'd like to test that theory.'

'I'm still not sure whether to help.'

'What do you know?'

'Not much. But more than you do now.'

'Whether I fail or succeed, I won't mention your name.'

'It's not as simple as that. Information has a price out here. You would have been spotted by any number of people on the way here. If Simba was angry and motivated enough, he would trace your journey to my doorstep.'

'Then I'll make sure that doesn't happen.'

'How can you guarantee it? You are one man.'

'I have a strange past. Just like yourself.'

'Will you share it with me?'

He wasn't sure why, but he told her everything. Not just the basics. Not just the general outline. He sat at the table for over an hour, rattling off a story that wouldn't even have been believable if he toned it down. But he told it with all the raw emotion and passion that he'd felt at the time. He moved through his early childhood, the loss of his mother, the suicide of his father a couple of years later, the instant enlistment in the United States military as soon as he was of age, the discovery of his genetic talent, the honing of his reflexes, the constant bouncing from division to division as his skills were put to the test, continuously resulting in outperforming expectations.

Then the urgent movement found a home in a brand-new division, nicknamed Black Force. The clandestine outfit served as an anchor for transforming himself into a physical project. They'd treated his life as a game, to be optimised and improved in ways he hadn't considered imaginable. He'd embraced the suffering that had come along with that and become something wholly unique, something at the very edge of what was humanly possible. Like a video game character with every characteristic set to maximum. He'd sacrificed any semblance of a social life or time outside of work, and the result had been truly spectacular. He had all the genetic traits. A high IQ. Natural athleticism. An unparalleled reaction speed. A sickening work ethic. And the covert world had used those traits as building blocks to forge a monster.

And then he'd used that talent over ten years of physical and mental hell, but he'd done more for his country and for innocent lives that anyone looking in on the tale could possibly fathom. He couldn't put it into words. He listed an estimate of the amount of missions he'd been on — somewhere in the hundreds. But he couldn't describe how each particular outing had pushed him in brand new, unique ways. Indescribable, he said. But he knew how far the mind-body connection could go, because he'd experienced it first hand. He'd pushed through barriers he didn't even know existed. He'd been in more pain than he thought survivable.

And it had all taught him the limits of the human mind.

That was the most valuable part of his career.

He'd found the metaphorical line in the sand, telling you it was impossible to go any further.

And he'd steadily pushed it back over ten years until he couldn't see where it rested anymore.

So he wrapped up by saying, 'That's why I doubt what you're telling me. It might be impossible for most people with combat experience to give Simba a fight. I have no doubt he's entrenched in hired guns. He's probably paying them well. They've probably been through their own personal horrors. That's the nature of their surroundings. But they're not me. Without sounding arrogant, no-one is me. I've met one man who came close, but he's not in the picture anymore.'

32

Danai said, 'Was he a colleague?'

Slater said, 'Much more than that.'

'What was his name?'

'Jason King.'

'Why isn't he here?'

'That life breaks anyone. He snapped. He's focusing on living a normal existence with all the discipline he's built up over the years. And nothing's going to pull him away from that path.'

'Why haven't you tried that?'

'I did. Briefly. But it's not who I am.'

'What happens if you kill Simba? What then? You will never be satisfied.'

'I don't ever want to be.'

Danai said, 'What will be next?'

'I haven't figured that out yet. But there's a man in close proximity to me who tortured and killed people who didn't deserve it, and then let the rest of the country starve for having the gall to criticise him. I've heard two separate accounts of that sort of behaviour. That sounds like someone who I can't let slip through the cracks.'

'He's spent a lifetime building his own life through the suffering of others. He won't part with it lightly, Will.'

'I don't expect him to. Where can I find him?'

'There is a bull auction, not far from here. It runs every Wednesday. Simba attends them all with a small army of his men. It's an opportunity to flash his cash. To allow word to spread, so that no-one gets any ideas about taking back from Simba what is rightfully theirs. He's effective at that. No-one would dare touch him.'

'Except me.'

Slater mentally calculated. He hadn't been keeping track of the date for a long time. He found the last discernible reference point, and worked his way forward.

He said, 'Today's Tuesday.'

Danai smiled and shook her head. 'If it took you that much effort to work that out, I don't think you are fit to tackle Simba.'

'I consider myself an idiot savant.'

Danai said, 'Or just an idiot.'

They both laughed, and settled back in their chairs, and some of the intensity disappeared out the open window. They didn't need to focus on harrowing subject matter all the time. Slater knew what he needed to do now. In some strange way he had a new life purpose. Unlike most, his purpose seemed to change with each passing altercation. He always found new enemies. It was an unending circle, destined to loop round and round forever for as long as he lived.

Danai, in her unique and motherly way, seemed to sense exactly what he was thinking about.

She said, 'Are you wondering whether you're the problem?'

He stared at her. They hadn't spoken in a long ten minutes. Each digesting the other's tale. Taking what they could from it. Projecting it in their mind, like filling in the outlines of a story. Making their own personal movie out of it.

He said, 'More or less.'

'You think because you're always going from enemy to enemy, you might be the one with the issue.'

'It seems a little pathological, don't you think?'

'My English can only go so far, but this is how I see it. You are good at what you do. You help people. If you are true to your word and kill Simba, you are helping so many in this region. And then you will move on and find another. And there is always another. But that is not your fault. There will always be those people around. They are part of the population everywhere you go. It is natural. It is not your fault they exist. And it is not your fault you are so good at seeking them out. You might think you are like a magnet—'

Slater cut her off by widening his eyes. 'Actually, that's exactly what I've been feeling.'

'You are not a magnet. You just don't turn away when it's easy to pretend something isn't happening. I like that about you.'

Slater said, 'Thank you.'

'You mean it?'

'That's one of the best compliments I've ever received.'

Danai half-smiled. 'I don't know about that.'

'Can I ask you a question?'

'Of course.'

'Would you rather I walked away, or went after Simba? If you had full control over the choice.'

'You already told me I wouldn't affect your decision.'

'Maybe I've changed my mind.'

'Do you do that often?'

'No.'

'Why this time?'

'I respect you. I want to give you the choice.'

'What is the choice, exactly?'

'You know my story. I know yours. You're informed now. You understand where I've come from and what I've done. You know I'm not a man who puffs my chest out and pretends I can waltz into places and fix situations. I'm a man who *can* fix situations. So now you get to choose whether you want me to go after Simba or not. Because you're level headed enough to look at the long-term ramifications, and I'm probably not. Will it be good for the region if he's taken out of the picture?'

She thought about that for a long moment. Then she said, 'You have no idea.'

'What does that mean?'

'It would mean more to most of us than you can imagine.'

'I can imagine,' he said. 'I've spent half my life in war zones. Usually behind enemy lines. I know what people like Simba do to a population. I know why he needs an army of men to protect him. How many do you think he has?'

She shook her head. 'A few dozen, at least. But it's impossible to keep track. He doesn't let anyone in. He is a very private man. He owns acres of land all over the region. And he breeds them tough. He only shows up in public when he needs to display some kind of power. Whether that be through intimidation, or flaunting his wealth at auctions.'

'Rand said he's really looking to get into a legitimate industry.'

'It is possible it might be real. The days of oppression are slowly receding, and...'

Then she cut herself off mid-sentence, and paused, and smiled, and said, 'That was a good phrase by me. My English is better than I thought. I don't usually get the chance to practice it like this. So thank you for that.'

Slater smiled too.

She said, 'Anyway, those days are in the past. The inner circle of the elite will stay rich, because nothing was on record. None of the disappearing funds can be explained, but they'll hold onto them. Simba will be able to keep all the wealth he made off the backs of the rest of us. The country can't repair itself that fast, and it definitely can't bring justice to everyone. But there's a chance that there'll be a future where Simba will need to explain how he's got enough to pay a mercenary army to protect him. All the outcasts of the old guard who worship him, but need compensation all the same. The hordes of Green Bombers that are still hanging around. They'll always work for Simba. But he might need a legitimate explanation for their presence in future. So maybe that's why he's putting his funds to use. He's one of the only men with enough wealth to scoop up all the best bulls at auction. If he becomes a major player in the beef industry, he can launder his dirty money through that.'

'You said he owns acres of land. Does he live on them?'

'He owns enough buildings to house half the country. No-one knows where he lives. That's the beauty of his plan. He treats them like safe houses. He moves from location to location. Most of the moves are decoys. There were a few brave members of our community who tried to track him.'

'Are you deliberately speaking in the past tense?'

'Two of them disappeared.'

'When?'

'About six months ago. They thought they tracked Simba's location. They started spreading rumours. Tried to round up a gang of disgruntled settlers. To start a small revolution of sorts. They thought maybe we would be inspired by the coup d'etat last year. They thought we'd have the gall to try and strip Simba of everything he had.'

'And did you?'

'Fear is a strange thing.'

'It froze you all?'

'Maybe some of us would have rounded up the pitchforks eventually. But we all hesitated. And by then it was too late. They were a pair of teachers from the local school — the ones who found Simba. They were kind, good people. They vanished a couple of days after they started spreading his location.'

'Did you ever find out what happened to them?'

'Oh, yes. Their bodies turned up the next week. Flayed first. Before death. And then strung up on telephone poles.'

Slater clenched his right fist together, watching the white scars on his knuckles light up with exertion.

Then he said, 'What time is the auction tomorrow?'

33

D anai's husband, Akash, showed up a couple of hours later.

The sun was halfway through its downward trajectory, disappearing behind the hills. It bathed the dirt road and the surrounding terrain in a deep amber light, adding something close to serenity to the atmosphere. Slater had spent the time replenishing his energy, fast asleep on his back on a small sofa Danai had led him to in an adjacent sitting room. When the front door opened, his eyes came open instantly and he swung his bare feet off the cheap vinyl.

The small man stepped into the room, led by his wife. She'd already explained the presence of the mystery man over the phone, speaking in hushed Shona. As soon as Slater had departed the kitchen, he'd hovered in the doorway and watched her retrieve the ancient bulky mobile device from a drawer underneath the cutlery.

Now Akash stepped into the room, nodded politely, and offered a hand. Slater shook it. The man's grip was soft yet reassuring.

Slater scrutinised him. The doctor stood no taller than five-foot-six, hunched over, wearing a cheap suit coat and workmanlike cargo pants. His eyes were set deep in his skull, and his face was weathered and battered from years of hardship. As Danai had explained, one side of his face didn't function properly. When he smiled, one half of his mouth tilted upward, and the other remained where it was, as if locked in place. One of his cheeks sagged slightly. He was bald, with a compact frame and a podgy build. But he had kindness in his eyes, and Slater latched onto it instantly.

Slater said, 'It's a pleasure to meet you, Akash.'

Akash just nodded and smiled.

Danai said, 'His English is not as good as mine. He is embarrassed to try to talk to you in his second language.'

'Tell him I'm not worried about that,' Slater said.

The old man said, 'I understand.'

'I'm here to help.'

'Thank you.'

'It's quite alright. Is there anything you want to tell me about Simba?'

'Bad man. No good. He do this to my face.'

Slater raised his eyebrows. 'He did that himself?'

Danai said, 'Akash used to have a unique relationship with Simba. He doesn't like to talk about it.'

Slater said, 'I understand.'

Akash said, 'He no like me. He make my life bad. From day one.'

'I'm sorry this happened to you.'

'You know where he is?'

'Your wife gave me some clues.'

One half of Akash's face scowled, and he said, 'She no know anything.'

Then he skulked out of the room, seemingly more

hunched than before. His wife followed.

Slater backed up a step and sat down on the sofa and waited for the tension to dissipate.

A few minutes later, Danai stepped back into the sitting room. 'I apologise for that.'

'It's quite alright.'

'He is angry all the time.'

Slater lowered his voice. 'Can he hear us?'

'He's showering.'

Slater nodded. 'I understand where it comes from.'

'Simba used my husband as an example all those years ago. To show what happens when someone supports the MDC. They did that, from time to time. It was one of the best ways to strike fear into people. Simba would show up every week, and drag Akash out into the street, and get his Green Bombers to round up the whole neighbourhood to come and watch. And he would beat him until he was bloody and raw, and then make him clean up the blood. And then he would send him back into the house, with the promise to visit the same time next week.'

'How long did that go on for?'

'A couple of years.'

'Christ. At least it's over now.'

Danai gave him an imperceptible look.

Slater said, 'What?'

'We still get the occasional visit.'

'From Simba?'

'No,' she said with a laugh. 'He rarely shows his face in public anymore. Too dangerous, given the way the country is headed. It's still the ZANU—PF in charge, but they're distancing themselves from Mugabe. So Simba only appears at the big events. Like the bull auctions. But he sends the men working for him. Sometimes we know them. Because they used to be Green Bombers. And we used to know all the Green Bombers around Marange. Sometimes they recognise us. A few of them have apologised. How's that for a bitter reality?'

'As in, they've defected from Simba?'

She chuckled again. 'Of course not. They still take everything we have. Everything that's left over after we pay for basic supplies. The Green Bombers try to tell us they don't mean it. But they do it all the same. Because they would never dare go against the boss. Like I said, they worship him.'

'Can't you go to someone about that?'

She gave him a look that represented all the resignation and anguish she'd experienced over the years. 'Who?'

He nodded. 'I'm not delusional. I get it.'

'We're on our own out here.'

'I can help you.'

'How?'

'Is it always Simba's thugs that visit you?'

'Of course. The rest of the men who used to be Green Bombers vanished when they couldn't find work. The country hasn't repaired itself yet, but you can't carry around those ideologies anymore. All the scum hanging around Marange have an employer.'

'Are you absolutely certain about that?'

'They wouldn't survive out here otherwise.'

'Is there any way you can draw a couple of them out here?'

'Why?'

'I'd like to take some players off the field before the auction tomorrow.'

'That's it?'

'And I need a gun.'

34

N ight fell.

But the heat remained.

Slater crouched in the vegetation on the other side of the street. He was squatting in an overgrown row of bushes, surrounded by weeds and the low-hanging branches of nearby trees. All the concealment rested in front of an empty shell that used to be a house. The lot sat practically opposite Akash and Danai's humble abode, only a few feet to the right of the property but across the dirt road.

In the darkness, Slater was invisible.

He hadn't noticed the abandoned lot when he'd first approached, too fixated on finding the correct house on the left of the street. Now he burrowed further into the shadows, and swept his gaze over the rest of the street, and realised half the houses in the neighbourhood had fallen into varying states of disrepair. Only a sparse few were popu-lated, with dull lights shining behind grimy windows. There was an unquestionable air of desperation in the village.

Slater imagined Akash's work as a doctor put them in a narrow percentile who could comfortably support themselves and raise children. Zimbabwe was on an upward trajectory, but it was nowhere near fully recovered. Perhaps that was why Simba and his minions targeted them. They were some of the rare few who could afford to be extorted.

The rest had nothing.

The veins along Slater's forearms rippled. He'd clenched his fists open and shut in anticipation for the last fifteen minutes, building up the lactic acid in his arms. He hadn't shown it on the surface, but the conversation with Danai had infuriated him. He'd been able to see the raw anger in her eyes. And it wasn't over her own fortune. It was over the fact that the diamond fields could have brought a comfortable standard of living to an impressive portion of Zimbabwe, but instead it disappeared straight into the pockets of those who didn't need it in the first place.

Slater had no problem with capitalism.

He was worth four hundred million dollars, after all.

Taking from the rich and giving to the poor for no reason whatsoever would make him a hypocrite of the highest magnitude.

What he had a problem with was disgusting, sickening corruption.

He hunched lower as headlights flared at the top of the street. A rustbucket of a pick-up truck came down the dirt track a few moments later, kicking up small dust clouds under its fat tyres. It coughed and spluttered and came to rest parked menacingly across Danai and Akash's front lot. Two men got out — both dark-skinned, both tall, both fat.

But it wasn't the kind of gluttonous flab Slater saw frequently across the first world.

These men were both powerful, used to working with their hands, battered and knocked about and forged into shape by the circumstances and their surroundings. But at the same time, they were eating good. It made them effective powerhouses, packed with weight, all of it useful for shoving and poking and prodding and getting their way. Slater eyed their forearms in the harsh glow of the headlights — he'd found it the most effective way to determine strength. Their forearms were giant slabs of muscle, resting above tough calloused hands. They were hard men.

They would pose problems if he faced off with them across the road, despite their lack of visible weapons. Slater was a powerhouse himself, with all the combat experience in the world, but he was starkly aware of the reason for the existence of weight classes in professional combat sports. He didn't take that knowledge lightly. He could be super-human in his capacity, but all it took was one lucky punch from a guy weighing north of two hundred and fifty pounds to shut the fight down completely.

So he waited.

Both men wore identical olive uniforms — matching khakis and short-sleeved shirts with pockets on the breast. Their khakis were tucked into dirty black boots. The boots were giant steel-toed contraptions. The uniforms were over-sized and misshapen, hanging strangely off their frames, somewhat disguising their physiques. Slater couldn't work out how much of their bodies was muscle, and how much was fat.

To his surprise, they spoke to each other in stunted English. Perhaps they each originated from regions of Africa with different dialects, now united under the same ideology. Or just here to earn a paycheque. Slater figured he'd decide their punishment on the fly. If they seemed like they were just going through the motions, following the orders of a ruthless boss, then he'd let them walk away with superficial injuries, a strong warning, and a message for their superior. But if they seemed particularly malicious or cruel...

He thought he knew how the confrontation would go.

But he held back all the same.

The slightly larger man said, 'Why they call?'

The slightly smaller man said, 'Don't know. Simba say they need to tell something.'

'What they want?'

'Don't know.'

'This the MDC woman? And doctor husband?'

'Yes.'

The slightly larger man said, 'What if we do what we did two year ago?'

'Simba okay with that?'

'Simba don't care. Simba's annoyed they call in first place.'

'This not same Zimbabwe. Maybe they complain.'

The slightly larger man looked all around at the desolation, trying to prove a point. 'To who?'

The slightly smaller man nodded, and Slater thought he saw the guy lick his lips. 'I go first.'

'Fuck you. I always go first. Rule.'

'Okay. Make sure she okay for me, though. Don't hurt too much. You too violent sometimes.'

Oh, Slater thought. *So that's what this is.*

He came out of the bushes as they set off down the small dirt trail leading to the front door. No-one noticed. There was no-one around to see. No-one around to protest. It must have worked well for these two in the past. The nearest police were miles away, and wanted nothing to do with issues like this. Now it worked in Slater's favour. He matched their pace, then quickened it as they closed the gap and the slightly larger man raised a fist to smash against the cheap wood.

Boom.

Boom.

Boom.

The door rattled in place. Slater moved faster, realising he was a couple of steps behind the trajectory he considered ideal. Then he slowed down a beat. He was walking too hard. His footsteps were too loud against the dirt track.

He hunched lower and closed in on the pair of foul-smelling ex-Green Bombers, and up close he was able to recognise the sheer amount of bodyweight he'd been pitted against. No wonder Akash and Danai had been helpless to resist against these men in the past. One guy was six-three, and the other six-four, and their frames were solid.

But, snuck up on from behind, they went down all the same.

And their attention was seized by the door in front of them. They were both practically salivating at the prospect of having their way with Danai.

The door opened.

Slowly.

Inch by inch.

The person answering it was timid.

The slightly larger man became impatient, and he reached forward and shoved a palm flat against the wood and forced it inward, generating a soft gasp of shock from the person answering.

A feminine gasp.

Danai.

She stepped back, and Slater caught a glimpse of her

eyes, wide and terrified. Probably wondering whether these two men had already dealt with Slater. Wondering if her calm reality was about to come crashing to a halt.

Then Slater reared up out of the darkness and unleashed all he had.

35

At the last second Slater spotted their chunky utilitarian equipment belts, and he made out the rough shape of a knife and a pistol at each man's waist.

So he held nothing back, because if he came up short with the initial flurry of violence, it would be a long, cruel night for him in the aftermath.

He treated it like a dance. A vicious, macabre dance. Danai wouldn't like it. Slater figured she'd never seen a no-holds-barred fight to the death up close. Not right in front of her face. She might have seen her fellow countrymen gunned down in the street, or seen their bodies afterwards, but there was nothing like experiencing a fight between two-hundred-plus pound men from a couple of feet away.

There was nothing beautiful or impressive about the sound of breaking bone, or the *crunch* of teeth getting knocked out, or the *thwack* of a skull being slammed into a blunt object.

Slater hoped she and Akash were averting their eyes.

He closed the last few feet of empty space, still undetected. Both the newcomers' eyes were fixed on Danai. They both seemed to feed off her helplessness. She stared up at them and visibly gulped, and then Slater was right there in the mix.

Go.

He smashed the heel of his right boot into the soft left calf muscle of the slightly smaller man. Pinpoint accuracy. With all the power of a trained, hardened killer. He felt the sole of his shoe strike the muscle fibres with a blistering intensity. It had its intended effect. The muscle cramped. The guy's calf simply locked up, seizing in place with all the pain and discomfort and shock that came along with it. Nearly crippled by the agonising sensation, he buckled involuntarily at the knees. First his left leg went down, accompanied by a strange wobbling of the ankle, like his body was trying to get rid of the cramp before informing his mind. Then his right leg followed suit as the initial shock threw his balance off.

He stumbled forward, only a half-step, but this was a game of inches.

Slater wrapped a powerful hand around the back of the guy's skull and shoved him with all his might.

The man went through the same motion at five times the speed, and he hit the side of the door frame with his nose.

Which was never a good body part to block an impact with.

There was a sickening *crack* as a couple of important delicate bones met the wooden frame in just the right place, and the slightly smaller guy went down like he'd been shot in the face with an automatic rifle.

By that point a full second had elapsed, so the slightly larger man was beginning to realise what was happening.

He'd probably sensed the change in atmosphere first — there was something palpable, something primal, about being in the midst of a trained assassin looking to cause maximum injury or death.

So he spun to face Slater, twisting in a fast half-circle, but instead of swinging with an instinctual punch he went for one of the weapons in his belt.

A terrible, terrible move.

He only had one hope of winning, and that would have been to put maximum effort into a right hook. Then he would have intercepted Slater before he had a chance to move on from the first guy, and a well-placed hook with that amount of weight behind it might have killed him if it had landed.

But he didn't throw a punch.

Or a kick.

Or a knee.

Or an elbow.

Or a headbutt.

He panicked — maybe due to the sound of his buddy's nose breaking, or the shock to his system as he realised they were getting attacked, or sheer idiocy — and went for his gun.

Or his knife.

Slater didn't care either way.

He cocked an elbow and took careful aim, which only took him a fraction of a second. He isolated the jaw, lining it up square in his vision so he ensured he didn't have a hope of missing. He soaked in the sight of the neck muscles straining, the eyes wide and unblinking, the breathing heavy. He loaded up.

And he let go.

Horizontally, like a knife slashing across a throat. But

instead, an elbow across a jaw. He hit the man so hard in the face he thought he broke his own elbow for a moment. But it was just the sound of delicate bones shattering in and around the guy's chin. The big man went down even faster than his colleague, arms going limp and legs giving out.

Danai screamed.

Slater was on them in a heartbeat, methodically ripping guns and knives from their belts. He found a couple of old-school revolvers tucked in holsters, and realised the weapons were more for show than practical use. They were ancient Smith & Wessons, probably awfully effective back in the day, but now failing to serve as much more than an intimidation tactic. Slater hurled the guns into the hallway, tossing them past Danai's immobile form. She stood still as a statue inside the doorway.

Slater moved to the knives, and found they were infinitely more impressive. They were genuine Ka-Bars, probably at least a couple of decades old, but still in excellent condition. He figured there were a thousand possibilities concerning how they'd ended up with the Green Bombers, but most of the situations involved ex-U.S. soldiers heading over to Africa in search of mercenary work getting relieved of their possessions once they arrived.

Slater threw one Ka-Bar through the doorway, making sure to leave it in its leather sheath so it didn't slice up Danai by accident on the way past. He unsheathed the other and stood still, in between the two thugs. He waited patiently for them to make it to their feet.

It took one minute and thirty seven seconds.

36

They were in bad shape.

Slater waved the knife under each of their noses. Both of them barely noticed. Their faces were swelling beyond comprehension, their eyes glazing over, wet with involuntary tears. They stood like empty husks of the men they used to be. There was none of the aggression and control they'd possessed just a couple of minutes earlier. Now they stood with their shoulders slumped and their gazes averted and their expressions sheepish, whilst simultaneously wracked with pain.

Still facing them, Slater said, 'Danai.'

'Yes?' she said.

Her voice shook. Slater could barely hear her. He figured he'd nailed his diagnosis a few moments earlier. The violence would have been horrifying up close. Maybe she'd seen her husband beaten by these men in the past. But there was a difference between slaps and light punches designed to intimidate, and full-contact blows designed to destroy bone and tear muscle and permanently cripple adversaries.

Maybe she hadn't even realised a human body was capable of such things.

Slater said, 'Take a good look at these two.'

She did.

He said, 'Do you recognise them?'

'Yes,' she said.

'What did they do to you two years ago?'

'I don't want to talk about that.'

'But you're absolutely sure this is them?'

'Yes,' she said.

Slater tapped the knife against each of their chests, and then he said, 'Walk back to your car.'

They paused, seemingly confused. Likely wondering whether it was some kind of sick joke. As if he would hit them again if they had the gall to think they could move. They glanced at each other, and then at Slater. Neither spoke a word.

Slater knew exactly what it was. He'd dealt with a hundred similar instances, if not more. Physically imposing thugs in third world countries had none of the restraint most criminals built up through skirting the law. They'd had their way with anyone in the region for years, and they couldn't quite wrap their heads around someone standing up to them.

Not just standing up to them.

Utterly humiliating them.

So now they were stuck in mental thought patterns they had no experience with, going round and round in circles, wondering where they'd gone wrong and how doomed they were now that they'd lost control of the situation for what might be the first time in their lives.

Slater said, 'Walk back to your car.'

This time he meant it.

They got the message. They set off, slow and patient, their every movement controlled. They were deliberately trying not to antagonise. Slater realised if his hypothesis was true, then they hadn't been on the receiving end of a blow in a long time. Maybe they'd forgotten what pain felt like. And this was a different level of pain. This was the pain that would stay with them for years, haunting their dreams as they reminisced about the time the stranger from the night shattered their nose and devastated their jaw.

But they wouldn't get that chance.

Because if there was something Slater couldn't stand, to the extent that silent fury coursed through his veins, it was rapists.

More than anything else on the planet.

Mostly due to an intimate history with the industry.

He would never get his mother back.

He followed the pair to their pick-up truck, seething with rage.

Barely disguising it.

He told them to get into the rear tray.

They took care vaulting up onto the ridged metal. The back of the truck sagged and groaned under their weight. Slater leapt up alongside them with the dexterity of a cat. Far separated from the ragged breaths and laborious, shock-ridden motions of Simba's thugs.

He held the Ka-Bar down low.

He wanted them to realise what was coming.

And they did.

The slightly smaller guy figured it out first. Probably because a broken nose was a whole lot better than a broken jaw. At least he could speak if needed, and maintain a cohesive grip on reality. The slightly larger man was practically semi-conscious already. He had a glazed expression in his eyes and couldn't seem to focus on anything for longer than a couple of seconds. He stared around at the darkness like he'd been lobotomised. Maybe he had. Maybe Slater had scrambled wires in his brain with the elbow. It was certainly conceivable.

But the smaller guy decided there was only one reason why Slater wanted them in the rear tray. Because a sum of close to five hundred pounds between the pair of them was a hell of a lot of weight to move when it was all corpse.

Easier this way.

Less hassle.

Less fuss.

The smaller guy lunged forward.

Slater half-smiled.

He skirted back across the tray and his heels hit the rear door. It almost went down on its hinges, but he corrected his momentum at the last second. The guy's hands found empty air, and he snatched at nothing. He seemed to realise it had been his last stand. He cowered away from the inevitable counter-attack but Slater shoved the knife blade through the bottom of his chin all the same. It skewered up through soft flesh and struck bone and brain.

Slater wrenched it out and the guy collapsed, bleeding from the underside of his head.

Slater stepped over him and moved in on the larger guy.

This man had his wits about him. Maybe it was the stink of death. But he shook his head from side to side, causing enough temporary pain in the lower half of his face to shock him back to the present moment. His eyes crystallised and some level of alertness returned.

Good.

Slater wanted him to know what was coming.

He repeated the act, and when he lowered the massive

corpse to the undulating metal alongside its twin, he threw a quick glance in either direction to make sure none of the neighbours had deemed it prudent to become nosy.

But there was no-one in sight.

Those who lived in these parts were all cooped up in their houses.

He vaulted out of the tray, wiped the crimson blade on one of the olive uniforms, and tucked it back into its sheath. He put the whole contraption in his waistband and strode back up the thin dirt trail to the front door.

Danai stood there, unmoving, unblinking.

She said, 'I don't think I believed you when you told me your story. I thought you were exaggerating.'

'I wasn't,' Slater said.

'I can see that. What happens now?'

'Now I have a gun.'

'I mean in terms of the bodies.'

'I'll take care of them.'

'What are you going to do?'

'This is rural Zimbabwe. I'll figure something out.'

'I can tell you some good locations if you never want them to be found.'

'Best you don't.'

'Why not?'

'Plausible deniability.'

She looked at him funny. Perhaps because of the long words, or perhaps because of the shock.

He said, 'So you can truthfully say you don't know what happened to them if you're asked.'

She nodded. 'Right. Understood.'

He watched her carefully, and said, 'Do you think any differently of me now?'

'Why should I?'

'I just killed two men right in front of you. It wasn't pretty either. I beat them up and then I stabbed them. That can change the way people look at you. Even if they weren't the most savoury characters.'

She shook her head, almost emotionless. 'I don't care about what you did to those men.'

'They hurt you?'

'They did worse than hurt me.'

'Why didn't you tell me about that before?'

'I figured I could leave certain details out. I figured you would get the picture. I don't like talking about those times.'

'Were they frequent?'

'Every now and then.'

'Ever Simba personally?'

'No. But I've spoken to enough young women he's had his way with. He used to take them at will. Back when he used to run this region.'

'Can he still do that?'

'Maybe not as openly anymore. But I'm sure he still does it.'

Slater said, 'I can't wait to meet him.'

Then he backed out of the doorway and vanished into the night to dispose of the bodies.

37

Two hours later he knocked at the door again.

Danai opened almost immediately.

Slater paused in the doorway, surprised. He said, 'I thought I was going to wake you. I was preparing an apology.'

She said, 'I will not sleep tonight. Neither will my husband.'

'If I scare you, I can leave.'

'Where will you go?'

Slater looked around at the darkness. It had taken most of his energy and mental fortitude to walk back to the village in the black of night. He considered himself emotionally tough, and didn't figure anyone could label him as easily deterred, or easily frightened, but something about the utter desolation around Marange had set him on edge for most of the trek. The moonlight had barely illuminated the ground a few feet in front of him, and the ghostly night wind howling across the plains had sent shivers down his spine. His mind had conjured up all kinds of cheap tricks on the endless dirt trails, and he'd been ready to murder rogue

bandits at several points throughout the journey. He'd
dumped the truck in the bowels of what constituted a small
canyon, backing it up to a jagged maw in the landscape and
letting it gently roll off the edge into nothingness. And then
he'd walked all the way back on foot, through plains that
were ordinarily deserted in the daytime.

During the night, rural Zimbabwe had become a whole
different beast.

In essence, he was spent.

He said, 'Good point.'

With a half-smile she said, 'You don't scare us.'

'I can't see how I wouldn't.'

'You are a violent man. But you are a violent man with a
good heart. And that's not something that comes around
very often. I know it's portrayed in the American movies all
the time. But reality is something different. It's a worthy
ideal to hold but most men do not involve themselves in
trouble unnecessarily. And if they do, they do not have good
hearts. They are looking for fights. They are looking to let
out some of their anger. But you are violent in a way that is
controlled, and it is something I haven't seen before. You
have made my story, and Rand's story, personal. But you
haven't let yourself get carried away with emotion. That is
what I think about you. I think you are one of the last of
your kind and I would be happy to host you in my house for
as long as you need.'

The hot wind howled down the trail.

Slater said, 'Wow.'

'You seemed to think I had a very different mental image
of you. I just told you how I feel.'

'I appreciate it.'

'Do you hear words like that often?'

'Almost never.'

'Have you always been so rigid in your beliefs?'

'What do you mean?'

'Have you ever been in a situation where you need to do the morally wrong thing to survive?'

'No.'

'Never?'

'I've never needed to.'

'You ... what's the expression?'

Slater said, 'I don't know.'

'You stick to your guns,' Danai said. 'That's what I'm thinking of.'

'I do.'

'And you're still here.'

'Yes.'

'So you're very good at what you do.'

'You saw what happened just now.'

'Those two men were the most feared in the region.'

'They're at the bottom of a valley now.'

'Along with their car, I see.'

'Yes.'

'You said you don't hear words like that. Before. When I complimented you.'

'Most people would just consider me a killer.'

'I think there is a difference.'

'It's a fine line.'

'If there was anyone who could do a successful job at walking it, it would be you.'

'Thank you.'

'Would you like to come in?'

'I'd love to. I'm tired.'

'I'm afraid we don't have a spare bed. We sold the beds when the kids left. But you can use the couch in the other room. The one you took a nap on.'

'That will do fine.'

'I'll try to find you a blanket.'

'Don't bother,' Slater said. 'I'll sleep fully clothed.'

'You sure?'

'Apparently I just killed the two most feared men in all the region. Simba would have known what they came here to do, so he'll give them discretionary time. But not a ridiculous length. I need to be prepared for anything.'

'There are a million ways to die in Zimbabwe,' Danai said. 'I do not think Simba will assume it was us. He knows what we are. We have never fought back. We have always held our tongues. He will not think we are trying to resist him. You are the last person he would expect us to take in.'

'Why do you think that is?'

'Cockiness,' Danai said. 'He has not faced resistance in a long time. Because of his own brilliance, I must admit. It's a terrible thing to say, but it would be foolish to deny that he is brilliant. He has been waging a war against half of Zimbabwe for countless years, and he hasn't a scratch to show for it. You cannot do something like that without manipulating people. And he is very, very good at it.'

'I know,' Slater said. 'Rand told me about the settlers that came for him on the night they cut his arm and leg off. Simba had worked them into a state of frenzy. With the help of a Political Commissar known as Rangano.'

Danai hissed at the last sentence, pursing her lips.

Slater hesitated. 'What?'

'A Political Commissar...'

'I take it he isn't one anymore.'

'Of course not,' Danai said. 'But I told you I heard a whisper of his name. Rangano. When you first mentioned it to me...'

'Is it ringing a bell now?'

'There were rumours he was one of the inner circle. The ones that hoarded all the diamonds.'

'Would he be sitting on them now?'

'No way to know for sure. That part of the world falls under the shadow that Simba created. No-one dares to talk about it, or even think about it. They think if they mention the cruelties done to them in the past, they'll get a nighttime visit from men who used to be Green Bombers. And they're probably not wrong. But the genius of Simba's mental warfare is that he doesn't even need to get into physical confrontations. Zimbabwe is recovering, but he and all the others are just as much the same dictators as they used to be.'

'Back when I was employed, we referred to it as psy-ops,' Slater said. 'It's all psychological. Our government did it to our enemies, from time to time.'

'Does it work?'

'Almost always.'

'But not on you.'

Slater shrugged. 'I'm doing my best to use my own version of it.'

'How so?'

'I ran into a group of men in olive uniforms on the way here,' he revealed. 'I left one of them alive. With a busted nose. I sent him back to Simba with a message.'

'So he will know you are coming tomorrow...'

'I didn't give too much detail,' Slater said. 'And I know how to blend in.'

'You would hope so.'

'Describe the auction to me.'

'In the morning. You look tired.'

'I am tired. It's been a long day.'

'I will show you to your room.'

'I know where it is. Thank you, Danai.'

'For what?'

'Allowing me to help.'

Danai managed a half-smile and gestured for him to step past, through the doorway. 'I don't think you are helping me. I think you are helping yourself.'

'How so?'

'To me, you seem like a tortured soul. I think not getting involved in my business would be worse for you than for me. You need to move. You need to fight. Without it you are nothing.'

He took her up on her gesture, sauntering into the spare room.

He gently pushed the door shut behind him, sat down on the sofa, and put his head in his hands.

He thought hard.

And he realised she was right.

38

The sun rose just after five the next morning, creeping in through the thin see-through curtains draped over the front window.

Reclined on his back, Slater opened his eyes, awake in an instant. He felt for the weapons he'd wedged in between two of the cushions, and breathed a sigh of relief as he found them. He listened for sounds of any suspicious activity, but all was quiet in the house, and outside on the dirt road. No-one seemed to be up yet — if they were, they were taking care to allow their neighbours a few more hours of rest.

Slater sat up, cracked his neck, and rolled his wrists and ankles in small semicircles. He straightened his elbows and knees, tensing the muscles in all four of his limbs, paying keen attention to any niggles or tender areas. A rudimentary physical test. He'd beat three men to a pulp yesterday, stabbed two of them to death, and gunned down a separate trio. The hand-to-hand confrontations were the first thing to worry about — Slater might have come away unscathed in the moment, but experience had taught him a good night's sleep allowed disrupted muscle fascia and other nagging problems to present themselves. Putting all your explosive effort into a punch or an elbow or a kick when the difference between winning and losing was life and death took its toll on the central nervous system.

But Slater had been in life or death confrontations for most of the last decade.

And the human body was an adaptable organism.

So his quick physical check-up came away with no problems whatsoever.

He took his shirt and pants off, stripping to nothing but his underwear, and then set to work stretching out. He opened up his hips with a variety of vinyasa yoga salutations. It took less than half an hour, but the heat drew the sweat from his pores like clockwork. The nature of his lifestyle would cause anyone, no matter how physically fit, to deteriorate quickly if the muscles were left untouched. Hip flexors tightened, shoulders hunched, and cramps set in. Especially with a routine like Slater's. Maximum effort, full capacity strikes could leave you sore for months. So he never neglected this, no matter how uncomfortable it made him. The alternative wouldn't be pleasant for his physical and mental health.

Working with nothing but his own body and the floor underneath, he clambered to his feet drenched in sweat, breathing heavy. He looked down and saw his diaphragm expanding in and out with each breath. The tight musculature coating his abdomen expanded and constricted in turn. He wiped his brow with the bare crook of his arm and then sat on the floor, opting to drip sweat into his own lap rather than tarnish the sofa Danai had so generously offered him.

A moment later the door swung open.

Slater raised his gaze to the doorway and said, 'Mind if I use the shower?'

Danai tried to avert her eyes, but she couldn't. She said, 'Not many men built like you around here.'

'That's not what gives me the advantage against Simba.'

'I know. But it must help.'

'It takes a lot of work.'

'I can imagine. The shower is this way.'

Slater didn't know when he would have the chance to bathe again, so he spent twenty minutes under the cool stream of water, washing the fetid sweat and dirt and stress out of his skin. He'd discovered altercations like the ones he'd experienced the previous day drew a strange new level of sweat from a man. Reinvigorated, he dried himself and dressed in a fresh change of clothes from his duffel bag — different colours, same style. He never bought anything flashy, but he made sure to select the best material money could buy. Simple colours, maximum efficiency. Comfortable dry-tech sports khakis and a short-sleeved tee. He tugged the expensive gear over his head and stretched out until it fit perfectly, and then he came back out into the kitchen where Danai and Akash were preparing a simple breakfast.

He sat down at the table, and Danai gave a warm smile and said, 'I'll have something for you in a few moments.'

Slater held up a hand.

'It's okay,' he said. 'I don't eat in the mornings.'

She looked at him funny, just as Ron and Judy had. Befuddlement at his meal timings seemed to cross all cultural barriers.

He just shrugged.

She said, 'Are you feeling okay?'

He said, 'Fine.'

'The bull auction starts at nine on the dot.'

'That's early.'

'It's a competitive industry, especially now the country is going through a resurgence. The buyers are expected to take it seriously and show up on time.'

'Where exactly does this auction take place?'

'At the vendor's property, about five miles east of here. Further away from the diamond fields.'

'Can I walk there?'

Danai shrugged. 'You walked here. I can't see how it would be any worse.'

Slater passed over his phone, already open to the maps application, and urged Danai to pinpoint the exact location of the vendor's property. She wasn't familiar with the technology, but it didn't take her long to pinch and swipe and zoom in and zoom out until she had a basic grasp of the fundamentals. A little slower than Rand, but she got there in the end. She went east five miles, rapidly approaching the border of Mozambique, and then she zoomed in and stabbed her finger at a small patch of land on the other side of the Odzi River.

Slater took the phone back and dropped a digital pinpoint in full view of Danai. He presented the screen to her, silently asking a question.

She nodded. 'Right there. There will be signs.'

'I can't read Shona.'

'There will be people. There are no people out there usually.'

'One more question.'

'Yes?'

'What does he look like?'

'Simba?'

'Yes.'

'He's big.'

'Bigger than me?'

'Yes.'

'Anything else?'

'He is about three inches taller than you.'

King's height, Slater thought.

She said, 'He's heavier than you too. It's the same as the men from last night. Muscle and fat. But he is very powerful.'

'Any features you can tell me about?'

'He has very green eyes. That is all you need. You will find him in any crowd based on that alone. The rest of his appearance might have changed. As far as I can remember, he had fat lips and short hair woven into spiky dreadlocks. And a squashed nose. Like it had been broken in the past. And very yellow teeth. Some of his teeth are missing. It is strange, because most women might consider him handsome if he took care of himself. Because of his eyes. But he doesn't care about that. He pumps himself full of steroids, so he has a gut, but he is powerful. And the teeth and nose ruin his face.'

Slater paused, then said, 'He will send men to find out what happened to his last two guys.'

'I will tell them they never showed up here. I told you — Zimbabwe is a dangerous place. Especially out this far. That's why I was so surprised to see an American when you showed up at our doorstep.'

'I think I've proven I can take care of myself.'

'You certainly have.'

'You sure you'll be okay?'

'Depends if you are successful.'

Akash nodded, his expression weary. 'Do not fail.'

'I don't intend to.'

'Please,' Akash said.

Then the man turned back to preparing his breakfast. Hunching away from the conversation. No longer wishing to take part in it. His eyes went downward and a sigh caught in his throat.

Slater turned back to Danai. 'You should be fine, whether or not I succeed.'

Danai shook her head. 'No. That's where you're wrong. You have to succeed. We won't be fine if you don't.'

39

S later said, 'There's no way to prove those men showed up here. No-one saw.'

She chuckled. 'Simba doesn't need proof. He will come here and take out his anger on us if his men don't show up. He will not care whether we played a part in it. They were on their way to us, and that is all that matters.'

'That seems nonsensical.'

'Simba has always been nonsensical. That's part of his ... what did you call it? Psy-ops? It's half the reason everyone is on edge all the time. He will take out his anger at random. At least, he used to. He needs to be more careful about it now. The country is shifting underneath him. But there is still a whole lot he can manage discreetly. Some of our friends have disappeared up to only a couple of months ago. There is nothing we can do about it.'

'To strike fear into the populace.'

'He cannot openly take credit for it anymore. But this is what he does.'

For the second time in twelve hours, Slater said, 'I can't wait to meet him.'

He poured a few glasses of water out of a chipped plastic jug in the centre of the table, gulping them down one after the other to hydrate for the journey ahead. Then he wiped his lips on his sleeve and rose off the chair.

Akash watched his every movement, and then the old man smiled and waved farewell and hobbled out of the room without further fanfare.

Danai stepped past the kitchen island and said, 'I apologise for his quietness. He does not like to talk to people he does not know intimately.'

Slater held up a hand. 'There's nothing to apologise for. I'm the same.'

'He could be more polite. Like you are.'

'I haven't been through what he's been through.'

'It sounds like you have.'

Slater shrugged. 'Maybe physically. Mentally, emotionally, it's a whole other story.'

'Why?'

'Every time I've run into a situation like this, I've been able to do something about it.'

Danai smiled her trademark sad smile. 'You have hope.'

'I do.'

'I hope Simba does not strip that from you, like he has to so many of us.'

Then she showed him the door, and he left without saying another word, because there was nothing else that needed to be said. They could talk for days about hypotheticals and possibilities and the way things could go and the problems Danai and Akash had in store if Slater came up short. But they already knew all that. It hovered there in the silence, raising the stakes, elevating Slater's heart rate. He knew if he failed, it would all be traced to their doorstep. He would bring a world of suffering and unimaginable cruelty to them when they hadn't even asked for help in the first place.

He was keenly aware of that.

So he wouldn't fail.

It wasn't in the list of possible outcomes.

There was nothing but victory, in every sense.

He went to the spare room and retrieved one of the old-school revolvers from the night before. It was a Smith & Wesson Model 17 K-22 Masterpiece, with six .22 cartridges sitting in the chambers, and a cylinder that swung out to the side to reload. Slater took the six cartridges out of the other identical revolver and wedged them one by one into a tiny pocket at the front of his khakis, right near the waist.

A swing-out cylinder revolver wouldn't be his first choice of weapon, and a quick frisk search of the two corpses the night before had revealed an absence of speed loaders. Therefore, he would have to insert the spare cartridges one by one into the chambers if he needed to reload in a hurry. It would be a logistical nightmare, especially if he found himself empty in a shootout.

But that was all he had to work with, so he tucked the K-22 tight into his waistband and slipped one of the Ka-Bars into the other side. Without any holsters, he would simply have to put up with the discomfort. Having a knife and a gun in easy reach was a hell of a lot better than keeping them in his duffel.

He retrieved a belt from his bag and secured it tight around the two weapons, then left the other empty K-22 and the spare Ka-Bar on the sofa cushions. No use needlessly arming himself with unnecessary duplicates. He wasn't about to dual wield revolvers in an open skirmish, and he figured if he was getting into a shootout at the bull auction he had worse problems to deal with in the first place.

The K-22 bulged out against his waistband. It was a bulky, sizeable gun. He dropped the hem of his T-shirt over the weapons and breathed a sigh of relief that the garment was long enough. Then he stepped back out into the hallway. Danai and Akash sat at the dining room table a dozen feet from where he stood.

They watched him.

He put the duffel on his back and nodded to them.

They nodded back.

Nothing to be said.

It had already been voiced.

All of it.

They all knew the stakes.

Slater turned to the door, and then he froze, and turned back to the older couple and said, 'I won't let you down.'

Danai got a look in her eye, as if recalling what she'd seen the night before. The savage movement, the crippling blows, the smaller guy's skull bouncing off the door frame.

She said, 'I know.'

Slater stepped outside into the hot morning sun.

40

S later looped his hands inside the straps of his bag and set off in the direction of the Odzi River.

He followed dusty trails and weaved through trees and drank sporadically from a plastic bottle of water resting at the top of his pack. The sun climbed higher in the sky and people started to materialise outside their houses and shacks and huts. Most were stooped, seemingly shielding themselves from the sun, dressed in simple garments stained with dirt and dust. Slater shared their skin tone, but his athletic frame and overall vigour jarred with the majority of the population of the Manicaland Province. He was in peak physical condition, and the people he passed by weren't.

A rather simple contrast, but one that meant everything all the same.

They stared and gawked and turned away when he nodded politely to them. He carried on until the village fell away, replaced by outskirts, followed swiftly by rural nothingness. The hills rose in the distance, vast and green, and Slater figured Mozambique's invisible border rested somewhere in the scenery. The wind picked up and the dust swirled, hot and thick in the air. Sweat flowed freely from his forehead and his palms and his chest, but he ignored it.

It was now a familiar sensation.

He reached the Odzi River after an hour's walk, which constituted a dark muddy leviathan twisting and snaking through the landscape. Its rapids seemed toxic, churning dirt and muck through its waters. He trekked along the riverbank for close to a mile before he found a rickety footbridge spanning a particularly narrow stretch between the two shores. There was no-one in sight. No guards manning the ends of the bridge collecting tolls.

Slater didn't know what he'd expected.

He crossed, climbing another dusty trail that spiralled away endlessly in either direction, parallel to the border. He checked his phone, squinting to make out the display under the harsh glare of the sun, and caught a glimpse of his own reflection in the process. His eyes seemed as bright and energetic as ever, but there was definite wear and tear in his expression. He noted his lined cheeks and the faint dusting of peeling skin coating his forehead. The beads of perspiration stood out, bright and wet, at each corner of his hairline. The hair, as usual, was shaved down to the scalp. He wasn't balding, but it annoyed him incessantly when he grew it out.

He tucked the phone away and turned left, figuring he was only a mile or so out. He quickened his pace. Best to arrive early and find a quiet private corner of the auction site to bury his head in the sand until the proceedings got underway. From there, it was anyone's guess. He had no plan, no concept of how many men Simba would bring, and he hadn't seen a photo of the guy. Neither Rand nor Danai had one on hand.

Just a description.

Green eyes. Spiky hair. Fat lips. Bigger than Slater. A steroid gut, formed through years of testosterone abuse. Perhaps some human growth hormone thrown in the mix. Thick with muscle and fat.

He sounded like a freak, based on Danai's description.

Slater wondered how many of his features she had exaggerated.

He spotted some kind of commotion in the distance, perhaps two hundred feet away. A dust cloud rose above the tree line. A pick-up truck or a similar vehicle, turning off the main trail. Heading in the direction of the border. Slater checked the map on his phone again.

This was it.

He adjusted the bag on his back and settled into character. He breathed a silent sigh of relief for the amount of physical cash he'd carried into Zimbabwe, figuring he'd need to rely on it if he found himself stranded somewhere rural without access to an ATM. Now he counted his blessings. He adopted the role of a wealthy foreigner, injecting as much false confidence into his stride as he could muster, and walked faster as he approached the dust cloud.

The brown haze dissipated, replaced by nothingness, but Slater didn't need to use it as a reference point.

He had his phone for that.

He spotted the vendor a hundred feet from the mouth of the private driveway. He could barely make out the features of the distant silhouette, but the man exuded the aura of money, even from this distance. Just as Slater likely did for the locals he passed by. This man wore a plaid dress shirt tucked into blue jeans, and he stood with his shoulders back and his chest stuck out. Like he was ready to take on the world. Like he had nothing to worry about, standing at the head of a trail in rural Zimbabwe, surrounded by desperation. He was dark-skinned and bald, but as Slater got closer he saw the man's eyes sparkle with opportunity. He looked healthy, without any stoop or ailments.

Slater stopped a dozen feet away from the man.

'Are you the vendor?' he said, laying his American accent on thick, inflating it twofold.

The guy cocked his head. He said nothing, sizing Slater up, his hands in his pockets.

Slater repeated the question.

The guy said, 'You speak just English?!'

Slater nodded.

The guy said, 'Where from?'

'America.'

'Ohhhhh,' the guy said, raising his eyebrows, widening his eyes. A sickly smile spread across his face. 'You long way from home.'

'Are you the vendor?'

'I don't know what means. You in wrong place. You go.'

'Bulls,' Slater said.

The eyebrows went higher. The eyes went wider. The smile grew larger. 'Bulls?'

'Yes,' Slater said. 'Bulls.'

'Right place,' the man said.

'So you are the vendor.'

'Yes,' the guy said, even though he still had no idea what it meant. 'I vendor.'

'How long until the auction?'

The smile started to fade. And then it turned to a scowl. 'You no come auction. Auction private. For buyers that ... trust.'

'Buyers you trust?'

'Yes.'

The sickly smile came back.

As if to say, *Sorry, wish I could help.*

Slater slung the bag off his back. He dropped it into the dirt, and unclasped the flap on top, and stuck his hand into its contents and burrowed around, and came out with close to twenty thousand U.S. Dollars in crisp hundred-dollar bills, bound together by thin bands.

He said, 'Bulls.'

The guy smiled the widest smile Slater had ever seen, and said, 'You buyer I trust.'

41

The guy stood there, excited and hesitant at the same time. Slater put the money back in the bag and crossed his arms over his chest and cocked his head.

The vendor shifted from foot to foot.

He said, 'I no know English good. What you need to know?'

Slater said, 'Nothing. I'm fine. I came with all my credentials. No other reason for being here. I'm ordinarily not one to venture this far out. Most of my business is conducted overseas. But your name came up with recurring frequency, so I figured I'd make the trek. It's a business expense after all, isn't it? I'll take any advantage I can get in this day and age. But if you need to know about me, I have a keen interest in premium, genetically pure bulls. I think they are the principal foundation for success in the beef industry, and I'm a man who enjoys my success. I like to thrive. I imagine you do, too. So let's keep things relaxed. I know what I'm here for and I won't cause any trouble. I'll purchase the livestock that catch my eye, and we can arrange the requisite transportation in the aftermath. How does that sound?'

He made sure to inject as much unnecessarily verbose language into the spiel as he could muster. Better to throw the guy off from the start. Because Slater's knowledge of the bull industry sure as hell wouldn't hold up to a coherent interrogation.

The guy nodded along, even though he probably understood less than half of what Slater was saying. But he got the general gist of it, and Slater's confidence crossed all language barriers.

So the vendor smiled again and stepped aside.

Which was an entirely symbolic gesture. The mouth of the driveway was wide enough for ten men to walk past without resistance. But it meant Slater was accepted, and granted entry to the property, so he didn't underestimate it.

He smiled and nodded back, and picked up his bag, and held his chin high, and kept his shoulders back, and strolled on past. Pretending this was a perfectly normal place to be. Acting as if he belonged. Over the years he'd discovered it was nigh on the most important part of being in the field. He'd lost count of the number of times he'd capitalised on sheer ignorance and laziness.

What the vendor should have done was question where the hell Slater had come from and why the hell he'd come out to rural Zimbabwe if most of his business was conducted overseas. This was the middle of nowhere, and the sudden appearance of a mystery buyer didn't add up.

But dollar signs trumped everything in business.

On the way past Slater revealed the twin hundred dollar bills he'd peeled off his stash and kept in his palm. He tilted his hand toward the vendor, and opened it, and waited for the man's eyes to dart to the bills.

Then he passed them over.

'A friendly tip,' he said. 'For your discretion.'

'What this mean?' the vendor said, but his eyes had already lit up, so Slater knew the justification wouldn't be an issue they'd linger on.

This man spoke money.

'I want good prices on these bulls. So I don't want you to tell anyone else there's a new guy here. Because then they'll start planning and scheming about how they're going to outbid me as a group. You know what I mean? They'll want to band together and drive me away, because I'm competition. And I can't let that happen.'

'No tell them,' the man said.

Slater nodded, and raised a finger to his lips.

A universal gesture.

The guy nodded.

He mirrored the same gesture. A finger to the lips.

Then he took his hand away from his mouth.

'You will see auction site,' he said. 'Walk down and wait. Start in one hour.'

'Thank you.'

'I have good bulls today.'

'I've heard you have the best.'

The guy should have said, *From who?*

But instead he gave a false sheepish shrug and a knowing nod.

Slater set off up the driveway. There was ochre dirt underfoot and the skeletons of trees on either side of the trail and the bustle of activity ahead in the distance. A hundred feet later the trees opened up into a natural clearing, home to a ranch-style compound made up of nearly a dozen outbuildings and a giant main house. Everything was made of caramel-coloured wood, scorched by the sun over

the years, and a hot wind blew through the thin smattering
of trees arranged in a ring around the complex. It kicked up
the dust underfoot and stung Slater's eyes. He held up a
hand to shield himself from both the glare and the silt, and
he searched for anything he could identify as a location for
a bull auction.

He found it without much effort.

It was one of the outbuildings — another massive structure made of horizontal wooden slats, with two vast open-
ings along one side leading into what effectively constituted
a giant barn. He heard faint snorts and the sound of large
beasts shuffling in place. Slater approached with relative
caution, figuring it was best to be wary of anyone he might
run into that would question his legitimacy. But he found
the interior largely deserted, save for a couple of workers the
vendor had hired to clean up the building before the big
occasion.

Slater ducked inside, and took in the details of his
surroundings.

He needed to know everything.

Here, he would come face to face with Simba for the
very first time.

42

There was a sweeping ground floor covered in loose straw, and an array of bullpens arranged in semicircular fashion around it. Slater pictured the ground as an arena of sorts, and the spectacle was completed by a raised viewing platform that ran around three sides of the barn, all made entirely of wood, propped up by supports. Like a giant U running around the interior perimeter.

He twirled in a full circle, admiring the setup. To his left and right, identical staircases led up to the viewing platform, where potential buyers could look down on the scene as one bull at a time was released from their smaller enclosures. From there, the beasts could parade around like they were on some kind of prehistoric catwalk, and selections could be made based on which livestock had the most potential.

Slater couldn't see the bulls themselves. The beasts were tucked away behind chipped and battered sliding doors made of steel. As if giant chunks of metal had been smashed into something resembling a flat surface and wedged into place with the help of rolling tracks underneath. But he could see the outlines of their heaving backs, and the tips of their horns, and the general ruckus caused by their massive weight shifting around their isolated pens.

He sensed opportunity in the air.

It was eerily similar to the awkward initial hour of a party, where no-one had showed up yet, but expectations were strong.

He chose the right-hand staircase and ascended quickly. The workers sweeping the barn floor with brooms paid him no attention whatsoever, and he figured the vendor had made it explicitly clear not to antagonise the buyers. To the man who owned the place, this was his life's work. He wasn't about to let a couple of minimum-wage workers ruin the whole thing by offending a potential customer.

Slater scoffed at that thought — truthfully he knew out here there was no such thing as minimum wage. The sweepers would be lucky to be paid with a hearty meal.

Work was scarce, and business was ruthless, and men were cruel.

Those who were cunning enough to take advantage of people would thrive.

That was the way the world would carry on forever.

Unless Slater got involved.

He set himself up at the end of the U, facing out over the parallel sides, and the rest of the barn. From there he had a sweeping view of the whole interior, and prime position for the fabled auction. He put his pack on the floor, resting it against the solid wooden stomach-high balustrade. Then he rested his elbows on the railing and waited.

He considered himself particularly adept at waiting.

Time ticked by, and slowly but surely new arrivals bled into the barn. Slater didn't bother turning away from any of them. He knew it was all but guaranteed Simba would show up close to last. Auctions were as much about confidence as anything else. And Simba's years of encouraging oppression would have taught him reams about maintaining control over those around him. He would also show up with a guard of honour, but they wouldn't present it as such. They might pretend they weren't bodyguards, and weren't armed. But he would go nowhere alone. Not in the new Zimbabwe. Not when his entire being was riding on his position as a man of great power.

He had to maintain that above all else.

So a smattering of healthy-looking Zimbabweans trickled in through the two separate entrances, both facing Slater. A couple nodded greetings to one another, but most headed straight for the viewing platform and concentrated on their own business. They mirrored Slater's actions, setting themselves up at equidistant intervals, maintaining as much space as possible between each man. Then a few women showed up, just as stern and serious, just as interested in the bulls behind the gates. None of the men snorted in derision, or laughed, or turned them away. They simply concentrated on themselves.

The new Zimbabwe.

Slowly, piece by piece, bringing itself out of the twentieth century.

But not quite yet.

Because men like Simba still reigned without consequence.

The barn continued to fill, and Slater kept his eyes trained on a vague space in the centre of the straw floor below. He had mastered the art of patience over a decade in the field. Operations were always solo, and sometimes that meant laying low until an opportunity arose. Sometimes for days at a time. Doing nothing but waiting in a half-awake, half-asleep state, but with the brain primed to flip into attack mode at any moment.

Just waiting for the opportunity.

And he did so now. He felt the weight of the K-22 Masterpiece resting against his hip, and the soft touch of the Ka-Bar's leather holster against the other.

He breathed in, and out, and focused on the sequence of movements he would go through if Simba walked into the auction and instantly recognised him.

In truth, his options were limited.

Especially if he brought help.

But Slater had never achieved anything by playing it safe.

So he stood with silent furious energy rippling through his veins, and then the viewing platform started to fill, nearing thirty occupants, and still there was nothing...

And Slater started to realise he might have made a massive error in judgment.

He'd taken Danai's word. Maybe things had changed. Maybe Simba didn't care about bulls anymore. It was the only thing Slater had based his approach on. Maybe it was all different, and right now Simba was furiously calculating where his men from the night before could have disappeared to. Maybe that was his only focus. Maybe Slater had trekked five miles away from Danai and Akash just to allow them to be slaughtered when Simba came hunting for answers over what happened to his men.

Beads of sweat appeared on Slater's brow.

It was stiflingly hot in the barn, but that wasn't the reason.

The vendor walked through the left-hand door. The bald man gestured to one of the workers, then to the big double doors behind him. He repeated the process with the second worker, and the second set of the doors on the right.

Sealing the venue.

Before things got underway.

Slater tensed up, calculating how fast he could run five miles.

He had a suspicion it was already far too late.

The workers split up, one on each side, and set to work raising the door stoppers skewered into narrow indents in the barn floor. The guy on the left moved faster than the guy on the right, and started swinging the door along its predetermined path. About to seal it shut.

Slater stepped away from his pack, figuring it was better to abandon the clothes and money than allow them to weigh him down over the course of the run. It would be hot as hell, and it would put his endurance to the test, but he simply had to do it. He'd sworn to protect Danai and Akash, and he was letting them down almost immediately by failing to do his due diligence.

He started to move to the left, approaching a burly man in his early fifties with weather-beaten skin and rough hands. The guy was leaning forward on his elbows, same as the rest of the buyers on the viewing platform, but his bulk denied Slater passage.

Slater reached out a hand to shove the guy out of the way, consequences be damned.

Then the worker stopped the door halfway through its trajectory and ushered a late arrival into the barn.

Simba walked through the doors.

43

The big man stepped into the room, and Slater looked down at the first bull in the pen. He kept his eyes trained on the animal, mustering all the scrutinisation he could, as if he knew exactly what he was looking for and why. In his peripheral vision he saw Simba's eyes on him. They lingered there for a moment, and then they drifted away, preoccupied by other details of the auction house, scanning the rest of the occupants.

Slater didn't breathe a sigh of relief.

He always knew it would be fine if Simba showed up.

He was aware of the disconnect between fantasy and reality. In a fantasy, the villains knew everything. They spent every waking moment compiling information on their enemies, and they recognised everyone's intentions the second they stepped into a room. They saw through ruses, they identified strangers, and they acted decisively. In reality, life was more complicated than that. Simba had men working for him and responsibilities to take care of and dirty money to handle and a legitimate business to run.

He didn't lord over everything.

One of his men had returned to him with a broken nose, speaking of three dead comrades, claiming a muscular black man had handled them with ease the previous day. But if that was the only description he had to work with, then he could apply it to half the men in the auction house. They were all wealthy, and they all worked in a physical industry, and they were supremely successful at it, so they had the ability and resources to keep themselves in shape. Slater eyed a couple of men with similar builds along the row.

Besides, there were a million other things to worry about from Simba's perspective. Namely, securing the finest bulls to kickstart his legitimate empire. He'd probably forgotten all about the two men he'd sent to take care of Danai and Akash. Their wellbeing would come to him in a realisation several hours from now, in between the hundred other things he had to take care of, and by then it would be far too late.

By then, either he or Slater would be dead.

Rigid with anticipation, Slater thought about going for the revolver. He could probably hit Simba with a couple of rounds before bedlam erupted. But in such an open space, it would prove disastrous.

There were over thirty men and women in the building, and Slater couldn't account for which of them were armed.

Simba was flanked by two bodyguards on either side. They presented themselves as harmless sideshows to the main attraction, like hangers-on in a celebrity's posse. But they couldn't change their eyes — four identical sets that darted around the room with the understanding and aware-ness of trained protectors. Slater passed his gaze across the room, lingering on nothing, but he paid keen attention to the bulges at their sides. They were all armed. That was four men right there, guaranteed to have had some kind of firearms training in the past. And Slater doubted they were all carrying swing-out cylinder revolvers. More than likely, Simba took his own protection seriously. Therefore he reserved semi-automatic or automatic pistols for the guards closest to him, leaving the strays with K-22 Masterpieces to take care of their own business. Hence the thugs targeting Danai and Akash the night before.

Hence the cumbersome weapon at Slater's side.

He was locked in an old-fashioned Mexican stand-off, even though the other party wasn't aware they were in one.

What he wouldn't give to have a Glock at hand.

Simba thundered over to the left-hand side of the barn and took up position at the top of the flight of stairs, coming to rest at the leftmost point of the viewing platform. A smart move. It put him right near the entrance doors if he needed a hasty escape. His men formed a guard of honour around him, uncaring about where they ended up, as long as it was within close proximity of their boss. They had no interest in the bulls. Their sole purpose was to protect the man paying the bills.

The workers sealed the doors shut and the widespread natural light fell away, replaced by shafts of sunlight filtering in through cracks in the door frames and the windows set high up in the barn's walls. The air turned musty and hot.

The auction house became a furnace.

The vendor crossed to one of the pens, ensuring all his paying customers were a safe distance away from the danger zone.

Then he opened up one of the steel gates, and led an enormous black bull out into the centre of the barn by its nose ring. He tethered the rope attached to the ring to a metal picket skewered into the floor, and the beast shifted restlessly in place, staring around at nothing in particular.

Its musculature rippled in the lowlight, exposing all of its detail to the viewing party.

The vendor rattled off a list of facts about the animal in Shona, his voice swallowed up by the hot wood, and then the bidding began.

44

The bids came fast and fierce, and within ten short minutes, three bulls had been sold.

They were led back into their pens by the workers. Genetically pure and premium quality, Slater quickly realised the beasts were prone to aggression. One of them nearly broke free from its nose ring as it tore away from the entrance to its pen, and both workers leapt back in shock, nearly losing their balance in the process. Slater watched their wide eyes and startled expressions and figured they'd been on the receiving end of a few too many bumps and knocks from the bulls in the past.

The vendor stood back by the entrance and watched with a keen eye.

Almost amused by their trepidation.

The man directly to Slater's left — the one he'd almost pushed aside — made a bid for the fourth bull, shouting a number into the empty void, drowning out the other interested parties. Slater glanced across, noticing a particular inflection in the way the man spoke. He thought the guy might speak English.

Then Simba outbid the man, screaming a higher integer, irritating his competitors.

Separated from Simba by at least fifteen people and a few dozen feet, the man deemed it safe enough to curse him out without detection.

Under his breath, he said, 'Motherfucker.'

In English.

Slater skirted a foot to his left, still resting his elbows on the railing. He said, 'You speak English?'

The guy looked across. His face was even worse off than Slater had originally estimated. It had been bombarded by sunlight for what seemed like the better part of twenty years, and there were pockmarks and hard lines and flaking skin all over his cheeks and forehead. But his eyes were sharp, and he regarded Slater with all the intensity of a wizened veteran of the industry.

He said, 'So you're not mute after all. You haven't said a word this whole time.'

Slater said, 'I'm a quiet guy.'

The man's accent was thick, but the underlying English was fundamnetally sound and coherent. He came off as a native Zimbabwean trying his absolute best to learn a second language, much like Danai. And he seemed to be doing a damn good job of it.

Slater said, 'Are you from around here?'

'Close by.'

'How do you speak English?'

'I learned it.'

'Why?'

'Times are changing. The country's going one way. We use U.S. Dollars now. It's already an advantage to speak the language. Soon it'll be the norm. I need any advantage I can get. Just business.'

'You sound dedicated to your trade.'

'Have to be.'

'What do you think of Simba?'

The guy looked at him, then surveyed the room, then stared right back at Slater. He said, 'I've been sizing you up since I stepped in here. You're hunching over in a way that's not natural. Like you're not used to it. Got something to hide?'

'Maybe,' Slater said.

'You're built like a brick shithouse.'

Slater smirked and said, 'Did an Australian teach you English?'

'No. But I Googled their slang.'

Slater smirked again.

The surrounding cacophony of noise reached a crescendo as Simba settled into a furious bidding war with a pair of buyers on the right-hand side of the viewing platform.

The man leant in closer and said, 'My name is Winston.'

'No it's not.'

'It's what I go by now. Changing times.'

'My name's Slater.'

'You from America, Slater?'

'Sure am.'

'What are you doing out here?'

'This and that.'

'You look like you could kill me with your bare hands. But I'm just about the only one who can notice, because most of you is hunched behind the balustrade. Are you hiding from someone?'

'Trying not to present too large of a target.'

'There's been a couple of rumours sweeping across this province over the last twenty-four hours.'

'And what would those rumours involve?'

'Someone's walking around beating up almost anyone he gets his hands on.'

'Is there a description attached to these rumours?'

'Not yet. It's all very vague. Whispers in the night.'

'Then you shouldn't pay attention to it.'

'You have a keen interest in Simba.'

'I don't like the look of him.'

'Many don't.'

'I want to know more about him. I thought I'd ask you.'

'I don't know much about him. He keeps everything under wraps. There are whispers about him too, though.'

'What are the nature of these whispers?' Slater said. 'Because between us, the other whispers you're hearing are accurate.'

Winston eyed him warily. 'I'd be careful if I were you.'

'Don't worry about me. Tell me about Simba.'

'He used to work for Rangano. That's all I needed to know to hate him.'

'I haven't heard that name in a couple of days. My focus has been on the man across from us. But I hear they were an item back in the day.'

'Not romantically.'

'That's not what I meant.'

'Although I think Rangano goes both ways.'

'I don't care which way he swings. I want to know why I should get my hands on them. With equal ferocity.'

'You don't have a reason yet?'

'I do. But I'm looking to extrapolate my theory to as many sources as I can find. Corroborating evidence. That sort of thing. Reduce the bias.'

'There's no bias. Rangano is a monster.'

'Give me a single example.'

'Why?'

'I just told you.'

'No,' Winston growled, shaking his head, keeping his voice low. 'You don't go after men like Simba and Rangano because of rumours. You go after them if you're a madman who doesn't value your own life. Like some of the victims' families, maybe. They would be dumb enough to try and take them on. But not you. This does not make sense. Not one bit. You don't know them.'

'But I've heard enough about them.'

'Then you really are a fool.'

'Maybe,' Slater said. 'But it's worked for me so far.'

'If you want to get yourself killed, I'm not going to stop you.'

'Can you help me?'

'How?'

'Get creative.'

'I'm not laying a finger on Simba, or Rangano, or any of their men. They're untouchable out here. I have family that live in the country. They will be placed in danger if I help you.'

'Good thing I'm alone then,' Slater said. 'And good thing I have no family.'

45

Winston shot daggers at Slater and said, 'What's your story?'

'Now's not the time for that.'

'I hope you pull it off.'

'Why?' Slater said, drilling his gaze into the man. 'Why do you hate them so much? Why is everyone so afraid of them?'

'You don't know by now?'

'I'm getting the picture.'

'When they threw Mugabe out of power, Simba and Rangano were left without jobs. They weren't sure where they stood in the new Zimbabwe. On paper, everything had changed, but reality isn't as simple as that. So they did not know what they could get away with. So they tested it.'

'On who?'

'My daughter. It was sheer dumb luck. She was in the wrong place at the wrong time. A gang of disillusioned Green Bombers took her and brought her back to Simba's compound and raped her. Simba and Rangano joined in.'

'Did they kill her?'

'No. They dumped her at my doorstep later that evening. Because it was the new Zimbabwe, and they were going to test their powers step by step. They wanted to see what I would do.'

'What did you do?'

'I helped her recover. The physical injuries healed after a few weeks, but the emotional scars are still there. And this was over a year ago. I think those scars will always be there. As long as the memories remain.'

'And then what did you do?'

'I went to the police.'

'What did they do?'

'Nothing. They filled me with empty promises, and then they concluded Simba and Rangano had them in the palm of their hand due to their wealth. And the country had enough problems as it was. Shifting tides and all. So they never got back to me, and no-one was ever charged, even though my daughter knew exactly where she was taken and what was done to her and who did it.'

'Does he know it's you standing across from him right now?'

'Who — Simba?'

Slater nodded.

'He's probably done that to a hundred women. Rangano's probably done it to a hundred women and a hundred men. Things are different out here. You don't know how much money they have. It's obscene. In your country there are strict laws and regulations around money. Out here it's everything. If you have money you own everything. You own the police, you own the politicians. You own it all.'

Slater lowered his head and said, 'That's not so different from my country.'

Winston eyed him warily.

'Human nature,' Slater said.

'It's a harsh world.'

'That's why I'm getting involved. Even though I have no skin in the game. None of it's personal to me. But hopefully I can make the world a little less harsh.'

'I will help you however I can, but I won't get involved myself. All I have is information.'

'About what?'

'Where Simba lives.'

'Does he live on the same compound as Rangano?'

A nod. 'Around twenty miles west of here. Near the border of the Manicaland and Masvingo Provinces.'

'Would you know where to point it out on a map?'

Winston shook his head. 'Not exactly. But I know the general area.'

'Do they try to hide the fact that they live there?'

A nod. 'They own land all over. No-one's supposed to know which tract they actually occupy.'

'But you do.'

Another nod.

Slater said, 'Can you lead me there?'

'I don't need to.'

'Why not?'

'They will return there today. They take their purchases back there after the auction finishes.'

'How do you know?'

'I followed Simba once.'

'That's a dangerous game to play.'

'I couldn't believe it was him. When he first started attending these auctions. He doesn't even know who I am. He didn't recognise me. Just disregarded me. Even though he ruined my daughter's life. He parades around in front of everyone as if he's oblivious to the things he's doing.'

'He's not oblivious,' Slater said. 'Trust me. I've met enough of his type. He just doesn't care.'

'It makes my blood boil.'

'So you followed him.'

'Six months ago. Or thereabouts. I parked at the edge of his land. There had to be a dozen workers tending to the grounds. Everything was bright green and lush and beautiful. Like an oasis. Especially when you compared the place to its surroundings. There were enormous mansions and smaller outbuildings and a small army of hired help. I had a gun.'

'I assume you did nothing.'

'Why would you assume that?'

'You're still standing here.'

'Well, you'd be right. I thought about using the gun on myself. Right there in front of his property. To send a message.'

'He wouldn't have cared.'

'That's what I realised. So I drove away.'

Slater paused, deep in thought. He mulled over something for a few beats, and then he started to speak, but he cut himself short. He kept thinking.

Winston said, 'What?'

'I spoke to you entirely by chance.'

'You did.'

'And you had a horror story to share about both the men I'm looking for.'

'I did.'

'Was that coincidence?'

'Were the other people you spoke to coincidences too?'

'I thought so at the time.'

'Everyone has a horror story about Simba and Rangano,' Winston said.

Slater said, 'Why hasn't anyone done anything about it?'

'Intimidation and manipulation.'

'Psy-ops.'

'What?'

'Don't worry,' Slater said. 'I think it's about time I took care of this.'

He reached for the K-22 in his waistband.

He wrenched it free.

46

Below the wooden balustrade, the six-speed revolver was obscured from Simba's view.

The big man pierced his gaze across the viewing platform with his bright green eyes, soaking in every detail. Slater imagined a path to the man's forehead with the barrel of the Smith & Wesson. He figured it would be simple enough to score a direct hit from this distance. There was no wind or dust — in fact, no extraneous problems whatsoever. Apart from the heat, which had caused beads of sweat to collect in Slater's eyebrows, risking running down into his eyes. But he'd dealt with worse shooting conditions for most of his life, so he didn't doubt his ability to gun Simba down where he stood.

He brought the gun up.

It would be bedlam.

But he could deal with bedlam.

A rough calloused hand with thick fingers — Winston's hand — shot across the space in front of Slater, catching his wrist in an iron grip. Pinning his shooting arm at a forty-five degree angle. Keeping the K-22 positioned just below the top of the railing.

Slater wrenched with all his might.

The veins in his neck bulged.

He got nowhere.

Simba noticed. The green eyes pierced into Slater, scrutinising all his micro-expressions, searching for a sign of imminent danger.

The big man could tell *something* was happening.

But he couldn't quite figure out what.

Slater turned to the left and saw Winston staring him dead in the eyes, one hand wrapped around Slater's wrist. The wizened man was straining with a similar level of exertion. And he had phenomenal strength for his age. Slater recalled Winston's short biography. He had lived in the region his whole life. Working in the beef industry. Dealing with the beasts day and night.

Farm strength.

Winston muttered, 'Not here.'

Slater hissed, 'Okay,' through gritted teeth.

They both relaxed their grip. Their gazes drifted back to the barn floor in unison, where a massive black bull glistened with muscle, almost shiny in the lowlight. A multitude of buyers across the viewing platform were locked in a bidding war for the prime specimen. Slater pretended to pour his concentration into the spectacle. But he kept Winston in his peripheral vision, and silently seethed at the missed opportunity.

As soon as Simba gave up on watching the pair of them, and turned his own attention back to the bulls, Slater muttered through tight lips, 'Let me do what I came here to do.'

'Not here,' Winston repeated. 'You are a fool to try that.'

'You got a better idea?'

'I just told you where to go.'

'His compound?'

'It's your best chance.'

'At what?'

'Taking care of all the business you want to attend to.'

'And what is it you know about my business exactly?'

Winston turned to regard him with a derisive look. 'You hate injustice. That much is clear. You shoot Simba here, and his men will kill you where you stand. There's four of them over there.'

'I have six bullets.'

'You will miss. Everyone will be screaming and running after the first bullet. And then whoever survives from Simba's side will fire into the crowd without hesitation. That's how they operate. Many people in here will be killed. In fact, almost everyone will start shooting. You and Simba and his men aren't the only ones who are armed.'

Winston tapped his waist, revealing a leather holster with the hilt of a black semi-automatic pistol jutting out.

'Competitive business in rural Zimbabwe is a different beast,' he said. 'You would do good to learn that before you go firing shots in a place like this.'

'This might be the best chance I'll get.'

'Let's say you succeed. Then there's still Rangano. And he will know what happened the very same minute you start shooting. Calls will be made. And then he will vanish, along with his private army. He'll disappear off to one of his other properties and go to ground and no-one will ever find him.'

'What if I only care about Simba?'

'You asked me about Rangano. You care about the whole

outfit. All of it. You won't be satisfied unless you get all of them.'

'So I take the fight to them? To their compound?'

'They'll be clustered together in one location. All of them. All the bad eggs. That's what you want, isn't it? And there's no collateral damage.'

'None at all,' Slater mused.

Then Winston screwed up his face and said, 'Except…'

Slater just raised an eyebrow.

Winston said, 'There are rumours.'

'About what?'

'That Simba has slaves.'

'Slaves?'

'People disappear. Their bodies aren't recovered. They have to go somewhere. But he gets an impossible amount of work done. Looking in from the outside — it's madness. It's like he has entire factories working for him, but there's no proof of anything. He wanted to get into the bull industry, and suddenly an entire cattle farm appeared on his main property, with barns and bull pens. Built from the ground up. That's more work than the Green Bombers can take care of.'

'How do you know that? I heard he has dozens of Green Bombers.'

'Brainwashed thugs,' Winston said. 'All of them. They're cannon fodder. They can aim a gun, and swing a knife, and throw a punch. And that's about all they can do.'

'How many do you think he has?'

'No way to know for sure.'

'I guess I'll have to find out for myself, then.'

Winston said something, but it fell on deaf ears. Slater let the raucous din of the bull auction envelop him, the energy reaching a fever pitch as more than five different people shouted and gesticulated from competing sections of the viewing platform.

Winston's words fell away, replaced by background noise, because by that point Slater was turning over possibilities in his head, most of them concerning a one-armed man who had never seen his daughter's body.

And never confirmed her death.

47

The bull auction came to a conclusion nearly an hour later, and all the buyers stuffed into the viewing platform filed out of the barn as the final beast was locked away in its pen. Slater saw the vendor urge his workers to open the doors, and then the scene descended into a frenzy as everyone set to work figuring out logistics. There was clearly no established order to the proceedings, despite the fact that the weekly auctions seemed to have been a staple for quite some time.

Slater didn't mind.

The chaos helped him.

Without it, he would have been doomed.

No, not doomed.

There was always a way. No matter how outrageous or complicated it was. But, despite his penchant for abandoning stealth at the first available opportunity, Slater was experienced enough to realise it had its time and place. Like right now, for instance. He could embrace his usual ways and turn the aftermath of the auction into a bloodbath, but after a harrowing journey through Colombia and North America a few months ago, he was hesitant to rack up a staggering body count as soon as he had the chance. And Winston's proposal made a hell of a lot of sense. An isolated property with a defended perimeter would work well. He could turn that place into a bloodbath without a moment's hesitation.

But he had to get there undetected first.

He sauntered down to the ground floor along with the rest of the crowd. They all spilled out into the hot sun, streaming through both sets of double doors. At the front of the procession, Simba peeled away with his guard of honour and took up position down the side of the barn, loitering in the great shadow cast off the building. Slater made to follow him, but thought better of it. He carried along with the ebb and flow of the main crowd, pretending he hadn't a care in the world.

Then a hand reached out and snatched his arm.

Hard.

He wheeled on the spot, pulse racing, and found the vendor staring him dead in the eyes.

'You no buy,' the man said.

Slater threw a glance over his shoulder. The timing was perfect. There was a group of five farmers right behind him, obscuring him from Simba's withering, all-encompassing gaze.

Slater came out with the twenty grand in U.S. currency and shoved it into the vendor's pocket.

Forcefully.

At first the guy recoiled and a certain primal venom flickered behind his eyes, as if his brain was telling him, *Don't let the strange man do that.*

But when he looked down and saw the bills disappearing into his pocket, and Slater stepping away instantly, and pretending nothing happened at all, a sly smile spread across his face.

'You want something,' the guy said.

'Simba,' Slater said.

The vendor shook his head. 'I do not put my clients in danger. You want bad for Simba.'

'Not here. And not yet.'

'No can do it.'

'Then give me my money back.'

The vendor shifted from foot to foot, and then beckoned for Slater to walk with him, following the crowd down the trail to a small makeshift parking lot burrowed into the perimeter of the clearing. An array of vehicles coated in dust were arranged at random intervals. Up the back of the gravel lot, an enormous modern livestock trailer sat behind a massive four-wheel-drive pick-up truck with elevated suspension and muck caked on thick over its frame.

Slater said, 'The money?'

The vendor scrunched up his face, unwilling to part with the cash, and said, 'Okay, fine. What you want?'

'Is that Simba's trailer?'

'Yes. He bring it here. He not patient. Everyone else come back later for what they buy.'

'Get me inside that trailer.'

'How?'

'Put your thinking cap on.'

'What?'

'Figure it out. It's twenty grand. Come up with something.'

'I no have keys.'

'You're loading bulls into that trailer?'

'The ones he buy. Yes.'

'You have time alone with it?'

'Group effort.'

'Then distract them when they're leaving.'

The vendor looked at the dissipating crowd, and then back at Simba. The big man still loitered in the shadow of the barn, sucking on a hand-rolled cigarette, drinking in lungfuls of the tobacco. A couple of his guards were smoking too. They all seemed distracted enough.

The vendor said, 'Okay. Go into trees behind trailer. Walk down to front fence. Wait there. I try something.'

Slater nodded and turned to thank the man, but he found a mask of sweat and an expression of mortal fear in place of the previously jovial features.

He said, 'Are you okay?'

The vendor said, 'No.'

'What's wrong?'

'Simba bad man. Might not work.'

'It'll work. It's twenty grand.'

'My life cost more than twenty grand.'

'That's a lot of money to get me in a trailer.'

'Okay,' the vendor said.

He branched away from Slater, vanishing into the crowd. Slater skirted around the maze of trucks, weaving across the gravel. The sun beat down on the back of his neck, and he regulated his breathing. His heart raced. His mind reeled. The conversation had been short and sharp and burdened by the language barrier. He had to concede that nearly everyone he'd run into had given him a similar warning. Simba was not a man to trifle with. Slater didn't dare under-estimate him.

So he crossed fast to the trailer, and on the way past he noticed a thin horizontal gap eight feet off the ground, running around the top portion of the carriage. To circulate fresh air through the pens inside. There were small metal bars set at regular intervals, but Slater figured there was just enough space for a man to squeeze through if they had no fear of getting stuck halfway in.

Slater certainly had that fear.

But he'd be willing to circumvent it if the opportunity arose.

Yet now wasn't the right time. The process would involve vaulting up onto the lip, and then leaping up and grabbing hold of the upper lip of the wall, and then hauling himself all the way up by his arms, and then going head-first in through one of the gaps between the bars, and then wiggling and squirming like a dying fish in an attempt to get in, and then plummeting top down into the trailer, likely resulting in serious injury if he fucked up the acrobatic manoeuvre and came down on his neck.

And if he tried all of that now, half the buyers at the auction would see.

So would Simba and his crew.

So he carried on past, striding like he had a purpose, vanishing into the skeletons of trees lining the ranch complex. He weaved through thin branches and pointed himself in the general direction of the front gate, and set off that way. He ducked his head low and shifted the pack over his shoulder blades and tried to minimise his visibility, suddenly distinctly aware of how strange it would look if anyone saw him ducking into the trees.

But then he made it a few dozen feet from the tree line, and he was in the clear.

The sounds of murmuring and footsteps and car doors slamming fell away.

Replaced by an intense silence, stressing the isolation of the region.

Slater looked all around, and quickened his stride.

There were a hell of a lot of places to bury a body out here.

48

He set up shop fifteen feet inside the tree line at the mouth of the driveway.

Pick-up trucks and smaller, battered sedans rumbled past, turning out of the ranch and churning dust as they set off back to their homes. All personal vehicles, designed to bomb around the rural trails, conducting business. Leaving the heavy duty transport vehicles on their properties until the auction results had been settled. It would be a brazen waste of fuel to cart the massive trailers and trucks out to the bull auction before they'd even locked in a purchase.

Simba was the only man who'd done it.

That told Slater more than enough about the nature of the ex-ZANU—PF official. He was reckless and confident and sure of himself. He had money to burn. And he didn't anticipate walking away from the auction with nothing. No matter the price. No matter the number of buyers. He would come away with a genetically pure collection of premium bulls, probably for breeding purposes, even if he had to pay double or triple the regular price to get it.

Which also meant he was impatient.

Or pressed for time.

So he might be more desperate to build a legitimate empire than Slater originally thought.

He found a suitably smooth patch of dirt and lay prone between a pair of spindly trees, protected from the sun by the web of branches over his head. But the heat remained, palpable at midday, as the blazing ball of fire far above reached its apex in the sky. The flies and mosquitoes buzzed all around him, and the soft chirping of a random array of wildlife sounded all around him. There was nothing visible besides the insects, but the barren waste-land got under his skin all the same. He shifted in place, suddenly overwhelmingly uncomfortable, and waited with bated breath for Simba's trailer to come blazing down the path.

It took far longer than he expected. The minutes ticked by, and he counted them out in his head. He pulled his phone from his pocket and checked the time. Nearly one in the afternoon. He sighed and bowed his head, and a bead of perspiration ran off the bridge of his nose and splashed into the dirt. He ignored it. He rolled onto his back and stared up at the cloudless sky through the canopy of dead wispy branches.

He breathed in, and out.

He rolled back onto his front.

Frustration set in.

And hunger.

But he was used to fasting, so he figured it wouldn't be a big deal until later that evening.

And then a low rumbling started far in the distance, at least a hundred feet up the trail. Slater tensed up and went through the same nervous mannerisms. He adjusted his back. He shuffled his knees on the ground. He cracked his wrists. He got ready to pounce.

If the vendor couldn't follow through with his promises, concessions would need to be made.

Slater wondered how he'd do it.

He could leap on the speeding trailer, gun down the security, jam the K-22 Masterpiece into Simba's ear, and force him to head back to the compound by gunpoint.

But this was a smart man he was dealing with.

There would be panic buttons, and emergency protocol, and evacuation routines.

In all likelihood, they would return to an empty compound.

As much as he hated stealth, he conceded it was his best bet in a situation like this.

A single word ran through his head.

Fuck.

He repeated it, over and over again on an incessant endless loop in his brain. He hated the quiet tension and the beating heart and the sweat and the reactionary nature of snooping around places he didn't belong. Much better to smash the door down and rely entirely on his uncanny, near-superhuman reflexes. It had worked well in the past.

There's a time and place, he told himself.

Neither of which were the current moment or location.

The giant pick-up truck rumbled into view, dragging the bulk of its trailer behind it. Billowing dust clouds spilled from the fat tyres, and Slater thought he caught a glimpse of restless bulls shaking and rattling the trailer through the narrow portholes on either side. Or it could have been his imagination.

Regardless, he shrank into the dirt — despite the trees providing an effective form of concealment — and hoped like hell the pick-up's occupants weren't paying close attention to the view out the grimy windows.

Slater stared as the truck barrelled past, his mouth agape.

Where the hell is the vendor?

Then the truck slammed on the brakes.

The trailer groaned and almost jackknifed as the vehicle pulling it down the trail froze in place. The tyres locked up and skidded to a stop, and the pick-up came to rest nearly diagonal across the trail. The rear window rolled down and one of Simba's guards stuck his head out into the open, peering back up the trail with wide eyes.

He yelled something in Shona, and was met with no response.

In the driver's seat, Simba screamed at the men in the back seat, also in Shona.

Seeking answers to some unspecified question.

Slater adjusted his angle, and squinted, and focused all his perception on the slim gap through the rear window to the driver's seat.

He saw a phone pressed to Simba's ear.

Then the vendor came sprinting down the trail on foot, puffing and panting as he ran, another phone pressed to his own ear.

Some kind of last minute request before the trailer was carted away.

Maybe a vague report of a problem with one of the bulls.

Slater managed a wry smile.

49

The vendor made it all the way to the passenger window, around the other side of the pick-up truck. Due to the elevated suspension he barely made it to the height of the sill, but he mounted the step running around the lip of the cabin, roughly a foot and a half off the ground. Slater saw the top of his bald head protruding above the thin metal roof, dotted with sweat beads.

He couldn't see what the man was saying. The passenger window was down, given the conversation occurring between the vendor and the occupants of the vehicle. But the driver's window was up, and it was tinted. It blocked Slater's view of proceedings.

It was now or never.

But he quickly realised it wasn't going to work.

Slater couldn't see in, but they could see out. He imagined Simba sitting in the driver's seat, locked in conversation with the vendor on the other side of the truck, but sweeping his gaze around his surroundings at regular intervals, wary of a potential ambush. He hadn't succeeded in life without being aware of his circumstances, especially in a place like this. The trees were spaced too far apart to allow for a mad dash to the trailer. Even if Simba wasn't looking, he'd catch the flash of movement in his peripheral vision. Slater stayed on his belly and grimaced. Perspiration kept flowing off his forehead. He wiped it with a dirty palm, and even that amount of movement made him wary of the truck parked just a couple of dozen feet away.

He was too close and too far at the same time.

This wasn't a forest. It was a graveyard of dead trees. It barely passed for cover. He couldn't move if there was the slightest risk of detection. There was a sizeable gap between the end of the tree line and the pick-up and trailer.

No man's land.

And Slater was blind to the enemy.

He swore under his breath.

Then the driver's side window buzzed down too.

There didn't seem to any particular reason for the gesture. Maybe the air conditioning was broken, and Simba needed a hot breeze for the drive. But it gave Slater a direct line of sight through the cabin. He saw Simba in the driver's seat, face tilted toward the passenger side. But not all the way. He wasn't directly involved in the conversation. The vendor was up on the lip of the truck, speaking to the passenger. The passenger had his head turned all the way, but Simba and the three men in the rear seats were growing impatient. It was clear as day. They were looking this way and that, highlighting their disinterest at the hold-up. They hadn't come this far in rural Zimbabwe without being cautious of unnecessary stops on deserted trails.

Your excuse isn't good enough, buddy, Slater thought. *I need a better distraction than this.*

Simba put a giant forearm on the windowsill and

growled across at the passenger. A gentle reminder to wrap the conversation up. It clearly wasn't worth their time.

Slater bowed his head, cursing the uselessness of the man he'd paid twenty grand to cause a distraction.

Not good enough at all.

And then the vendor knocked himself out.

Slater looked up, and saw the man slip. At first he thought it was genuine. He caught a fleeting glimpse of the vendor dropping off the platform, and then the guy's jaw smashed into the sill on the way down, eliciting the same kind of *bang* as when you slammed a car door closed as hard as you could. He disappeared from sight, a few teeth probably rattled in their gums, his consciousness almost certainly stripped from him.

Lying prone in the dirt, Slater had a clear line of sight underneath the truck body, with its jacked-up suspension and oversized wheels. He saw the vendor hit the dust on the other side of the cabin, but he landed horribly, with no capacity to protect himself. He'd knocked himself out cold with the impact with the sill, and his head came down like a bowling ball on the hot earth. He landed on his back, then his head struck the ground, and he lay still.

He would come back to reality in half a minute. No one stayed unconscious for long. The injury looked gnarly, but he'd be okay. He might have a headache for a few weeks. Perhaps a concussion. It would fade.

The passenger shouted an exclamation, and opened his door to check on the supposed fool.

Simba should have thought better of it. By all accounts he was a cruel ruthless man, and the vendor's wellbeing likely didn't cross his mind. But he threw his door open and vaulted out of the cabin all the same. Some sort of morbid curiosity. A fascination with unconsciousness. Everyone had it, whether they liked to deny it or not. You saw someone faint in the street, and it seized your attention like nothing else. And the incident had happened right there, only inches from the passenger, like a movie on the big screen brought to life, with all the dire physical consequences that accompanied it.

All five of the thugs piled out of the car and rounded to the passenger side, fascinated by the vendor's ability to do serious damage to himself with the slip of a foot.

Slater almost smiled at the ridiculousness of it all.

The vendor had asked himself if his consciousness and general wellbeing was worth twenty thousand dollars, and had clearly decided it wasn't.

The ultimate distraction.

All in the name of profit.

Slater got up and sprinted for the trailer.

50

H e didn't have long.

The vendor had thrown himself to the wolves, but curiosity and fascination only lasted so long. As soon as Simba and the lone guard who piled out of the back seat on the driver's side rounded the hood of the pick-up, Slater lurched off the mark.

He got his feet underneath him and ran flat out, staying low, keeping as quiet as he could. Ten steps in he made a rapid calculation and shrugged off his pack. He dropped it in the dirt, discarding it without a moment's hesitation.

Without the cash he'd given the vendor, it was worthless. Just a heaped collection of spare clothes. Not worth the hassle of forcing it through the gap in the trailer. It would waste time he didn't have. His phone was in his pocket, and his wallet, and his passport, and that was everything he needed on the planet.

Now lacking possessions entirely, he broke out of the tree line and darted into no man's land, suddenly exposed. His heart beat a million miles an hour. All the thugs had to do was look through the open windows of the pick-up's cabin. There was a direct line of sight to Slater. He saw the backs of their heads, but they were focused solely on the unconscious vendor sprawled like a corpse in the dust. Just as Slater had suspected.

Curiosity.

Intense fascination.

This guy just KOed himself, they were thinking. *What an absolute moron.*

Slater made it to the trailer and leapt onto the step. The suspension sagged and let out a tiny, muted groan. He froze, clinging onto the upper lip of the gap. The wind howled hot and steady down the trail. Someone muttered something on the other side of the vehicle. Slater clung for dear life, wondering whether it was better to take care of business now or attempt this mad infiltration.

He reached for the K-22 in his waistband.

Ready to blow apart the head of the first guy to round the corner, wondering where the noise had come from.

But nothing happened.

The wind died down, and the muttering faded away, and absolute silence descended over the trail. Then there was the sound of spluttering and choking, followed by a sudden gasp, and then heavy breathing. Slater had enough experience to know what was happening.

No-one was dying.

The vendor was returning to consciousness. Shocked by what had happened. Slater wondered if the man had ever been knocked out before. The result might affect him deeper than he'd anticipated. It was a strange, foreign sensation that you never got used to, no matter how many times it happened. Like a grotesque time jump.

One moment he'd deliberately slipped off the step, and

the next he was awake on the ground with a monumental headache, with five burly men standing over him.

Slater heard one of them mutter something reassuring in Shona.

He took his hand off the hilt of the K-22 and went for it.

He grabbed the lip of the gap and strained upward, activating his biceps and shoulders. Veins strained, and he took all his weight on the flimsy material. It was some kind of sheet metal, but it bent and warped as he put two hundred pounds of bodyweight on the curved lip. He shoved his head through the gap, followed swiftly by his shoulders, and then his arms were pinned underneath him. He wedged through, inch by inch, legs flailing, feet kicking.

He looked down and saw a mammoth of a bull directly underneath him.

The beast snorted and rotated on the spot, butting up against one of the walls. The muscles on its back rippled. Its horns stuck out, thick and dirty and pointed. It couldn't crane its massive neck, so it stood there like a silent guardian, aggravated by the cramped nature of the makeshift pen. Slater threw a quick glance left and right and realised the trailer was separated into four separate storage spaces. Each was populated by a black bull, all premium breeds, all giants. All had humps on their shoulders. Every inch of space was taken up by the pens.

He baulked.

It would be a tense ride back to Simba's compound.

There was no way to separate himself from at least one of the animals.

But he'd gone too far now. He couldn't backtrack. Physics wouldn't allow it. So he kept shifting through the gap, shoving his chest through, and then skirting along his stomach. Sooner or later his momentum would shift forward, and he'd topple into the trailer.

He looked down again, and realised he had nowhere to land.

He froze up, horizontal, wedged uncomfortably between the roof and the lip pressing into his abdomen.

He nearly groaned in protest. Panic rose in his chest, short and sharp. Piercing through to the core.

And then there were the sounds of commotion, echoing in through the opposite gap in the trailer. Footsteps and shuffling and muttered complaints. Simba and his thugs, angry at the hold-up. The vendor had come awake, seemingly no worse for wear, and the group of five were floating back towards their truck.

Soon they would round to the driver's side, and see a pair of legs sticking out of the trailer, and draw their guns and blast him to shreds where he lay wedged into the gap like a seesaw.

But he couldn't land on the bull.

Yes you can.

Only option.

He swallowed raw fear and forced his way through, and momentum caught hold of him and sent him plummeting into the trailer.

He twisted in mid-air to save crushing his neck, and landed in the foetal position on the upper back of the beast. He sunk into muscle and bounced off, and the bull reared up and snorted and shook violently to throw the strange weight off its hide. Its horns slashed at the air, missing Slater by a couple of feet, but he hit the wall of the pen with a staggering impact and bounced off that too. He landed in straw, legs splayed at an awkward angle, and he instinctively rolled away from the giant bull alongside him, pressing himself against the detachable sliding partition that separated each pen.

The bull stamped and shook its head and gored the wall, grating his horn along the metal. It smashed its head from side to side like a battering ram, perturbed by the new arrival, hunting for Slater's head.

Slater burrowed down into the crook between the floor and the wall and dripped sweat onto the straw.

He breathed out a ball of pure tension and lay deathly still, and the bull stamped again and rattled the trailer and smashed its horns into the wall only a few inches above Slater's shoulder.

Then it pawed the trailer floor, right near his head, smashing a hoof into the metal.

He visibly recoiled, but he kept as silent and as still as he could, and after a long and horrifying pause the bull straightened up in the rectangular pen and rested its bulk against the wall and snorted, and then all went still.

Slater breathed in, and out. He thought he might pass out from the sheer stress of the situation.

He'd caused an awful ruckus. There was no hope of success. Simba would open up the trailer to investigate, and that would be that. Slater had uncanny reflexes, but now he was trapped in a stifling tin can with one exit up the back, and Simba had five men and a hell of a lot more firepower than he did. He'd put all his eggs in one basket, and the basket was about to get torn to shreds by a hail of gunfire.

But instead of checking on his livestock, Simba smashed a fist several consecutive times against the trailer from the outside. He barked a vicious string of Shona, insulting his prize possessions for their aggression.

And Slater realised the man knew less about bulls than he'd expected.

He'd chalked the commotion in the trailer up to a change in surroundings. He thought the bulls were uneasy. He was screaming at them to shut up.

Then the five men clambered back into the pick-up truck and put it into gear and rolled off the mark. The trailer lurched and the bulls snorted in response to the sudden jerking motion. Slater skewered himself deeper into the floor, minimising his target area in case the bull felt the need to stomp him to death. He couldn't think of a worse way to go. He pictured the hoof drilling into his stomach with all the weight of a prized beast behind it, crushing all the organs in his mid-section, leaving him to suffocate in the fetid heat.

Pouring sweat, armed with a six-speed revolver and a Ka-Bar knife, heart thrumming hard in his chest, alert and focused at the same time, Slater settled in for the ride and wondered how the hell he kept getting himself into impossible situations.

51

H e spent much of the journey wondering how Simba and Rangano were able to afford so much land.

The way it had been described to him, it seemed the pair were practically moguls. But they were a Political Commissar and a ZANU—PF official, neither of which seemed to constitute a gross fortune. Sure, they had exploited farmers and ridden the trend of oppressing a particular class of people for the sake of a dictator in power, but there was little wealth to horde and redistribute. As far as Rand's story was concerned, they'd been more concerned with reckless destruction than any actual attempt to steal resources. If they wanted to do that, they wouldn't have targeted farmers.

And they had nothing to do with the injustice in the Marange diamond fields, given what Danai had said. That particular brand of greed had applied only to the heads of the diamond companies assigned by the government. They were the ones who couldn't account for the cash. They were the ones who had sent it up the pipeline to the very top, whereupon it had been flushed out to God-knows-who.

The inner circle.

The elite.

That wasn't Rangano, and it sure as hell wasn't Simba. They were the foot soldiers, the ones who got down and dirty. So how the hell had they gotten so rich?

The bull snorted again, spraying him with a fine mist. Slater gagged and shrank away from the beast. The trailer hit a pothole and bounced, its suspension rattling hard, nearly driving the animals into a frenzy. He fought back the tendrils of claustrophobia and focused on his breathing. Compartmentalising it all. Doing what he did best. Dealing with a horror show as best he could. He considered it one of his most refined talents.

They drove for close to an hour. The time passed excruciatingly slowly. Every second was wrought with tension as the animal shifted restlessly next to him.

Then Simba took a turn far too fast, throwing Slater across the pen. He bounced off the bull's hooves and spiralled into the opposite wall, and was forced to deal with another bout of aggression from the big animal. But then it thrashed his head in the wrong direction, and the nose ring caught against its rope, and the bull snorted a couple of times, settling into place, disturbed by the pain in its septum.

Slater lay still on his back, staring up at the metal roof, disorientated but alive.

He didn't move a muscle.

Eventually they slowed and the potholes disappeared, replaced by a smooth undisturbed track that seemed to run on forever. Slater controlled his breathing, conserving his energy, and waited for the inevitable stop.

If Simba and his thugs threw the trailer open straight away, he'd have to move fast.

The journey continued right up to the lee of a massive building, given away by the shadows plunging over the gap running around the top of the trailer. Darkness enveloped the interior, and the bulls shifted again, rattling the metal floor. Slater heard the sounds of doors opening and closing, and hushed conversations, and grumblings, and the ordinary minutia of daily life. He slipped the K-22 Masterpiece from his waistband, and the Ka-Bar, and held them tight. One in each hand. He levered himself upright into a crouch, his chest only inches from the bull's ribcage.

He stared deep into its left eye. It regarded him with a reserved curiosity, its energy expended by the long cross-country trip. But if he moved suddenly it would gore him without hesitation, an instinctive reaction to such close proximity to a foreign threat. Slater gripped the Ka-Bar tighter and considered trying to silently slaughter the animal to prevent a grisly death of his own. But there would be no chance of that. It would squeal and shriek and thrash in its death throes, which wouldn't bode well for the subtlety he was going for.

So he remained still.

There was a series of dull impacts up the front of the trailer. Latches being removed, and tethers being separated. Then the sound of the pick-up truck driving away from the trailer rose above everything before fading into the distance.

Replaced by silence.

Now or never.

Slater shimmied over to the same gap he'd come through on the way in. There was no particular reason for selecting the same partition. Familiarity, perhaps. He'd done it once, and he couldn't be certain that he wouldn't get trapped in the other partitions. He had a good track record with this gap. He knew he could get through it. So he waited another few beats, and heard nothing but silence. He looked at the weapons in his hands, and grimaced. Out of necessity he tucked them back into his waistband. He needed both hands free for the awkward manoeuvre.

And now he felt vulnerable as hell.

He shifted nervously from foot to foot...

...and his ankle tweaked hard.

He jerked up like he'd been electrocuted and stumbled to the left, unable to help himself. For a terrifying moment he thought the same injury had resurfaced, and he half-expected his foot to collapse. Bones re-breaking, muscles re-tearing. But none of that happened, and after the moment passed he came to the conclusion he'd experienced phantom pain. But he'd thrown himself off-balance all the same. He tried to right himself, and stumbled again, and crashed into the bull's side.

It smashed its horns into the wall a couple of feet behind him, grunting in protest as it carved a jagged line down the metal.

And then it tried to turn around in the pen.

Slater scrambled for the gap, expecting the bull to gore him at any moment.

52

H e got his hands on the lip and hauled himself up, feet scrabbling against the metal. It was slick and hot and his palms were sweaty.

The bull wedged itself against the walls of the pen, trapped by the tiny space it had to work with, but it threw another headbutt all the same. Its horn smashed the metal only a few inches to the left of Slater's leg. He abandoned all hope of maintaining his composure and hurled himself through the gap, head-first again. It was the only way to escape. There was no time to scout the area. He had to hope for the best.

Once again his hands got trapped, and he struggled to squeeze his shoulders through. Then his chest followed, and his stomach, and then there was a precarious moment of balance as he tried not to topple forward out of the trailer without the use of his hands.

He paused for breath, and to compose himself.

He stared all around.

Oh, shit.

He blanched and tried desperately to shimmy back into the trailer, but it was too late.

The broad-shouldered man was halfway through the process of sprinting directly at Slater, opting to charge toward his adversary rather than retreat and regroup.

The guy wore the same olive uniform and red-and-green beret of the Green Bombers. He was bigger than the four guards accompanying Simba to the auction. A sentry, left over to silently guard the trailer as Simba parked the car.

But without a weapon.

There was likely no need. The perimeter guards had to be armed at all times, but it was less crucial for the men deep in the bowels of the property. His job description didn't involve protecting the bulls from armed assassins. His role was to make sure none of the beasts managed to escape in the interim. He was inventory management — nothing more, nothing less.

Hence his shock when Slater appeared in the gap.

Slater tried to reach back and get a hold of the Smith & Wesson's grip, but he found himself hopelessly trapped between the metal bars. Calculating angles and possibilities in the space of milliseconds, he committed to shimmying forward. It was the only available option.

And it was a bad one.

He got his shoulders through the gap, then his chest, then as he was working on his mid-section the Green Bomber leapt onto the ridge above the rear tyre with surprising dexterity and athleticism.

Slater swung a wild fist at the guy's face, but he missed completely.

He was horizontal, and aiming downward, and trying to balance, and working on freeing himself from entrapment. Far too many variables. The swing was one of many things he struggled to concentrate on. It sailed on harmlessly by, almost sending him tumbling outward. His heart leapt into his throat.

He lined up another shot, but he'd already put himself on the back foot, and the guard wasn't entirely useless.

The man reached up and grabbed two handfuls of Slater's shirt and wrenched him out of the gap. His stomach and hips and legs came out of the trailer like he'd been fired from a cannon and he toppled to the earth. He passed over the top of the Green Bomber's head, twisting and flailing in the air, like a cat dropped from a considerable height.

Unfortunately, he didn't have the same dexterity as a feline.

He turned half a revolution in the air before he came down in the dirt on his rear, hitting the earth with enough force to smash the breath from his lungs.

Jolted by the impact, it took him a couple of seconds to get his bearings. His brain tried to process his surroundings and the position of the hostile, and simultaneously started to conduct a rudimentary check for injuries. He'd come down hard on his coccyx, and falling from a considerable height was nothing like the movies, especially if you didn't land on your feet, or roll with it. For a fleeting moment he figured he'd shattered his tailbone, given the intensity with which the landing had startled him.

But then the initial wave of pain fell away, replaced by a dull throbbing, and he shot to his feet.

Too late.

The Green Bomber came off the trailer, sporting the same athleticism he'd mounted it with, and covered the distance within the range of a single second. Slater had his arms up and his defence mounted, but it all came too fast, too soon.

The guy hit him with the momentum of a defensive line-backer, leading with both arms held straight out, using his massive bulk to send Slater straight back into the dirt.

His brain moving a million miles an hour, Slater toppled backwards, coming dangerously close to smashing the back of his skull into the hard-packed earth and knocking himself out. But this time he managed a backwards roll, and threw his legs over his head, and bent at the torso, compressing his ribcage, and used the momentum to kick himself backwards, and then he was upright again.

Stunned, hurt, slightly battered.

But upright.

There was a gap now between the two parties. Five feet, maybe. The Green Bomber started to charge again. Reality was moving at an incomprehensible speed, and Slater had only just started to get a sense of how big the guy was. The initial tackle had sent him to the dirt like he weighed noth-ing. He figured he would come away with a staggering amount of bruises. He wasn't used to being hurled around so effortlessly.

He got a brief glimpse of the oncoming figure and put him at six-six, two hundred and fifty pounds. Or there-abouts. An incredibly large man.

Everything happened in milliseconds, again.

As usual.

He started a reflex movement with his left hand toward his waistband, searching for the Ka-Bar knife, keeping his eyes trained on the giant sprinting at him. But all the theory in the world didn't hold a candle to reality, and he knew most street fights came down to momentum, and he also knew he was firmly on the back step here. If he got knocked to the ground again, he might not manage to get up in a hurry. And as good as his jiu-jitsu was, he didn't fancy his chances at defending from the bottom against a guy who outweighed him by fifty pounds. And he'd probably be concussed if he hit the ground again. He might already be. There was no way to know for sure. Everything unfolded in the blink of an eye in combat.

And he couldn't get a sense of the where the knife was. He couldn't feel it at his waist. Not the slightest sensation. He couldn't even be sure it was still there. It could have slid right out from underneath his belt in the carnage, and he had no way to tell besides looking down, and he wasn't about to waste a valuable second taking his eyes off the guard.

And if he went for the knife, and it wasn't there, he would be in a world of trouble.

He didn't fancy getting beaten to death in an isolated ranch-style compound in rural Zimbabwe.

So he changed direction instantly and went for the gun instead. He knew it was there. He could feel it pressing into his hip, wedged tight between his belt and his underwear. He snatched down with an open palm and found the hilt and wrenched the K-22 out of his waistband.

He brought it up just as the Green Bomber charged into range, barely thinking, relying solely on intuition, and he manoeuvred the barrel and yanked the trigger as soon as he felt the trajectory was somewhat accurate.

The big guy closed the gap.

Furious noise blared.

It was an assault of sight and sound.

The body hit him like a dump truck.

53

S later couldn't brace himself for impact, because all his concentration was fixated on the accuracy of the gunshot.

Two hundred and fifty pounds hit him square in the chest again, and he flopped back with the dexterity of a rag doll, taken off his feet for the second time in the space of a few seconds. The body followed him down, preventing him from rolling with the landing. He hit the dirt on his upper back, and his skull lashed the earth.

He went dizzy, and semi-conscious, and confused, and disoriented.

And then the body came down on top of him.

It hit him with the sort of unbridled heaviness that signalled a corpse ten times out of ten. There was no bracing for the fall, or sticking the arms out in front, or turtling up to take some of the force out of the landing. The body struck Slater, chest to chest, adding to the momentum of the fall. Then the blood hit him, pouring out of the guy's throat. Slater strained with his free hand and rolled the dead man off his chest. There was no resistance. The man had succumbed instantly to the bullet smashing and tumbling its way through his neck. Maybe it had ricocheted up into his brain. No way to know for sure.

The guy rolled off onto his back and stared up at the cloudless sky with a vacant expression.

His eyes glazed over.

His jaw hung loose and slack, as if he was shocked by his own bad luck.

Slater worked his jaw left and right, his ears ringing from the discharge. His hearing came back just in time to catch the remnants of the report's echo drifting over the landscape in every direction. Other than that, the grounds were silent. Impressively serene for a murderous thug's compound.

He swore under his breath.

There was no time for anything other than forward motion. He could see, and he could partially hear, and he wasn't stunned enough to give up and accept his fate. He was nauseous and suddenly cold and hurting all over, but the majority of it was superficial, in the sense that he could put it all aside if he absolutely *had to*.

And he had to.

He needed to move.

Right now.

Because he'd fired the first shot, and kicked off a war he had every intention of finishing.

First, his surroundings.

Amidst all the chaos, he hadn't even had the chance to figure out where he was.

In front of him was the trailer, detached from Simba's truck, resting alone in the wide dirt lot. The giant patch of churned earth was otherwise deserted. There were no other vehicles in sight. To Slater's right, he eyed a long low building with a thatched roof, covering the same amount of floorspace as a sizeable warehouse. It was a makeshift barn for the livestock with open walls, like a pavilion. He spotted open paths littered with loose hay arranged in a criss-cross pattern through the building, surrounded by bull pens, several of them occupied by enormous premium bulls no doubt purchased on a previous week of the same auction.

He heard their snorts, and their general unrest. The unmistakable sound of hundreds of pounds of pure muscle and power shifting in place, transferring their weight around the straw. Slater shivered. An involuntary action. He recalled a particularly brutal outing in Macau, almost a year earlier. An encounter with a pair of hairless Tsavo lions on the top floor of a casino. Now it all seemed like a fever dream. A ludicrous nightmare.

But it had been very real, and it had come very close to ending his life.

This was just as real.

He weighed up how long it would take to move the body and formulate a plan. He started scouring the bull pen for hiding spots. Shadows, and darkness, and opportunities to ambush whoever came to investigate the gunshot.

It didn't take him long to abandon that plan entirely.

The time for stealth was over. He bent down and peered underneath the trailer's elevated suspension. It gave him a direct line of sight to the main building in the compound. He saw a long structure that looked eerily similar to three houses thrown together at random, forming a ranch with a wide deck and a picture perfect view over the green hills. The ground Slater stood on was elevated a few dozen feet, resting in an inlet carved into the side of another hill, so he had a decent view of the entire compound.

He saw tiny silhouettes leaping off the front deck of the

ranch, nothing more than blips on the radar from this distance. They were on foot, and they were moving too fast for Slater to make out any significant details, but he knew it was nothing resembling good news. They would be armed, and they would be charged with adrenalin, and they would know almost exactly what they were walking into. A gunshot didn't leave a great deal of room for interpretation. There was no other way to react to it. Just a sudden hair-raising moment of clarity, followed by preparation for war.

Slater pictured himself stalking through the bull pen, trying to both figure out unfamiliar territory and systematically take out all the approaching men in unison.

That wasn't him.

It wouldn't work.

He always hit hard and fast right at the start, and hoped like hell he could take out so many of them in the confusion and chaos of the first few seconds that there would be no time for tactical planning. That was the benefit of his genetic reaction speed, and it had carried him through impossible situation after impossible situation for as long as he could remember.

But it never got any easier, and it never got any less terrifying.

So he tightened his grip on the K-22 Masterpiece, distinctly aware of the five remaining rounds, and he found the Ka-Bar resting in the dirt where it had fallen, right next to the trailer. He unsheathed the knife and balanced it in one hand, and he swung out the cylinder of the revolver, and he fished a spare round from the small pocket at the front of his pants and slotted it into the lone empty chamber.

Six rounds now, not five.

Perhaps the most important thing in the world.

Perhaps nothing at all.

But Slater hadn't got this far by leaving things to chance.

He took one look at the body, and one look at the approaching figures strafing across the open ground, and knew there was no time to move it to the bull pen.

So he used the remaining fifteen seconds to get to work.

54

There were five.

They all wore olive uniforms. A couple had berets on. They ghosted up the side of the slight incline and reached the open dirt lot in a row. Some sort of attempt at tight co-ordination. But no actual tactical positioning whatsoever. They left blind spots a mile wide.

If Slater had a couple of allies with him, it wouldn't have been a fight at all. But he didn't. It was one on five, and they had semi-automatic pistols, and a couple had Kalashnikov rifles, so there wasn't a hope in hell he could beat them in a game of sheer reflexes. He could probably kill four, if he got incredibly lucky, but he wouldn't get the fifth. And there was no hope of winging it. The fifth would absolutely kill him. All it took was a pull of the trigger, and a long three-second hold, and the ability to work the barrel from left to right. No precision required. One of the bullets would catch him and put him down. That was the beauty, and the simplicity, of an AK-47. It never jammed. It could handle all conditions. It was one of the most reliable weapons on the planet.

So Slater stayed where he was, and he waited for them to stumble on his trap.

Which wasn't a trap at all. Not to anyone with a few brain cells. A pointy-head in the upper echelon of the secret world — the type of men he used to work for — would dismiss it as laughable. But Slater didn't care what anyone did or didn't find ridiculous. He operated solely in the world of primal combat, where a couple of seconds spelled the difference between life and death.

And he understood exactly how to manipulate those seconds to his advantage.

Because everyone was human.

And everyone hesitated the same when they had to think long and hard about what they'd found.

The five men came around the side of the trailer ready to kill. They had their guns up. They had their eyes trained on any sign of the slightest movement. They had pure adrenalin in their eyes. They had stress chemicals flooding through their systems.

They found the body of their comrade, lying on his back in the middle of the dirt lot. A gaping wound in his throat. His lifeblood spilled across the earth around his head and shoulders.

Their eyes went to their friend, and lingered.

And then they froze.

Because he was naked.

Slater had made use of the time he had. Dragging the guy, who he figured weighed well north of the initial two hundred and fifty pound estimate, wouldn't have worked. He would have made it halfway to the cover of the bull pens, and then the five Green Bombers under Simba's employ would have crested the ridge, and Slater would have had to fight right there in the open, achieving nothing in the process. So he'd hacked at the olive uniform with the Ka-Bar and stripped him of his underwear and left his corpse there on its back, stark naked, genitals exposed, nipples pointed to the sky.

Which ordinarily wouldn't have achieved a thing.

But these newcomers weren't thinking straight. They'd come expecting a war, and they'd found something very different instead. They looked at their dead friend, and the back part of their brain paused a beat, and then they started extrapolating. They couldn't find an enemy, so they looked all around helplessly, and then instead of splitting up and sweeping the ranch building — which was the only feasible place Slater could have reached in time — their eyes went straight back to their colleague.

And then they started thinking, *What have we stumbled into?*

The nakedness indicated someone caught in the act of something unsavoury. Maybe shot to death in anger, after being discovered in the middle of an unscrupulous crime. Maybe a family member had been involved. Maybe an angry father had gunned the guy down for violating his daughter. This was a big compound, after all. There were a plethora of moving parts. There were people all over the place. Workers and guards and staff and...

Maybe, maybe, maybe...

They spent so much time thinking that they started to doubt themselves. A couple of them glanced at each other, and then back to the corpse. One of them shrugged. A man on the end mumbled something under his breath. Then they turned their eyes away from the body. Maybe flooded with some sort of half-hearted "respect for the dead" bull-shit. This was their co-worker, after all. If they'd all been

Green Bombers, then they'd shared the same ideologies. They were the same people.

They were friends.

Slater materialised at the height of their confusion. He leapt out of one of the empty bull pens and landed like a cat in the middle of one of the straw-covered aisles. He touched down in a particularly shadowy stretch, resting underneath a broken sodium light cast in darkness, and it afforded him the narrow window of opportunity to capitalise.

He raised the K-22 and fired twice.

There was a kick as the revolver jerked in his hand, but he had enough experience in combat to adapt to it. He didn't hesitate between the shots. He tried to calm himself as best he could, and relied solely on intuition. He targeted the two men with pistols, figuring it was necessary to take out the wielders of the weapons that would work best in close-quarters.

Deep inside the maze of aisles, surrounded by bull pens and shadows, Slater knew a bulky Kalashnikov AK-47 would prove a disadvantage. But these men wouldn't realise that. They'd watch their two friends die before their eyes, and they'd see the twin muzzle flashes coming from the only building in sight, and calculating what would work best in the firefight wouldn't even cross their minds. Plus there was the allure of the assault rifle. These were tough and uncompromising men, but they didn't spend their lives in combat. Most of what they did was based on intimidation and scare tactics. Looking imposing, instead of actually living and breathing the fight. They wouldn't understand why an AK-47 might not bode well in a claustrophobic indoor setting.

So as soon as Slater had squeezed off the two shots he hurled himself down the aisle, turning right at the first available intersection. He didn't have time to see whether both rounds had struck home, but he was fairly confident. He heard shouts and screams and frantic talk, and then a deafening volley of gunfire, and the unmistakable sensation of bullets whizzing past and displaced air blowing hot and fetid against his face.

But none of them struck home, because he was already out of sight.

Slater smiled in the darkness, crouched low against the partition.

The cacophony had sounded an awful lot like three voices.

Two down.

55

They came into the building in unison, storming underneath the open roof with intent in their stride.

Slater could hear every step.

They weren't worried about being quiet. They were starting to realise the glaring contrast between the two parties. The precision of their enemy, and their own lacklustre strategy. They were rattled and confused and shocked at the death of their three comrades, especially with the last two unfolding right in front of them. This was a brutal industry, with no room for weakness, but seeing your friends die rattled anyone. No matter how much they tried to hide it. So now they were angry and pumped full of the concept of revenge, whilst at the same time keenly aware of their disadvantage. They were opting for carnage, and hoping to overwhelm Slater with sheer numbers. Otherwise he would pick them off from a distance, tucked away in the shadows, like a sniper taking them out from a nest a mile away. And everything about that tickled them the wrong way. Best to go down in a blaze of glory than to never see it coming at all.

Which was exactly the sort of cocktail that Slater had been going for.

He waited until the sound of thudding footsteps was right on top of him, and then he shot out from cover on all fours and dove for one of the approaching Green Bomber's legs with an animalistic fervour. He tapped into a decade of powerlifting training and wrapped a calloused palm around the guy's ankle. Still on his knees, he wrenched with all his might.

Which, in Slater's case, was a sizeable amount.

The guy was still sprinting, hoping to catch Slater before he disappeared into the shadows, with no idea that his target had been lying in wait. So Slater used the man's momentum too, and he ended up tearing the guy's foot off the ground with such force that it almost dislocated his hip.

It was known as an ankle pick, but in the heat of the fight it was more power and less technique.

The man tilted backward at the waist like he'd slipped on ice, and all his computational processing ability went away from the AK-47 in his hands. He almost dropped the gun to break his fall, but at the last second he thought better of it. He wasn't about to let go of the rifle. Some kind of intuitive split-second planning.

Not the right idea.

He landed on his upper back from a considerable height, but the straw did nothing to break his fall. There was just a loose coating of the material over hard, packed dirt. Effectively the same as coming down on concrete. With no hands free to reach back and absorb the force of the impact, all the kinetic energy transitioned through his torso and into his neck. He lashed his head back involuntarily, and the back of his skull struck the earth.

There was a sound like a coconut falling out of a tree and hitting asphalt below.

Slater kept low and collected the Kalashnikov from the guy's limp hands. Just one continuous slick movement, scrambling over the top of the body. The man was either unconscious or dead. Knocks to the head were nothing to be trifled with. Slater was acutely aware of that.

He took the leather strap off the guy's shoulder and disappeared back down the same path. Everything was moving at warp speed, so there was no chance of deducing where the other pair were. Slater had been accounting for the possibility they were bringing up the rear, only a dozen or so feet behind the guy leading the charge. But they could have branched off down other aisles, or entered from other positions. He hadn't had time to look. Taking the guy off his feet and relieving him of his gun had taken less than three seconds from beginning to end. Everything outside of his immediate vision was nothing but an adrenalin-induced blur.

So he crouched back in the same position and waited and listened, prepared for anything.

A gunshot blared like a crack of thunder, close as hell.

Slater didn't flinch.

The bullet whisked through the space he'd been occupying a second earlier.

He casually leant back out into the open aisle, found his target in milliseconds, and depressed the trigger before the second guy could adjust his aim. The man's head jerked back and dark blood sprayed like a geyser, backlit against the bright entrance of the building. His corpse toppled forward and he tripped over his friend in his death throes. Stripped of his life before he even hit the dirt.

He hit harder than his friend, pitching forward with no resistance in the limbs. The headshot had been instantly fatal, especially at this range. He splayed across the dirt with a wet smack.

Slater crouched completely still.

There was no sign of the third man.

He stayed where he was, hovering awkwardly in no-man's-land toward one side of the T-junction. Exposed to all three aisles. Hesitant to go back to his old position and play the same trick twice. He squatted low, tightening his grip on the sturdy Kalashnikov, and listened hard.

He heard nothing.

And then he heard something.

56

B ut it was faint. Imperceptible. Tickling the edge of his hearing. Only barely within earshot. And he couldn't tell exactly where it was coming from. Somewhere to the left. From the other end of the path he'd hidden in, supposedly. He leant back that way and peered down the dark straight aisle. Nothing.

He froze again.

Patience.

There was another sound, coming from...

And then the bull in the pen on the corner of the T-junction snorted and thrashed in its shelter, slamming against the wall only a couple of feet from Slater's head. He jolted in place, shocked by the sudden explosive movement. It took him half a beat to process what had happened, and by the time he did the shock had already started to dissipate.

Like a jump scare in a horror movie, blaring with sound right when the protagonist was listening most carefully.

Then Slater heard the faint sound again, right as the noise of the bull started to fade...

Footsteps.

Much, much closer.

He could have capitalised on it and been lying in wait if the bull hadn't disrupted his rhythm. He silently cursed the giant beast and wheeled on the spot, figuring out where the last guy was approaching from, right as the man sprinted into range. The acoustics in the ranch building had confused him, and he hadn't been facing the correct way. He brought the gun up and fired at the same time as the other guy, who sprinted into the T-junction and let loose with a hail of bullets in a last-ditch effort to surprise Slater and put him on the back foot.

Slater's rounds struck home.

The last guy spasmed and his finger slipped from the trigger.

Just in time.

The cacophony of lead cut a path through the T-junction towards Slater's face, and then at the last second it fell short as the guy's death throes stifled the output. The stream of bullets stopped. A couple of them passed through the space directly above Slater's left shoulder. He made a vain attempt to throw himself out of the path of gunfire, but it was too late. Thankfully the stream never would have hit him in the first place. He'd held his ground against the last remaining man and it had paid off. So the wild tumble roll ended up being pointless.

Which made what came next all the more frustrating.

Slater rolled across his back and came up to his knees several feet away, heart thumping in his chest. There was nothing like almost getting shot. It carried with it every primal sensation known to man. Instant terror, no matter how many times it happened. If the guy had moved the barrel a couple more inches to the right, it would have been game over then and there. Will Slater, one of the most destructive government operatives in history, cut down in a rural compound in the east of Zimbabwe by a gun for hire.

So it took him a moment to compose himself, and that was coupled with the sensation of relief, because five men had come for him, and five had failed. He wasn't considering variables. Not in those milliseconds. That time would come later, when the dust settled and the fog of war cleared and he got tactical again.

But right then and there, he breathed out and managed a half-smile.

And he looked up and saw a giant of a man with deep piercing green eyes locked onto him, only a couple of feet in front of him. Looming over him. The newcomer had been sneaking up behind Slater, employing stealth to account for his lack of weapons. His hands were bare, but they were curling into fists, and already in motion.

Slater computed the scene before him, and reacted with all the output one could expect from a man who had been relying on his reflexes to get him through hostile situations for the better part of ten years.

He jerked at the waist and pivoted and started swinging the Kalashnikov around to aim, but the same limitations applied to him that he'd been hoping to exploit against the Green Bombers. Namely the confined space, and the hefty bulk of the rifle.

The barrel was halfway along its trajectory when Simba hit Slater in the face with a closed fist and sapped all the cohesiveness out of his limbs.

57

Slater's head snapped back like it was on a string and his vision went mad and nausea exploded in his throat and he lost all control of his legs.

He stood up briefly, then stumbled back and sat down in the dirt, landing hard on his rear. Still conscious, but hanging onto it by a thread. He looked up at Simba. He tried to bring the AK-47 up to finish the fight. To finish what he'd set out to do all along, ever since he'd left Ron and Judy's homestead a couple of days ago. He'd known instantly he had to kill Simba. Ever since Rand had told him his story. The encounter with Danai had been to make sure, but Slater had known all along. The man standing over him now was pure evil in the same way many of the foes he'd run into over the course of his life were.

They had no empathy. Which made all of life a game. Which made human life expendable. Which led to just a handful of the atrocities Slater had heard of over the course of his time in-country. Simba didn't kill and rape for the sake of it. He did it because it furthered his own agenda, whether through a perverse sense of pleasure at the thought of holding power over others, or because it benefitted him financially in some way. Slater wanted nothing more than to lift the barrel and put a bullet through his head. It meant more to him than anything he could think of. A raw, elemental serving of justice. Nothing better than that. His skillset allowed it. All he had to do was raise the gun.

But the gun wasn't there.

His hands were empty.

He looked down, and sighed, and spotted the Kalashnikov lying in the dirt a few feet away. Just out of reach. A wild lunge for it might do the trick. But it might as well have been a thousand miles away. Slater sat on his rear and folded his elbows onto his knees and breathed heavy and tried not to pass out. Simba walked over to the gun and kicked it away.

He stood over Slater.

Looking down at him.

Simba said in stunted English, 'You are the man giving me problem.'

His voice boomed. Like thunder.

'That's me,' Slater mumbled.

'Why you no fight?'

Slater coughed and spat into the dirt and tried to hold onto his sanity.

He said, 'You win.'

Simba raised an eyebrow. Hot anger seared his face. 'What?'

'You win. I'm concussed.'

A smile. The anger turned to glee. Manic, unbridled glee. Simba realised he was dealing with a shell of a human being. The murderous rage turned to a certain reserved wariness. Cockiness sprang forth.

'Want me to hit you again?' Simba taunted.

'No.'

'You are hurt. I see your eyes.'

Simba's own eyes pierced into Slater, the colour of the rainforest.

Simba said, 'What we do now?'

'I don't know,' Slater said. 'You tell me.'

'What wrong with you?'

'I told you. Concussion, maybe. I don't feel good.'

'I only hit you once.'

'My brain is volatile.'

'What?'

'I had an injury.'

'When?'

'Six months ago. Give or take.'

'Where?'

'Russia.'

'What you doing here?'

'Wandering around.'

'Why you try to cause me problem?'

'I don't particularly like you all that much.'

'Good. Mutual feeling.'

'How come you can speak English?'

'Not much. But some. Good for business.'

Thought as much, Slater thought. *That's the way it goes these days.*

'You going to try something?' Simba said.

Slater gently shook his head from side to side, and fought the urge to vomit. He said, 'I can't fight right now.'

'What wrong with you?' Simba repeated.

'I told you. Maybe a concussion.'

'You can fight through concussion. I have done. In past.'

'Not me,' Slater said. 'Not anymore.'

'I going to kill you now.'

'Then you should just do it instead of talking all day.'

'I like talk. Talk make you suffer. If it quick, you no get what you deserve.'

'Get it over with.'

'You kill my men. Lot of them. They are good men. Six new position, need replacing. Lot of work.'

'Sorry.'

'Not good enough.'

'I thought this would go differently.'

'So did I. I no think I lose men. I no take precaution. I hear rumour of you but I do nothing about it. I think you get lucky first time.'

'Yeah...'

Silence settled over the aisle. The straw crinkled under Slater's feet. He peered down at it. Suddenly cold. Exhausted of options. His fate reversed in the space of a fleeting moment. That was the way combat unfolded. Win or lose. All or nothing. A hundred or zero. No middle ground. He'd lost. Fair and square. He sat uneasily on his rear and thought about making a half-hearted attempt for the Kalashnikov, but he didn't think he could make a single rapid movement without disrupting his equilibrium.

The brain was a fickle bitch.

He cleared his throat, and fought the rising emotions in his chest, and sat deathly still.

He said, 'Can you make it quick?'

'What wrong with you?' Simba repeated. 'Why you so scared?'

'Head injury,' Slater said. 'I told you this. It fucks with your reasoning, and your perception of things, and your emotions. I can't think straight.'

'Okay.'

'Can you make it quick?'

'You deserve slow.'

'You want the truth?'

Simba shrugged. 'Might as well.'

'I'm scared.'

'Of course. You about to die.'

'I'm not usually like this.'

'Okay.'

'The knock to the head. It's fucking with me. Please just make it quick.'

'You shouldn't be in this business with brain injury.'

'I didn't think I was this sensitive.'

'You're not. I hit you hard.'

'How hard?'

'Very hard.'

'You usually hit people hard?'

'I do boxing in youth. It help.'

'Were you good?'

'The best.'

'Okay,' Slater said.

Somehow it took half the panic away. Slater realised Simba hit like a truck, so the semi-consciousness and confusion was justified. For some reason he thought the man had lightly tapped him on the skull, and his brain had effectively imploded. But it was somehow reassuring that the punch had caught him square in the forehead, and had been backed by years of technique, and a two hundred and sixty pound slab of meat behind it. So he wasn't permanently scarred by the injury in Russia. Not yet, anyway.

Anyone would be stunned and disoriented by a good knock from Simba, square to the temple, knuckles to forehead, brain against skull.

His health hadn't failed him completely.

Which was a stupid thing to grapple with, considering

he was about to die anyway, and it made him realise how much of his emotional response was mental imaginings. It was all castles in the sky. He'd invented the fear. He thought the same thing. *The brain is a fickle bitch.*

But that pulled him out of the depths of despair. Nothing palpable. Nothing anyone could observe on a scan, or a reading. But he switched from despair to hope, ever so slightly.

Simba stepped forward. Raised a fist. The air stank of manure and sweat and baked dirt.

Slater sensed sheer helplessness.

He closed his eyes, and the hope faded away. He waited to die. The next punch to the head would knock him clean out. He couldn't raise his arms to defend himself even if he wanted to. So he sat there and fought back a whole mixture of emotions and waited for the end. Waited for the *crack* and the sharp flash of light and then ... nothing at all.

Then he thought, *I got this far in my career through sheer goddamn willpower. I can go a little further. I can do a little more. I didn't do all of this for nothing.*

So he thought it through. He couldn't fight. He could barely move. All he could do was speak.

Simba stepped in, and the air crackled with electricity. Slater knew the sensation all too well. A life was about to be stripped. Death was in the air. Final and terrifying in its rawness. There was something elemental about it. It was different from a firefight, or a no-holds-barred brawl to the death without hesitation. Slater had sensed the same electricity from his own end countless times. It was cold and calculated and ruthless. It happened when he had a man prisoner, and decided a quick death from the bite of a bullet wouldn't suffice, so he would step in and loop an arm around their throat and start to squeeze and listen to them kick and gasp and fight the grip with their hands and finally succumb to a grisly fate with saliva dripping from their lips and bloodshot streaks in their eyes.

He rarely went for that option, but it was reassuring to know he had the capacity in times of need. If he didn't have a gun or a knife available, and his enemy was a bottom-of-the-barrel scumbag, responsible for more suffering than Slater could ever hope to dish out on him.

He got that same sensation here.

Simba reached down and wrapped a giant meaty hand around Slater's throat to hold him in place. It was futile. He wasn't going anywhere. He could barely turn his head from left to right. Simba held it there for a beat, and Slater gagged and retched and gasped for breath, and an electric spark shot into Simba's eyes.

He enjoyed this.

He cocked his other fist, and loaded it up, and got ready to smash Slater's forehead to pieces with a set of calloused knuckles.

Then Slater croaked out, 'You need me alive.'

58

Simba paused, and frowned, and furrowed his brow.

He said, 'Do not make me mad.'

'Why would I be trying to make you mad?'

'You say to make it quick. I respect you for that. No one go quiet and calm to their death. I like this about you.'

'But I just realised something.'

'What you realise? You no have my respect anymore. You weak.'

'If I had it my way, I'd have you kill me right now.'

'No. Now you pretending. You weak.'

The hand stayed wrapped firmly around Slater's throat. It tightened. Slater opened his mouth to speak, and Simba crushed the air right out of his windpipe. He rocked back on his haunches, choking for each morsel of ragged breath. The air was hot and thick and rancid. He gagged again.

Simba let go, and Slater nearly vomited. But he breathed in, and out, and composed himself.

He said, 'If you let me go, I will take you to Danai and Akash.'

Simba scrunched up his nose at the sound of the names. He said, 'Where are they?'

'I found them through a contact. I caught them red-handed. They had two bodies in their kitchen. I figured out they were your men. I agreed to hide them. The bodies, and then Danai and Akash, too. So you couldn't find them.'

Simba cursed and turned around and thundered a boot into the nearest bull pen. His toe struck the wood and the whole pen rattled. The giant bull within snorted in derision and butted the wall in return and thrashed about in the narrow confines. The hot air rattled too. Slater felt it draping over him, the temperature ebbing and flowing. All the sensations were heightened by the knock to the head. He could taste the atmosphere, and found himself acutely aware of the sweat flowing from his pores. He sat wallowing in his misery and waited for Simba's rage to fade.

He knew he was clutching onto his life by a thread. All Simba had to do was drive to their residence and find them sitting there at their kitchen table, at which point Slater would be all but useless. But that took time and effort, and all Slater cared about was the here and now.

So he said, 'You were close to those two men they killed, weren't you?'

Simba went to hit him. Which would have proved disastrous. It might have damaged Slater permanently. For good. At which point trying to crawl out of this miserable hole would be even more pointless. No use living with severe brain damage. And he could sense himself right now, standing on the edge of the cliff, teetering and swaying and about to plummet. Another hit would send him all the way over. There might be no coming back from that.

He flinched away, more scared than he'd ever been in his life.

Simba laughed at his unrest. 'You are hurt bad. You are no lying.'

'Why would I lie about that?'

'Faking it.'

'I'm not faking it.'

'I can tell. Yes, I was close. And close to these men here. Six here, two there. Lots of gaps in my army now.'

'They came to kill me. I just defended myself.'

'You shoot this one out there. Why he naked?'

'To make the others hesitate.'

Simba laughed and nodded, like the world was a cruel joke. 'You good.'

'I try my best.'

'Where is Akash? Where is Danai?'

'I hid them.'

'Where?'

'I can't remember.'

Simba stepped in and hit him in the chest. The blow slammed home with incredible force. Slater saw the fist coming, and braced for impact, but the crunch to his sternum shocked him all the same. He tumbled back and hit the dirt and the world went mad. He groaned and stared up at the thatched roof. It spun. Blood leaked from the corner of Slater's mouth. He levered up onto his elbows, and coughed and gasped for breath, and found it ... but at the same time he found an immense pain. It was sharp and foreign and it speared through his sternum. He gasped again, a little louder, a little more panicked.

Simba noticed.

The big man spat on Slater. A glob of saliva landed on his chest. Simba said, 'You weak.'

'I...' Slater started, and then panic hit him, flooding through his chest.

It was his sternum. He was sure of it. He soaked in every detail of the pain, like a knife through his chest, and he knew it wasn't heart-related. But it terrified him all the same. Just the nature of human instinct. No-one got a searing pain in their chest that prevented them from breathing or sitting upright and passed it off as something minor. His rudimentary knowledge of battlefield wounds chalked it up as costochondritis. Inflammation of the cartilage connecting one of his ribs to his breastbone. But it felt eerily similar to a heart attack.

So his eyes went wide and his breathing turned shallow and he forced himself not to panic.

The semi-consciousness didn't help.

He groaned and wryly noted the rate at which a fight could go in one man's favour.

If he'd turned around half a second sooner, Simba would be dead with a bullet hole square in the centre of his forehead.

But that wasn't what was happening.

Instead, Simba loomed over him.

Clenching a fist.

Threatening another blow.

Slater figured if the big man hit him again, he might actually have a heart attack.

He managed to croak out, 'I'm telling the truth. My memory ... isn't working right. I told them to go...'

He trailed off, and hoped it was convincing.

Simba snarled, and spat again. 'You no tell truth anymore.'

'I swear, I am.'

'You bad liar.'

'I'm not lying.'

'I want those two. I need them. They no get away. You help me find.'

'Yes.'

'Cannot do that if you dead.'

'No.'

Simba grunted in frustration, but he seemed to note how compromised Slater was. He must have figured it wasn't a ruse. It was hard to impersonate genuine terror. And the combination of concussion-related symptoms coupled with chest tightening and shallow breathing had created a kaleidoscope of panic.

Slater found himself unusually indisposed to deal with this particular version of his personal hell. He hadn't collected a cluster of symptoms like this before. Not in this unique pattern. He tried to deal with the panic and the dizziness and the shortness of breath all at once. It didn't work.

Simba hauled him to his feet, hit him in the stomach to double him over, and started to drag him out of the building.

Towards the main house.

59

Simba was many things, but he was not a fool.

He shoved Slater out of the building, into the harsh sunlight, and left him standing awkwardly there for just a few seconds as he retrieved one of the discarded Kalashnikov AK-47s. The rifle seemed small in his meaty paws. He pointed the barrel at Slater's torso, maximising the chance of hitting his target, and stayed ten feet back at all times. A smart distance. Too far for a lunge. Close enough to all but guarantee a direct hit.

He said, 'Walk.'

Slater didn't want to let on to the fact that he would have done as Simba instructed without being held at gunpoint. He was wrestling, deep in his own head, trying to convey a lack of serious injury whilst swimming up to his neck in metaphorical shit. He could barely put one foot in front of the other, but he didn't dare show weakness. He couldn't let Simba know that he wouldn't be able to defend himself if he tried. He needed the big man treating him as some kind of unspoken threat, albeit compromised.

But Simba didn't need to know just how compromised.

They set off for the main house, an awkward two-man procession, like a surreal horror show against an otherwise scenic backdrop. Slater with his eyes wide and blood dripping from his mouth, doubled over in pain from the chest inflammation, hands hanging limp by his sides, footsteps awkward and soft. Then came Simba, all two hundred and fifty pounds of him, with the rifle and the manic glint in his deep green eyes and the giant confident strides. Behind them the bodies lay strewn across the dirt lot and the inside of the barn, no thanks to Slater's handiwork.

They trudged down into deep green fields that matched Simba's eyes, and continued up to the wooden deck running the length of the ranch-style property.

Slater stumbled up the short flight of stairs, his movement ungainly, his mannerisms stunted. He came to rest at a sufficient viewing point, and just before Simba joined him on the deck he spent a moment admiring the view. The hills swept away into the distance, undulating as they faded. There was no sound — just a slight breeze, and the creaking of the wooden planks underfoot.

Simba clambered up the stairs, but his aim never wavered.

A morsel of clarity came back to Slater. The effects of the knock to the head, fading gently away. Not a concussion. A severe bump, but nothing more than that. He gained a little proprioception. He figured he could knock Simba unconscious in a fight now.

Or maybe not.

The big man had only hit him twice, but each punch had wreaked havoc. His chest hurt with each breath. His head hurt. His neck throbbed for some reason. He felt as if he'd been chewed up in the path of a locomotive. His vision still shimmered. His hands felt weak and raw. He was acutely aware of the AK-47 aimed at his chest.

Reflexes meant nothing now.

And the fear remained.

He knew it didn't make sense. He shouldn't be scolding himself so severely. Like he'd told himself earlier, another half-second or less, and the result would have been a very different story. But it didn't feel like that. Like he'd also told himself earlier, combat was all or nothing. Win or lose. A hundred or zero. No middle ground.

Just the harsh reality.

Slater said, 'What now?'

The front door burst open in his face. First the wooden door was tugged inward, and then the screen door was thrust outward, and then the deck got a whole lot busier. Three bulky men in olive uniforms trundled out onto the landing. They were all bald and angry, and sported ramrod straight postures. They barked questions at Simba, and he fired answers back. They stared at Slater with unrestrained fury.

Slater said nothing.

One of the three men hit him in the gut.

Slater probably could have defended the blow, given his slight recovery, but he didn't.

He let the fist crunch into the skin just below his stomach, and he doubled over and collapsed onto the deck. Half performance. Half not.

He groaned and held his mid-section and squeezed his eyes shut, as if pretending he couldn't see would stop the next attack. Half performance. Half not.

Simba said, 'That was for men you killed.'

Slater spat blood onto the dusty planks. He said, 'I assume there's a lot more where that came from.'

Simba just nodded.

He took a step closer, forming a roadblock between Slater and the three guards. He crouched down, looming over Slater.

Slater was curled in the foetal position, feeling awfully sorry for himself.

Simba said, 'We can make easy.'

'How?'

'Do deal with me.'

'What do you want?'

'Tell me Danai and Akash location. Then I shoot you here. Easy. No pain. But if you no tell me, I have to get location out of you. I have to make pain. I let these three do it. They have friend you killed. They angry about this. They live with friend you killed for long time.'

'Bet they've never faced resistance before,' Slater mumbled.

'What?'

'And neither have you.'

'I need answer from you.'

'None of you sheltered fucks know what resistance looks like,' Slater said, managing a bloody smile, staring up at Simba through half-closed eyes.

The pain was making him delirious.

But he wasn't about to cave.

Not anymore.

The moment of weakness had passed.

Replaced by what he'd been all along.

He said, 'I killed eight of your men and I'm just getting started. How many more do you have? How much time do you have to break me? You might want to think about those things. You're a smart man. You delegate your resources properly. You know you have limited time. How much are you prepared to waste on me?'

Simba smiled back and said, 'Lot of time. You no felt pain like I give. One of those men my brother. Another one my uncle. You kill two of my family. I make life hell for you. Just watch.'

He reached down to haul Slater to his feet.

Slater snatched for the AK-47.

It was the only chance he would get.

But there were a million variables against him. Namely the positioning, and the fact that gravity wasn't working in his favour, and the fact that he would have to kill Simba, followed swiftly by the other three, two of whom were armed. But above all that, the main obstacle was Simba's speed. Slater made the lunge, scrabbling out of the foetal position, outstretching both hands, and Simba simply tipped his weight back on the balls of his feet and levered out of the way, and the big man looked at Slater like he was stupid for even trying to resist.

And right about then Slater started to realise that he might have met his genetic rival.

In an alternate universe, Simba would have worked for Black Force. He would have scored off the charts in every test of reaction speed, just as Slater had. But instead of devoting his life to a noble cause, he'd ended up here. Standing on a deck in rural Zimbabwe. And through no fault of his own, Slater had ended up here too. Lying on a deck in rural Zimbabwe.

A classic tactical disadvantage.

Simba cocked his head, and Slater noticed a moment of silent fury rippling across his expression.

And then it was gone, replaced by indifference, with a hint of amusement.

And then Simba stomped down on Slater's chest.

He kicked just as hard as he punched.

It felt like Slater's breastbone exploded.

He rolled over in silent agony and the four-man team dragged him into the musty shadows of the house.

60

T he goons dragged him down a flight of stairs, with the only illumination coming from a weak bulb fixed into the uneven concrete ceiling. The walls and the stairs were concrete too. Like a dungeon. Something medieval. Primitive. The atmosphere aligned with the aesthetic. Everything stank, and the sense of death hung hot and heavy in the air.

Slater didn't like where this was headed.

Not one bit.

They carried him into a corridor, with the same cold concrete floor, and he thought about putting up another fight. But they had him by the arms, one on each side, and another had his legs, and Simba followed behind like a giant monster stalking its prey. Slater made out the shape of the AK-47, and he knew this wasn't the time for a fight. He had to be tactical about it. He had to choose his battles wisely. The lunge on the porch had been a shocking idea. He'd been caught up in the heat of the moment. It had been something about the dynamic. He was outside on the porch, under the hot sun, surrounded by a sea of lush greenery, with the wind blowing on his face. He'd known they were about to drag him inside, and he'd known he might not ever make it back out of the house. So he'd momentarily panicked, and he'd reacted to it. He should have conserved his energy.

He should have done a lot of things.

His chest was on fire. It burned with a lethality he couldn't put into words if he tried. The inflammation was ten times worse now. Because of Simba stomping on his chest. Now the big man had hit him three times. A punch to the dome, a punch to the chest, and a stomp to the chest. All three had dished out unbelievable damage. Slater felt like a broken shell of his former self. Like someone had chewed him up and spat him out and done their best to rearrange the pieces. Either Simba had power like nothing he'd ever felt before, or he was getting older and weaker.

He figured it was the former.

There was something about Simba's physicality that seemed almost superhuman. He walked like an Olympic athlete. No-one ran into that kind of grace and dexterity and sheer unadulterated power in the real world. Those genetic freaks took their talents to the big leagues. They made millions of dollars to play sports at the highest level and insulated themselves out of the public eye. They certainly didn't beat people up in the street, or turn to petty crime, or become international players. They were scooped up and put into the machine before that. So Slater didn't encounter them often. He'd been scooped up and put into the government's machine early on.

Maybe this was what people felt like when Slater hit them.

Barely holding onto his own sanity, he didn't protest as they unlocked a makeshift jail cell and carried him through into its confines. The walls were made entirely of metal bars, with thin gaps between each one, but despite the job's crudeness it proved effective. Slater quickly realised he wouldn't be going anywhere without their permission. But it gave him an unobstructed view of the rest of the basement level, which consisted of a number of similar cells arranged in two rows on either side of the central corridor.

A cell block.

Underground.

The three men shuffled out of the cell, and one of them pulled the door shut. He slid a bolt across the front of the cell and locked it with a key. He put the key in his pocket and sauntered back the way he'd come, followed swiftly by the other two.

Simba stayed where he was.

Peering in.

Gloating.

Slater let him gloat.

Because what the hell else was he to do?

Simba said, 'I will be back to take care of you.'

Before Slater responded, he crossed to the other side of the cell and sat down with his back against the cold concrete wall. He hurt all over. He'd taken vicious beatings in the past. Blow after blow after blow. He'd been shot and stabbed. He'd suffered every wound you could possibly think of, save losing a limb. And in some strange cerebral way, nothing rivalled this. Because it all hurt, but he'd only been hit three times. And Simba hadn't put his full effort into any of the blows. Some kind of genetic gift. Some kind of incomprehensible power.

So Slater was experiencing intimidation for the first time since he could remember.

He said, 'Where are you going?'

He thought his voice was quieter than usual, but it could have been imagined. He didn't quite know how to act.

'To eat,' Simba said. 'Hungry.'

'Aren't you worried I'll break out?'

Simba just smiled. 'Try your best.'

'I will.'

'I almost want to happen. So I can hit. One more time.'

Slater must have visibly twitched, because Simba's smile spread wider.

The man said, 'I will enjoy this.'

Slater said, 'You should shoot me in the head. Right now. From where you're standing. I'm serious.'

'Why?'

'I've been in situations like this before. I'm still here.'

'Was I there?'

'Not that I can remember.'

'That's why you still here. You no meet me before.'

'A couple of people said the same thing you were saying.'

'They here?'

'Not anymore.'

'I here.'

'Maybe not for long.'

Simba just smiled. 'Tell me something.'

'What?'

'Tell truth.'

'Always,' Slater said.

'You ever been hit like how I hit?'

'No,' Slater said, shaking his head. 'Never.'

The smile lingered. Menacing as all hell.

Simba said, 'Everyone tell me that. I hit hard.'

'You do.'

'I go upstairs. I eat. I come back down. You give me location. Anything other than this happen, I hit you many times.'

'I wouldn't want that,' Slater said.

'How is chest?'

'It hurts.'

'Good. I be back soon. You can keep other prisoner company while you wait.'

'Other prisoner?'

'She no want to talk right now. She been bad.'

Simba pointed a lecherous finger across the basement. Slater followed the trajectory and found a small figure hunched in the corner of the far cell. Barely visible in the lowlight. She was short and plump and wearing a simple dress made of cheap denim. She was white.

Simba said, 'She no clean properly. She usually do good job. Not today. She sit here for a while. Maybe she get to know you, then I kill you. Then she understand...'

He trailed off, searching for a word, moving his fat lips back and forth.

'Consequences,' he finished, and the smile spread wide.

He disappeared up the stairs, following his guards. The basement turned silent. Slater sat for a beat, savouring the solitude for as much as it was worth. The pain continued falling over him in waves. Like sheets of rain. Ebbing and flowing. A moment of respite, and then a piercing bolt of lightning. He pressed the back of his skull to the concrete and held it there. He counted to ten. He took a deep breath, and counted to ten again.

And again.

And again.

And again.

And again.

Sixty seconds total. He opened his eyes. The pain was

still there. His chest felt fit to burst. But it was manageable, just as everything in his life was. Every obstacle was surmountable. He had learnt that a decade ago. Break the task down into little pieces, and then chip away at it until it's done.

He was getting out of this goddamn cell.

Whatever it took.

He rolled his head over, now slightly more composed, and stared through the endless rows of bars. He watched the small slumped figure as she cowered in the corner. He didn't say a word. He just waited. Eventually she stirred and turned to face him and looked right back at him. He scrutinised her face. She had a puffy lower lip and the beginnings of a black eye, but otherwise her face was unblemished. She had pale skin and red cheeks and a certain look in her eyes. Slater tried to pinpoint what it was, and chalked it up to a certain mischievousness, despite the circumstances, despite the hopelessness. He tried to scour his memory to figure out what it reminded him of.

He'd seen the same expression in the midst of hopelessness.

A couple of days beforehand.

He waited until she locked eyes with him, and then he said, 'I think I met your father.'

She didn't say anything.

He said, 'Paige?'

She paused.

Judging him.

Sizing him up.

Then she nodded.

61

Cue the most uncomfortable conversation in the history of conversations, Slater thought.

He said, 'How long have you been here?'

'All my life,' she said.

Her accent was plain and unimpressive with no distinct inflections. But she spoke with a confidence that belied the circumstances. He could hear each syllable clear as day. She wasn't muted and squared away and submissive. When she'd turned to face Slater she'd straightened her shoulders, and they stayed straight. Slater guessed she was in her early twenties. She had a mess of red hair, pointing this way and that, wild and untethered. It matched her cheeks.

Slater said, 'Not all your life.'

'I had a life before this. But I don't remember it.'

'Would you like to go back to it?'

'What are you going to do about it?'

She spoke with the confidence of someone who'd been held captive for many, many years. Too many to fathom. Slater didn't even want to start thinking about it. He had enough problems of his own to deal with. This new shock had been sprung on him at the most inopportune time possible. He felt sick at the thought of it. He wanted to curl up in a ball and go to sleep. Maybe forever.

And then he realised that was the pain talking. He sat up, and he fought against the resistance, and he straightened his shoulders, just like she had. He turned to face her. Because whatever he was going through was nothing in comparison to her plight. Not even close. Not even on the same spectrum. Because Slater had the capacity to do something about his problems, and she didn't.

And that made him more furious than he thought possible.

He said, 'There are a few things I can do about it.'

She just smiled. Much like her father had. Much like Danai had.

A resigned smile.

She said, 'No you can't.'

'How long have you been here?' he said again.

'I told you.'

'Be more specific.'

'Eight years, according to the dates. Feels like thirty.'

'What do they make you do?'

'You want me to sum up eight years of hell in a few sentences?'

'I want you to do your best. Because I don't know when Simba's coming back down those stairs. And I need as much information as I can gather.'

'Why? What good will it do?'

'I just need to know.'

'Why?'

'I might be able to get out of here. And by extension I could get you out of here.'

'You won't.'

'You don't know that.'

'Has Simba hit you?'

'Yes.'

'Then you're not going anywhere. Because you understand what that feels like.'

'I can deal with it.'

'You look like you're in pain.'

'I am.'

'So I'd say you're not dealing with it very well at all.'

'I've been in pain before.'

'Not like this.'

'I hit pretty hard too.'

'Rangano hits harder than Simba.'

Slater froze. 'Is he here?'

Paige shrugged. 'He comes and goes. He could be. No way to know for sure.'

'Give me something here, Paige. I met with your father. Just a few days ago. He thought you died all those years ago. I had my suspicions, but I kept them quiet. I need to know anything you can give me.'

'All I remember is getting put in the basement, and then getting pulled back out again an hour later by a group of people I'd never seen before. And then they took me back here and I became their slave.'

'What do they do to you?'

'Nothing good.'

'What's it been like?'

She paused for thought, summing it all up, and then she said, 'I was taken when I was thirteen. I've grown up here. All my teenage years, and beyond. And I'm still talking to you about how much I hate them. Do you understand what kind of mentality that takes? You know how tempting it's been to give in to Stockholm syndrome? Yes, I know what that is. I read books. They've raised me here. Given me a ragtag education, too. As best as they could. Because I'm a good servant.'

'Servant in what capacity?'

'Does that matter right now?'

'Not really.'

'None of it matters right now,' she said.

'I'm going to get you out of here.'

'And how do you propose to do that?'

'Working on it.'

'You've got a look in your eye,' she said. 'Like you can do it.'

'I believe I can.'

'Then you're either very talented or delusional.'

'Have you ever tried to escape?'

'Dozens of times.'

'Didn't work?'

'Have you seen what's around here? One time I got ten miles away. Their security got lax so I ran straight out the front gate. They tracked me down and picked me up and carted me back. And I never got that sort of freedom again. My privileges were taken away.'

'When was that?'

'Three years ago.'

'Are you scared?'

'Do I look it?'

'No.'

'Because I accepted what happened a long time ago. Only way to keep my head above water.'

'How *aren't* you brainwashed?' Slater said, incredulous. 'You said it yourself. You've spent nearly half your life here.

How are you having a normal conversation with me right now?'

He knew exactly what his own conversational shortcomings were. And he knew it was because of the bump to the head. It made sense. If it played with his emotions, then it played with his sensitivity. He was aware of how he should be speaking to Paige. She'd been a prisoner of war for almost her entire childhood and many years after. She'd been raised in hell. It was a relatively plain house that didn't look too dissimilar from a traditional country abode from the outside, but the dynamic on the inside must have been horrifying. Slater didn't want to probe too deep about what had been done to Paige. For all he knew, they hadn't violated her once. It was wishful thinking, but it was certainly possible. He knew all about how men could be twisted and sick in certain ways and perfectly reasonable in others. Maybe Simba or Rangano didn't interfere with kids.

Or maybe they did.

But Slater wasn't in a position to coddle Paige through the process. He could barely string his thoughts together. He focused on the immediate issue, which was getting out of the cell, and determined the fastest way to do that was to draw some kind of information out of Paige.

'Paige,' he said.

She looked at him. No emotion in her eyes. Just resignation.

He said, 'If you could think of one thing — one piece of information — you could feed to someone like me to help me get you out of here, what would it be?'

She said, 'You can't get out of here.'

'I think I can.'

'You let them drag you into the cell.'

'Tactical retreat.'

'If that's what you call it.'

'Anything Paige — anything...'

She sighed, and furrowed her brow, and let the basement descend into silence. Then she said, 'Well, I guess ... some of the guards don't like Simba all that much.'

62

S later sat up, and he grimaced involuntarily.

Everything hurt.

He wiped dirt and sweat off his forehead and forced his mouth back into a hard line and said, 'What do you mean?'

'They don't talk in front of me. So I can't know for sure.'

'You've been here eight years. You've overheard something. Surely.'

She twitched, and flinched away, and he scolded himself for the brutal honesty. No use rubbing her face in it. But he needed answers. She could get all the counselling and therapy and psychoactive help she needed once she was off the property. Once she was safe.

She said, 'Nothing.'

'Paige...'

'I think it might have something to do with money.'

'You think?'

'I've heard snippets of conversations. I've been here long enough. Like you said.'

Then a flicker of utter helplessness flashed in her eyes,

and she screwed her figure deeper into the corner, as if tucking the shadows up to her chin. They'd given Slater endless training in dealing with hostages during his time in the government. Shock was a real and paralysing thing. But this was something else. This was a whole new ball game. This was another sport entirely.

The very concept of resisting was alien to her. It didn't make any sense. The thought of a life outside of what she knew was incomprehensible. Slater had full knowledge of the power of habit, and this was that concept taken to extraordinary new heights. Nearly a decade of serving the same masters. Nearly a decade of having her every move dictated. That wore on everyone, no matter how tough they were. It was a miracle she was even toying with the idea of escape.

She was right.

Stockholm syndrome should have seized her in its intoxicating tendrils many, many years ago.

So he switched gears. He decided to keep it short and sharp and simple. He said, 'They're not getting paid enough?'

She shrugged. 'I think they do alright. But there's whispers of dissent every now and then. Maybe that's what keeps me going. Knowing one day one of them might snap and get me out of here.'

'But it hasn't happened yet?'

'Have you *met* Simba?'

'I have.'

'It was a rhetorical question. The point is he's incredibly persuasive.'

'I've been getting that sense.'

'I don't know ... this is just a gut feeling...'

She trailed off.

Slater said, 'I could use a gut feeling right now.'

She looked at him and said, 'I think he's paying them peanuts. I don't think he's doing as well as it looks.'

'He seems to have money to throw around.'

'It would appear that way.'

'You know better.'

'He makes it look like he does. How did you find him?'

'I was at the bull auction.'

She sighed and nodded. 'He won't shut up about the bulls. He's convinced he can build an empire with them. But I don't think he's paying for them. I think he's making empty promises. For future deliverance.'

Slater paused, and thought. He said, 'If so, he's a phenomenal actor.'

'You think he has money?'

'I don't know what to think. I guess it doesn't matter what's real or not. What matters is whether the guards think Simba is broke.'

'You think he's lying to them?'

'I don't think he's barely scraping by. He wouldn't be so rash at the auctions if he was.'

'You don't think he's trying to save face?'

'I don't think he'd do it like that.'

'So he's acting broke?'

'He's a manipulator. Through and through. Everything's a game to him. If his men are gullible, he'll try to convince them he's just scraping by. And it'll probably work. Because he's good at what he does. In the meantime he can hoard his wealth until he doesn't need this kind of security anymore. He can probably scale it down when his beef empire takes off.'

'If,' Paige corrected.

Slater shrugged. 'He might be a piece of shit, but he's excellent at what he does. Just the nature of the world.'

'Are you on his side?'

'I'm on your father's side.'

'He's still alive?' she said.

Slater paused a moment.

Because it seemed like she had barely any interest in the subject.

He mulled it over. He put himself in her shoes. He thought long and hard about what might have taken place, and what kind of thoughts might have festered over the years. Simba must have added fuel to the fire. No doubt. A master manipulator wouldn't pass up a chance like that.

Slater said, 'Do you think your dad gave you up?'

She looked at him. For a long, long time.

Then she said, 'That would seem to be the case. He was desperate. His business was failing. I'm sure he tried to convince you otherwise, though.'

Slater thought about it, and then shook his head. 'Your dad wasn't lying when I talked to him. I can tell when people are lying.'

'I doubt that.'

'Try me.'

'Have I lied to you at any point during our conversation?'

'Right at the start. When you said you don't remember your old life. You remember it vividly. I could see it in your eyes. You were trying to cover up the pain and the hurt with denial. Because you think your father led you down to the basement to make it look like he'd been forced off his property. An elaborate ruse in your mind. Because you needed to be angry at someone out there. So it might as well be the guy who had the responsibility of protecting you.'

'It was bullshit,' she said. 'I could tell from the start. He brought me down to the basement, and an hour later there was banging and clanging, and the locked door burst open, and Simba and all his men were standing there. And they led me by the hand out of the room and told me everything was going to be okay and brought me here. My father wouldn't have let me go so easily. He would have tried to protect me.'

'He did,' Slater said.

She stared at him with some sort of fury in her eyes.

'You can't possibly know that.'

'I can.'

'Whatever he told you, he made it up.'

'How do you know?'

'I just know.'

'I just know too. How long are we going to argue about this?'

'You have no proof.'

'I saw proof.'

'Bullshit,' she repeated.

He said, 'If I get you out of here, your father won't be the same man you remember.'

'You're full of shit.'

'They hacked his arm off, Paige. And his leg, from the knee down. Right after he locked you in that basement. You think he cut his own limbs off to prove a point?'

She froze. She stared. She went pale. The rosy colour disappeared from her cheeks.

She said, 'Are you messing with me? Is this one of Simba's sick jokes? Hire an American to trick me?'

'I'm afraid not.'

'Is he okay?'

'As okay as he can be.'

'Has he been looking for me?'

'Right after they took you out of the basement they burned the place to the ground. He thinks you died.'

'In the fire?'

Slater nodded.

She burst out with a sob — the first hint of emotion she'd shown since Slater had met her. She seemed to try and catch it and stuff it back inside, but it came out, and her eyes swelled with tears, and she skewered herself harder into the corner. She lowered her head and the anguish finally spilled out. Slater couldn't fathom how long it had been bottled up for. She cried for what seemed like hours on end, and although he felt like a monster for doing so, Slater tuned it out.

Prioritise.

He focused on his own predicament. His chest was the main issue. The costochondritis wasn't getting any better. It had happened to him a couple of times before, after heavy deadlifts in the gym. Wrenching six hundred pounds off the ground, made up of iron plates on either side of a barbell, led to injury sooner or later. The swelling went down after a day or so. It wasn't a serious issue in everyday life. But right now, when he needed his body at one hundred percent, it was the end of the world. Metaphorically speaking. A glaring hole in his game plan. Which relied entirely on using brute force to work his way out of this mess. There was no other option.

The inflammation seared in his sternum, and if he didn't know any better he might think he was having a heart attack. He rested his back against the wall and tried his best to stifle the pain. His temples throbbed, too. A headache had sprouted to life. But his arms and legs were fine, and determination burned hot inside him. So he figured he could put up some kind of fight.

He just didn't know if it would be enough.

It was a hell of a dangerous game to play.

Paige kept crying, and footsteps sounded on the stairwell.

Thudding down to the basement.

Slater tensed up.

63

I t wasn't Simba.

Slater almost sighed in relief.

The ex-Green Bomber made it to the bottom of the stairs and looked all around. He wore the familiar olive uniform, and the red-and-green beret. He was short. Five-nine, maybe. And thin. All skin and bone under the khakis. He had frail skeleton fingers wrapped around another Kalashnikov AK-47. The rifle looked giant in his hands. His boots were tiny, too. The sleeves and pants of his uniform were baggy at the ends. Small calves, and forearms. A weak man all around.

In comparison to this guy Slater looked like an Olympic bodybuilder.

But the gun was loaded, and the safety was off.

Which meant everything.

The guard fished a ring of keys from his pocket, and crossed to Slater's cell door, and unlocked it. He stepped back instantly. Like springing away from an electrical socket that had given him a shock. He had the AK-47 up and aimed at Slater's chest in the blink of an eye. Paranoid about retaliation. Word must have spread about what Slater had done to most of Simba's troupe. They weren't taking any chances. Apart from the fact that this guy had been sent down to fetch him. They should have sent an army.

But that was the point of men like Simba. They couldn't be overly cautious about everything.

Simba had become wrapped up in an entrepreneurial mindset, probably considering issues like spreading resources thin, and not throwing too much of a safety net. It would be foolish to send three men down to collect Slater. It would look weak. And it would hurt Simba's pride. Because that would mean the big man hadn't hurt Slater enough.

It would mean three punches from a man like Simba meant nothing.

And he had his pride to uphold.

Slater feigned like he was hurt worse than he was. Admittedly, it was bad. But not worst case. Nowhere close. He slumped against the wall and stared at the frail guard with a foggy, milky expression. He held up his hands with his palms out in response to the barrel aimed at his chest. He grimaced.

The guard beckoned with the rifle.

'Out,' he commanded.

It came out wrong. Only one syllable, but he still botched it.

He didn't speak English. Simba had told him what to say.

Slater got to his feet, and looked in the direction of Paige, and muttered something about the weather. Then he described the landscape around the property. The green hills, and the blue sky, and the hot dirt. The guard watched him speak with a perplexed look on his face. When Slater finally wrapped it up, the man beckoned with the rifle again.

'Out,' he said again.

This time a little less confident.

By all accounts, Simba was a hard, cruel man. He wouldn't take failure as an option. And there was the possibility Slater was relaying important information. So did he carry on with the initial protocol and get pulled up for it later, or leave Slater to stew in his cell? The latter option ran him the risk of looking like a fool if Slater hadn't said anything important at all. He was torn. He stood there a few feet from the cell door and shifted from foot to foot, biting his lower lip. His cheekbones jutted out sharp and angular underneath his eyes. The sockets were sunken. He looked like a crack addict. Maybe he was.

Slater pointed to the pre-determined path past the guy, to the stairwell, and raised an eyebrow.

You still want me out?

The guy nodded.

Slater took a step forward, and let loose with another string of gibberish. But he put all his concentration into it. He put emotion and fear and joy and sadness into it all at once. He said something along the lines of, 'This morning I bought three bulls but Simba only wanted me to buy two, so I went back and he told me no, you can't do that, you have to make do with what you've got, which confused the hell out of me, right?'

Then Slater looked a question at the guard, as if expecting an answer.

Now he was in the doorway. No way for the guard to step in and close the door and work out what the hell he was going to do next. He would need to command Slater back inside the cell. Which he wasn't ready to do, because he was trying to decipher what his prisoner was blabbing to him about in English.

Eventually he shrugged and gestured for Slater to carry on past him. There was a few feet of space between Slater and the skinny guard. Enough of a gap to make things difficult. If Slater made any rapid movement at all, the guard would instinctively pull the trigger. And from this range, missing was all but impossible. The tension in the atmosphere reached a fever pitch. Slater took one step out of the cell. He threw a glance in Paige's direction. The colour hadn't returned to her cheeks.

He turned back to the guard.

You didn't cuff me. You didn't bring more men. This is your fault.

He jerked his eyebrows in Paige's direction, and shot a questioning look at the man, and smiled a wry smile.

A universal gesture between disgusting predators.

How good's having her in a cage?

The guard looked past Slater, just for a fleeting moment. Maybe he didn't get the chance to be around the girl very often. His loins might have stirred. His composure might have dropped.

The barrel wavered a fraction of an inch. To a common prisoner, nothing at all.

But Slater was far from a common prisoner.

He shot for a double leg takedown with every ounce of explosive energy in his body. Which turned out to be a hell of a lot. An elite athlete moving with determination and single-mindedness could appear superhuman in the flesh. Slater considered himself an elite athlete. His vision was nothing but a blur, but a half-second after dropping low and charging like an angry bull he had his arms locked tight around both the guard's skinny legs. He picked the man up like he weighed nothing and changed direction in the air and dropped him on the top of his skull on the concrete like a rudimentary version of a pro wrestling pile driver. Which was nothing like the soft manoeuvre performed on television by trained actors. Instead of insulating the landing with both his knees, Slater leapt into the movement and powered all his own weight down onto the guy's neck.

The guard's skull crushed against the concrete and made a sound like a bowling ball dropped from a second story balcony, and Slater followed him down and smashed a frantic elbow into the forehead for good measure, bundling down on top of him in a clash of furious limbs. The guy was probably dead from the impact of his skull against the ground, but Slater made sure by dropping the same elbow over and over again into his face until the guard's features were unrecognisable.

To an outsider, it would appear inhuman. Beyond brutal. Something reserved for those headed straight for the depths of hell. If there was such thing as an afterlife, killing a man with your bare hands put you straight at the bottom of it.

At least, from the perspective of someone unaccustomed to violence.

The real world was much trickier.

Much more of a moral grey zone.

Slater clambered off the body with blood dripping off his elbow, panting for breath, coming down from the massive adrenalin high of the encounter. The guard hadn't even squeezed the trigger of the Kalashnikov. It had spilled from his grip in an attempt to save his fall. It was lying there beside the corpse, discarded. Slater had killed the man in roughly four seconds.

He took a giant breath, but the inhale came in a rattling gasp. He knew if he'd been a second slower, the guard would have lowered the aim of the AK-47 and fired a cluster of rounds through his upper back. Slicing straight through his internal organs. Dropping him onto his stomach on the cold floor to bleed out and die in front of Paige.

Stripping her of the only morsel of hope she had left.

Slater stood in the silence, panting, and the disfigured face of the skinny guard beside him lolled to one side, rolling to the right to face Paige.

She held in a scream.

Slater said, 'I really didn't want you to see that.'

64

He said, 'Are you okay?'

She said, 'Me?'

He shrugged. 'I'm fine. Don't worry about me.'

'Do you do that a lot?'

'When I need to.'

'How did you ... move that fast?'

'Practice.'

'Okay,' she said, and took a few breaths in and out, in and out, in and out. Trying to compose herself. She set off listing the circumstances. 'You're out of your cell. I'm still in here. That guy's dead. What do we do now?'

Slater collected the AK-47 off the concrete. A pool of blood had almost snaked its way to the rifle by the time Slater scooped it off the floor.

'Did you know him?' he said.

Paige shook her head. 'He was new.'

'Do you think I'm a monster?'

'I don't know what you are.'

'It's not about to get any better for whoever's left upstairs. You know that, right? Do you still want out?'

She looked him dead in the eyes.

'Kill them all,' she said.

He nodded, and said, 'Will do.'

No questions necessary. He wasn't that kind of guy. He didn't need graphic detail. He just needed the right kind of look in a helpless person's eyes, and it told him everything that needed to be said. Without fail. Unquestionable. *Kill them all.* A direct implication of guilt concerning anyone within a mile of this place. Just as Slater had suspected. There was no way any of Simba's men could be unaware of what was going on. Slater figured Paige was justified in presenting an argument that she was brainwashed. If she had to. If she'd been forced to commit appalling crimes she could explain to a court that she'd been held against her will for eight years. That would twist anyone's head. But not Simba's men. They were here of their own free will, and due to their own lack of empathy. The big man wasn't keeping any of them prisoner. They had the choice to leave, whenever they wanted.

So Slater started for the stairs.

And then he froze.

He heard footsteps.

Paige inhaled sharply behind him.

Could it be?

But it wasn't Simba.

Another guard came trundling down the concrete stairwell. A larger man than the first. He was zipping up his fly. Perhaps Simba had told them to go down as a pair. He had a pistol in a holster at his waist. Perhaps he'd taken a bathroom break, figuring the prisoner was hurt bad enough to warrant a one-man expedition. The skinny guy could handle it okay.

Or not.

Slater shot him through the forehead. He had the AK-47 trained on the mouth of the stairwell and the newcomer strode right into his imaginary crosshairs. The bullet hit him square in the skull and the report blared in the windowless concrete space. Deafening in its intensity.

Slater hadn't wasted any time trying to silently subdue the guy. He treated every fistfight as luck. Sure, his reaction speed was off the charts, but reflexes slipped up eventually. No use making it unnecessarily difficult. And Simba didn't have an endless stream of henchmen on the ranch. He wasn't paying them enough for that. His resources were stretched thin enough as it was. Or they weren't, and he was bluffing about the whole thing.

Slater started to weigh up the possibilities.

The conclusion he came to was meaty. He figured he could use it as leverage. But he left it in the back of his mind, because right now it didn't matter in the slightest.

He kept the AK-47 trained on the stairwell, and kept his voice soft, and said, 'You should stay in the cell for now.'

Hearing no sounds of approaching hostiles, he glanced over his shoulder and saw Paige's eyes widening.

He knew why.

Her last hope of escape before she finally succumbed to Stockholm syndrome, slipping away. Disappearing into nothingness. Piece by miserable piece. He knew this was it for her. She'd spent eight years resisting the fight. And now a golden opportunity for freedom had presented itself to her. A killer in the next cell. A guy who'd overpowered the guards and now had her fate in the palm of his hand. And he was throwing it away. Why had she even bothered speaking to him?

She looked like she was about to cry.

He said, 'It's not what you think.'

'Oh, I'm sure,' she said, her tone dripping with scorn. 'You talk a good game, mister.'

'What good is it letting you out now?'

'What good is it doing it later?'

'Because if I get myself killed upstairs, you have deniability.'

'You're talking like that's a possibility. I thought you were Superman.'

'To an extent. Everyone's luck runs out.'

'I still don't understand.'

'If I let you out now, you'll stay down here anyway. What if I die upstairs, and they come down here and find you out of your cell?'

'It wouldn't be good for me.'

'So do you understand?'

'You won't come back.'

'I will.'

'Everything anyone's promised me for the last thirteen years hasn't been fulfilled. Why would you be about to start?'

Slater said, 'I'll come back.'

'Why isn't anyone coming now?'

'Because they're realising their errors. There's not many of them left. This is a siege now. They heard that gunshot. They'll be waiting at the top of the stairwell with all their guns pointed at the entranceway. I'll be a sitting duck. Now it's a waiting game. Who makes the first move? Do I go up, or do they come down? And the last two guys to come down here are dead. So that'll be a factor. And they have food and water up there. And a bathroom. So realistically they can wait as long as they like. And they can do it in shifts. They can have a man with his gun on the door for weeks straight, just by rotating. I don't have that luxury.'

'I could help,' Paige said. 'If you let me out.'

Slater thought about it. Then he almost smiled. At the stupidity of it all. He looked down at the lock, and shook his head in disbelief. The rush of combat made fools out of the most intelligent men. He said, 'I might have. If I could.'

She looked at the lock too. Then she sighed. 'Oh.'

'Who has the key?'

'Simba. He keeps a bunch of them in his pocket. He's the only one with access to different parts of the house. Like a power dynamic. He likes to keep his guards on their toes. But I think it's the same thing as his money situation. I bet it's just a bunch of empty rooms. I think he likes to seem more important than he is.'

Slater thought about that, too.

'Interesting,' he said.

'What are you thinking?'

'It plays into my theory.'

'What's your theory?'

'It's based on some things I've heard over the past few days.'

'Care to enlighten me?'

He kept his gaze fixed on the stairwell, and listened hard. No-one coming down. He'd hear it. Even if they were trying to sneak down each step. The noise would carry.

He said, 'Not right now.'

'Why not?'

'I'm preoccupied.'

'With what? You're just standing there.'

'I'm about to go upstairs.'

She stiffened a little, and he thought he heard a sharp intake of breath.

She said, 'Please don't get yourself killed.'

He glanced to his left. Down the other end of the aisle. There was a low wooden table, with a broom resting on it. He looked at his feet. As he suspected, the concrete was unblemished. Not a speck of dust on it. The cleanliness had been ruined by the pool of blood oozing out of the first guard's head, but Slater guessed it didn't matter now.

Someone in the house had OCD.

He crossed to the table and picked up the broom.

He held it by its handle, wielding the AK-47 in the other. The Kalashnikov was a far heavier item. The veins in his right forearm bulged.

He said, 'I'll be right back. I promise.'

65

He crept up the stairs inch by inch, experiencing every stress chemical at the same time.

Some small part of him wished he could stay in this state his whole life. If anyone could achieve it, they'd be the most hyper-aware individual on the planet. There was barely any light in the concrete stairwell, but he could see every millimetre of detail. He could smell everything, even catching a whiff of the blood on the floor downstairs. He could smell his own fetid sweat. His hearing was better, too. Sounds of shuffling and general unrest drifted down the stairwell, coming from the ground floor. Coming from the carpeted hallway around the entrance. There were men up there. Lying in wait. Anticipating a sudden firefight at any moment.

He lowered himself into a crouch, and got quieter. He had a knack for it. It didn't matter that stealth wasn't his forte. He was still exceptional at it. Because his life was on the line, and he'd spent most of his life in similar predicaments, and getting better at one aspect of staying alive generally increased your capacity to stay alive in any scenario.

Usually he had to improvise in the middle of an active war zone. He had to figure out his next move with bullets flying over his head and enemies at five different angles. That's where the reaction speed came in. That's why Black Force made it the baseline of all their initiation tests. In the chaos and carnage of a life-or-death struggle, those who could keep their head together came out on top nine times out of ten. Just the way the world works. Panic and flinching and rash decisions led to failure. If you tested off the charts with your reflexes, you could figure out what was happening faster than the other guy. And that was all it came down to in the end.

But this was better. Even if the circumstances were less than ideal. He figured he could deal with it. In reality he could probably throw himself into the line of fire and try to squeeze off an accurate shot before the other guy did. It might work, too. He'd done it before. When all other options had been exhausted. He knew how fast he could move. But there was the possibility of more than one field of intersecting fire. One guy at each corner, with a rifle pointed at the top of the stairs.

If that was the case, he didn't stand a chance.

Hence the broom.

He gripped the handle tight, and held it straight out in front of him as he crouched low. The door at the top of the stairs was half-open, but it opened outward into the corridor, not inward into the stairwell. Advantage number one for Slater. He could hit the door with his shoulder at a run, which took far less effort than having to reach out and haul it inwards in order to get past. And if he threw it outward, it blocked the line of sight of anyone standing on that side.

He figured his chances were about as good as they were going to get.

Still in a crouch, still making no noise whatsoever, he reached out and extended the arm holding the broom, until the broom head hovered a few inches above the top step. He gently brought it down on the step. Inch by inch.

When it struck the concrete, it made an imperceptible noise.

Just a *plink* in the silence.

Slater heard bodies stiffen, and the faintest creak of automatic rifles being raised into position.

He listened hard.

He figured out where they were.

He burst into action.

As soon as he realised there was no-one waiting directly opposite the top of the stairwell he stood up to his fullest height. He hurled the broom end-first like a spear at the opposite wall. He put everything into it. Like a pitcher hurling a fast ball. He had impressive shoulder dexterity and flexibility. It was a good throw. He threw it so hard that it smashed through the plaster on the other side of the hallway. It embedded deep in the wall, and the sound echoed down the hallway.

Two men fired at the broom.

Slater didn't blame them. It would have scared the shit out of anyone. Himself included. In fact, he almost flinched at the noise himself, even though he knew he was the cause. It sounded like a bomb going off in the midst of the quiet stand-off. So two rifles went to the source of the sudden movement, and two fingers squeezed the trigger.

Slater bounded up the last couple of steps, leant his upper half out into the hallway, and shot the closest man in the face with a three-round burst.

Then he ducked back into the stairwell.

It marked the turning point. Another small success. Another of their men cut down in front of them. Complete with all the blood and gore involved with taking three rounds from an AK-47 directly to the unprotected face. The survivors had to be at their wits' end. Slater thought he'd glimpsed two or three men behind the first guy, but he couldn't be sure. All his concentration had been focused on taking out just one of them. Because that would start the snowball effect.

Momentum was a fickle thing, and it was responsible for almost everything in life. The rich got richer. The poor got poorer. Success begets success. And losing comrades spirals into dejection, and doubt, and surrender. Slater had killed two at Danai's, and six in and around the bull pens, and two in the basement, and one upstairs. Simba had finite resources.

Soon it would all come crashing down.

Standing deathly still just inside the mouth of the stair-well, Slater slipped out of his shoes. They were heavy boots, and they were loose from the chaotic events of the morning. He stepped out of one of them, and then used his foot to paw off the other. He bent down and picked them up, still not making a noise. Simba's remaining troupe weren't thrilled. Slater could hear them muttering between them-selves, trying to discreetly organise their next move. Did they follow him back down into the basement? Was that where he'd gone? Had the prisoner only come upstairs to kill one man?

Slater tossed his shoes down the stairwell.

They almost made it to the bottom. He figured they covered fifteen or sixteen steps. When they hit one of the stairs near the basement, they clattered hard against the concrete. The sound echoed up through the stairwell and spilled out into the corridor.

Slater could almost *hear* them look at each other. He pictured eyes widening, pulses pounding. As they sensed opportunity.

He brought the AK-47 to his shoulder and lined it up with the mouth of the stairwell.

Two guys materialised in the doorway a second later.

At a full sprint.

Nowhere near ready to exchange gunfire.

They'd sensed Slater retreating. They'd pounced on it like ravenous vultures. They'd aimed to bolt down the stairs and catch him off-guard as he retreated. They hadn't expected him right there, only a couple of steps down, aiming an AK-47 at them.

Slater pulled the trigger, and worked the gun from left to right, and then shot out of the way to avoid their corpses crashing into him.

Both bodies tumbled end over end down the steps. No way to break their fall. They were dead. They slumped and pitched and crashed and finally came to rest at the bottom of the stairs in a broken heap, multiple bones shattered posthumously.

Slater thought he heard a soft gasp rise up the stairwell.

Paige, watching another two dead men crash into view.

He figured it was safe enough.

He moved to step out into the open, his gun up, ready to shoot it out with anyone who'd decided to linger around. But Slater figured his maths was right. He figured it was just Simba now.

He rounded the corner.

A chair hit him square in the upper body.

66

I f you've ever been hit by a chair — or any massive blunt object, for that matter — you know it's nothing like the movies. It doesn't shatter into a dozen pieces upon impact. It hurts like hell.

It caught Slater in the shoulder and bounced off him, but the sheer force spun him into the door, and he bounced off that in turn. When he realised he had his back facing the danger zone he twisted in a wild arc, trying to keep hold of the Kalashnikov in the carnage. The pain stunned him, and he figured Simba was the man behind the throw. No-one else he'd seen had the size and strength to pull off something like that.

But he hadn't seen *everyone* in the house.

And he recalled what Rand had told him about a 6'6" Political Commissar named Rangano.

Who turned out to be an old man. Slater saw him coming, and tried to raise the gun, but it was too late. He brought it up in front of him but his rotator cuff caught halfway, damaged by one of the chair legs, and the tendon screamed for relief, deep in his shoulder. It affected the trajectory of the Kalashnikov. All he saw was a bald head with a receding hairline, complete with grey tufts of hair above the ears, and an old wizened face, and deep sunken eyes, and a hard thin mouth twisted with rage.

So he figured it might be okay after all.

But then he saw the body attached to the head. Just as Rand had described. Six-foot-six, packed with strength, like a sculpture carved out of marble, with veins and bulging muscles and rippling sinew and giant hands. And an athleticism that lingered. This was the most powerful, hard-charging old man Slater had ever laid eyes on.

Rangano ran into him like a locomotive train crushing a car that had broken down on the tracks.

He knew it was the ex-Political Commissar. Right before the guy hit him, Slater got one look in the man's eyes, and he saw intelligence and cunning and intensity there that the rest of the guards lacked. And he was dressed expensively. He wore a short-sleeved button-up shirt tucked into dress slacks. Practically royalty, as far as his surroundings were concerned.

And unarmed.

Hence the wild throw, and the subsequent charge.

Slater could chalk that up to a number of issues. And they were the same advantages he ran into time and time again. Jumping to conclusions, for one. The fact that he was a single man, and Simba and Rangano had a horde of ex-Green Bombers grovelling around at their feet. There was comfort in that. Assumptions were made. *Sure, the prisoner had got out of his cell in the basement, but that's what my men are for. They'll take care of it.*

Hubris.

Before long it made a fool of everyone.

But Rangano had capitalised with impressive speed, and

that was what had taken Slater most by surprise. So he found himself splaying backwards, shocked by the blunt force of the hit, like a football player smashed off his feet. But he knew there was carpet behind him. So he concentrated less on the fall, and more on what to do after he landed. If he was tumbling backward toward concrete, it would have captured the majority of his attention. Instead he calculated where the AK-47 was — wedged between his body and Rangano's — and figured out whether it would be useful or not.

It wouldn't be.

The disadvantage of an automatic rifle in a close quarters fight.

He let go of it.

Rangano hadn't been anticipating that. He thought he'd have time. He thought Slater would spend a vital second fumbling with the rifle, trying to wrench it out from between their bodies, but he abandoned it entirely. Which went against all his natural instincts. But it freed his arms, so when he came down on his rear on the carpet, and Rangano sprawled on top of him, all two hundred and fifty pounds pressing like a deadweight on his chest, Slater found a useful second and a half to do something with his hands before Rangano had recovered from the fall.

He envisioned his elbow as a blade, sharpened for years for this very moment, and he swung it horizontally across the space right in front of him. Which was currently occupied by Rangano's forehead. Their noses were practically touching, and before the old man could use his weight and power and position to make Slater's life a living hell, the tip of an elbow hit him in the forehead and dragged a thin line across it, tearing the skin in a perfect horizontal slash.

Blood spilled immediately.

The next part of Slater's plan was paramount to his success. He had to assume Rangano didn't get hit often. He had to pray for the insulation that came with a position of power, and turned everyone fat and lazy. Judging Rangano's physique, he was neither of those things, but Slater had to hope like hell his fitness was at a commercial level, instead of the result of years of simulated combat training. If Rangano actively sparred, then he wouldn't be afraid to get hit, and it wouldn't be a foreign sensation, and he would keep his composure.

And Slater would die.

But it quickly became apparent that Rangano *hated* getting hit.

He pawed at his face, trying to wipe the blood from his eyes. It spurted out, covering Slater, covering the carpet. Slater bucked his hips, *hard,* putting all his desperate energy into gaining leverage, and he threw the old man right off him. Rangano sprawled across the carpet and almost put a dent in the opposite wall. Slater scrambled to his feet, closed the gap, and kicked him full in the face as he tried desperately to regain his vision.

He'd thrown his boots away.

He was wearing socks.

But it didn't matter.

He wasn't using his foot.

He made sure to hit Rangano with his shin, like bringing a two-by-four down across a mass of delicate facial features. There were a couple of *cracks,* and a muted gasp from the old man, and he went down like he'd been shot. It was probably a similar sensation. Slater's shin was sore.

He calculated the timing, and figured he'd been exposed for around five seconds.

And he heard movement behind him.

Everything moving at light speed.

He sensed the chair resting on its side next to him, still in one piece, and the Kalashnikov a little further away, loaded and ready to fire.

He acted straight away.

Not a moment of hesitation.

He picked up the chair, pivoted in a half-circle to build momentum, and hurled it with the strength of ten men back down the corridor.

Simba had just entered through an open doorway, and had a pistol in his hand, and had his shooting arm extended, and had the barrel pointed at Slater.

The chair hit him in the forearm.

It broke one of the bones clean in two.

67

There was a loud *pop,* and Simba dropped the gun.

He recoiled like a shellshocked guy in a drama film, his eyes going wide.

Nearly bugging out of his head.

The only thing Slater could concentrate on was the lactic acid burning hot in his shoulder socket. His rotator cuff was nowhere close to a hundred percent, and he'd just exerted it beyond anything one could achieve when their life wasn't on the line.

Simba brought his dominant arm to his chest, clutching it with his other hand, like protecting a prized possession. But shock was setting into his features, and a ball of stress seemed to lodge in his throat. He looked all around, and came to the conclusion that the chair had done serious damage, and then he looked down at the gun on the ground and wondered if it was worth trying to pick it up and shoot with his non-dominant hand. He'd probably never tried it. And he saw how close Slater was to the Kalashnikov AK-47.

It all happened in the blink of an eye.

Analysis.

Decision.

Run.

Simba took off. Which wasn't easy for a big man in a confined space with a shattered forearm, who also had to deal with a dynamic he hadn't experienced in quite some time. He was the hunted, not the hunter. He spun around in a half-revolution and nearly slipped on the floor as he took off. Slater saw him disappear and heard the squeak of a shoe on linoleum. He'd gone into the kitchen.

Slater took off too.

No hesitation, again.

The same choice to make, again.

Pick up the AK-47, and waste a valuable second, and almost certainly lose Simba by having to juggle extra weight and simultaneously navigate through a house he knew nothing about. Or catch him through sheer explosiveness and try to deal with him with his bare hands.

Neither option appealed to him.

But only one had a reasonable chance of success.

So in milliseconds he made the decision and broke into a flat out sprint. He bounced off the door frame and tore into the kitchen, almost too fast for his brain to compute the layout. Simba was right there, only a few feet in front. Ahead Slater saw a row of windows facing out into the hills, and alongside them a screen door lying ajar, leading out onto a private patio.

Simba made a beeline for it.

Slater pushed himself faster.

He almost tripped over the dining room table, but he darted around it and shot past the kitchen island and made it to the door almost in unison with Simba. He shot out a hand and lunged for the big man's waist. Snatching for his belt. He found it.

Crunch.

In his own shoulder. He nearly gasped as Simba continued at a furious pace, barely fazed by Slater snatching hold of him, and the man's strength and momentum almost tore Slater's shoulder from its socket. But he held on for dear life and skidded across the linoleum and snatched with his other hand. He found the belt again.

He wrenched backward.

Simba seized hold of the door frame and wrenched forward.

An old-fashioned tug of war.

Then Simba let go and abandoned escape, so abruptly that it took Slater by surprise. He rocked back on his heels as the momentum reversed and almost went down. Which would have been disastrous for his health, if he sprawled across the kitchen floor, defenceless.

He managed to keep his feet.

But it took him a moment to go from rocking back to rocking forward. He went down in something resembling a half-squat, and sprang back up. He'd almost torn Simba's belt off, but now he was ready for a fistfight. And this time...

Simba kept his dominant arm pinned to his chest — a sure-fire sign it was hurt bad — and twisted at the waist. He threw all his bodyweight into a left hook, with a giant fist swinging like a club. Meaty fingers. Hard knuckles. A thick wrist.

It hit Slater square in the chest.

Again.

It came with a sensation akin to half his internal organs bursting in unison.

He thought he felt his own heart snap in half.

This time he did go down.

And he stayed there.

All the breath stripped from his lungs, all the fight sapped out of him, all the momentum heading back Simba's way.

68

But this time, Slater kept his game face on.

He'd figured he would get hit in the confrontation. He knew how painful it would be. He knew the kind of power Simba had in his hands. So he'd mentally hardened himself prior to the altercation. Even though it sure felt like his world was ending on the inside, he kept his face deadpan and his expression unchanged and his posture as defiant as he could manage.

So even though he sprawled across the kitchen floor, it seemed as if he was ready for round two, and round three, and round four. It seemed as if he was ready to fight endlessly.

Simba noticed, and made another rapid calculation. Was it worth fighting, and potentially losing? Slater now knew for sure he had finished off all of the Green Bombers. Otherwise there would be no internal debate whatsoever. Simba would sprint at Slater and stomp on his chest over and over again until his breastbone cracked and his heart failed. And he could do that right now, if he wanted. Slater had no fight left in him.

Not until he caught his breath, and assessed his injuries, and tried to dull the abhorrent pain inside him.

But Simba didn't know that.

Because Slater had a good game face.

So he turned and bolted out the door, all his men slaughtered, his partner-in-crime debilitated, his resources expended. He could win this fight, probably, but what was the point? Best to regroup, retreat, and come back for vengeance when the odds were heavier in his favour.

There was the sound of footsteps on the patio, rapidly fading from earshot, and then they were gone entirely.

Slater sat up, alone on the kitchen floor.

His heart hurt. His chest hurt. His brain pleaded for mercy. For unconsciousness, or painkillers, or something to quash the agony. As soon as Simba disappeared from sight he let out a rattling gasp and reached for the nearest chair leg to stabilise himself.

It was the closest he'd come to a brutal death in quite some time.

A split second decision on Simba's part, and a fatal beating on the kitchen floor of an old ranch house averted.

He sat and breathed, half shocked, half relieved, and waited for the pain to numb so he could climb to his feet and deal with Rangano.

He knew precious little about the man.

But he knew enough.

So he waited it out, figuring an elbow across the forehead and a kick to the face had put the old man out of commission for at least a few minutes. And he listened hard for any sign of life from the corridor. He didn't hear a peep. Maybe Rangano's heart had simply failed him after all the steroids caught up to him.

You could only drink from the waters of an illegitimate fountain of youth for so long.

He looked in front, staring out through the open door frame, wondering what the hell was going on internally. He couldn't remember the last time he'd felt this broken. It was like his chest had split in two. The inflammation in the cartilage around his ribs had reached a fever pitch. He fought the urge to throw up.

His gaze trended downward.

He saw a small ring of keys, resting on the linoleum near the door.

Straight from the lip of Simba's pocket.

Rattled free during the tug of war.

He breathed a sigh of relief, and picked them up, and put them in his own pocket.

Then, with sudden clarity, the fog of battlefield trauma faded and he realised he might have made a crucial mistake.

Considering he'd left the AK-47 and Simba's pistol unattended on the hallway floor.

With panic in his chest to contrast the pain, he shot up and hurried to a position just a foot shy of the door frame. He listened hard, and heard nothing, and implemented the same tactic he'd used successfully during the standoff in the stairwell.

A distraction. Something odd. To throw any potential enemies off their game.

He thundered a boot into the side of the door frame. Heel against wood. Rattling the whole thing in place. The surrounding plaster vibrated. It made a colossal sound. When he took his foot away from the frame, he noticed the wood had splintered.

No reaction from inside the hallway.

No warning shot.

But Slater still didn't trust the situation.

He skirted to his left, tiptoeing across the linoleum, barely making a peep, and lifted the coffee machine off the counter. He held it in the palm of his right hand, muscles straining to handle its impressive weight. He took two steps toward the door frame as a rudimentary run-up, and hurled the coffee machine through the gap, bringing his arm around in a horizontal arc to send it hurtling down towards where Rangano should have been lying in wait.

He heard the coffee machine impact against the plaster wall, maybe ten feet along the hallway.

He leant around the corner and caught a split-second glimpse of the corridor. Then he ducked back, quick, in case Rangano had a barrel trained on the door frame. He was visible for maybe half a second. If the old man's reflexes allowed him to put a bullet in his head during that time, then fair play to him, Slater thought.

But no-one shot him.

Because no-one was there.

69

S later fetched Simba's pistol from just inside the corridor's entrance, and stood still on the carpet, listening intently for any sign of movement in the house. Even from the opposite end of the ranch. But he heard nothing.

He checked the gun in his hand. It was a compact Ruger P93DC chambered with 9mm rounds. An effective weapon. He could do a thing or two with it. It overwhelmed him with reassurance. There was nothing worse than being unarmed in an unfamiliar setting with trained killers stalking through the rooms all around him. But, he figured, it was all but unnecessary now. The house was deserted. Rangano was gone.

The old man had picked himself up and dusted off his semi-consciousness and cradled his broken nose and put up with his possibly broken jaw and hobbled away as Slater wrestled with Simba in the kitchen.

And now they were both gone.

Slater heard a car door slam, and an engine rev, and tyres spin on gravel — all in the space of a few seconds.

He ran through the kitchen, and out the door, and onto the patio, and he saw a black SUV rocket into view. It had circled from around the side of the house, and now it accelerated down the ranch's driveway, which had to be half a mile long. It kicked up a fat dust cloud as it tore away, containing the two men Slater had put his body through hell to kill. He raised the Ruger and fired two rounds at the fleeing vehicle, knowing the gesture was futile, but following through with it all the same.

He didn't care if he was expending ammunition needlessly. He was angry. He needed to let it out. He watched the SUV disappear into the horizon and blend into the endless green hills. He turned around and kicked the door frame, this time not looking to distract anyone. There was no-one left alive on the property. He was alone with a small army of dead men and his own nihilistic thoughts.

And a young woman in the basement with the horror story of all horror stories.

He shook himself out of his rage. It was selfish to dwell in his own head. It was the last thing he should be concerned about. He gathered himself and focused on constructing a mental image of his internal organs held together. He visualised it, and he pretended he was fine, and he hobbled through the house, noting the stink of blood and death. There were bodies everywhere. He ignored them. It was a unique talent, forged out of over a decade of surrounding himself with the corpses of those he had killed.

Sooner or later you became numb to it.

He descended the stairwell, keeping the Ruger low at his side, and stepped gently over the bodies of the two broken men at the bottom of the stairs. A sharp gasp tore through the basement, and Slater looked up to find Paige pressed as far back across her cell as she could manage. She'd pushed herself against the concrete wall, as if shrinking away from the consequences she'd convinced herself were coming.

When she saw Slater, she peeled off the wall and dropped to her knees, collapsing to the floor. She stared at him across the room. She said, 'You didn't lose.'

'Didn't win either,' Slater said.

'Did you kill them all?'

He nodded. 'Except the only two that mattered.'

'Simba and Rangano?'

He nodded again. 'You know Rangano?'

'Of course I know Rangano.'

'What's he like?'

'A monster.'

'I thought as much.'

'They're a partnership. Always have been. Always will be. But Rangano's getting up there in age. You wouldn't be able to tell by looking at him. He's a physical specimen.'

'I saw him.'

'Then you understand.'

'I understand.'

'He's the silent financier. I'm sure of it. He feeds Simba cash, and Simba wastes it. He must, if he can't pay his men.'

'He doesn't need to pay them anymore.'

'I see.'

'Besides, I still have my theory.'

'Are you ever going to share it?'

'Soon. I'd rather show you.'

'Show me what?'

'You said there are parts of this house no-one can visit.'

'I did.'

'I'd like you to show me them.'

'How am I supposed to do that? You said it yourself. Simba got away. You're not getting into those rooms, and you're not getting me out of this cell. You should leave. Save your own skin. Simba will be back soon. With his mentor. It's best for everyone if they find me still here, with the lock and the bars unblemished. No use trying to break me out if—'

She trailed off as Slater fished the keys from his pocket and held them up in front of her.

He said, 'Which one?'

She flapped her lips, and went pale, and said nothing.

He said, 'I understand.'

'Understand what?'

'This is freaking you out. As it would for anyone. This is breaking habits that have been drilled into you for nearly ten years. I went through something similar when I tried to get out of my old career. And it didn't work. It's the hardest thing on the planet to go against all you know. I still haven't broken my old habits. That's why I'm here. I figured it's better for me to have a life of hardship if it grants me the opportunity to do things like this. There's a silver lining for my habits. But there's no silver lining here for you. You're conditioned to obey and every part of you is screaming at you right now not to help me. Because if you don't tell me which key then maybe you can delay me long enough for Simba to come back and everything to return to normal...'

'That's not what I'm thinking,' she said.

'Maybe not consciously. But deep down you know it. Your whole world's about to change. Like I said, I don't blame you.'

'This is terrifying,' she admitted.

He saw it in her eyes.

He said, 'I know.'

'You said you couldn't break your habits.'

'Me not being able to rid myself of mine led me to helping you get out of yours.'

She pointed at a particular key. 'It's that one.'

Slater stepped forward, and slid it into the lock, and twisted, and the door sprang open. He grabbed one of the metal bars and pulled it outward. He stepped back.

Paige wandered out of the cell. There was fear in her eyes.

This was the very definition of walking into the unknown.

Her first taste of freedom for as long as she could remember.

70

S he froze a foot outside the cell, and looked all around, and said, 'I don't like this.'

'Being out of the cell?'

'I never get put in the cell,' she said. 'It's not that. It's that there's no-one watching over me. Except for you.'

'If you need time, you can take it.'

'You shouldn't be telling me that.'

'Why not?'

'Because Simba will come back. Sooner or later. You don't want to be here when that happens. You don't want to give me time.'

Slater kept the Ruger down by his side, and he put a reassuring hand on Paige's shoulder, and squeezed. He said, 'All of this is going to be hard. I'm not a shrink. I wouldn't know where to start. But I know who would.'

She lifted her eyes to his. 'I can't do that.'

'Why not?'

'This whole time I hated him. He was my scapegoat. I convinced myself it was his fault.'

'Your father didn't sell you out. I can tell when people are lying. And, like I said, he's missing half his limbs...'

Not the right time, he scolded himself.

Her eyes misted up with tears.

He hugged her tight. He let her cry into his chest. He kept the hand on her shoulder and held her as her shoulders heaved up and down. She sobbed, and it went on and on, and eventually she pulled away with bloodshot eyes and said, 'I don't know how I'm going to deal with any of this.'

'One part at a time,' he said. 'I'm not the one to help you through it. I told you already — that's not my specialty. My specialty is getting people out of situations like this.'

'You said you stumbled into this.'

'I guess I did. I don't really know what happened. I have a knack for finding myself in places like this. It's not a bad thing.'

'You look hurt.'

'I am hurt.'

'What happens now?'

'You know what we need to do.'

'If you take me back to my dad, Simba will find us eventually. He'll make it a hundred times worse. You're better off leaving me here. It's better for everyone.'

'Simba won't be around to find you.'

'You said you lost him.'

'I can follow him.'

'How?'

'You've been here eight years,' Slater said. 'Where would he go?'

She opened her mouth to speak, and then she froze. The same primitive instinct. The same mental pathways telling her what to do. Whispering in her ear that it might be in her best interests to keep her mouth shut, and play the fool, and keep sensitive information to herself. Slater saw her brain computing — one half resisting against the tyranny she'd experienced for over a decade, and the other half pleading with her to leave this place behind and start anew.

It was a war he had no concept of, and probably never would.

So he didn't speak.

He let her think.

The silence dragged out. She seemed to notice he'd given her time, so she went deep inside her own head, battling her own demons as best she could. Her face was blank, but her eyes told the story. There was a storm behind them. Something raging between her temples.

Slater took her by the hand, a perfectly placatory gesture. Nothing even remotely romantic about it. He led her up the steps and out of the basement, and he told her to close her eyes as they reached the mouth of the stairwell. There was blood and corpses all over the carpet. He sensed her shaking her head.

She said, 'I want to see them.'

'Did they hurt you?'

'Simba didn't let them. I was all his.'

'I'm so sorry.'

'You said this wasn't your job.'

'No, it's not. But I can still be sorry.'

'I appreciate it.'

'Are you glad they're dead?'

'Yes. But these are just the grunts. Like I told you. They do what Simba says. Half of them are too dumb to know right from wrong.'

'Which can still be awfully dangerous.'

'I'm not saying you shouldn't have killed them. I'm saying that Simba is a master manipulator. You know why he only hires Green Bombers?'

'Why?'

'Because they were brainwashed to hate a certain class of people under the old regime. They're easy to manipulate. The hate is bred into them. They all hated me. All I did was clean the house and act as a maid, but they looked at me like I was scum. Like I was lower than scum.'

Slater couldn't think of anything to say but, 'I'm sorry.'

'They're Simba's pawns. And Rangano's. Those two know what they're doing. Those two are some of the smartest people I've ever met.'

'I agree.'

'Which makes you think they'd know right from wrong.'

'That's not the same thing as being intelligent. I've learnt that over the course of my life.'

'They might be too smart for you.'

'Is that why you don't want to tell me where they are?'

'What makes you think I know?'

'You know.'

She let the silence drag out. Then she ducked her head, deliberately cutting off the conversation, preventing it from progressing any further. She barged past him, down the corridor and into the kitchen, then through to the screen door on the other side of the room. Slater trailed behind her, taking care not to get mad, understanding the sensitivity at the heart of it all. Paige seemed to quicken with each stride.

She was building momentum.

The first step was the hardest, and she'd taken it.

She was actively disobeying.

She was latching onto her own progress and pressing forward. And then nothing could stop her. She made it out onto the patio and overlooked the surrounding scenery.

She'd seen it before, but never through the eyes of a free woman. She stared at it with an intensity Slater couldn't quite believe, and a deep shuddering exhale poured out of her.

She turned to Slater and spoke.

71

S he said, 'They have a safe house fifteen miles from here. I'll point it out on a map. There's no chance in hell I'm going there. But you can if you want. If you do, make sure you kill them both. Please. I've never wanted anything more in my life. They'll have protection. These weren't their only men. I'm sure they have more all over the place. Money is cheap to someone like Simba.'

'You said he was flat broke.'

'I suggested it. But I don't know if I believe it myself. It's like he's playing a double bluff. That's my official opinion. Like he's pretending he's doing well, but every now and then he lets something slip through the cracks in conversation with his men. And they pick up on it. I see them glance at each other in surprise. As if they're thinking, *Did we just see that?* But then I give that scenario a moment's thought, and it makes me realise that Simba's far too smart to do something like that. If he was broke, no-one would ever know. So he wants them to feel that way.'

Slater nodded. 'It makes sense. He gives off the impression that he's falsely confident. His men latch onto it because they think they've caught their boss in a moment of weakness. But they don't understand he's been playing them all along.'

'But why?'

Slater fished the ring of keys out of his pocket and stared down at them. He said, 'How long has Rangano been around?'

Paige said, 'Forever.'

'Your dad described him, too. He was around when they took the farm, eight years ago.'

'He's always been around.'

'Have they ever fought?'

'Not that I've seen. And I wouldn't think it was possible. They're aligned like twins. They think the same. They act the same. They even have the same aura. Big and imposing. It's worked for as long as I've known them.'

'But Rangano's older.'

'He was higher up back in the day. A Political Commissar. I think he picked Simba out of the ranks of the ZANU—PF and groomed him. He knew what to do with someone he considered a successor.'

'I see.'

'What does this have to do with anything? We need to get out of here.'

'I need to confirm my theory.'

'What's your theory?'

Slater said, 'Stay here.'

'I want to see.'

'I need you to keep watch now.'

'Why don't I go? I know the house.'

'Because I spoke to someone yesterday who I already consider dearly important to me,' Slater said. 'She's suffered endless injustices, and if I'm right, this will just be one more grievance to add to the mountaintop. I need to see it with my own eyes. It can't be you.'

'How will it change things?'

'I'll feel a bit better about killing them.'

'Is that the right attitude to have?'

Slater looked at her. 'You don't hold back, do you?'

'I guess I'm not used to talking to people.'

'You're doing fine,' he said, adding a reassuring smile. But it quickly fell away when he considered what might follow.

He said, 'Wait here.'

She nodded.

All the confirmation he needed.

He ducked back into the house. The stench of death hung in the air. It was hot. The danger had fallen away, and without having to worry about his own mortality he could focus on the superficial details. Like the sweat pouring off him, staining his clothes, and the heat choking his throat, and the musty air lingering in the kitchen. He could smell the blood. He moved quickly through the house, striding down corridors and slamming his palm down on any door handle he came across. Each of them opened, one after the other, revealing a master bedroom and a series of dormitory-style rooms with rows of bunks, and a collection of bathrooms, and a few storage rooms containing uniforms and guns and extra supplies. He made a mental note to stock up on as much firepower as he could feasibly carry, but for now he left the rooms alone.

When he reached the far end of the ranch, he sensed the disuse. There was a narrow claustrophobic corridor with thick white carpet and white walls and a white ceiling. It seemed like none of the residents had stepped foot in this section of the house for years. Which was exactly what Slater was looking for.

He stepped up to the first door he came across and tried the handle.

Locked.

He pulled out the ring of keys and tried them one by one, as patiently as he could. One after the other they jammed in the lock and refused to move, until he finally slotted one of the last ones home and it gave a satisfying *click* as it turned.

He pushed the handle down and opened the door.

He stepped into the room that Simba and Rangano had kept sheltered away from all their henchmen for the entire time they'd owned the ranch.

It was full of diamonds.

72

There were hundreds of them, all fat and raw and uncut, piled up in cheap plastic containers that were slotted neatly into four storeys of metal racks. The shelves ran all the way around the windowless room. It was pitch dark inside, but even though most of the diamonds were grimy and foggy and stained, yet to be processed, he still noticed the glint coming off the shelves as the light from the corridor spilled into the room.

He stepped inside and turned on the bulb overhead.

All it took was a simple flick of a switch.

Weak yellow light poured over the room's contents. Slater kept one hand on the door handle and covered his mouth with the other. Something along the lines of a shocked expression crossed his face. He noticed it, largely because of the fact he rarely let himself display his true emotions. But he was alone in here. Other than Paige, he'd killed everyone still left on the property. Simba and Rangano were elsewhere, but he'd get their location soon. For now, he stood and contemplated what he was looking at.

It wasn't just diamonds.

It was the hopes and dreams of a region, crushed under the feet of Simba and Rangano to create a little more room in their pockets. Slater was no expert, but he put the monetary value of the stash as somewhere in the tens of millions. At least. Perhaps hundreds of millions. He couldn't know for sure. Not without someone who knew what they were doing. And he hadn't the time to go seek an expert. He just needed a brief flash of understanding.

And he had it.

He wondered how many people might not have starved to death if a Political Commissar in cahoots with a ZANU—PF official hadn't hoarded most of the region's wealth behind closed doors. Slater didn't need to know anything else. He'd seen the look in Danai's eyes. The desperation, and the frustration, and the bitter hopelessness. All of Marange had been counting on the profits from that find. It might have injected stability into the economy. It almost certainly would have put roofs over heads. It would have kept kids and babies from starving in the street, their corpses littering the side of the road, the famine sweeping over their neighbourhoods.

And here were the profits, festering in darkness in a spare room on a ranch.

Slater didn't say a word. He just looked at the diamonds.

There was movement behind him.

He spun in the doorway, frantically raising the Ruger to shoulder height, but he kept his finger off the trigger when he saw the small figure cower away from the sudden reaction.

He said, 'I told you to keep watch.'

Paige said, 'There's no-one coming. You know that. I needed to see.'

'It's diamonds.'

She paused to mull over that information. 'Was that your theory?'

'Yes.'

'And that makes you want to kill Simba even more?'

'Yes.'

'I guess I can't see the importance. You already knew he was a monster.'

'I just needed to see this.'

His frame filled the doorway, and she must have thought he was actively trying to hide something darker. Like a barricade standing between her and further trauma. She shouldered her way past him, and surveyed the room, and he stepped back and let it sink in that he was telling the truth.

She said, 'I just ... don't understand.'

'I don't expect you to.'

'Did he take this from people who needed it?'

'Yes.'

'And you met some of them?'

'He let a whole region go to waste to hoard riches for himself. And he did it with the help of Rangano, and the blessing of the men at the top. That's the purest evil I think I've ever seen.'

'What are you going to do?'

'Kill him.'

'Will you make it slow?'

'That's not my style.'

'I'd like you to.'

Slater looked at her. 'That's not me. I've never done it, and I'm not about to start.'

She looked back. 'You mean it, don't you?'

'Yes.'

'You told me you were sorry. About what's happened to me.'

'I am.'

'If I asked you to make it slow,' she said. 'As a return for all the times he made it slow for me. Would you do it? For me.'

Slater said, 'I wish I could. But I told myself I would never make it sadistic. Not for you, not for me, not for anyone. And if I break that promise, I start down a path I really, really don't want to go down. Because that will stretch the boundaries a little more. And step by step I'll get further away from where I started. I'm afraid that's something I can't waver on.'

'He doesn't deserve to be shot in the head. He deserves so much worse.'

She bowed her head, and tried not to cry.

Slater said, 'I told you the Green Bombers came into my theory.'

She raised her gaze. 'Simba hid this wealth from them, didn't he?'

'Those dorms,' Slater said. 'Are they for Simba's men?'

She shook her head. 'No way. They're for guests. The guards live out back. I clean their quarters. I mean — I used to clean their quarters. They're disgusting. It's a shed with a bunch of mattresses. It's boiling all the time. Everything's covered in sweat.'

'And they put up with it,' Slater said. 'Because of the act he put on. Because he convinced them he was bleeding money. When really he's just applying the same logic he always applies. Amass wealth, by any means necessary. And cut costs, by any means necessary.'

She nodded. 'I told you. He's a master manipulator.'

Slater pulled out his smartphone — by some miracle, he

hadn't cracked the screen in the skirmishes — and opened the camera function. He took photos of the room. Inch by inch. He covered everything.

Then he put his phone back in his pocket and said, 'Let's get out of here.'

73

W hatever Simba saved on wages, he splurged on weapons.

Slater didn't blame him.

With as many enemies as Simba had, loading up on a literal arsenal of weaponry didn't seem such a ludicrous concept.

Slater collected a loaded MK16 SCAR from one of the spare rooms — it was supposed to be a weapon exclusive to the U.S. special forces, but there were a dozen backchannels that could have resulted in one of the rifles showing up on the black market in Zimbabwe. Veteran expats, contractors, mercenaries, false goods in cargo planes ... the list went on. Slater gave the weapon the once-over, slightly in awe at the firepower in his hands.

But he doubted he would have to use it.

He thought he knew how the rest of the day would unfold.

Paige found an old rusty pick-up truck in the garage and fished the keys out of one of the smaller, more obscure drawers in the kitchen. She told Slater that Simba kept everything well hidden. He believed her. He got behind the wheel and fired the ancient Dodge to life, leaving the SCAR balanced precariously on the centre console with the safety on. Paige clambered into the passenger seat beside him, and eyed the gun warily.

She said, 'They'll all have firepower like that. Don't think you're special. If Simba and Rangano are going to their safe house, then they'll pull out all the stops. They won't be confident anymore. And that makes them dangerous.'

Slater said, 'I'm expecting a wall of them at the front gate. With weapons equally as fearsome as mine.'

'Then how are you going to do it?'

'I'm going to walk right up to them.'

She stared. 'What?'

'You heard me.'

'Care to explain?'

'I told you I'd get it done,' Slater said. 'And I'll get it done. You don't need to worry about the details anymore. You need to keep Simba and Rangano as far from your mind as you possibly can.'

'That's not going to happen,' she said.

'I know. But they're as good as dead. *If* you tell me where they are.'

'I'll tell you.'

He fired up the engine, put the pick-up into gear, and rolled its rusting chassis out into the sunlight. They set off down the trail, leaving the ranch behind. Paige twisted in her seat and stared through the grimy rear window as the structure rapidly receded into the distance. She drew in a sharp breath, and held it in. Slater glanced over, and noticed her face turning red.

He said, 'Breathe.'

'Sorry,' she mumbled. 'This is hard.'

'I know.'

'Last time I saw the house in the distance, it didn't work out well for me.'

'You said you got ten miles away. What happened?'

'I found an old woman, and pleaded for help. And she called Simba and told him to come pick me up.'

'Jesus.'

'He owns the region. He controls everything. He's good at what he does.'

'Not anymore.'

'I have a feeling you're going to fail. You're not taking this seriously.'

'How do you know that?'

'You don't seem invested.'

'I don't like to show emotion.'

'But you feel it?'

'I haven't heard many more harrowing things than the stories I've been told over the last few days.'

'Did you react to them?'

'Not in the moment.'

'But afterwards?'

'I react to things differently to most people.'

'How so?'

'I'm going to go put a bullet in Simba's head. And Rangano's. Then I'll feel better.'

'They deserve much worse than that.'

'And I'll try to give it to them.'

'You told me you had a code.'

'There's ways around it.'

'How?'

'That's why I took photos.'

'What's that meant to achieve?'

'We'll find out.'

'*You* will. You said it yourself — I can't risk going with you. If you fail, then I'll fall right back into his hands. I need to be as far away from them as possible. Both of them. Forever. I'm never going back.'

'What do you want to do now?'

'Drop me anywhere. I don't care. An inch or a mile from here. And I'll just run.'

'That doesn't sound like the smartest plan.'

'I don't care. I just need to be by myself. I need to be alone. To try and make sense of all of this.'

'You need to meet someone who cares very much about you.'

She turned to him, and made to respond, but then she clammed up and descended into her own thoughts. He could see her thinking hard.

He said, 'What?'

She said, 'I don't know your name.'

'Will.'

'I can't believe we didn't cover that at the start.'

'I called you by your name. That would throw anyone off. You assumed you were on speaking terms with the person addressing you. It wouldn't have even crossed your mind.'

Silence dragged out, and Slater focused on the view out the dusty windshield. He could sense her eyes on him, but he weaved and twisted along the dirt trail until they passed the perimeter of the property and hit the open road. He held the wheel with one hand and used the other to fish his phone out of his pocket. He set a destination he was relatively familiar with and tossed the phone onto the dashboard, allowing the voice commands to guide him. He knew where he was going. He'd been there before.

Paige's eyes stayed on him.

Finally he looked over. 'What?'

'You really did know my name at the start, didn't you?' she said. 'I didn't imagine that.'

'I knew it.'

'This isn't all some sick joke.'

'It's not.'

'What's my father's name?'

'Rand.'

The colour drained from her face, and her eyes went wide, and she turned away — all in the same motion. She now knew it was the truth. In fact, she probably already knew. Anything to distance herself from the ugly reality — the knowledge that she'd resented a man who'd only cared deeply for her, and had been traumatised himself by her disappearance. He'd assumed the worst as much as she had. He'd figured she'd died. She'd figured he'd sold her out.

Neither were correct.

Both of them would have to come to terms with the new world.

Both their lives would change.

But putting a broken family back together was better than the alternative.

Better than having no family at all.

Slater focused on the road, and his stomach churned restlessly, and he drove toward Ron & Judy's, where he imagined a man with one arm and one leg would be sitting in the corner, drinking a beer, expecting never to see the African-American stranger again.

Figuring the lunatic had got himself killed chasing tales he had no business injecting himself into.

Little did he know...

74

S later pictured something different in his mind to what actually unfolded.

He expected some sort of giddy emotional reunion, with the background music swelling to a crescendo as they sauntered inside the homestead and came face to face with the father Paige hadn't seen in nearly a decade. But the reality was something a little less grandiose. Something a little more harrowing.

Because there was that one undeniable fact — eight years had passed.

Like it had never existed in the first place.

But it wasn't as simple as that. They each probably wished the time had simply vanished, like a giant hole in the timeline, never to be seen again. Instead that time had been filled with grief and loss and misery for both of them.

Eight long years.

If it hadn't happened, Rand would have all his limbs intact, and his mental health sound. He wouldn't have dipped to the depths of crippling pain, both physical and emotional. He wouldn't have learned the limits of the human psyche. And all of that paled in comparison to what Paige had gone through.

So there was no happiness as Slater and Paige pulled up to the picturesque house and parked in the dirt lot.

Just a certain reservedness.

And nervous anticipation.

Paige said, 'Are you sure he's in there?'

'He's been doing the same thing for years. He's in there.'

'I'm not ready.'

'You're as ready as you're ever going to be.'

'You don't know that.'

'The longer you leave it, the harder it'll be the pull the trigger. Metaphorically speaking. You'll keep hesitating, and then that'll become a lifetime of hesitation, and then he'll die alone and miserable.'

She bit her lip, and chewed it, and fought back tears. 'I don't know how I'm going to make his life any better.'

'You can't honestly mean that.'

'I'm a wreck. What I've been through...'

'Would you rather overcome it alone, or with someone who cares deeply about you?'

She didn't respond to that. Probably because it didn't compute. She was still in shock. She'd only recently become enlightened to the fact that her father wasn't a sadistic monster who'd sold her out for a few dollars. To her, that had been the reality all along. It wasn't going to be easy to rewire those circuits. They'd been soldered in place with years and years of repetition. She'd convinced herself of a lie. It was like leaving a cult. It took time to acclimatise.

She said, 'Are you sure he cares?'

'Never been more sure.'

'Let's go, then.'

She sounded anything but confident. But it was the

words that mattered. Not the way they came out. He kicked his door open and stepped out of the truck, and she did the same. A little less bombastic. A little more reserved. But at least she was moving. Slater led her up onto the porch and savoured the hot afternoon air, and before he went in through the double doors he took a moment to breathe. He looked all around. The old homestead was in the same shape as when he'd left it. But it felt like five years had passed. Certainly he figured he'd aged a few years — emotionally, at least. He coughed once and wiped his forehead on his sleeve, and gave himself the once-over. It wasn't pretty. He was coated in flecks of blood and his clothes were stiff from dried sweat, and his limbs felt heavy, as if he'd fought for his life. Which he had.

He stepped in through the entranceway, and felt the cool breeze on his bare forearms, drifting through the open rear doors. He spotted Ron behind the bar, and nodded briefly to him. The man looked like he'd seen a ghost. He'd probably expected Slater to succumb to a grisly fate. As had Rand. As had Danai. Judy was nowhere to be seen. Probably out the back, tending to the grounds, or changing the beds, or focusing on all manner of other domestic issues a house of this size that was open to the public required.

Slater's gaze went past Ron. He saw a man sitting in the corner of the room. With one arm. And one leg.

The man's head was bowed.

Slater put his hand on the small of Paige's back for reassurance, and ushered her forward.

Then he stepped back with a lump in his throat and waited for the inevitable.

75

They saw each other at the same time.

There was the inevitable first glance — a look that revealed everything to Paige, and nothing at all to Rand.

She knew he was the only disabled man in the room. She knew exactly who she was looking for.

He didn't even know he was supposed to be looking for anyone. He saw her, and his eyes warmed, and he gave something resembling a placatory nod of greeting, and started to turn away. His eyes froze a few feet off her, and they went straight back.

The renowned double take.

And then they hung there for what seemed like forever, both to Paige and to Slater.

Slater sensed a shift of movement behind him, and he glanced over his shoulder. He saw Judy frozen in the doorway behind the bar, eyes wide, as if instantly aware of what was happening. He saw Ron put a hand on her chest and gently usher her back into the kitchen. The old man followed, sensing their need for privacy.

There were no other patrons in the homestead at this hour.

The three of them were totally alone.

Rand stared at his daughter, but nothing seemed to compute. His eyes drifted from Paige to Slater. Asking him a million unspoken questions.

Slater just nodded.

Paige was the first to lose it. She tried her best to remain stoic, but eventually the facade melted away, and a giant heaving sob wracked her body. As soon as it happened, Rand stood up, revealing the extent of his injuries to the young girl he'd been trying to protect all those years ago.

She took one look at his missing arm and the metal prosthetic jutting out of his knee socket, and she sobbed harder.

He limped across the room and put his arms around her, and the whole world seemed to condense into the gesture. Slater figured a bomb could have gone off behind him, and he never would have noticed. He couldn't take his eyes off the embrace. He was a loner at heart, but even he could comprehend the magnitude of the hug. It was two separate worlds reuniting, bringing together all the pain and anguish that had accompanied each separate timeline.

Slater turned around and walked straight out of the homestead.

He sat on the porch, and let the late afternoon sun fall over him. He turned his face towards the orange glow and closed his eyes. He sat there, serene. Not worrying about what was going on inside. This wasn't his story. He was the judge, jury, and executioner, but he wasn't the counsellor. He wouldn't know where to start. There would be the initial phase of shock, and disbelief, and guilt, and then maybe acceptance, if they were both lucky. Then they could look outward for help. They could seek advice on how to proceed. They could start to repair their broken relationship piece by piece. They could try, perhaps in vain, to move on from the horrors of the past.

Maybe it wouldn't work.

But they could try valiantly all the same.

Slater didn't know how long he sat there. Eventually the absolute silence gave way to the soft rustle of movement. Ron and Judy, back out in the open, perhaps preparing drinks for two very shocked, very traumatised guests. The faint sounds drifted through the open double doors behind him, but he didn't turn around. He kept watching the sun. There was the low hum of quiet conversation, punctuated by long silences and the occasional guttural sob. It could have been an hour that Slater waited. It might have been two. He didn't mind. If he had anything in life, it was patience.

Then the late afternoon gave way to a golden sunset, and shadows fell over everything in sight. In the orange twilight he sensed a stirring behind him, and he figured someone was coming out. He refused to turn around. He didn't know what the conversation had been like. He didn't know where they would begin. He wondered if it was a good idea to even *address* what had happened when it was all still so raw and fresh.

Rand materialised beside Slater. He'd approached quietly. Slater hadn't even picked up the added weight of his metal prosthetic on the wooden porch. The man sat down beside him, using his only hand to manoeuvre himself into a somewhat comfortable position. Neither of them said anything for a long while.

They just watched the sunset.

Then Rand said, 'I don't know what to say.'

Slater said, 'I had a situation like this only a few months ago.'

Rand looked himself up and down, then glanced over his shoulder, as if taking in all the variables of the situation. He said, 'Seriously?'

Slater managed a wry smile and said, 'Maybe not exactly like this.'

'You mean in terms of being at a loss for words?'

'I had to say goodbye to someone very dear to me,' Slater said. 'Someone I'd sacrificed everything for. I considered her a daughter.'

'What happened to her?'

'Nothing eventful. But I had to let her go. It's the nature of my lifestyle. She couldn't come along with me. She couldn't see all this. What I do is hell.'

'Maybe for you,' Rand said. 'Not for everyone else. I ... still don't know what to say.'

'That's the point I was getting at,' Slater said. 'We didn't know what to say either. When we had to part ways. It felt like words couldn't do it justice. You're probably feeling the same now. But we came to the conclusion that probably the best thing to say was nothing at all. It said more than if we tried to put it into words.'

Rand nodded, and brought a half-finished bottle of beer to his lips. He'd carried it out onto the porch. Slater figured it wasn't his first. He drank heavily, and then offered it to Slater.

Slater shook his head. 'The day's not over for me. I've still got work to do.'

'Paige mentioned you're going after them.'

'Did she say who?'

'Simba and Rangano.'

Slater nodded. 'She says she knows where they are.'

'I'm not going to talk you out of it,' Rand said. 'And that might be selfish. Because I want you to live a long and happy life for rescuing my kid. But at the same time I want them to die horribly and painfully. And I can't say I'm confident that you'll win this. Now that they know you're coming. So my gut tells me to warn you off it. For your own safety. But my heart tells me to let you go for it. Because if you go your own way, and walk away from this, I don't know who the hell will bring them to justice. They're untouchable out here. Always have been.'

'That's where I come in. I don't care about who's considered untouchable.'

'How are you going to do it?'

'I'm going to drive right up to the front gate.'

76

'Paige mentioned that you said something along those lines,' Rand said. 'I assumed you were joking.'

'I'm not.'

'You're going to get yourself killed.'

'Maybe.'

'Are you okay with that?'

'If I wasn't at peace with dying I probably wouldn't be living the lifestyle I do.'

'You should consider giving it up some day.'

'I tried that.'

'How'd it go?'

Slater shrugged. 'Not for me.'

'Do you want to talk to Paige?'

Slater glanced across. 'What would I say?'

'She thinks this is all a dream. She thinks she's going to wake up back in her cell, or wherever the hell they kept her. Maybe you could bring her back down to reality. So she doesn't think you're a figment of her imagination.'

'She's in shock,' Slater said. 'But even if she's not, you

can let her think that. It's best if I don't hang around. It's never worked out well for anyone.'

'I'd like it if you spoke to her.'

'I wouldn't. You two have your whole life ahead of you. Don't let me interfere with that.'

'You wouldn't be interfering.'

'I found her and brought her back to you. That's the only purpose I want to serve. The rest is on you now.'

Rand looked at him for a long time. 'Did you know?'

'That she was still alive?'

Slater shrugged. 'It was a possibility. I never expected to find her.'

'I don't believe that.'

Slater stared back at him. 'You want the truth?'

'Of course.'

'I thought she might be alive. As a slave. But I didn't think I'd find a functioning human being. I thought I'd find a physical and emotional wreck. I thought I'd find someone so destroyed that I'd have to put a bullet in her just to be merciful. But you gave your daughter the foundation she needed to stay strong in the face of whatever the fuck Simba and Rangano did to her. She's a healthy young woman. Never take that lightly. Never underestimate what you did for her. You raised her to be resilient. She never broke. Anyone else would have. I would have, if I was imprisoned eight years. If I was locked up for most of my childhood. She didn't cave in. So you two will rebuild a life together. I've never been more confident of anything. But I need to have as little to do with that as possible. I need to stick to my job. I'll go and take care of Simba and Rangano, and then I'm gone. Like I never existed.'

'If you don't take care of them,' Rand muttered. 'They'll

find me. Eventually. It won't take long. And they'll find Paige again.'

'I won't let that happen.'

'I don't know how I can trust you with that. I don't want you to carry that sort of burden.'

Slater got up.

'I don't think you have a choice,' he said.

'Couldn't stop you if I tried?'

'Something along those lines.'

Slater held out a hand, and Rand shook it. These instances never went the way he expected. He thought there might be more poignant words. He thought they might talk for hours. But they both recognised there was no need for it. There was only the need for one final gesture of goodwill, but it was an act that had been warped and twisted by the stories Slater had heard. Now he didn't want to murder Simba and Rangano on Rand's behalf, or Danai's. He'd seen the suffering they'd dished out with his own eyes. Now he wanted to murder them all on his own. So this wasn't vengeance. It was something more personal.

Slater nodded to the man, and behind Rand, he saw Paige saunter out onto the porch. She'd had a couple of drinks. He could see it in her eyes. A necessary social lubricant, considering the circumstances.

Slater smiled and said, 'Actually, I do need to talk to you.'

She cocked her head. 'You weren't going to?'

'I didn't think it was necessary.'

'You saved my life.'

'I've been hearing that a lot since I left my career.'

'It doesn't mean anything to you?'

'Of course it does. But I've got nothing to offer you. No parting words of advice. Nothing along those lines. Best that I disappear into the shadows and you all forget I existed.'

'It doesn't need to be like that,' she said. 'It doesn't have to be poetic. You can just say goodbye.'

'I don't know how. Not without sounding like an idiot.'

'Just say it. When you need to. I'll understand.'

Slater nodded. Then he stepped up onto the porch and passed his phone across. It was already open to the maps application, displaying a satellite feed of the region, with a checkpoint hovering over the ranch they'd just come from.

He said, 'That's where you were being kept. Can you figure out where their safe house is based on that? Drag your finger over the screen.'

She had around about as much trouble as Danai had, and Slater realised she was far from a typical twenty-something. She had been socially isolated and kept as a maid her whole life. She probably had zero access to technology during those years. Simba wouldn't have risked it. She could have found a way to skirt around the firewalls and call for help. Easier to prevent her from learning how any of it worked. But she must have seen the ranch's residents using devices, because she picked it up fast. She tapped and poked and prodded the touchscreen until she figured it out, and then she systematically followed the dirt road as it snaked through the countryside. She made a couple of wrong turns, and backtracked cautiously.

It only took three minutes in total. Slater considered it an effective use of his time. Usually there was a myriad of puzzles and deductions that resulted in finding his final checkpoint. Now it was as simple as asking a traumatised young soul about the location she'd overheard them speaking of. It wasn't any easier. Just a different kind of difficult.

She came to rest on a smaller compound, with a collection of buildings displayed as nothing but specks on the satellite map. She pointed it out, and Slater nodded his thanks and took the phone back.

She said, 'Please don't screw it up.'

Slater said, 'I won't.'

Rand said, 'You know the consequences?'

Slater looked at him and said, 'I'll die. That's usually all the motivation I need.'

'For us.'

Slater nodded.

'I won't screw it up.'

'They deserve to die,' Paige said.

Ordinarily a vague statement that could be applied to a host of subjects, both sarcastic and serious. Slater knew how serious she was. He could sense the weight of the words. He nodded to her, too.

Then he said, 'Goodbye.'

They said it back.

Just as Paige had instructed.

Because he didn't quite know what else to say. He understood the gravity of what he'd achieved, but it wouldn't hit him until weeks or months later. The nature of being a loner. The only time he could fathom what he'd accomplished was after he'd had time to internalise it and process it on his own. Until then he would keep relentlessly checking tasks off his wretched to-do list until his body fell apart from the stress or he finally reached the end.

His current list only had one task left to complete.

He walked away from them, leaving them to forge a new future.

He got in the pick-up truck and held the smartphone in one hand and twisted the wheel and drove away. He didn't look back. It wasn't in his nature. If he latched onto the emotion running thick in the air, he might stay a while to help them settle into their new life. He might crack jokes with Rand and take care in re-integrating Paige back into the real world. But then he wouldn't leave. And he knew how dangerous that concept was.

So he kept driving, and he rested his elbow on the SCAR for reassurance, and held the phone out in front of him, and glanced over at it intermittently. He controlled the wheel with the other hand.

The sun descended into the horizon and the orange glow turned purple, then a light blue.

In the semi-darkness he roared toward the safe house.

77

I'm going to drive right up to the front gate.

He'd said it twice. He hadn't been lying either time. For good measure, he checked his phone battery when he figured he was a mile out.

He had enough charge to see him through to the end, and that was all that mattered. He might get himself killed with the ploy, but he wanted it to have nothing to do with his phone conking out halfway through the ordeal.

He wasn't sure why he was doing it this way. Because it was poetic, perhaps. But Slater had never done anything for self-satisfaction. He wanted to get the job done, each and every time, as simple as could be. But that also played into it. He figured this carried the least risk. He had a SCAR, which proved a fearsome weapon in the hands of someone like Will Slater, but if Simba had been keeping an arsenal of fire-power at the ranch, he no doubt had a similar haul at the safe house. In which case the Green Bombers he'd pulled together in a last-ditch effort to protect himself would be armed to the teeth. All sorts of automatic weaponry, and tactical positioning, and knowledge of the land. All wrapped up in a neat package with a ribbon tying it together.

As if to say, *check-mate*.

You lose out here.

Ten times out of ten.

And he would.

Maybe, considering his reaction speed, he might win one out of ten encounters. But that wasn't a risk he was willing to take. If that was his only option, he never would have attempted it. Storming the ranch earlier that morning had the accompanying element of surprise. He'd been able to place Simba and his men firmly on the back foot. And then he'd kept them there, as their forces whittled down. And then he'd failed all the same. It had taken a last-ditch breakout and rampage through the house to secure a victory, and Slater had no desire to repeat anything like that.

And he figured his current approach would work seven out of ten times.

Much better odds.

But still not perfect.

A seventy percent chance of overwhelming success, and a thirty percent chance of getting laughed at and carted off to another cell and tortured to death for all the trouble he'd caused.

Slater managed a half-smile.

He'd spent his whole life playing odds like that.

It seemed to work out for him.

Correlation wasn't causation. There was no guarantee of success here. But he went forward all the same. Because he hated Simba and Rangano with a passion. All the way down to his core. He couldn't quite pinpoint why. He'd met monsters in his life. Hundreds of them. They hadn't troubled him like this. Maybe because Slater hadn't seen the consequences of Simba's actions in the flesh. He'd only heard tales, and stared deep into the eyes of an old woman who'd seen the horrors his decisions had led to. And maybe it was the sheer pointlessness of it all. Simba wasn't living lavishly. He wasn't enjoying himself. Not that it would have made it any better. But he'd locked up a staggering haul of diamonds in a spare room and never let anyone see them, because...

...why?

For security, perhaps. A safety net. A Plan B. If all goes to hell, sell the diamonds. Was that worth it, in the face of the poverty of the people he'd stripped them from?

Of course not.

Hence Slater's rage.

He drove all the way up the dirt trail, passing the skeletons of trees in the twilight, and he kept the SCAR on the centre console. He didn't touch it. He spotted a barebones perimeter fence in the distance, highlighting the boundaries of a vast property skewered into the hillside. Another ranch, or so it seemed. Slater peered past the fence, into the half-gloom, and figured the satellite photos were outdated. They'd showed a cluster of buildings, but here there was just a single weatherboard house resting like a lonely beacon in the undulating hills. He could see it clearly. The porch light was on, and a couple of lights inside, too.

He turned his attention back to the fence. There were guards waiting. Nothing but silhouettes against a darkening blue sky. Like rock golems standing as watchful protectors over their realm. They had weapons at their sides. Their dark faces peered out at the trail, and saw the approaching pick-up truck, and stiffened in anticipation.

Slater left his lights on. He showed no sign of hostility whatsoever, and he figured the Green Bombers wouldn't light his vehicle up with automatic gunfire without checking who the occupant was. They didn't want to kill any old passerby. Those days were over. Zimbabwe was slowly pulling itself out of the unsupervised past. You couldn't massacre anyone you pleased anymore. You had to be subtle about it.

So Slater kept rolling forward up the slight incline, touching the gas when required, and finally he pulled to a stop a few dozen feet away from the wall of security. There were eight of them in total, spaced evenly apart across the trail. All had assault rifles in their hands. Some Kalashnikovs, some more modern weapons. All of them looked like they knew how to use them. The edge of the headlights' glow caught their frames. Most of them were tall and skinny and wide-shouldered. Emaciated, but wiry. Hard men, with hard lives, and hard jobs. Men who wouldn't hesitate to do whatever their boss commanded.

Such as kill all hostiles.

Unwinnable, in Slater's humble opinion.

He killed the engine but left the headlights on. He swung the door open and stepped slowly out of the car. Guns came up. Just precautionary, though. Because who the hell would approach like this if they intended on storming the compound? Slater killed the headlights next, and there was just enough natural light left in the sky to accentuate his own silhouette on the trail. They all stared at him.

He took the SCAR off the centre console, and held the other hand palm open in the air.

He tossed the rifle towards them.

Then he put both hands in the air.

78

They watched him with intense curiosity.

Slater had never felt so uncomfortable.

Eight sets of eyes, all gaunt and bloodshot and sinister in the lowlight. They tightened their grips on their weapons. They seemed to sense the opportunity in the air. But they didn't pounce on what appeared to be an unarmed man, because it all seemed too strange. Slater wouldn't have come here to surrender. If he considered the fight impossible, he would have turned and run.

Slater figured this was the most important moment of his life. Any weakness, and he wouldn't get to go through with what he intended. And he would die a grisly painful death at the hands of a pair of men who no doubt wanted nothing more than to rip him limb from limb. So he took his time, and he kept his demeanour composed, even though his insides were anything but. With cold sweaty palms and a heart rate through the roof he walked straight towards them, with his hands way up in the air.

A couple of them pointed their guns at him.

Slater wondered if they would shoot. They had every

reason to. It would be simple enough. Gun him down where he stood, and drag his bleeding corpse up the trail to the doorstep, and present it to Simba and Rangano, and accept a handsome reward for their forward thinking.

But that didn't happen.

Probably because there would be no reward.

Not now, not ever.

All part of Slater's theory.

He reached them, and he pulled up on the dirt trail maybe six feet from the eight-man procession. Testosterone crackled in the air. The party stank of stale sweat and rotting teeth. They were unkempt and overworked and at their wits' end.

All part of Slater's theory.

He said, 'Who speaks English?'

The guns stayed where they were.

No-one spoke.

They all looked at each other.

Then they turned back to him, and stared.

Shit, Slater thought.

A minor speedbump.

No matter.

Slater pointed to his pocket.

He said, 'Phone.'

The largest guard — probably six-four, hunched and lanky like a praying mantis — said, 'No.'

His voice was gruff and tinged with misery, like he'd been through a life of hardship with nothing to show for it.

All part of Slater's theory.

Slater said, 'Phone. Important.'

He stressed it with his eyes. He didn't shy away from staring them all dead in the face. He showed no hint of being subservient. He didn't blink. He nodded at all of them as if Simba had asked him to come, like it was the most important thing in the world that he was allowed to access his phone.

It piqued their interest.

The largest man said, 'Okay.'

'You speak English?' Slater said.

'Few word.'

'But you understand it?'

The guy raised a hand and tilted it back and forth.

Slater said, 'I need to show you all something.'

'On knees,' the largest man grunted.

But all eight of them stayed where they were.

Like they didn't know exactly what to do.

They'd expected furious confrontation or nothing at all.

All part of Slater's theory.

He didn't get on his knees.

He said, 'Phone,' and pointed to his pocket again.

The largest guard nodded, like, *What the hell? Why not?*, and said, 'Slow.'

Slater held two fingers like pincers to highlight his innocence, and drifted them slowly down toward his pocket. Eight gun barrels followed the move. He knew they would fire at the slightest hint of aggression.

Unwinnable.

Just as he'd expected.

He pulled out a phone. Not a gun. And therefore he stayed alive. They all relaxed a little, and he figured he probably could have used the phone as a decoy and dropped five or six of them with a blistering volley from a pistol he'd secured to the small of his back with duct tape. But he hadn't prepared for that, so it wasn't an option. He'd trusted his gut.

He hoped, at the end of the day, he had something to show for it.

Instead of mounting offence he navigated to his camera roll and opened up the long string of photos. The brightness of the display accentuated his features in the encroaching darkness. He cradled the slim device in one hand, and tilted his free palm towards the procession. Indicating he meant no harm. A lump formed in his throat. If this didn't work, he had just signed his own death warrant. And it wouldn't be a quick death.

He selected the first photo he'd taken in the ranch. It showed a plain white corridor with thick carpet underfoot and a number of closed doors leading to a plethora of spare rooms. He turned the screen around and presented the photo to the group.

They looked at it.

79

The largest man stepped forward, and Slater caught more of his features in the glow emanating from the phone screen. His eyes somehow seemed more gaunt now. More bloodshot. There were scabs and scratches and cuts all over his neck and exposed collarbones. He was dressed in a simple loose T-shirt that hung off his frame as if it had been designed that way. There were holes in the shirt.

With time to focus on his adversaries, Slater figured this man was barely holding his life together. He could see the strain in his eyes. The heat and the nighttime solitude had started to get to him. After all, why the hell should he be forced to wait out here at Simba and Rangano's expense, especially if they were barely paying him enough to survive?

The same principle applied to the other seven.

They crowded around the screen, and Slater sensed the opportunity starting to leech out of the air. They surrounded him, all eight of them, and the stink of their unwashed bodies washed over him.

Slater gripped the screen tighter, and looked expectantly at the largest Green Bomber.

The man nodded.

A gesture of recognition, and approval.

I know that corridor.

Proceed.

This better be good.

Slater swiped at the screen with a single grimy finger.

The next photo appeared.

A little further down the corridor. Like a slideshow from the seventies. Stuttering, frame by frame. Slater remembered the path he'd taken. In the second photo, he was approaching one of the doorways, perhaps halfway down the corridor. The white panelled wood was half-ajar.

Slater looked to the guards for approval.

A few of them nodded now. They were getting the hang of it. And maybe one or two of them were starting to get the idea. If they put in any kind of respectable hours on Simba's property, they would know which doors were locked. They were starting to understand where Slater was headed. The largest man's eyes widened. Maybe he'd never seen that particular door open before.

Slater swiped again.

The next photo he'd taken just inside the doorway. The shelves were in full view, as were the plastic containers stacked with grimy diamonds. But the camera had captured the room in its entirety, and the finer details were obscured. The largest guard hunched over the screen, squinting against the glare, and Slater noted the tactical positioning. He could have looped his free hand around the back of the man's neck and brought it down to meet his knee, then stripped him of his gun as he collapsed and killed four or five of them in the carnage before absolute chaos erupted. The guard's interest had got the better of him. He'd made himself vulnerable.

But Slater didn't do any of that.

Instead he swiped again.

The next photo consisted of a close-up of one of the containers. Now there was no denying the value of its contents. Some of the diamonds were coated in a cloudy film, and some were littered with fine debris, but there was no mistaking the chunks of minerals piled high. These men had lived around the Marange diamond fields their whole lives. They had seen many such objects before. None in such great quantity. Nothing like this.

Slater held out the phone, completely at the mercy of the men around him.

But they didn't care about him anymore. They cared about what they saw on the screen. He could see it in their eyes. There wasn't just anger there. There was an utter hopelessness, coupled with disgust. As if they were all thinking in unison, *How could I have wasted so much of my miserable life serving a man who pretended he couldn't pay me?*

Then it all became real apparent, real quick.

Slater studied them harder. He scrutinised their eyes. Every pair was transfixed on the tiny phone screen cradled in the largest guard's hand. They were paying him no attention at all. He could have walked away, right then. Just turned around and strolled off down the dirt track, leaving the truck and his weapon behind. But he stood still. He let the gravity of the situation sink in.

Your boss could have paid you handsomely this whole time.
Instead he kept you well below the poverty line.
It was all a ruse.
You starved and bled and lived a life of hardship as he had

enough wealth sitting in a spare room to make you and all your
families comfortable.

Slater didn't need to say a word.

It transcended the language barrier.

It transcended everything.

The largest guard swiped back and forth between the photos, as if checking to make sure they weren't doctored. But he found no discrepancies. He passed the phone around. Inch by inch, the rifle barrels ebbed toward the floor. Away from Slater. But there was still a thin veil of skepticism. Hanging in the air. They couldn't trust this intruder entirely. None of them had smartphones. Maybe some of them had never even seen one before. Not of this quality. So maybe the photos were doctored after all.

To make sure they believed him, Slater slid the ring of keys out of his pocket, and held them out.

The largest guard took them. He waved the glow of the phone screen over them. Making sure they were the same keys he'd seen Simba carrying, all this time.

He gave a nod of approval.

He passed them back to Slater.

The first step.

Completed.

None of them spoke English, but none of them needed to. One by one they took the phone in a preordained pecking order — scrutinising the photos, making the connection between the cloudy diamonds and the Marange fields. They had to know they were looking at tens of millions, if not hundreds of millions of dollars. The stash wasn't new. Simba hadn't recently come into wealth. He'd had it all along. And they'd starved and pleaded and begged for more money the whole time. Simba and Rangano had adamantly refused. No matter what. Maybe some of their

family members had starved to death. This was the new
Zimbabwe, after all. And they were determined to keep
identifying as Green Bombers. So work opportunities would
be scarce. They had to take what they were given. Which, in
this case, was the scraps Simba would have ordinarily fed to
his prized bulls.

Now, Slater thought. *Step two.*

He pointed to each of them in turn, one by one. They
watched him every step of the way. They saw he was
unarmed. They made no move to detain him. He jabbed a
finger at each of the eight men, and then he held up a closed
fist with the thumb sticking straight up in the air. A
universal gesture.

Thumbs up.

You guys are okay.

Then, with as much fury as he could muster in his eyes,
he pointed past them.

To the ranch house.

He held up a closed fist, inverted, with his thumb
pointed toward the dirt.

Thumbs down.

They're not okay.

There was a silence that dragged on for eternity.

Dark thoughts and hypotheticals churned in the hot
night air.

Slater thought he could taste his own fear.

Then the largest guard nodded, and stepped aside.

Then he went even further.

The man bent down and retrieved Slater's SCAR from
the dirt.

He handed it over.

He nodded his approval.

He grunted, 'Go.'

Slater walked straight past the eight men and set off down the driveway toward the safe house.

The group watched him as he disappeared into the night.

All silent.

All deep in thought.

All their lives and beliefs changed in a single demonstration.

80

S later came out of the night like a demon clawing its way out of the underworld.

He strode like a man possessed, which he figured he was. He would never forget the eyes of the men that had let him past. They weren't guards anymore, or Green Bombers. They were brainwashed minions. They were slaves just as much as Paige had been. Slater had never seen suffering like that. On the surface they seemed fine. On the surface ... they seemed evil. But they weren't. They were hard men with hard lives raised in impossible circumstances, holding onto an ideology because it was all they had left in the world.

Slater hated every part of this business.

He hated every part of the moral grey zone.

None of it made sense. None of it fit into a neat jigsaw puzzle. Instead it was a brutal mess, with pieces scattered all over the place. But there were certain characters in the landscape who transcended that moral grey zone.

Namely, the two men sitting in the safe house. Smug and

confident in their protection, even though their security was barely making enough to keep themselves alive.

The outside light spilled over Slater. The darkness receded and he leapt up onto the porch in a single bound, clearing the three steps with one stride. He had adrenalin in his veins. The injuries he'd sustained meant nothing anymore. He figured he could shoulder his way straight through the wall, if that was what it took. He figured he could smash the plasterboard apart with his bare hands and strangle Simba and Rangano in unison, no matter how hard they hit, no matter how confident they were.

But, even in his deepest, blackest rage, he was a little more tactical than that.

So he kicked the screen door in like it weighed nothing, sending the thin mesh twisting off its hinges, complete with a groaning and tearing that signalled his arrival as if he were the Grim Reaper itself.

He heard a frantic scurrying in the kitchen.

He strode through the entranceway and rounded the corner in one sweeping motion, catching Simba and Rangano halfway through their mad dash to the kitchen bench. There were two guns on the countertop. Both Glocks. The two big men froze in place when they saw the SCAR barrel aimed at them. They were each at least six feet from their weapons. They'd been sitting at the kitchen table, deep in conversation, when it had all gone to hell. Rangano had a busted nose and dried blood caked across his upper lip, and a thin crimson line across his forehead. It had only stopped bleeding recently. Simba was unblemished, apart from the rudimentary sling wrapped around his arm, pinning it to his sternum. His deep green eyes bore into Slater from across the room.

He said, 'You persistent.'

With a half-smile.

As if he expected to negotiate his way out of it.

Slater shot him through the shin.

Blood and gore and flecks of bone sprayed across the shiny tiles, and Simba went down without any resistance. Rangano figured it was an appropriate time to make a final lunge for his weapon, but Slater had been anticipating that. Maybe the old man wanted a quick, merciful death. Like suicide by cop. Make a blatant move to go for a gun at the most inopportune time, and get lit up with bullets for your troubles.

Thankfully, Slater was a little smarter than that.

He was already aiming low by the time Rangano burst off the mark.

He shot the old man in the left shin, then the right.

Twin explosions of gore.

Rangano collapsed too.

Blood flowed across the tiles and welled in the cracks. The big men lay on their backs, staring at their ruined lower limbs, panting for breath. Both of them hyperventilating. Both of them going into shock. Slater thundered across the room and stood over them. He made no wasted movements. He concentrated with all his intensity on soaking in the expressions on both their faces. More than anything, he wanted to remember this.

A shuffle of feet, right behind him.

He barely heard it, because of the unsuppressed reports blasting through the enclosed space just a few seconds earlier. But something at the very edge of his earshot trickled into the back of his brain, and a primal instinct kicked into gear, and he spun around with manic intensity.

He caught two Green Bombers right as they stepped into the doorway, their own pistols raised.

But not aimed at Slater. Aimed a couple of feet off, at a random space. They hadn't isolated their target yet. Slater had beaten them to the draw.

They saw the SCAR barrel trained on them, and they lowered their weapons with a defeated sigh. The last guards, thwarted at the final hurdle.

Slater kept his voice low and said, 'Go wait by the front gate with your friends. They'll explain.'

The two guards stared. They were both short thin men with hollow cheekbones and wide eyes. Their hair was buzzed short. Then one of them seemed to get the gist of Slater's message, even if he didn't speak English. He nodded, his eyes even wider now, flooding with relief, and he slapped his friend on the chest. They put their guns down and sauntered out of sight. Slater heard footsteps on the porch outside, and then the *squelch* of shoes on loose dirt, and then nothing.

He turned back to Simba and Rangano.

The big men stared up at him, fighting to hold onto consciousness. They were both opportunistic. They knew if they passed out, they were as good as dead. They fought and clawed for their own lucidity with every scrap of rabid desperation they had in their bodies. Slater watched them gnashing their teeth, flaring their nostrils, blinking hard. They kept bleeding all over the tiles. Slater sensed warm blood pooling around his boots.

He stayed where he was.

He said, 'Do either of you feel like begging for your life?'

Silence.

Slater said, 'It might be in your best interests.'

'Please,' Rangano croaked.

It was the first time Slater had heard the old man speak. It came out weak and timid due to a mixture of blood loss and genuine fear for his life. Maybe he really thought the money and power had insulated him. It might have, amongst the general population. No-one around here would think of trying anything against the all-powerful ex-Political Commissar.

Slater would.

He said, 'How's your English?'

Rangano said, 'It is good. Please. Be reasonable here. We can work something out.'

Slater nodded, like he was considering it.

He swung the barrel of the SCAR around to aim between Simba's eyes.

'You got anything to say?' he said.

Simba shook his head.

Resolute to the end.

Committed to his ways.

Slater blew his skull apart with a three round burst.

81

Rangano cried out in anguish as the brain matter of his closest companion and protégé sprayed all over him.

Simba's corpse lay still.

Calmly, Slater turned the barrel back to Rangano.

'He didn't beg,' Slater said. 'So I killed him. You want to stay alive?'

'Yes!' Rangano cried, almost sobbing. 'Yes, of course. I cannot die here. We can work something out. We can do a deal. I have money. I have everything. I can give you whatever you need. Please.'

'That's good,' Slater said. 'Keep doing that. The second you stop begging, I'm going to shoot you in the face.'

It lasted fifty minutes in total.

Slater counted out the seconds. He stood like a rock golem over the crippled old man and let him pour his heart and soul out into the silence of the kitchen. Rangano's desperate pleas rang off the walls, echoing in the tiled space, like hymns sung by the damned.

Slater didn't outwardly gloat. He kept his expression neutral, and simply watched.

Rangano tried every angle.

Every possible avenue.

He exhausted all options.

He promised riches, and women, and power, and then he changed tactics and tried to appeal to Slater's sensibilities. Surely he wouldn't kill an old man in cold blood? Surely he would accept a surrender, because that was what a good warrior did?

Then he changed tactics again.

He started down the path of supposed nobility, and acceptance into the afterlife. If Slater wanted any chance at a pleasant life after death, then he couldn't, in good conscience, gun Rangano down where he lay. And then, when that path was exhausted, Rangano's lucidity began to fade. But the will to survive was strong, because he kept droning on and on with increasing desperation as the lifeblood ebbed out of his lower legs.

Sweat broke out across his forehead, and his eyes took on a certain milky hue, but he kept going.

He rambled and chattered and eventually descended into utter insanity. All in less than an hour. He spoke until his voice turned raw and hoarse, talking about nothing in particular, just clutching onto life with everything he had left.

Eventually the Green Bombers got curious.

They were all waiting outside.

One by one they trickled into the kitchen, only interested in observing the situation from a distance. They hovered in the doorway, and noted Slater standing over the blabbering cripple that used to be their all-powerful boss. He didn't seem so imposing anymore. One by one they flowed out of the house, seeing all they needed to see. Understanding what they needed to understand.

Slater never looked in their direction.

If they were going to shoot him, then so be it.

But none of them did.

That was Rangano's last strategy. Get a couple of his guards to switch sides again. In something resembling a fugue state, his hazy eyes wandered to the doorway, and he met the curious stares of the men in his employ. He held out a weak shaking hand in their direction, repeating the gesture for each of the guards who entered the house. They all ignored him. He promised them the same things he'd promised Slater. Great riches, as much power as they desired, a field of beautiful women. They all watched him with a certain wonder, then turned and ignored his cries and promises.

Then Rangano got angry.

Insanity gave way to a rage so dark Slater figured his own anger paled in comparison. Rangano's pupils expanded, black as night, and he swore and cursed and spat with every morsel of aggression in his body. And he had a whole lot. He'd gone his whole life using it to his own advantage. Now it poured out, and he lambasted Slater from his head to his toes, using language Slater hadn't even known existed.

Then, piece by piece, it began to fade.

The cursing turned to muttering, and saliva stopped spraying from the corners of the old man's lips, and his eyes grew hazier and milkier, and his nostrils stopped flaring, and the lucidity fell away as his body emptied itself of its final reserves.

The gas ran out of the tank.

He had nothing left. He'd exhausted every option, every

possible alternative, everything that could have saved him, but hadn't.

Then he stopped talking.

Rangano closed his lips for the last time, and it was as absolute a defeat as Slater had ever seen.

The old man was a broken, miserable, dejected wreck of his former self.

Good.

Slater shot him in the face.

He put the SCAR down on the kitchen floor, and put his hands on his hips, and sighed.

It wouldn't bring anyone back.

It wouldn't undo any of the suffering.

But damn, it felt good.

He stepped out of the giant puddle of blood and walked out of the kitchen. He turned left and stepped through the door frame. There were ten men on the porch. Like a guard of honour. All dressed in olive uniforms. Some wearing red-and-green berets. Lost souls who'd been raised and trained to hate, and didn't know any better. Men who'd held onto an ideology like their life depended on it. They weren't evil. They just didn't know any better. Maybe in the past, Slater would have killed all of them. But that person didn't exist anymore. Simba and Rangano were pure evil. These men were...

He didn't know. He recalled reading about the harrowing nature of Nazi Germany as he lay cooped up in bed in the Russian Far East, recovering from a concussion. You'd think most Germans would have secretly despised the regime. But humans aren't as simple as that. Most thought it was the right ideology. More importantly, almost no-one spoke up. You get used to your surroundings. You acclimatise to wherever you are in the world. You latch onto a belief system and get swayed by social compliance if it's the prevailing attitude. As these men had.

Slater nodded to all of them. They were now technically unemployed. They'd have to figure out something. It might involve stepping away from their past beliefs. It might involve shattering what they thought was their reality. He'd leave them to sort it out on their own. If they could do it, then they might be able to make something of their lives. If not...

Well, that was none of Slater's concern.

They let him leave. He'd achieved everything he'd set out to do. He nodded to them, because that was all he could think to do, and shuffled past.

Exhausted to his core, he stepped down off the porch and blended back into the darkness. He walked along the driveway until he reached the front gate, and found the pickup truck right where he'd left it. He climbed up into the driver's seat and sat still, but eventually the tiredness hit him in a wave, and he leant forward and rested his forehead on the wheel.

Just as he'd done in Brooklyn, months earlier, after parting with a young kid that meant the world to him.

Eventually he sat up and started the engine and switched the headlights on. They illuminated a short stretch of the dirt track leading up to the front gate. He reversed and twisted the wheel and made a three-point turn, so he was facing the other way, and he set off down the trail.

After less than a minute of driving he reached a T-junction.

He could turn left, and trundle back in the direction of Ron and Judy's homestead. There he would find a warm bed and an intimate atmosphere and a series of meaningful conversations with a disabled ex-maize farmer and his long-lost daughter. He could hang around, and laugh and cry with them over drinks, and help them integrate back into something constituting a normal life. Perhaps it was his duty. He'd pulled Paige out of hell, after all. Who was he to leave her stranded with someone who needed all the help he could get — someone who had to attempt to mend the broken bond between parent and child?

The homestead was familiar, and safe.

If he turned right, he'd enter uncharted territory. He'd broaden his horizons, and expand his narrow field of view, and perhaps drive all the way to the border, whereupon he'd find new lands to explore. He'd no doubt run into a thousand injustices along the way, all of which needed his attention, all of which he'd happily involve himself in. Because that was all he had done, both during his career and after. And he knew he was lying if he tried to pretend he wasn't any good at it.

His head hurt and his chest burned with inflammation and his shoulder felt like it might be dislocated.

If he went right, then those injuries would just be the start of his problems.

There'd be many more where that came from.

If he went right, he'd maintain the pace he'd set for all his adult life.

And, if anything, Will Slater was a creature of habit.

He twisted the wheel to the right, and stepped on the accelerator.

MORE WILL SLATER THRILLERS COMING SOON...

Visit amazon.com/author/mattrogers23 and press **"Follow"**
to be automatically notified of my future releases.

If you enjoyed the hard-hitting adventure, make sure to
leave a review! Your feedback means everything to me, and
encourages me to deliver more novels as soon as I can.

Stay tuned.

Join the Reader's Group and get a free 200-page book by Matt Rogers!

Sign up for a free copy of '**HARD IMPACT**'.
Meet Jason King — another member of Black Force.

Experience King's most dangerous mission — action-packed insanity in the heart of the Amazon Rainforest.

No spam guaranteed.

Just click here.

BOOKS BY MATT ROGERS

THE JASON KING SERIES

Isolated (Book 1)

Imprisoned (Book 2)

Reloaded (Book 3)

Betrayed (Book 4)

Corrupted (Book 5)

Hunted (Book 6)

THE JASON KING FILES

Cartel (Book 1)

Warrior (Book 2)

Savages (Book 3)

THE WILL SLATER SERIES

Wolf (Book 1)

Lion (Book 2)

Bear (Book 3)

Lynx (Book 4)

Bull (Book 5)

BLACK FORCE SHORTS

The Victor (Book 1)

The Chimera (Book 2)

ABOUT THE AUTHOR

Matt Rogers grew up in Melbourne, Australia as a voracious reader, relentlessly devouring thrillers and mysteries in his spare time. Now, he writes full-time. His novels are action-packed and fast-paced. Dive into the Jason King Series to get started with his collection.

Visit his website:

www.mattrogersbooks.com

Visit his Amazon page:

amazon.com/author/mattrogers23